PEPPER BASHAM

The HEART of the Mountains

BARBOUR
PUBLISHING

The Heart of the Mountains ©2022 by Pepper Basham

Print ISBN 978-1-63609-325-3
Adobe Digital Edition (.epub) 978-1-63609-327-7

All scripture quotations, unless otherwise noted, are taken from the King James Version of the Bible.

This book is a work of fiction. Names, characters, places, and incidents are either products of the author's imagination or used fictitiously. Any similarity to actual people, organizations, and/or events is purely coincidental.

Cover image: Rekha Garton/Trevillion Images

Published by Barbour Publishing, Inc., 1810 Barbour Drive, Uhrichsville, Ohio 44683, www.barbourbooks.com

Our mission is to inspire the world with the life-changing message of the Bible.

Member of the
Evangelical Christian
Publishers Association

Printed in the United States of America

Praise for *The Heart of the Mountains*

Pepper Basham weaves a stunning tale of suffering and hope set in the heart of Appalachia. Blending romance, humor, and history, *The Heart of the Mountains* reveals a God who not only heals the broken but redeems hearts in ways no one can imagine.
- Tara Johnson, author of *All Through the Night, Where Dandelions Bloom,* and *Engraved on the Heart.*

The Heart of the Mountains is a world created with exceptional skills by Pepper Basham. It immersed me in the mountain life until I could see the scenery, smell the plants, and hear the mountain breeze and the bird calls. All of that was wonderful, but more than that was the way I felt as I read. The hurt, the love, the longing, the loss, the fear, the joy. Basham created a beautiful, emotional work of art. I enjoyed every word.
- Mary Connealy, bestselling author of *The Element of Love*

Pepper Basham's *The Heart of the Mountains* has a perfect title, as her story reveals the hearts of her characters as they face one challenge after another in their mountain community. You'll hardly have time to catch your breath from one exciting scene to the next. Great characters, great setting, great background history. Great story! You won't want to miss it.
- Ann H. Gabhart, bestselling author of *Along a Storied Trail*

Exciting. Moving. Humorous. Touching. *The Heart of the Mountains* touches every sense. With characters that are strong and determined and a story that moves like honey dripping from the comb, Pepper Basham has nailed this Appalachian story. Set in 1919, Basham draws the reader in with the strength and sassiness of Cora Taylor. She grasps the era, the mountains, and heart of the people of the mountains. This must read will find you flipping page after page and sad when it ends. Pepper Basham's work is exquisite.
- Cindy K. Sproles, author of Christian Market Book Award, Novel of the Year, *What Momma Left Behind*

The Heart of the Mountains is a beautiful story of second-chances, redemption, and finding home. Filled with breathtaking scenery, heart-tugging encounters, and tender romance, this latest story by Pepper Basham will leave you feeling as if you've just spent time in the dangerous, yet fascinating, Appalachian Mountains.
- Gabrielle Meyer, author of *When the Day Comes*

Dedication

To my Papa and Granny "Rat." Though I never had the chance to meet them, their story has inspired mine.

Acknowledgments

As always, this story has an entire backbone of people who helped me make it a reality. I CANNOT thank Joy Tiffany, Beth Erin, or Carrie Schmidt enough! This story was the hardest one I've ever had to write as I pushed through the grief of losing my brother to pen this tale, and these three ladies just kept encouraging me ALL THE WAY!!

Laura Frantz is as lovely as she presents online, y'all. I am so grateful to be blessed with her friendship and kindness.

The Pepper Shakers will FOREVER make it on the acknowledgments page because they continually believe in each and every one of my stories. I've been quieter than usual this past year because of various struggles, but they have always been ready to cheer me and my fictional family on!

Garrett and Jo Pittman encouraged me to visit Cataloochee Valley, where I not only discovered the wonderful inspiration for Jeb McAdams's house, but uncovered another wonderful piece of Appalachian history to help with my research for this story.

I'd like to thank all the people who prayed for me while I tried to write this story through the grief of losing my brother. I will never be able to thank all of you, but I am so grateful for your kindness.

I am so grateful for Becky Germany and the team at Barbour for allowing me to bring this story to the page. The Barbour team has just been the sweetest group of people with whom to work and I'm grateful they've believed in these stories.

My Spencer family have a wealth of family history stories and have always been generous enough to allow me to take the truth from our family and give it a fictional spin. Thank you all so much for the stories and encouragement, but most of all for your love and faith. (And Aunt Penny, thank you for all the extra info you have to share!)

As always, my closest cheerleaders are the ones who live in my house. I'm so grateful they never tire (or rarely tire) of my love for the worlds and people God allows me to create, while still trying to navigate the very real ones.

And lastly, to the One who loves the unlovable, cherishes the outcast, finds the lost sheep, and redeems the broken. I pray that He is the true "heartbeat" behind the stories I write, but mostly, the story I live.

Chapter One

October 1919

Running away from an arranged marriage to the wilds of the Blue Ridge hadn't gone as Cora Taylor expected. Of course she'd anticipated a remote world, perhaps even a step back in time, but utter destitution was another thing altogether. When she'd stepped from the train onto a platform with no depot, and one of the rather gruff trainmen ushered her toward a rugged-looking building across the tracks with a sign that read GROCERY, Cora contemplated returning to her cozy, cushioned seat aboard the steam engine and disappearing into the West.

And she could have, perhaps, if duty and love for her dear brother didn't tug her heart away from modern comforts to the ramshackle building before her. The train moved on, leaving her trunks in a haphazard heap on the platform and her surroundings coated in a cloud of smoke. She released a sigh, adjusted her hat, and took a survey of her current options.

As the smoke cleared, the emptiness of the setting took a decidedly isolated turn. And those mountains! They crowded close, like guards blocking her escape on every side. Hadn't her brother written of the beauty of these hills? The lavish welcome of the landscape?

Clearly, he'd forgotten a few details.

She unfastened the top button of her blouse and studied the train track as it disappeared around a bend of trees. Perhaps coming all this way had been a monumental mistake. But then Dexter Arnold's face flashed through her thoughts and she stiffened her resolve to remain as far from England as humanly possible. Nothing could be as bad as a lifelong commitment to that thick-headed, withered-hearted pansy of a man.

She stared at the mountains, daring them to stop her. Then she slung her leather medicine bag over her shoulder, grasped the handle of her other bag with a tighter grip, and marched toward the grocery. Her boots left the rickety steps and immediately sank to the ankles in mud. She squeezed her eyes closed, drew in a deep breath for strength she wasn't sure would be enough, and then slogged through the mire to finally reach the grocery store steps.

Only a few small windows filtered daylight from the front of the store throughout the tiny space. Several barrels stood scattered across the floor. A counter ran the length of the wall to Cora's left and shelves covered the one to her right. Canned goods, an assortment of tools, a few handmade baskets, a container of…she stepped closer…potatoes?

"Well, you're quite the sight to show up in our little store, ain'tcha?"

Cora turned to find a petite woman behind the counter, her wiry, blond and silver hair making a failed attempt to stay in the bun at the back of her head. She smiled, and her face curled into a thousand wrinkles.

"Hello."

"We ain't seen the likes of them fancy duds in these parts in a while." The woman waved toward Cora's crimson traveling suit. "You must be *some*body."

Cora blinked at the indecipherable phrase and took a few steps forward, hand outstretched. "My name is Cora Taylor."

"Well, howdee do," the woman said more like an exclamation

than a question. She took Cora's hand. "You even sound fancy, don'tcha?" She gave Cora's hand another shake. "I'm Avis Ayers, and this here is the only store you're gonna find for a few miles." Her bright blue gaze trailed down Cora. "Though I don't reckon you'll find much to suit your tastes in these parts."

Cora scanned the room. "This looks like a fine establishment, Mrs. Ayers. I'm sure it meets the needs of the people here."

"That's right. We're storefront, post office, smithy, and hotel."

Hotel? Smithy? The little building barely held the collection of items crammed into every part of the store. How on earth did it serve as a hotel too? Cora decided to bypass her curiosity. "I'm here to visit my brother and uncle. Perhaps you've heard of them. Reverend Anderson and Jonathan Taylor. Is there a wagon I can hire to help take me and my trunks to—"

"Oh mercy, you're Teacher Doctor's sister!" The woman laughed and pressed a palm to her chest. "Well now, I've only seen him a few times, but I should have knowed you'd be kin. You have the same eyes, though your hair's a might bit darker than his, ain't it?"

Cora reached up to touch her light brown locks, more like their father's color than mother's blond. "Yes. Would you happen to know of a wagon I could hire for use to get to his home?"

Mrs. Ayers shook her head with a frown. "Ain't no wagon makes it up the trail to Maple Sprangs on this side of the mountain. You have to take the wagons from the next stop or on to Flat Creek."

"This side of the mountain? Next stop?" Cora gestured back toward the train platform. "But the sign said Maple Springs."

"Maple Sprangs *Junction*," the woman corrected with a nod. She tapped the counter as if to make her point. "The junction's been here for years as a stop for travelers who plan to hike into Junction Cove, down that aways." She pointed toward the far side of the store, as if Cora would know the place of reference. "Maple Sprangs is the next stop. Round the bend, yonder."

Oh good heavens! She'd traveled thousands of miles, over land, sea, and rail, only to make a mistake here at the end? Perhaps she should have told Jonathan she was coming, but, of course, she hadn't even known she was coming until Father's ultimatum, which forced her to climb out her window in the middle of the night, send the butler in for her trunks, and make a clandestine escape down the streets of London.

At least she'd left a note for Mother.

And had the poor butler swear to secrecy for fear of her revealing some unflattering information about his eating habits.

"And when would the next train come through to take me. . . 'round the bend'?"

The woman's smile brightened as she began scooping flour into a sack. "Well now, it's Tuesday." She pinched her lips closed and squinted up to the ceiling in thought. "That'd be Thursday."

"Thursday?" Cora slammed her palm on her head, flattening her knit cap against her curls with a crunch. "As in two days from now?"

"That'd be so. No time a'tall."

Cora squeezed her eyes closed and internally counted to five. Was it possible for things to get worse? She shook off the idea and braced her shoulders. She hadn't survived the Great War to let a little thing like a missed train stop detour her. Certainly not! If Jonathan could find his way to Maple Springs by himself, surely she could too. "So, can I walk there from here?"

The woman's expression softened. "No need to walk, dearie. We can get you fixed up with transportation, and that's a fact." She dusted off her hand on her apron and waved toward the back of the store. "Hezekiah's got a mule that can cut the five-mile mountain trek down to half the time."

"A mule?"

"Mule's name is Thunder." She tied the flour bag and shuffled around the edge of the counter. "He ain't much to look at, but he's a smart'un. Stout too. Will take you right up to Maple Sprangs and find his way home once you let him loose again."

Cora stared at the woman for a full five seconds as comprehension seeped through the odd phrases like "five-mile mountain trek," "mule named Thunder," and the possibility of riding the "stout" animal for five miles up a mountainside toward a place she *hoped* ended with seeing her brother and uncle. She looked down at her attire, thankful for her choice in wearing a full skirt instead of one of the newer, more fitted designs, especially if she was going to. . .

Wait a moment! Was she truly contemplating riding a mule into an unknown forest in the hopes the mule and this woman knew where he was supposed to go? She swallowed through the horrible imaginings running through her head at her possible demise in the future and clung to the truth that she'd survived six months as an ambulance driver at the Front and a year as a nurse in all sorts of situations. How bad could Maple Springs, a mule, and these mountain folks really be?

"My. . .my trunks are on the train platform by the rails. Should I. . .should I find a way to bring them. . ." Cora scanned the store, searching for a suggestion that didn't include her attempting to haul two trunks over the sludge to the store's steps.

"Hezekiah!"

The name burst from the woman without warning and shot Cora back three steps, nearly sending her tripping over a barrel of peanuts in the middle of the floor. She dropped her bag and steadied herself against the barrel just as the woman shouted again. "Hezekiah! Get on in here."

A crash sounded from a back room and then a massive man, with a face much younger than his size, lumbered forward. He wore a pair of dusty overalls with a stained white shirt underneath, and his blond curls hung in erratic ringlets down into a pair of piercing blue eyes.

"This here's my youngest," Mrs. Ayers announced, her smile brimming so wide her eyes almost disappeared into wrinkled depths. "He's strong as an ox. I'll have him get your trunks and then fix up Thunder for you, so you can git on up the road. You'll be courtin' dusk as it is."

Cora glanced out the window. The afternoon sun still hung high in the sky.

"Sit on down there on that barrel of pickled eggs and have you a bag of peanuts while Hezekiah fetches your things." Mrs. Ayers dusted off her hands and nodded toward a smaller barrel near where Cora stood. "I'll run grab ya some fresh cold milk and a beef jerky. Ain't no use to you ridin' off famished when you've got a full day ahead of ya."

Cora squinted down at the barrel. Pickled eggs? With another glance to heaven and a resigned sigh, she collapsed to a seated position. "Thank you, Mrs. Ayers."

The woman nodded and disappeared into the back of the store as her son exited the front. The quiet of the tiny, dusty store swept over Cora, bringing the myriad situations she'd experienced in the last half hour to the forefront of her mind. A tickle scratched at her throat. Her lips twitched. She looked out the window as Hezekiah raised one of her trunks into his massive arms, his face as red as a beet, and plodded through the mud as if he walked down Oxford Street in London.

Then the very idea of Hezekiah walking down Oxford Street forced the tickle into a laugh. She pressed her fingers to her lips to attempt to control the sound, but whether from the utter ridiculousness of her circumstances or the exhaustion of her travels, her chuckle transformed into a cackle before she could stop it.

"Well now, at least you've got your humor, girl." Mrs. Ayers waddled into the room, a tin in one hand and a small bag in another. "I've always said that a merry heart can weather the roughest of storms."

Cora swiped at her eyes and stood from her pickled-egg-barrel seat.

"Now, I packed you some jerky and an apple in this here bag." Mrs. Ayers pushed the paper sack into Cora's hand. "And take a good swig of this before you get on your way. Fresh from the spranghouse."

Cora looked down at the proffered tin and, with a slight hesitation, took the cup from Mrs. Ayers. After giving the contents a discreet sniff, she raised the tin to her lips, and the creamy liquid cooled a trail down her throat.

"Oh, Mrs. Ayers. Thank you for this." Cora raised the tin in salute. "I haven't had fresh milk since I was a little girl visiting my grandparents' farm." She took another drink.

"You ain't had fresh milk since you was a little girl?" Mrs. Ayers shook her head with a *tsk.* "No wonder you're as scrawny as a fencepost."

Another laugh bubbled out of Cora before she could stop it. "Am I?"

"I put a biscuit in the poke too." Mrs. Ayers waved a finger at the sack. "It'll be some fine eatin' along with that jerky." She peered out the nearby window, her smile returning. "Ah, and here's Hezekiah comin' round the side of the store with Thunder in tow. Come on now, girl. So you can be on your way afore too long."

Cora followed Mrs. Ayers to the door, and within a few minutes and a couple of embarrassing attempts from Cora to straddle Thunder with some decorum, Mrs. Ayers gave a few simple directions and pointed toward a trail winding up behind the store.

"Now, if you get lost, just turn around and come back down to us. You'll eventually run into the train tracks and can find your way back to the store." Mrs. Ayers patted Cora's knee as she spoke. "And stay on the main trail. The cougars, bears, and coyotes are less likely to bother with you there."

"Cougars?" Cora's throat suddenly squeezed tight. "Bears?"

"Now, they're more troublesome of a evenin' than midday, which is why we need to get you on your way, don't we?" She slapped Thunder's hindquarters and the mule took off at a relaxed saunter. "You're such a slight thing, I reckon he can go a might bit faster than usual."

Faster? This was faster? Her lips twitched.

"Stay on the trail, ya hear!"

Cora clenched her travel bag in front of her with one hand and held to the reins with the other. With a little twist, she turned to send Mrs. Ayers a smile. "Thank you for your kindness."

The petite woman and her giant son stood with the mountains and the train rails in the background, and Cora couldn't help but wonder what sort of story she'd entered.

Her gaze followed the rails and then turned toward the forest ahead of her, her smile falling with the darkening approach of the trees. Were mountain cougars the same as jungle cougars? At least she knew what a coyote looked like, but she'd never even seen a bear. She rested her travel bag against her stomach and slid one hand into her medical satchel. Her fingers searched over some vials, cloths, and medicine bottles to the back corner of the bag. Oh dear, she'd packed her pistol in one of her trunks. She groaned. What good would it do there?

She'd gotten the small pistol at the Front from a fellow nurse. Only fired it twice. Killed someone once.

Heat drained from her face.

And that had been enough.

She shook away the memory and focused on the surrounding forest as the trail began its marked ascent. Peculiar birdsong brightened the journey—sounds she didn't recognize from home in England. Squirrels scurried across the path. A rabbit hopped to her right.

After spending hours on various trains to arrive in North Carolina, the gentle quiet of nature cradled Cora's annoyance at her current debacle with a gentle caress.

This world breathed with life.

Visions of the wasted, lifeless frontlines of the Great War never strayed far from her mind, even though she'd been away from it all for almost six months now. Experiences like those attached themselves to the most mundane of tasks, withered fingers of brokenness and desperation clinging to the everyday.

Several older, more experienced nurses had helped her learn how to cope with the pain. The memories. Her mother's gentle words of faith had calmed many of the nightmares, and Cora had learned to focus on the good within those memories instead of reliving the devastation.

So this unfamiliar forest of green and growing things brought a welcome reminder that not all the world looked as bleak as the war-torn battlefields of France.

She smiled as the scent of mint drifted on the cool autumn breeze, and she loosened the scarf about her neck, so the coolness would kiss her warm skin. Thunder kept his steady momentum, his grunted breaths puffing in time with his steps up the hillside. About an hour into the journey, the terrain took a rockier turn. Gray boulders of various sizes scattered through the woodlands, some covered with a rich, emerald moss, and a few even boasted some lavender flowers blooming among the creases and clefts. Her initial reservation about this remote world softened at the gentle beauty as another tuft of mint-scented breeze brushed her cheeks.

This reminded her more of her brother's letters. The lush landscape. The quiet and beautiful world. A haven, he'd called it. "Not such a bad trip, is it, Thunder?"

The mule's right ear twitched as her question broke into his rhythm.

"But I must say, I'm ever so grateful Jonathan has a house that isn't too far from the main trail. He's told me of some mountain homes that are miles away from the trail." She caught a glimpse of a smoky-blue horizon through the veil of trees on her left, and her pulse gave a responsive flicker. Jonathan had written of the mountain views with deepest admiration, even sharing that his words could never do the myriad hues or grand horizons justice.

She caught sight of a distant peak in a frosty shade. Low-lying clouds?

Suddenly, Thunder came to a stop, both ears raised to alert.

"Do you miss my talking? Is that it?"

Thunder grunted, but it wasn't like any sound she'd heard a mule make before. More like a grumble or a growl. Thunder's ear twitched again. The grumble purred closer and not from Thunder. It came from Cora's right. A swath of cold spilled down her spine as she turned in the direction of the sound, and her body stiffened from hat to heels. Perched atop a pile of boulders stood a gorgeous, golden cat-like creature, massive, with defined musculature from its broad shoulders to its hind legs. Its amber eyes shone over the distance, taking in Cora and Thunder and likely wondering who would make the tastier treat.

So, *that* was a cougar.

The creature didn't move. Cora couldn't move. But Thunder seemed to recognize the threat, because with nothing more than a squeak, he took off at a run. Cora screamed and snatched a tighter grip on the reins, barely keeping her travel bag from falling.

When she looked behind her, the cougar was no longer on his perch. She scanned the forest. Where was he? The feline could easily outrun Thunder, though the mule moved at a pace that surprised her.

A glint of gold appeared in Cora's periphery. The cougar glided among the trees at her right, glinting in and out of vision from the wooded shadows, his presence closing in. Thunder must have noticed, because with a strangled noise, he turned left, off the trail, toward what looked to be a clearing, nearly sending Cora off his back. She screamed again as she grappled to keep her seat.

The cougar edged closer, giving her a clearer view of those monolithic paws pounding ever nearer. She was so focused on the golden-eyed creature, she wasn't prepared for the scene in front of her when she looked up. Just ahead, the trees disappeared to reveal nothing but a bright blue sky, an endless, gray-hazed horizon, and a rocky ledge. . .a ledge to which Thunder charged in blind terror.

Cora screamed, "No!" The cougar nipped at the mule's haunches. The sky came into full view. The ledge dropped off into nothingness, and those beautiful mountains were going to be the last thing Cora saw if she didn't do something quickly. A tree stood at the edge of the outcropping, one of its limbs branching out as if to offer her assistance. As the cougar made another attempt at Thunder's leg and the mule dove forward toward the ledge, Cora released her grip on the reins and her travel bag and pushed upward, catching hold of the limb just as mule, cougar, and travel bag careened over the edge of the cliff.

Her scream echoed back to her in full, uncontrolled terror, then all went quiet. With a shaky breath, Cora opened her eyes to survey her fate. The branch hung at a precarious spot between the rocky ledge and the ravine, so if she attempted to drop to the ground about five feet beneath her, there was no assurance on which side of the ledge she'd land. Her medicine bag pulled against her shoulder, and her hat, which already held a loose perch on her head, came unpinned by the next gust of wind and joined the plight of poor Thunder.

She attempted to slide down the limb closer to the trunk and farther away from a possible freefall, but the branch protested her movements with a bristly crack or two. Perhaps she wasn't as scrawny as Mrs. Ayers had thought.

With a look up into the cerulean, autumn sky, Cora attempted to keep her wits about her, though the circumstances enticed the taste of hysteria to emerge in the form of uncontrollable tears. She hated crying.

"Dear Lord, I know You must think I'm very brave and strong to have lived through all the many difficulties I've experienced over the past year." She adjusted her hold. The tree cracked again. "But I believe Your faith in me may be exaggerated. Or, at least I feel it is." She swallowed through the tears threatening to emerge into her voice and scanned the darkening forest. "Please send help."

Chapter Two

Artillery fire sliced through the smoke. Jebediah McAdams pushed across the mauled field laden with wounded and dying American and German soldiers. Only a few more steps and Amos would be safe. This time, Jeb would save his friend.

The drumfire of explosions beat on every side and then a terrifying squeal penetrated the deafening thrum. Was that a missile? Jeb pushed forward, though weariness made his moves sluggish, his cry silent. Amos was only an arm's length away.

And then, the unthinkable happened all over again. An explosion erupted directly in front of Jeb, separating him from Amos just like every other time, and Jeb knew that when the smoke cleared, his friend would be gone.

A sob racked through him, but the silent cry which usually accompanied the dream was replaced by a high-pitched scream from somewhere outside his head. Jeb attempted to push deeper into the dream, determined to see if he could save Amos, but the scream resounded again, so desperate it jerked Jeb fully awake.

He looked around the workshop. Hazy daylight filtered through the two windows and lit dust floating in the air at a pace much slower than his pulse. He pushed back in his chair and his attention landed on the empty cup of whiskey he'd downed before falling asleep at his crafting table. He'd stopped at one dram this time. More control. But he had to be vigilant or the nightmares and reality twined together to destroy his good intentions.

God help him. He would not become his father.

He scrubbed a palm over his face and stood, trying to remember what woke him in the first place. The scream resounded again. Nearer.

East.

Jeb pushed back from the table so hard he upset his chair and it slammed against the dirt floor. He ran from his workshop—Puck at his heels—and paused only long enough to grab his pistol from the porch of his house. The cry echoed through the forest. He increased his pace, branches and roughage slapping against his work-worn trousers.

Another noise brewed through the air, raising the hairs on the back of Jeb's neck. A mountain lion's growl.

Puck's dark fur bristled, and he rushed ahead of Jeb toward the mountain path and Parker's Edge.

Jeb gripped his pistol more tightly.

Another cry, more desperate than before, followed by. . .the squeal of a mule? Puck disappeared ahead through a blind of trees. A few briars caught against Jeb's trousers, slowing him down, but he followed the faithful dog, breaking through the forest into the afternoon light.

What he saw made him wonder if he was still stuck in a dream.

The mountains looked the same. Open sky and miles of rolling, multicolored peaks, bright with autumn leaves. The sunlight glowed with similar hues he'd seen before. Even the familiar breeze hinted with the welcome wild-grape scent of kudzu blooms.

But what didn't fit into the normal view was a woman dangling over the ravine with her deep red skirts blowing about her like a flag. Jeb stood a full five seconds, blinking in the sight, attempting to make sense of it. He even gave his head a thorough shake.

A quiet whimper and a solid creak of the tree branch propelled him into motion. Dream or not, he'd save her. Then at least, he could save *somebody*.

Puck didn't seem to notice the crimson-waving anomaly. The mutt frantically sniffed the periphery. And though Jeb kept his pistol at the ready, he knew that if the cougar was hungry enough to chase this woman through the forest, he wouldn't have disappeared just because his possible meal ended up in a tree.

Jeb couldn't see the woman's face. Her dangling position oriented her toward the view, but just some quick observation confirmed she wasn't anywhere close to being a local. And those were some fancy boots, even if they were tinged with mud.

He took a few steps closer, examining the problem. She hung at the cliff's edge. If she dropped or the tree branch broke, she had a fifty-fifty chance she'd end up on land, but with those dainty-heeled boots, Jeb wasn't likely to put much faith on her balancing against the rocks.

Her light brown hair caught glints of reddish gold in the sunlight as it curled and spun in wild directions, half of it still in some sort of bun. But even that was coming more undone by the second, and her hair seemed to grow as each curl bounced loose. As he drew closer, he could make out a few of her words.

"On the count of three. One...two..." She moaned. "Let go of the branch. That's what must be done."

He blinked a few more times. What on this whole side of creation was an English woman doing hanging from a tree over a ravine in Maple Springs?

Maybe he'd had more drams of whiskey than he remembered.

"One...two..." She drew in a breath. "You can't hold on much longer now, can you?"

Despite the humor coloring her words, Jeb heard the tremor in her voice. He knew all too well the familiar sound of forcing more confidence out of one's mouth than one felt. He'd lived it almost every day he'd been stationed in Europe. Sometimes, he'd even needed to remind himself to breathe.

He still did.

He cleared his throat.

She jerked to turn her body, and the tree limb cracked again.

"Don't move." Jeb stepped forward, palm out. He slid his pistol into his pocket and raised his other hand to join the first.

He slipped closer to the edge so that the woman could see him. Her eyes were pinched closed, brow and nose wrinkled, and her small fingers held a white-knuckled grip on the branch. The massive bag slung over her shoulder most assuredly didn't help her plight.

"I'll catch you."

She pried her eyes open and Jeb met one of the most stunning gazes he'd ever seen. Eyes, aged-wood gray with hints of a pale blue, stared back at him from a face too small for them. Perhaps fear made them seem larger, but they gave her an almost childlike look that didn't fit the rest of her figure.

"Are you sure?"

Her question disrupted his study of her, and he cleared his throat. "I reckon it's your best option 'cause sooner or later, you or the tree is gonna tire out."

She opened her lips to respond, but the tree branch made the decision for her. With a massive crack, it broke beneath her hands and sent the woman, her bag, and all that hair flying directly toward Jeb.

Her body hit him, knocking him back a step too far and sending the heel of his boot teetering over the edge of the ledge. With a quick turn, he shifted his weight, swinging her for a second out over the ravine and firming his footing before pulling her back against his chest as they both tumbled to the rocky ground.

She landed on him, her hair spilling over his face and wrapping him in some soft, sweet scent of flowers, like he'd stuck his head in a bouquet of daphnes. He'd never smelled anything so good in all his livin' days. Not even Mama's peach cobbler compared.

With a bit of a huff, the woman pushed up from his chest and attempted to stand, staring at him the entire time. In her hurry to untangle from Jeb, she tripped over his foot.

Just before she tumbled over the edge, he grabbed her by the hand. One of her boots poised on the tip, the other dangled over the cliff. Her hair flew all around her in a wild mass, and time slowed. Curls swirled around her pale face, her unusual eyes wide, the azure sky framing it all. Much better than any dream he'd had recently.

She wrapped her other hand around his and he pulled her back into his arms.

For an instant, she stared up at him, her face uncommonly pale, her eyes larger and deeper than before. Her bottom lip trembled. "You. . .you smell like licorice."

Licorice?

Jeb opened his mouth to respond that the scent was likely the horehound candy he carried in his shirt pocket, but before he could, the woman looked back over the ravine, whimpered, and then, with a quiet moan, went limp in his arms.

The horehound candy comment wouldn't have fit the moment nohow.

He shifted her in his arms and examined her face. Her full lips slightly parted, allowing her breath to fan his face. She sure was a pretty thing. He cleared his throat and looked around the forest. Quiet as before.

He moved her more comfortably into his arms and slung her bag across his shoulder in the process. He'd never held a woman in his arms. A little sister or his mother, maybe even one of the freckle-faced tagalongs from church, but a beautiful stranger?

And what was he supposed to do with her?

Puck tipped his head to the side, one ear pointed northward as if he were asking the same question.

Reverend Anderson, Jeb's nearest neighbor, had set off early that morning for some sort of preacher call, so Jeb couldn't take the woman there. Laurel's house was nearly an hour's walk. His shoulders sank, and he looked back at the trail from which he'd just come. With a deep breath, he made the trek to his house, having an internal argument with himself the entire way.

What if someone stopped by to visit and found a woman asleep in his house? He shook his head. Not that folks visited much up near his secluded spot, but he knew the dangers of rumors. It had led to his sister, Laurel's, unexpected marriage. Though, that had turned out to be a good match, from what Jeb could tell. But Laurel and Jonathan Taylor had been friends before having a shotgun wedding.

Jeb didn't even know this woman's name.

With careful steps, he entered his house. Too large for a single man and much "fancier" than a mountain man ought to have, from what his daddy said, but keeping busy kept Jeb's mind from pondering too long over those war memories. And working with his hands kept his fingers from reaching for whiskey. Besides, he felt alive when he worked with wood. Mama said it proved God's calling.

Jeb had started building the two-story white farmhouse when he'd first returned from war, and though it was close to finished, it was still a work in progress, and half-empty.

Puck followed Jeb down the little hallway, completely ignoring Thistle, the resident mouser, who'd slipped into the house sometime during the day and took up residence on one of the handmade spindle-back chairs. Jeb's usual companions. Quiet ones. He liked those best.

The woman remained quiet as he placed her on his bed and carefully, after a few fumbling tries, took off her dainty boots before covering her with a blanket. He ushered Puck from the room and then turned at the doorway, taking in the unexpected addition to his day.

Her wild hair lay sprawled on the pillow, but the easy rise and fall of her chest confirmed her well-being. And her face didn't look as pale as before. He studied her a second longer. She'd been so light in his arms.

He sniffed. And her fragrance lingered on his clothes.

A whimper came from Puck, sending Jeb stumbling backward

and nearly falling over the door's threshold. He cleared his throat and looked down at the dog. "Come on," he whispered, casting another glance toward the bed. "We'll go sit on the porch."

At least then if somebody wandered by, they wouldn't find Jeb inside the house with an unconscious, nameless woman. He already had a long list of regrets and a few tagalong rumors. The last thing he needed was to darken his world with an unwanted wife.

Licorice?

Why would Cora dream of licorice?

Something brushed against her face. Most likely her own wild hair, but she didn't remember leaving it down before going to bed. In fact, she didn't remember going to bed at all. She reached up to push at the errant strand against her cheek, and her fingers touched fur. Fur?

Her eyes popped wide to find a set of purplish-blue cat eyes staring down at her.

What on earth!

She pushed up from the bed and the cat scurried off, leaving her to examine her surroundings. A simple rock fireplace stood across the room from her, its wood-beam mantel boasting a few unique items: a carved squirrel, rabbit, and. . .was that a man in overalls holding a shovel? How curious! Cora shook her head and looked down at the bed, at the frayed quilt covering her body. Her breath grew shallow. Where was she?

With another cautious look around the room, she shoved the blanket back and studied her clothes. Wrinkled, but nothing misplaced or missing, except her boots. Her hand went to her shoulder. But her bag? Where was her bag? The cat's movements drew her attention. Her bag waited on a chair by the door and her boots on the floor nearby. She swallowed through her tightening throat and attempted to ease her breathing. How did she get here? Wherever *here* was?

The last events before she lost consciousness began to flip through her mind. The cougar! The mule!

And a stranger who'd caught her and then. . .

She'd fainted?

She gasped, pressing her palm to her chest. She *never* fainted.

But just the memory of nearly falling off the massive cliff spun her head. She took another deep breath and then, a sweet sound permeated her thoughts. A melody. Haunting and drifting toward her from outside. A cool breeze ruffled the white curtains in the room, so she stood from the bed and stepped nearer.

An open field stretched to a line of trees, but even through the wood, she could make out the sky and mountains beyond. She was high up on the mountain, evidently. A rock building stood a short distance from the house with a brown horse grazing within a connected fence. Another building, also made of stone, nestled at the edge of a stream. Something glittered on top of that building, catching sunlight. A wooden fence appeared to mark the property line, or, perhaps, it housed some group of animals she couldn't see. Sheep, maybe?

The sound, a violin, pulled her attention to the left. The edge of a porch came into view, but she couldn't see enough of it to answer her question as to who played the music. After a year as a volunteer nurse and six months at the Front, she'd curbed some of her youthful "high emotions" with more logic, but waking up in a strange house in a strange part of the world after being chased by a cougar up a mountainside and then nearly plummeting to her death off a ledge seemed a fairly logical reason for "high emotions," regardless of what her father might say.

Whoever had rescued her from the tree clearly had no designs to hurt her or he would have done so by now. If only she'd taken her pistol from her trunk and placed it in her medicine bag! What was the use of owning one and learning how to use it, if she didn't carry it with her?

She shot a glance heavenward, as if God were shaking His head in confusion as well.

The melody drifted forward, as soft and gentle as the breeze, and something in its turns and trills tugged at her heart in a strange way. She smoothed a palm against her neck and then studied the room, catching her reflection in a small mirror nearby.

Her hair stood on all ends, curls defying gravity. Good heavens, she looked positively wild. Even if she'd entered the untamed Appalachian wilderness, she didn't need to look untamed herself.

She made quick work of smoothing her hair into a bun, almost pinning all the curls in place. Almost. But there were always the rebel few. She pulled on her boots and picked up her bag before stepping gingerly around the doorway.

A large room greeted her, complete with a massive rock fireplace in the center of the facing wall. Large windows allowed light from different directions to brighten the sparsely furnished room, with white-slabbed walls and a few exposed wooden beams overhead.

It was a lovely space. Too barren for her tastes, but lovely.

A stairway curved up to her left and, through another doorway, she noted a cookstove and table. She'd expected unkempt and filthy surroundings, but this place appeared in perfect order. Whatever woman kept house here certainly knew how to do it right. Cora cringed a little. Much better than she herself could do if she had to keep her own house. When she'd worked in a mansion-turned-hospital in France, Cora had had the hardest time keeping her room to Nurse Barclay's specifications due to her note-taking habits and ever-present drawings. It was much easier to go over her notes if they were scattered all over the bed, and floor, if necessary. Nurse Barclay did not agree.

With quiet steps Cora approached the open front door, the strains of the violin pulling her forward. She paused at the threshold, taking in another view of surrounding forests with a small path cutting from the front of the house. Another outbuilding stood to the left, the clucking sound alerting her to its occupants.

A man sat on the far left side of the porch, his legs hanging over the edge despite an unoccupied rocking chair behind him. He was positioned in such a way that she could only make out part of his profile. His shoulders stooped as if he carried some invisible weight upon them, but he moved the bow across the strings of the violin with ease. Skilled and gentle.

Was he the same man who had rescued her? She scanned the area. No one else appeared to offer another option. Suddenly, the music stopped, and he turned.

Dark blue eyes met hers, then skimmed her from head to boot tip. As he unfolded himself from his seated position, he grew into a larger man than he'd appeared as he'd cradled the violin. Broad shoulders, strong stature. A man well suited to the hard life she imagined happened in these mountains.

She raised her chin and offered what she hoped was a smile. "Hello."

He studied her, holding the violin to his side, seemingly as uncomfortable as she. "Ma'am."

The quaint greeting spoken so quietly somehow eased the tension in her shoulders, but that didn't last long, because a bark erupted from one side of the house, and a dog with dark fur burst up on the porch toward her.

Cora pressed back against the doorframe, preparing for either a greeting or an attack.

"Puck. Back."

The dog paused but still edged forward to give Cora's skirt a good sniff before sitting on his haunches and staring up at her, his brown eyes offering a plea for attention.

"He ain't much for hunting, but he's a good snake dog."

"Snake dog?" Cora's throat closed around her high-pitched response. "Do you need one of those here?"

"You can get on without one, I reckon." The man gestured

toward the dog. "But they're awful nice to have around."

Cora nearly whimpered. Legs gushing blood, she could handle. Bombs exploding overhead, she'd managed. A few instances of being roughly handled by ill-mannered soldiers, she'd overcome. But snakes? She hated snakes. Did Jonathan or her uncle have a snake dog she could borrow?

The man shifted in the silence and then took a step forward, hand outstretched. "Jeb McAdams."

"McAdams." She took his hand, the rough edges of his palm slipping over hers. "Would you happen to know Laurel McAdams Taylor?"

Those blue eyes sharpened. "I do."

Clearly, elaboration wasn't his strong suit. "My name is Cora Taylor. I am Jonathan's sister."

"The nurse." He released her hand.

"Well, nurse-in-training, at any rate." She hoped her smile softened his frown. "I was partly through with my nurse's education when the war ended and. . ." *My father gave my future away to the highest-bidding bachelor.* But Mr. McAdams and the rest of Maple Springs didn't need to know that particular information. "I wasn't able to complete it, so I decided to find my brother and see how I could make my skills useful here."

He studied her, gaze holding hers as if he read all the things she didn't say, then with a step back, he glanced up at the sky. "Your uncle's place is about a half mile." He gestured with his head toward the forest. "You can make out the roof from here."

Cora peered up the hillside to see a slip of smoke rising from a chimney in the distance. "Oh, he isn't far at all."

"Closest house to mine." Mr. McAdams kept his face forward as he moved away from the porch, presumably for Cora to follow. "He was smart to build higher up on this side of the mountain. Less damage from running water and more daylight come winter."

"More daylight?"

He sent her a look from his periphery. "The shadow of the mountain can bring on dark much faster than you might think. Especially in winter."

"Oh." She glanced behind her at the well-situated house and the mountain rising up behind it. "But what about Jonathan?" Cora moved to catch up with the man, his dog, Puck, at his heels. "I would so like to see him."

"Night'll catch us before we can get to his place." Mr. McAdams stepped to the side to hold a gate open for her. It was then she realized his entire garden was fenced in and nearly immaculate. "Preacher can get you there tomorra."

The sky was beginning to fall into evening hues. How long had she been asleep?

"Yes, of course. Thank you."

He nodded and started down the hill, slowing his pace now and then to allow her to catch up. Well, he wasn't one to fill the silence. She fidgeted with her hair as the shadows fell longer across their path.

"Is Puck named after Shakespeare's character?"

He turned toward her and the slightest tip came to his lips. "I'd imagine so."

"You don't know?"

"My sister gave him to me as a welcome home gift, and she'd already named him." He nodded. "But I seem to recall she named him after some character in a book she'd read. She likes to read."

Cora's smile bloomed. "Yes, it seems that was the beginning of my brother and your sister's friendship, as I recall. Books."

"They have no lack of 'em, that's for sure."

"I suppose there are worse things to have in plenty." She flinched at the sudden memory of the wounded and dying soldiers being rushed into her medical tent.

"There sure are." The somber turn of his voice matched her thoughts. She studied him more closely. Had he mentioned Puck was a homecoming gift? Could that have been coming home from the war? He carried himself as one of the many men she'd met who knew unspeakable loss and nightmarish grief. If what she'd witnessed was only a third of what they'd seen, she couldn't even imagine the horror.

Her gaze dropped to his hands. Strong, work-worn hands that still made beautiful music on a violin. What sort of man lived in such a world and played with such feeling? Was that common for this desolate place?

"Thank you for. . .for catching me when I fell."

He faltered in his step, his profile turning toward her again. "I reckon the mountain lion was to blame?"

Mountain lion? Ah, the cougar! "Yes, he lost me a bag of clothes, an overpriced hat, and an unfortunate mule."

His lips twitched. "Good thing you didn't follow that mule. This ain't a place for. . ." He drew in a breath and pressed his lips closed.

Oh, she'd heard this argument before. Typical man. "For what?" She stopped walking, forcing him to copy her. "Or, should I say, for whom?"

He steadied his gaze on her, slow in his response. "It ain't for folks unfamiliar with the terrain." His shoulder bent a little, and he sighed. "This is an unforgiving land, Miss Taylor. Best you keep that in mind during your visit."

He resumed his walk without another word. Had he no idea what she'd lived through the past year as well? Casualty Clearing Stations in the middle of war-torn devastation. Exhausting days of work followed by nights filled with the moans of the dead or dying. True, she'd not encountered any mountain lions or bottomless ravines, but his words echoed with the same skepticism she'd experienced most of her life. What could a young, "pampered" woman of the city do to help the war effort? How could her weak constitution possibly survive such hardship?

Her jaw tightened and she marched to catch up with him. "It is true I am not familiar with your mountains, but I can assure you I am no wilting flower, Mr. McAdams. I do not faint as a rule." She waved behind her. "In fact, back there on the ravine was the first time I've ever fainted and I have been through enough difficulties with the war, not to mention corsets, to have been tested aplenty. So whatever constitution you are assigning me in your head right now, I suggest you think again."

He turned toward her, his mouth pressed tight, and those brilliant eyes narrowed. "I have every respect for the nurses and volunteers who took care of me and my fellow soldiers in the war, Miss Taylor." His lips twitched again. She flicked her attention from them and folded her arms across her chest. "And I ain't settled on one thought about you except the fact that you're a stranger here and it's my duty to see you safe to your uncle's house."

She swallowed back her readied retort at his gentle answer. "Well, I thank you." She resumed walking, the faint outline of a cabin coming into view among the trees. "I just wanted to make sure you understood that I'm no weakling. You just happened to catch me at a very unexpected time or I would have never fainted, you see. I believe heights are the problem."

He nodded but didn't respond, merely led the way into the clearing, where a log cabin stood nestled among the trees. This house was much smaller than the one she'd just left. Not even half its size, but a front porch lined the entire front of the house and the golden glow of lamplight welcomed her forward, away from the growing shadows.

"You understand, of course?" she continued, following him up the porch steps. "About the fainting?"

He turned to her then, his height and nearness causing her to tip her head back to see his face in the shadowed dusk. "Miss Taylor, I think you're allowed a faint or two after being chased by a mountain lion and nearly fallin' to your death, no matter what part of the world you're from."

He turned and knocked on the wooden door before she could respond. Likely ready to be rid of this talkative foreign lady who was much too ready to defend her fainting at all cost. She rolled her eyes skyward and stifled a groan. Why was she forever trying to justify herself? Why couldn't she just allow her actions to speak loudly enough for her goodwill and capabilities?

A rustle from inside the cabin preceded a shake of the door as it opened to reveal her Uncle Edward Anderson. It had been over nine years since she'd last seen him, and if her mother hadn't kept a photograph on display at home, she may not have known him at all, but he shared her mother's eyes. Soft green, and welcoming. Sudden warmth pricked at her eyes.

Family.

Her uncle's gaze traveled from her face over to Jeb and back, before realization dawned. "Cora?"

She released her held breath and nodded, her smile brimming. "It's been so long."

Without invitation, she surged into his open arms and buried deep. Years had separated their physical meeting, but hundreds of letters had kept them connected. She hadn't realized how much until she felt the vibrations of his warm chuckle against her cheek.

"What a surprise!" He drew back and held her by the shoulders, looking her over again before drawing her back against his chest. "I can hardly believe it!"

Cora stepped back and swiped at her eyes, keeping her attention away from the quiet stranger at her left. Just seeing her uncle grounded her in this wild wilderness *and*, somehow, brought to the surface all the pent-up emotions she'd felt from the time she'd left England. But the last thing she needed was Mr. McAdams to witness any high emotions at all, especially after he'd observed her near-death experience followed quickly by a most embarrassing fainting spell.

Heat resurrected in her face.

"Oh, dear girl." Uncle Edward's gravelly voice smoothed warm and deep, and he studied her afresh. "It *is* good to see you. You've grown into the very image of my mother."

Grandmother. Cora almost smiled and then gasped. "Grandmother." She reached for her throat. "Oh dear! Her scarf."

"What is it?" Uncle Edward's smile dissolved into worry frowns.

"The scarf Grandmother gave me. Well, you see, it blew off while I was hanging from a tree over a ravine." She pinched her lips closed to keep them from wobbling. That scarf had been one of her most precious possessions. An heirloom.

Oh, these mountains were no good to her at all!

"Hanging from a tree over a ravine?" her uncle repeated.

"As far as I can figure, Preacher, she was chased up the trail by a painter. She lost the mule over the edge, but I ain't sure what happened to the lion." Mr. McAdams shifted his attention to Cora and then back to her uncle. "I found her holdin' on to the tree and brought her here to you. We wouldn't've made it to Doc's place afore night caught us."

"And the last thing my niece would need is to have another such mishap in one day. Good thinking, Jeb." Uncle Edward nodded to Mr. McAdams then turned his attention to her. "You couldn't have been in better hands than those of Jeb McAdams, Cora. He's one of the best sort in these parts."

Jeb looked down to the ground, his discomfort in the compliment giving off a sense of humility, maybe even gentleness. Cora almost smiled.

But Uncle Edward continued. "And thank you for seeing her here, though I'm afraid she'll be sorely disappointed."

Cora flipped her attention back to her uncle. "What do you mean?"

"Jonathan and Laurel leave before sunrise to take handcrafts into town for the day, so you won't be able to visit with them until Friday. And I leave tomorrow for my circuit preaching route and won't return until Saturday."

Served her right for showing up unannounced, didn't it?

"But I don't see why you can't manage a night or two here alone. You've been at the Front." Uncle Edward waved toward the cabin. "My cabin has everything you need, and I feel certain Jeb won't mind keeping an eye on things while I'm gone."

A look passed between the two men.

"Not at all."

"And would it be too much trouble to escort Cora to Jonathan's house on your way to the mill on Friday morning?"

Mr. McAdams sent her another glance before nodding to her uncle. "No trouble a'tall."

"Thank you, Jeb. I'm glad *you* happened upon her." Her uncle's emphasis sent Cora's thoughts spiraling through what might have happened if some other mountain man with less—integrity? gentleness?—would have come across her instead. Her stomach pinched, and the burning in her eyes magnified.

Had this truly been her only choice to escape an unwanted marriage? How long would she be forced to stay in these mountains until her father stopped searching for her? Or until Dexter Arnold lost interest, whichever came first.

She shuddered at the very idea of his beady little eyes and condescending stare.

"A chill's settin' in for the night." Jeb ducked his head and backed away toward the porch steps. "Sir." He nodded to Uncle Edward and then raised his eyes to her. "Ma'am."

The word melted through her again. So. . .tender. How strange.

"I best let you two catch up."

And with those words, he made his way back to the path, his dog, Puck, at his side.

Cora pressed her palm against her chest and breathed out a long sigh. She'd met a great many men in her life, and most of them she could easily place into a category: aristocrat, snob, soldier, playboy, gentleman, and so many others. But as her gaze landed on

Jeb McAdams's retreating back, he seemed as much an anomaly as these hills.

And she didn't want to have very much to do with these hills, if she could help it.

Chapter Three

U ncle Edward pulled her forward into the house and led her to a chair. Though the cabin was small, it held a cozy air with a few additions her uncle must have brought with him from England. He settled her into one of the wingbacks by the fire, and she pressed her back into its softness.

A rug nestled beneath her feet and a small ornate table stood to the left, between her chair and the fireplace. Oil lanterns joined the fireplace's glow to give a cheery golden light to the room. A narrow stair disappeared to the right of the kitchen and led to a loft which opened to the room below.

Uncle Edward stared down at her, his green eyes holding questions, and then he patted his palms against his trousers. "Now, before you start to explain this unexpected visit, let me get the tea."

A smile touched her lips as she pressed her head back against the pillowed chair. Didn't Mother say that tea solved everything? Or at least, it helped get one's mind ready to solve things.

The scent of the fireplace mixed with steeping tea reminded her of those summers long ago when she'd pretended to be a "farm girl" at her grandparent Andersons' house in Derbyshire. How had she ever thought those memories could prepare her for living in this Appalachian wilderness? She shuddered at the memory of the cougar's growl as it closed in on her.

But she wasn't so ill-prepared, was she?

She'd helped birth sheep and sheared a few too, milked cows, brought in firewood—when she wasn't distracted by the puppies—and then there were her most recent experiences. Slogging through mud in France, tending broken bones as cold rain pelted her face, protecting herself from a rogue soldier.

Her throat dried at the memory.

"Now." Her uncle's soft voice pulled her gaze to him as he set a cup of tea on the little table and took his spot across from her in the matching chair, his own cup in hand. "What is the real reason you found your way to Maple Springs unannounced?"

"I suppose you wouldn't just believe it's because I missed you and Jonathan?"

His lips quirked into a frown, though his eyes still twinkled a little. "I have no doubt you missed your brother, dear girl, but I think there's much more to the story than that."

She took a sip of her tea, biding her time, but there really was no use. It wouldn't take long for a letter to arrive from Mother to her dear brother detailing the wild escape of his niece to the wilderness of Appalachia.

She released a slow sigh. "I ran away."

"You ran away?" His repetition edged on a low rumble and he leaned back, massaging the chair's arms as he did. "What did your father do?"

Of course, he would guess. The generic group of their family's acquaintances may not know her father's controlling bent, but family members knew. All too well. He'd been attempting to overpower and intimidate them for years.

Cora met his eyes. "Do you remember how Grandfather used to say that you can tell a man by the way he treats his mother or sister?"

Uncle Edward's brows rose, but he nodded.

"Well, Dexter Arnold treats his mother and sister abominably.

Not only that, he smells like bacon grease and has yellow teeth."

Uncle Edward rubbed his beard, the tension around his eyes softening a little. "And I'm assuming, based on your father's desire to marry off his children to the most lucrative options, Mr. Arnold was to be your husband?"

"Of course he was." Cora took a sip of her tea and groaned. "Though, I had wondered why Father never pursued a spouse for me up to this point, as he had Jonathan and Charles. It seemed he was just waiting to see which men survived the war before setting me up with the most unsavory bachelor of his acquaintance."

"And I suppose you told your father no?" His lips quirked beneath his mustache.

"Have you any doubts?" Cora's grin stretched wide. "And quite clearly, to both Mr. Arnold and Father. And yet Father published the announcement of our engagement the following week."

Uncle Edward released a rush of air from his nose. "And so you came here."

"Exactly. Of course, I'd wanted to see you and Jonathan and meet my new sister-in-law, so this provided a perfect excuse." Her smile tightened into mock sweetness and she batted her eyelashes for effect. "And I can help Jonathan with his medical work here in these mountains." Though, after the introduction she'd had, she was feeling a bit doubtful on that score. "Plus, if I remain here long enough, I have high hopes Mr. Arnold will either think I'm dead or find a woman more suitable to his fancies."

Uncle Edward braided his hands together and leaned forward, resting his elbows on his knees. "The mountains are an excellent hiding spot, but, as you've seen so far, life here is not as simple as you may have thought."

"I can't go back, Uncle." She shook her head, holding his gaze. "I won't. And if you won't allow me to stay here, then I'll be forced to travel West and find my place there."

"No need to rush headlong into a defense, Cora dear." He raised his palm, the corners of his eyes crinkling with his smile. "You are welcome here for as long as you need, but keep in mind, you've entered a world for which not even war can prepare you. Good things as well as bad reside within the hills and hollows of these mountains, things you don't understand."

"But I *want* to understand. I haven't spent almost a year in the worst possible places to allow my skills to go wasted."

"I have no doubt you will be used. Perhaps even sooner than you can imagine." He chuckled. "Adventure and danger are often thrust on a person here. There's no need to go and seek them." His expression sobered. "But keep in mind, these people are often suspicious and tied to their traditions and old ways. You are a woman of action." He waved toward her, his brows giving a slight shimmy at his implication that her grand escape from matrimony was sufficient proof. "There is no fast thaw with these people. Slow and steady faithfulness and authenticity reach them. Keep that in mind."

Cora set down her tea and nodded, searching his face. "Then you'll let me stay?"

His laugh broke out. "You may not have seen me in years, Cora, but how can you doubt my desire to protect your future? Even if it means I must bear the brunt of your father's ill will, should he discover you." He stood and took her hand, bringing her to a stand. "You are as dear to me as Jonathan and, though I cannot protect you from the harshness you may uncover here in Maple Springs, I can provide you with a place to lay your head."

He gestured toward the small bed in the corner of the room. "You are welcome to use either that bed or. . ." He raised his gaze to the loft. "The one in the loft, which will provide a bit more privacy, should you desire it?"

She glanced at the small bed on the main level. Clearly, it was her uncle's. Her attention slipped back to the narrow loft and she thought, for a fleeting moment, of her four-poster bed back home. With a sigh, she squeezed her eyes closed and then spun toward her uncle, putting on a smile. "I'll take the loft."

"Are you certain?"

"I am." She walked with him to the kitchen, her teacup in hand. "And when my trunks are delivered, I'll actually add some delicious English staples to your kitchen."

Her uncle's eyes brightened, a smile waiting on his lips.

"Huntley and Palmers shortbread and—"

"Digestives?"

Cora laughed at the boyish hope on Uncle Edward's face. "And digestives."

He took her by the waist and swung her around. "On my way out to my circuit tomorrow, I'll have the wagon sent here straight away." He set her down and patted her arms. "And, I suppose I ought to let Mrs. Ayers know about her mule."

"I'll pay for the costs. He truly was as noble as he could be, I'm sure."

Uncle Edward's grin tipped beneath his mustache. "I'll make sure to pass your sentiments along." He chuckled and waved toward the room. "And you should be fine here until Friday, surely. There's plenty to eat." He looked in the direction of the kitchen, where a few tins waited on the counters. "Gifts from my parishioners all across the mountains. Mrs. McAdams's dried apple stack cake is particularly nice."

Cora swept another look around the small house, preening a little at her uncle's faith in her skills. Likely, there was a little chicken coop outside, a well, and a cow to milk. With apple stack cake and a few beef jerkies in her bag, she should be fine to keep close to the house and explore this little part of the world until she could get to Jonathan's house. Then he'd help her navigate this new world.

Uncle Edward gave her a few more instructions, handed her a quilt, and gave her a kiss on the cheek before she climbed the narrow stairway to the loft. The area proved surprisingly cozy, with an iron-framed bed complete with a pillow and a couple of blankets already in place. A trunk waited at the end of the bed, and a little dresser stood to one side, between the bed and the small window beneath the low-lying eave.

The window was propped open by a stick, allowing the cool mountain breeze and a few night sounds to flow into the space. Cora stepped to the window and peered out, her raised position giving her the slightest glimpse of a dark silhouette of mountains and a fathomless starry sky. The air was tinged with some sweet floral scent mixed with pine. She breathed out a sigh, releasing more of the tension she'd carried throughout the day. She may not like the heights and dangers of these mountains, but there was something comforting about the quiet beauty of a starlit night and the crackling of a steady fire.

With quick work, she used water from a little basin on the dresser to wash some of the dust off and placed her gown over a rocking chair poised in the corner of the room. She draped her dirt-stained stockings and underskirt over the trunk, determined to give them a wash in the morning. Wearing a newer petticoat design that hit her at the knee, she crawled into the small bed. The weight of the quilts pressed down on her like a hug and, despite a few indefinable night noises beyond the window, she fell into a quick sleep.

꿈꿈꿈꿈

Cora blinked her eyes open, taking in the unfamiliar room. Cabin? Raftered ceiling? Memories from the day before filtered through her mind with an added shiver at the memory of the cougar. Heaven help her. She sighed and sat up in the bed. Light streamed in from the tiny window, and the smell of the fire drifted from below. The quiet of the house proved her uncle had probably already left for his circuit preaching route.

How had she slept so long? From the look of the sun, it had to be almost midmorning? She couldn't remember the last time she'd slept so deeply. Especially since the war.

Not wasting any more time, she dressed, attempted to wrestle her hair into a bun, and, finally, inched her way down the steep stairway to the main level of the cabin. The fire flickered with a dying flame, so she stoked it alive again and added a log from a small stack nearby. Her uncle had left the kettle hanging from the crane, keeping the contents warm, so Cora fixed herself a cup of tea and explored in daylight what little there was of the tiny cabin.

Somehow, her uncle's special touch gave the rustic surroundings a homey feel. Neat, tidy, with little handcrafts here or a homemade wall-hanging there or a special item from England carefully on display. This wasn't so bad, was it?

And then she felt the morning urge to use the toilet, and her momentary sense of contentment vanished. One of the definite benefits of city life was the ease of certain. . .necessities.

She pushed open the cabin's back door which led to a tiny stoop, nothing like the wide front porch. To the right stood a small structure with a few chickens poking around it. Nearby, a fenced area held a larger building, likely the barn.

Her attention slid to the left. A narrow, well-worn trail led to the edge of the forest where a small shed stood. The door on the structure showcased a crescent moon.

She squeezed her eyes closed. Jonathan had spoken of these "outhouses" or "Johnny seats." It shouldn't surprise her. She'd had to use them when she was a girl at her grandparents' house in Derbyshire. Even as a nurse near the Front.

But for some reason, the idea of walking toward the forest to enter a somewhat slanting little shack in the middle of nowhere held no appeal whatsoever. The pressure in her stomach built, and she put down her teacup. With a lift of her chin, she marched toward the building, keeping a wary eye on the forest.

The chickens clucked behind her, a few squirrels skittered up a tree nearby, and the way the sunlight filtered its golden hues through the veil of trees softened the foreboding look of the thick woods. She slowed her pace and breathed in cool morning air. A good night's sleep and a cup of tea was an excellent way to start the day. And the sooner she became accustomed to the culture of these mountain people, the easier it would be to make a temporary home here, even if it meant using a Johnny seat.

She gave the wooden door handle a solid tug and stepped over the threshold of the outhouse only to be met in the shadows by a pair of glistening white eyes. Her mouth opened to scream, but the only sound that emerged was a strange growl from the creature in front of her, perched on the toilet seat.

She'd never seen anything like it before. Like a cross between a large cat and a small bear? Big black circles framed each glistening eye, like a bandit mask. What sort of creatures did these mountains produce? She shuffled back over the threshold, almost falling, and had barely made it through the door back into the daylight, when the creature leaped forward.

A scream erupted from her then and she raised her arm to protect herself, but the creature landed on the ground and dashed away into the underbrush of the forest. She stared at the place he'd disappeared, her body quivering from residual fear. Keeping her eyes on the forest, she reached down and picked up a stick. The chickens' noises rose like laughter, and she turned toward them, stick raised.

"Don't get too cocky." She pointed the stick at the few chickens outside the coop. "I know your future."

Her warning failed to quell their chatter. She drew in a deep breath and turned back to the outhouse. After a thorough look inside, and keeping her stick at the ready, she entered and closed the door. Goodness, how had her brother ever managed to survive this place? If she'd almost died from a cougar on the first day and nearly been attacked by a cat-bear on the second, she felt rather daunted by trying to make it to a third.

Though she was proud of at least one thing.

She may have lost her composure, but she'd managed to hold on to her water. And, at the moment, small victories mattered. Unlike Mr. McAdams's home, her uncle's small yard had no fence barrier and the forest crowded a bit closer than Cora liked. She took a cautious walk around the space, briefly exploring the other buildings and examining the outside of the house. Despite the bitter taste in her mouth over her morning scare, she had to admit there was something charming about the log house, especially as the cool breeze brought the scent of earth and citrus to her. She slipped around the side of the house to find a small parcel of land dedicated to what she supposed was her uncle's flower garden. A wild array of color dotted the small plot near the rock chimney of the house, with varieties Cora had never seen before. Sunflowers she knew, as well as goldenrod, but an entire army of purple blooms rose like decorative spikes from the ground surrounding the other two yellow plants. A bush near the side of the front porch boasted a glorious burst of red berries, which complemented the wooden logs of the house in a most appealing way. Cora grinned. If she had her own cabin, she'd frame her porch with such a bush too.

The sky above shone with an almost otherworldly blue, framed in by trees of dark green. A few filtered with golden leaves, hinting at what her brother had called a "quilt of autumn color." Her gaze shifted over to the right, and the faint roofline and upper windows of Mr. McAdams's house came into view.

What must he think of her? Fainting.

She pressed her palm against her bun and cleared her throat, mounting the front porch steps. Something fluttered on the rocking chair by the front door. She stepped closer and her bottom lip came unhinged. Her carpetbag waited on the chair, her scarf tied to its handle. How did they get here from the bottom of the ravine? Her fingers slid over the scarf to make certain it was real.

Her attention shot back to the house below the hill. Had he scaled down the cliffside and gathered her items before dawn? Why? She was nothing more than a stranger to him. A headstrong, fainting stranger.

She untied the scarf and brought it to her face, the faint scent of licorice within its folds. A strange prickling burned the backs of her eyes. She didn't quite know what to do about this. She blinked away the sudden film across her vision and cast one last glance to the house below before taking her bag in hand and going inside.

She desperately needed another cup of tea.

Jeb guided his mustang down the mountain trail, the sun already higher in the sky than was usual for his trek, but he couldn't get Cora Taylor out of his head. He'd been praying God would send him something to distract his thoughts from the war memories, but the entrance of a feisty Englishwoman hadn't been on his list.

He took off his hat and scratched his head, his body moving easily with Hickory. He'd bought the horse within a week of getting back home, and the stallion had proved a smart and steady personality amidst Jeb's oft uncertainties. The horse's name certainly helped. Hickory wood was sturdy, durable. Strong.

Exactly what a horse—or a person—had to be in these mountains.

Miss Taylor flickered back to his mind. She may be a spitfire, but it'd take a lot more than that to survive in these hills, even if only for a few weeks. Especially with the start she got so far. Though, the fact she hadn't broken down into tears proved she had more strength than her fancy boots hinted at.

And Jeb wasn't quite sure what he'd have done if she'd broken down in tears nohow. It was one thing to take one of his sisters in his arms, but a strange woman?

Heat crept up his neck at the remembrance of carrying her into his house and putting her on his bed. Shoot fire, his pillow even smelled like her hair. All sweet and flowery.

Hickory snorted as if laughing at Jeb's wild wonderings.

"I gave you an apple as a treat for making the trek down the gorge," Jeb said. "Ain't no need to make more of a fuss."

Hickory's ears twitched, likely from the word *apple*.

Jeb breathed in the air, trying to clear his head of flower thoughts and the lingering darkness hovering at the edge of his mind at all times. The sounds. The silence. The loss. Reverend Anderson had encouraged Jeb to ponder on God's truths and good memories to counteract the bad ones, and some days, that worked.

It was the nights, when the dark crowded in and his hands couldn't keep his mind busy. When God's truths failed to penetrate the explosions and screams. And what little sleep he did gain came after battles and sometimes with the aid of a dram or two, which he'd relied upon in the war. But he refused to become his father. No child should be raised in a home of pins and needles and nightly rages.

Woodwork soothed him some.

Prayer too.

And these mountains. They'd called him from all the way across the world, even though his very small life had expanded to seeing and knowing much more than this tiny place. He had to find a way to overcome this, and God promised to help.

Even if that help took a heap longer than Jeb wanted.

The trail took a turn and then opened up to a broader path, soon spilling out to a crossroads, where the Rock Creek Mill stood just a ways off the road. The three-story wood-framed structure had become another home for Jeb since returning from the war, and the owner, Elias Harris, had become a good friend.

Though he'd borne the ridiculous verbal jabs from a few of the locals at befriending a black man, the larger population of the mountains didn't make much fuss about it. Truth was, they were all too poor to care what color a man's skin was if the man could help provide wood for building and flour for cooking. And thanks to Elias's quick mind and innovations, he'd taken the old wood mill and fixed it up to do both, converting part of it to steam. With it being less than five miles from Maple Springs and only a mile from

Rock Creek proper, the location ensured Elias had plenty of business and offered returning soldiers productive work in the process.

A young girl came skipping forward from the small cabin near the mill, her dark hair caught in a halo of braids around her small head. "You comin' in late this mornin', Mr. Jeb."

Jeb slid from Hickory and guided him into the pen near the cabin, the girl on his heels. "I had an errand to run first, Miss Dolly."

One of her hands went on her little hip and she raised a brow. "Well, Daddy's fit to be tied a'waitin' on you to git here. Had one man take to bed with the fever and 'nothern ain't shown his face in two days, and Daddy needs a body to cart wood into town."

"I'll get right to it, Miss Dolly." Jeb tipped his hat at the girl, who was no more than ten, but her personality added a few years. "'Specially if that's one of your excellent molasses cookies you've brought to me."

She preened a little at his praise though she attempted to hide her smile. "Don't know as you deserve it for bein' so late."

She caved at Jeb's exaggerated pout and handed him a handkerchief with, if he guessed right, about three molasses cookies. She raised on tiptoe and lowered her voice. "But don't tell Paul I gave ya three when I only gave him two."

"Not one word."

He slid the handkerchief in his pocket and strode down the path to the mill, the rhythmic sounds of the turning wheel and grinding corn welcoming him long before he reached the door. Jeb took the steps into the narrow entry, daylight slipping through the windows to dash away some of the dimness of the vast room. A pine log came across the carriage, and the saw sliced into the wood with its high-pitched whine, filling the entire space with a Christmassy scent. Jeb stepped around the massive carriage machine and caught a glimpse of a tall, dark figure on the other side.

He raised a hand to get Elias's attention, the sound of the saws easily drowning out any words. The massive man, who was a few inches taller than Jeb and a few more broader, dipped his head in welcome. Navigating the wood, saws, and carriage, Jeb slipped around to find Elias manning the edger saws and getting some wood slabs fit for delivery. Elias finished the edging and motioned for Jeb to step outside, nodding toward Paul, a former soldier who'd served on the eastern front, to take his place. The younger man moved into position, his dark eyes haunted.

Jeb wondered if his own eyes looked the same.

"I half wondered if you were laid up with Grady." Elias's deep voice resonated with humor, but his eyes searched Jeb's face. "Or worse."

Elias had seen him worse. Drunk stupid a few times, when Jeb had first returned home, but the man had given Jeb a job and a listening ear. Those two things along with the Almighty and a loving family probably saved Jeb from becoming more reliant on whiskey. Finding purpose by working with his hands helped too.

"No, nothin' of the sort." Jeb rubbed his palm against the heat creeping back up his neck. Ain't no way he'd tell Elias what he'd really been up to. "I had an errand to run, but wasn't too far behind my usual time."

Elias nodded, still searching Jeb's face until he seemed satisfied. "I'm glad you came. We got three orders due in town, and that's not including what you're takin' to the clinic."

Jeb followed him to the wagon, which had been filled to the brim with fresh lumber, each section separated and marked for delivery. Elias's palm rested on Jeb's shoulder, stopping him from moving forward. "Eb Carter was found this morning."

The look on Elias's face told Jeb more than he wanted to know about the outcome of a fellow veteran. "How?"

Elias released a long sigh, shaking his head before answering. "Hanged. In the barn."

"Who found him?" Jeb groaned, praying it wasn't one of his young'uns.

Jeb pinched his eyes closed at the image.

"You sure you're fit?"

Jeb met Elias's gaze head on. "I got my struggles, friend, but I ain't so far gone as that." He nodded. "Maybe, at one time, I might have felt so, but not no more. Not for a long time now."

Elias stared a moment longer then took a step back. "Well then, get goin', if you're going to have my team back to me afore dark."

Jeb grinned and took the carriage, drawn by two mares, the short trip into Rock Creek. The small town, closest to Maple Springs, had doubled in size over the past year since the rail station had added a stop to the place. Two rows of buildings lined the dirt main street, some wood frame, one or two brick, and then, of course, one was a stone church that'd been there long before the railroad came through.

Jeb made his stops as quickly as he could and then unloaded the last stack of lumber near an unfinished, wood-frame structure at the edge of town. His smile spread as the skeleton of the building took shape. Jonathan and Laurel's idea. A shop for selling local hand-crafts with an attached clinic. Close to the rail station and right near a growing town, so shipping would be easier.

His sister and her English husband had taken a dream by the horns and made it come to life.

Jeb sighed, his smile fading. If he could stop his nightmares long enough, maybe he'd realize what dreams he still had too. The reason why God let him live instead of so many other men.

He looked beyond the structure to a little cabin halfway up the hill. Amos's. Amos had left it to Jeb, but Jeb hadn't quite figured out what on earth to do with it or how he'd have the strength to go into that place again. He'd barely stayed five minutes when he'd first returned to the mountains after the war. But that was over six months ago, and Jeb needed to visit again. Sort out what to do. He owed Amos that and much more.

Maybe next time he was in town to work on the clinic, he'd

make time. He nodded to himself as if he'd made the decision, even though his heart pumped a retreat rhythm in his ears.

Daylight had disappeared behind the darkened mountain-horizon by the time Jeb took off Hickory's saddle, fed and watered him, and left the horse to rest for the night. His feet moved sluggish steps to the porch, Puck bouncing at his side for some attention. The wind bent the trees in an erratic dance, hinting of a coming storm. Thistle darted between Jeb's steps to get into the house, the feline well aware of the taste of rain in the air. Jeb placed his hat on a hook by the door and loosed his suspenders so they fell by his hips, and then he pulled the cookies from his pocket. Two left.

"Well, let's go make certain the windows are closed tight upstairs."

Puck darted toward the stairway and Jeb followed, patting the solid railing with a little pride in his work. The house was too big for him, but maybe God would fill it one day.

"I wouldn't mind none." He looked toward the ceiling. "Onct I got my mind on straight again."

The upstairs landing opened to a small hallway with two bed-rooms on either side, each with two windows. Enough to allow warmth, light, and a cross-breeze, if needed. He'd tried to plan it all, using his savings carefully because, well, for some reason each little piece of this house seemed to matter in his healing process. He hadn't been able to pin down a reason why yet, but that didn't change the fact.

At the last room, his attention caught on the roofline of Preacher Anderson's house. He hadn't checked on Miss Taylor all day long, but surely, if she'd stayed around the house, she was fine.

A glimmer of light glowed from the upstairs window. Probably where she slept.

The image of her curly hair splayed over his pillow popped to mind out of nowhere and he shook his head to dislodge it.

Something caught his attention. There was another light coming through the woods, directly toward Preacher's house. A lantern?

His gaze flew to the sky, the dark clouds growing darker by the second and trees bowing their branches lower and lower from the wind's strength. No one needed to be out in this weather, let alone an Englishwoman who didn't know anything about the mountains.

Jeb pushed the remains of the cookie into his mouth and dashed down the stairs.

Why did he have the sudden premonition that Cora Taylor might be the death of him?

Chapter Four

As Uncle Edward had promised, Cora's trunks arrived at the cabin around noon on the back of a wagon headed by a man who looked as though he was much closer to eternity than the rest of the people she'd met in Maple Springs. But he jumped from the wagon like a man half his age, and despite his leathery skin and slight size, walked with such purpose in his step, Cora wondered if he'd been in the army.

Another body emerged from the back of the wagon. A boy. Maybe twelve or so. Lean, with ill-fitting clothes and a head of hair so unruly Cora barely noted a set of small eyes beneath the dark mass.

"You don't look like no granny woman." The older man shook his head as he and the boy heaved the first trunk into the house.

"Granny woman?"

The scent of sweat and earth accompanied the man. He took off his straw hat and wiped his hand across his weathered brow. "That's what Preacher called ya when he beckoned me to fetch your boxes."

The man's accent held a curl of something familiar. Was it Scottish?

"Preacher called you a nurse woman, but Grandpaw ain't never heared of 'em, so's he figured that's what a city-born granny woman was called." Cora turned and found herself lost in the boy's curious eyes, a surprising shade of pale green. A shocking combination with the deeper tones of his skin. How curious. Most of the people she'd seen so far had very fair skin, or sun-touched gold. His held a warm, olive tone.

A nurse woman? Cora's mouth quivered into a smile. "And what is your name?"

"Fig Tate, ma'am." He dipped into a full bow with dramatic flair, inciting Cora's chuckle, his dark curls waving forward.

"Boy, git on over here and help me, afore the other half o' the day is gone."

Fig's grin wrinkled his nose, and he gestured toward the older man. "And that there's Fergus Tate." He jogged back to the wagon bed and helped Mr. Tate with the other trunk. Fergus. Very much a Scottish name.

Cora shifted on her feet as she watched them teeter beneath the size of the trunk, and then she rushed forward. "I can help."

"No place for womenfolk." Mr. Tate sniffed. "We'll tend to your parcels as Preacher said, so git on."

Her back stiffened at the dismissal, a defense waiting on her tongue about all the ways she was forced to do many "menfolk" things during the war, but she wasn't on familiar ground right now. And the longer she stayed in this Appalachian world, the more unfamiliar things became.

"You reckon to catch yourself a mountain man from the looks of it?" Mr. Tate grunted as he carried the trunk through the cabin door. "You brung 'nough to set up your own house?"

Set up her own house? Her stomach turned as the second trunk dropped against the wooden floor. Maybe she'd gotten a bit carried away with her packing. "I don't have any plans of catching a mountain man or setting up house with one, Mr. Tate."

The man chuckled, a glimmer in his pale eyes and then, with a tip of his head, he marched out the door. Fig's grin resurrected and he started to follow, but Cora stepped after him.

"So, a granny woman is a person who helps tend the sick?"

"That's right." His gaze traveled down her and back up, brows disappearing beneath his long locks. "But I ain't never seen one the likes of you and that's a fact."

"Meaning?"

He shrugged one shoulder. "Fancy clothes and nary a wrinkle."

With that, he ran off after his grandpa.

Cora stood in the doorway, watching the wagon make a slow retreat back into the forest. The pale blue afternoon sky dusted with a few clouds. She'd explored every piece of the cabin that morning, admiring the homespun rugs and quilts. The handmade pottery. Even a few pieces of furniture had to have come from the hands of an excellent wood craftsman. Despite her dislike of Maple Springs, something about these intimate glimpses of beauty within this dangerous world softened the edges of her skepticism.

What *was* this place? And how could her brother love it so much?

She set to work going through her trunks, first taking her pistol out and ensuring it was in working order. Then she changed into clothing much more suitable for her new surroundings. Clothes she'd purchased while nursing. "Sensible" things, Nurse Barclay had said. A sturdy skirt and simple shirt. Boots, without ornate heels. Then she fitted her medicine bag with some of the necessities she'd brought in order to prove to her brother that she truly had learned some skills over the past year and a half. And she placed her pistol snug within the bag. For safekeeping.

It took her much longer to situate her things while keeping the fire going and attempting to sort out how the stove worked. By the time she'd scalded some leftover corn bread and tried to cover the burnt taste with some cold ham, darkness had crowded around the little cabin.

Out of nowhere, the wind erupted with sudden force, giving the fire an extra flicker in the hearth. It wasn't the fact that she was alone in a strange place. Of course not. She'd been alone before.

Many times. However, the incessant moaning of the wind just beyond the impossibly black night outside the windows proved the *real* problem, and Cora attempted to correct things by pulling all the curtains closed and tossing a blanket over the one window without curtains.

She'd barely finished a cup of tea when a strange glow came from behind one of the front curtains. Golden. Lantern light?

She stood, teacup clenched in her fingers.

The glow grew brighter. Nearer.

Uncle Edward wasn't due back until Saturday.

She placed the teacup on the table and grabbed her medicine bag, feeling for her pistol, just as a resounding knock shook the front door.

"Nurse Woman!" a thin, young voice yelled from the other side of the door. "Are you inside, Nurse Woman?"

Nurse Woman? What on earth? Cora took a few steps toward the door, fingers tightening around the pistol.

"It's Fig Tate. Brung your trunks to ya today."

The little boy from this morning? Cora thrust the pistol into the pocket of her skirt and pulled the lock-board away from the door. A cool gust of wind pushed the door open with more force than Cora had meant, causing her to stumble from its sudden weight. Before her, capless and pale, stood the young boy, his large light green eyes finding hers.

"Fig?" Cora looked past him for another person, but saw only darkness. "What are you doing here? It's much too late for you to be out a—"

"Mary Greer's baby's comin' early." He stared at her expectantly. "We can hear her cryin' from across the way."

"I'm sorry?" Cora kept looking at him. He kept looking at her.

"Grandpa went for Granny Burcham, but she ain't home, and Teacher Doctor ain't back from town yet."

Teacher Doctor. And then a sickening realization dawned.

Nurse Woman.

"You. . .you want me to come?" She breathed out the question, more to herself than to the boy.

His eyes narrowed, and he took a step back toward the porch, as if he was doubting her abilities as much as she was. She stiffened at the very idea. She'd nursed many people. Some women. But *none* in childbirth.

Still, she *was* a woman, and she knew the basics of it, somewhat. And she did have medicine. Her chest pulsed with her breaths. If she wanted to be taken seriously in this place she couldn't turn the boy away when someone clearly needed help, right?

She nodded to herself. Right.

"Of course I'll come." She grabbed her coat and snatched up her medicine bag again, adding some nearby cloths to it, just in case.

Fig sent her another incredulous look before turning up the collar of his threadbare jacket and stepping off the porch. A sudden gust nearly took her breath away, or perhaps it was the way the silhouette of trees waved overhead like black claws against the faint gray of the sky, but she jerked the door closed and trained her attention on the lean boy disappearing down the trail.

With a glance up to where Jeb McAdams's cabin stood and a quick prayer heavenward, she followed the lantern light into the black forest. A rumble of thunder growled into the night, and she relinquished a resigned chuckle.

Well, at least God had enough confidence in her to send her off with a drumroll—the wind moaned anew—or. . .maybe it was the beginning beat of a death march.

Fig didn't talk, merely held the lantern high enough to allow Cora light to barely see in front of them. Which was a mercy, since the boy walked so quickly, Cora nearly tripped to keep up. Not ten minutes into their trek, sprinkles of rain slipped through the trees and began an increased assault on her hat and shoulders. Fig didn't slow at all. In fact, he seemed to move faster, dodging tree roots and rocks with excellent skill. He had to have dodged them, because Cora stumbled over almost every one.

The wind blew the rain around her and into her face, but she refused to slow her pace. If the boy could march through this dark, wet forest at staggering speeds, then she could. And with more appropriate footwear, at least she wasn't in danger of twisting her ankle nearly every step.

A turn in the trail led upward. Cora couldn't see anything beyond the lantern light, and the black shadows crept closer from all sides. If the war had taught her nothing else, it was how to control her fears, so with an internal prayer and a direct focus on the boy in front of her, she closed off the "what ifs" in the shadows. She had to. A survival skill.

A sudden cry pierced the darkness, slicing against the thunder and dashing a chill up Cora's spine. It was a pitiful noise. Pain-laced. It called to Cora's heart, setting her feet in motion. She bypassed Fig and rushed toward the sound erupting again from a tiny structure. Faint light glowed from a single window beneath a narrow porch roof as Cora took the creaky steps to the front door.

Wind pushed her over the threshold, but she came to an immediate stop. Fig squeezed in behind her. She blinked into the low-lit room. One lantern hung on a hook on the wall and firelight glimmered a golden dance across the floor, but the feature in the room that captured Cora's attention was the small young woman clutching the back of a chair. Her extended abdomen was outlined beneath her billowing nightgown and her dark hair fell loose around her shoulders. With the firelight playing off her pale face, she looked almost haunting.

Fig turned wide eyes to Cora and then backed out the door. "I'll. . .I'll be goin' now."

"Wait," Cora called after him, but the boy closed the door, leaving Cora and the young woman staring at each other, Cora's eyes likely as wide as hers. She looked so small and young. Could she even be sixteen?

The poor girl suddenly stiffened and grabbed at her stomach as another whimper turned into a wail. What had Fig called the girl? Mary?

Cora moved closer, waiting for the girl's cry to die down. "My name is Cora Taylor." She took a step closer. Sweat beaded on Mary's forehead. "I'm a nurse. Fig thought that maybe I could help you."

"You...you a granny woman?" came the girl's trembled response.

Cora shrugged a shoulder. "I helped doctor soldiers during the war."

"You was in the war?" Mary's eyes widened.

"Not in it, as far as fighting, but I helped with the sick and wounded." She scanned Mary's body, her throat tightening at the thought of all the things she didn't know.

"Mama said babies just come and all a body's gotta do is get through the pain."

"Well, what do you say we prepare for your baby by heating up some water and cleaning some cloths." Clean cloths were always a good idea. And likely good for this too.

Mary's body stiffened as her whimper extended into another moan, and this time, she almost collapsed. Cora caught her just in time and both of them nearly sank to the floor, but with a careful turn, she was able to help the girl get to the bed. A trail of liquid marked their path.

Cora squeezed her eyes closed for a moment in quick prayer before helping the girl adjust herself on the bed. "Cloths?"

Mary nodded toward the table, where a few rags lay in a pile. She must have been preparing. Oh good heavens, the idea of the poor girl managing birth all alone in this cabin shot a fire through Cora. Where was Mary's husband? Or mother? Anyone?

Yet, Cora was here. Who knew nothing about birthing babies.

And, God help her, she'd have to do.

She got to work putting a pot of water over the fire and then took the bottled alcohol from her bag as Mary whimpered through another pain. That was two pains in less than five minutes. Hadn't she heard of that being significant? Weren't the pains supposed to get closer together as the time neared?

She glanced down at the morphine in her bag. No. Mary needed to be alert and aware for this, even if she was in pain.

"You. . .you talk funny," Mary whispered.

Cora turned around with a smile. "Well, I'm from England, like your Reverend Anderson and Mr. Taylor."

Her brow furrowed with suspicion. "You ain't no kin to that Teacher Doctor, are ya?"

Cora trained her features as she rolled up her sleeves. "What on earth could be the trouble with Mr. Taylor?"

"My man ain't keen on the teacher. Says he's spreadin' lies and magic."

Magic? Cora turned to the young woman and was about to ask her to explain when she began to tense again with another pain. Cora moved to her side and tried to pull from her experience. "Breathe, in and out. Slowly."

The girl took Cora's hand and held her gaze with such desperation, Cora dared not look away. Mary mimicked Cora's breaths and made it through the pain without screaming, though she moaned through her breaths. With what little Cora knew about birthing babies, she imagined moaning was the very least the poor girl could do. Cora pinched her knees together at the very idea of what was about to happen to Mary. Of course it had to hurt!

"That. . .that helped," Mary whispered, giving Cora a look of awe.

Her large round eyes took up so much of her pale face. Cora pushed up a smile and squeezed her hand. "Good. I want to help."

Mary nodded. "The last'un came too early. Never made it to this part of birthin'. I. . .I don't know what to do."

Neither did Cora, but she refused to show it. Mary had already been pregnant once? And lost the baby? Cora steadied her expression with what she hoped was confidence. "For most cases, nature takes its course, so perhaps you should relax back against the bed and..." Cora swallowed. "Raise your legs so we can prepare."

The faux-confidence in her tone must have convinced the girl because she placed her head against the headboard just as another pain seized her body. Cora helped her breathe again. The pains were closer. That wasn't even two minutes.

Just as Mary's body began to relax, the door burst open, wind rushing into the room and sending the fire into a frenzy. Out of the darkness emerged a petite person shrouded in dark colors from the black scarf around her head to the dark brown boots on her feet. Cora stood, stepping toward the end of the bed as a barrier between the stranger and Mary.

The figure pulled back the scarf to reveal two dark eyes within a leathery face, with wiry gray and white hair pulled back into a tight bun. The woman took in the room, her attention shifting from Mary back to Cora, her eyes narrowing as she focused. Cora's breath stalled, the elderly woman's penetrating gaze holding her fast, as if reading her thoughts and finding her wanting.

A whimper from Mary tugged Cora's attention, and she rushed to the girl's side and took her hand. They breathed together a few times, until the pain appeared to subside. Had it been a minute since the last pain? That had to signify something important, didn't it?

"How close are them pains?"

Cora looked up at the stranger. She'd closed the door and stepped closer into the light, her thin face wreathed in wrinkles. As she drew nearer, the lightness in her step contrasted her bent position. A large basket crooked over her arm.

"That. . .that one was barely a minute from the last," Cora answered.

"I'm hurtin' somethin' awful, Granny," Mary whimpered as Cora wiped the girl's sweaty brow.

"'Twill all be done soon 'nough," came the woman's matter-of-fact response, and without warning, she pulled something from her basket and raised it above her head.

Cora barely had time to process what was happening. The spry woman raised a hatchet into the air and rushed toward the bed.

Why, oh why, hadn't Cora thought to take her pistol out of her bag? She blinked at her own thoughts as the wild woman drew closer. Well, because she hadn't expected to die by the hatchet of a madwoman while helping to deliver a baby for a mountain girl in the middle of the wilderness.

Without thinking, Cora threw her body over Mary's, waiting for the slice of a blade to hit her in the back, but the impact never came. Instead, the old woman drove the hatchet into the wooden floor of the house, just beneath the bed on which Mary lay.

Cora pushed back from the bed and stood, her attention moving from the hatchet to the woman, who'd stepped over to the fire as if she hadn't just taken ten years off of Cora's life.

"You put the cloths in here to boil?" Her dark gaze turned back to Cora.

Cora worked up a reply. "Yes."

The woman nodded and reached back into her basket. She brought a small piece of some brown, withered strip to Mary. "Chew on this, girl. 'Twill help with the pain."

The girl shoved the strip in her mouth and whimpered as another pain came.

Cora stared at "Granny" as the woman took her time moving from one thing to the other, without any hurry in her walk. Who was she? Cora's breaths shivered. Or *what* was she?

A sudden knock from the door resounded over Mary's quiet cry.

"Things about done in there?" A man's voice boomed forward as if the thick wood didn't separate him at all. "I ain't got no notion to spend my night out hyere on the porch."

Granny's attention sharpened, and she focused on Cora. "Ain't no rushin' babies, boy. Healthy babies can take time to be borned.

You already lost one 'cause o' your hotheaded ways."

A round of unsavory comments followed from the man behind the door. "Git on with it then, cause I ain't stayin' out here on the porch, no matter what you say, woman."

Granny rounded the bed and took Cora by the arm, her grip stronger than her stature would suggest. "You best git out o' here right now."

Cora's attention flew to the window, knowing full well a forest, several miles, and a dark night separated her from her uncle's cabin. "Now? It's night and. . .and I can help you here."

"If you want to live to see the mornin', you best git out o' this house afore Clark Greer comes through that door."

Cora stumbled back from the woman and shook her head. "I. . . I don't know the way home."

"Moon's out now. Keep it to your back and follow the trail." She pushed Cora toward a back door she hadn't noticed. "Leastways, you'll have a chance."

"A chance?" Cora grabbed her bag and jerked it up on her shoulder as the woman opened the door.

"You stay here, and you won't have no chance." She shoved Cora out onto a little stoop that didn't have a covering, and a chill which had nothing to do with the cool wind shivered up Cora's body. The darkness of the night failed to compare to the pitch within those trees.

Granny thrust a lantern into Cora's hand. "Don't light it till you're away from the house." She gestured ahead. "Trail begins by that rock pile, yonder." She gave Cora a push. "Go. Now."

Cora stumbled down the few steps to the ground and turned, but Granny had already closed the door. The moon shone in the sky to Cora's right, clouds passing over it as the cool wind continued to blow. She turned her attention toward the "rock pile" and the forest just beyond, noting a tiny path that slipped around the side of the rocks and into the trees. A sudden rush of tears warmed her eyes and she tightened her grip on the lantern. She didn't belong here.

How could God have placed her in this moment? Didn't He know she couldn't navigate the dark on her own? She'd survived the war without any lasting scars except this. The dark. Alone. The dark was the place of dying breaths and shattering explosions. Of ghosts.

She turned back to the cabin door, weighing her options. Something sinister lurked behind Granny's words. Had Mr. Greer hurt other strangers in the past? The way he'd voiced more concern about his sleeping spot than his wife's welfare spoke volumes. How much less would he care for a foreigner in his house?

Cora raised her gaze to the moon again and drew in a deep breath. An infant's cry shuddered through the silence. Cora smiled at the strength in that cry. Good and strong. If she'd only been able to wait a few more minutes, she'd have seen that little baby. Was it a boy or a girl? Did the baby have hair?

A slam exploded from the other side of the door, followed by the angry voice of a man. Air pinched in Cora's throat and she took off at a run toward the rock pile. She'd barely skirted around it when the back door of the cabin opened and the large silhouette of a man filled the frame. Cora crouched lower behind the rocks, holding her breath. Even though she couldn't make out the man's face, somehow she felt him searching for her. She slipped her hand into her bag and pulled out her pistol.

She'd had to defend herself once before.

She could do it again.

Long seconds passed and then, with a sound like a growl, the man closed the door. Cora waited only a moment before she dashed off down the narrow path that split through the trees. She stumbled over roots or rocks in the dark, barely keeping her balance as one hand clutched the lantern and the other her pistol. Unfamiliar night noises she'd heard from the safety of her bed last night took a terrifying turn without the shelter of walls and the glow of a fire nearby.

Even the moon, with its pale light barely making a sheen

through the thick branches above, failed to offer much comfort. But at least it was behind her. Her fingers trembled as she drew a book of matches from her nursing bag and lit the lantern, its glow only making the surrounding darkness more haunting.

The sound of her breaths seemed amplified. Her footfalls rustled against the fallen leaves, joining with unfamiliar noises from just beyond the lantern's light.

With a deep breath, she marched forward, keeping her attention on the path ahead and desperately praying her uncle's house proved much nearer than she feared it was.

Chapter Five

Where was she?

Jeb moved as fast as he dared. Though the moon scattered faded light in various shades of shadow, the narrow terrain of this part of the mountain took unexpected twists and turns, with a few precarious drops to the right toward the river below. Why on earth Cora was headed to Copperhead Peak, Jeb hadn't any idea.

Puck kept to Jeb's side, his ears perked to attention as he occasionally pawed at the dancing glow of the lantern light against the forest's darkness. Night sounds trilled from all directions. Cicadas, crickets, a distant owl, a frog or two. A small critter rustled the brush at Jeb's left, skittering out of the light and nearly sending Puck on chase.

The recent rain brought out the earthen smells of damp moss and old leaves. Jeb wrinkled his nose at the scent of skunkweed and galax, stronger because of the fresh dampness. The path ahead deepened with the thickening forest, and Jeb slowed his pace. What if he'd been going the wrong direction all along? This may have been the main trail to follow from what he could tell as he'd caught glimpses of lantern light in the distance, but. . .

He shook his head. Someone had come to fetch Miss Taylor for some unknown reason, and she hadn't been in the mountains long enough to make enemies.

His stomach dropped. Or had she? He peered ahead into the

darkness. Crow Ridge wasn't a place for the likes of Cora Taylor. A glimmer of light flickered ahead and then disappeared. Jeb stopped and looked down at Puck, whose ears stood to attention.

The light flickered into view again. Puck sniffed the air, a rumble erupting low in his throat. Jeb placed his lantern on the ground and shifted his rifle from his back into position before taking the lantern back in hand.

"Steady, boy. We don't want no enemies, if we can help it."

Puck calmed at Jeb's gentle voice and walked toward the glowing light. The night sounds died down, as if they anticipated a fateful meeting too. Jeb tightened his grip on his rifle, the turn in the path preventing him from seeing anything except the approaching light. He stepped around the rocky outcropping and came face-to-face with the end of a pistol. A very shaky end of a pistol.

His body drew completely still and his gaze followed the steel tip all the way back to a pale face. Soft curls, loose and wild, sprang in all directions and made him think of his Granny's stories of faerie children of the woods.

"Oh," came a gasp as the pistol shook like leaves in a storm. "Jeb!"

His name erupted from her lips like a little whimper, and she lowered the gun. The shaking seemed to catch on because by the time she'd returned the pistol to her bag, her whole body was quivering like a newborn kitten.

Blood began a heated return to his body and he worked out some words through his dry throat. "What on earth are you doin' all the way out here?"

Cora didn't seem to notice the edge in his voice. He hadn't meant to sound irritated. But before he could prepare himself, she'd run directly into him and buried her head in his chest. For a second, he just stood there, frozen to the spot and not at all sure what to do next. He may have dreamed about holding a woman in his arms a few times in his life, but a weeping Englishwoman hadn't been part of the dream. Though now he thought about her and felt her body tremble closer to his as if. . .as if she trusted him. As if he'd keep her safe. The idea began to grow on him a little bit.

But just a little.

He released his hold on the rifle, allowing it to dangle from the strap across his shoulder, and wrapped his free arm around her. She burrowed deeper, her curls tickling the bottom of his chin and bringing the sweet scent of wildflowers. After his previous breath of wet skunkweed, she smelled downright sublime.

He dared not move. A part of him didn't want to. But his mind kept searching for exactly what he *should* do next. Or say?

"I'm real glad you didn't shoot me."

Her sobs turned up to a wail for a minute. He pinched his eyes closed. Well, that sure fire wasn't the right thing to say.

"It's alright," he cooed, his palm smoothing down her back and getting tangled in her hair as if his fingers knew exactly what they wanted to do. He jerked his hand away from those soft curls and loosed his hold, barely touching her now. "We'll get you home."

Those words seemed to fare better.

She quieted, her sniffling growing softer. He tried real hard not to think about how soft she felt against him. And he tried real hard not to wish for his fingers to go exploring back into her hair again. But the longer she cozied up against him, the less he tried not to think about what he kept on thinking.

"I'm. . .I'm so sorry." She stepped back and wiped at her face with her hands. "I don't know what came over me. I mean, I. . .I don't handle the dark well ever since, well, you know."

Her watery gaze flashed to him and he recognized a fellow survivor. He nodded.

"And. . .and then, the baby was coming, and I've never delivered a baby. If the woman had needed an amputation or assistance with a bullet wound, in those cases I'm extremely proficient." She wiped at her eyes again. "And I felt I could sort out most things about birth, you understand?"

Jeb didn't really want to understand, but he nodded just the same, because it seemed to work so well the first time.

"Then just about time for the baby to arrive, or at least that's what seemed to be happening, this granny blew into the house and forced me out on threat of my life." Her volume rose along with her brows. "Have you any idea?"

If Jeb nodded, then he'd be lying. He hesitated a second and then slowly gave his head a shake.

"Well, it was terrifying."

He released his held air. Shaking his head seemed to work too.

"But not as terrifying as her tossing me out of the cabin in the middle of the night because some horrible man might kill me if he found me there." She raised her shoulders in a helpless shrug. "Kill me? He doesn't even know me and he wants to kill me? What is this place?"

All heat fled his body again. "Clark Greer?"

She blinked a few times, the lantern glow highlighting a few lingering teardrops on her lashes. Something pinched inside his chest.

"Yes, that was his name." Her brow wrinkled with her frown. "He was horrible. Not a care in the world for his wife who was giving birth to his child. All he was concerned about was not sleeping on the porch. Can you believe it? You and I, who've slept God knows where in the middle of the war, and this hateful man cannot bear a few hours of discomfort for the sake of his wife and baby!" Her voice rose, and the lantern light seemed to grow her stature a little. Her voice quavered again. "It's detestable."

Jeb reached into his pocket, took out his handkerchief, and offered it to her. He didn't have a notion what would be the right thing to say, so he guessed at the end result of it all. "I reckon you'll want to get on back to your uncle's house."

She took his offering and followed as he turned down the trail.

An owl screeched to the right and Cora jumped toward him,

grabbing onto his arm. He reckoned being at the Front prepared folks for some things, but not others. Actually, when he thought about life in the mountains, there were some things even war didn't fit a person for. He didn't look in her direction. She didn't release her hold, so he kept walking, slowing his pace to match hers. The wildflower scent invaded his thinking, a surprising complement to the smells of damp earth and wet pine. He liked it. Made him think of sweet things.

Quiet accompanied their steps for a little while, but Jeb's mind spun with questions, comments. Anything. The silence deepened. The only thing he could think of, besides how she felt in his arms, was the fact she'd almost come face-to-face with Clark Greer. The idea churned uncomfortable heat into his chest. Some men lost themselves in the shadow of these mountains. Some thrived. Some turned mean.

Others grew dark.

And dark was dangerous.

"Do you know him?"

Her question pulled his attention away from the lantern light ahead and back to her pale face, the glow haloing her hair in oak gold. "Well enough to stay away."

She fell silent, but he didn't reckon it'd last long. He didn't know a whole bunch about Cora Taylor, but he knew enough to figure that being quiet wasn't something she wasted time doing.

"But what about his wife?" Her voice took on an edge. "His baby."

"I don't know how he might handle his own, but he ain't too keen on strangers." He glanced over at her and then turned back to the trail. "Your brother got on the wrong side of the Greers."

She stopped walking and turned to him. "My brother?"

"He didn't mean no harm, but folks like Clark's daddy, Ozaiah Greer, and all his kin don't take kindly to folks bringing outside notions into the mountains, especially with their young'uns and the school." He gestured for her to resume their walk. "It started when your uncle commenced preachin' words different than they'd heard their whole lives, even if Preacher could show folks from the Bible that his words were true."

"That's ridiculous."

"Ridiculous or not." Jeb nodded. "Don't mean they still won't keep to their ways. 'Round here Grandpa or Granny's words can hold a lot more sway than the Almighty's."

Her dainty jaw stiffened with her back. "I can't believe my brother loves this place like he does. It's barbaric and. . .and. . . dangerous."

Jeb bit back his grin. "It sure can be."

"How could he have written letters about this dreadful place that made me want to come?"

He increased his pace to keep up with her sudden change.

"Grand, breathtaking vistas, kind, generous-hearted natives." She snarled out the words. "I almost fell to my death off of one of those breathtaking vistas, and the only generous-hearted native I've met so far is you."

That sounded a heap of a lot like a compliment, but he didn't have time to ponder it before she went on.

"Mary Greer was barely out of her childhood, and to be lorded over by such a man." A sound like a growl came from her throat. "Is it so difficult to treat each other with respect and equality? Does it have to resort to some sort of power struggle? Why is it that no matter which country I'm in, women are constantly being controlled or mistreated by men?"

Jeb refused to speak one word. He felt certain saying anything was a bad idea. Though, her declaration raised more questions about the woman. Of course, as his grandpa once said, *If you have questions about a woman, just be quiet. Sooner or later, the answers will come right out of her mouth. Most times, you can count on sooner.*

But the strange woman didn't continue. In fact, she fisted his handkerchief in her hand and stared ahead, those shoulders of hers drooping a little as she walked. She had to be tired. After all the traveling followed by the crazy.

The sky had cleared enough to showcase stars, and the moonlight cast a halo on the wispish clouds as they passed. Jeb cast a glance over at the quiet woman and then cleared his throat.

"Follow me a minute."

"What?" She stumbled a step as he pivoted on the path and turned to the left. "That is not on the path, Mr. McAdams."

He stepped farther away from the path, Puck at his heels. In a few seconds, he heard the rustling of leaves and bushes behind him as she followed, alerting every critter within a half mile of her presence, from the sound of it. Nursing near the Front sure didn't teach her how to walk in the woods.

The ground shifted from muddy earth to rock and he placed his lantern to the side so that the light wouldn't dim the view ahead.

"Mr. McAdams, I don't know what you're doing, but it's quite late and I—"

Miss Taylor pushed through the bushes and came to a stop, the light of the moon glowing down on her unhindered. Out in front of them, just beyond the edge of the rocky outcropping, lay a silhouette of mountains upon mountains bathed in frosty moonglow. Stars twinkled above and a cool breeze brushed up from below carrying the scent of rain and earth and the faint scent of pine.

He gestured forward. "A grand vista."

She pressed her fist against her chest, her eyes wide, those curls of hers springing out around her face, and Jeb had the strange feeling that showing her the vista wasn't such a good idea. For him.

"It's. . .incredible." She lowered her lantern to the ground and took a few steps farther out toward the view, but not too far. "I don't think I've ever seen so many stars."

"There's somethin' about the world after a storm." He pulled his attention away from her and ruffled Puck's fur with his palm. "Seems

71

like everything looks clearer. Brighter." His attention raised back to her standing on the rocks with the sky and mountains behind. He cleared his throat and looked away. "Ever seen a bear before?"

Miss Taylor turned her head toward him. "I've already come face-to-face with a mountain lion, Mr. McAdams. Can't we leave bears out of it and just talk of stars and vistas?"

Jeb dipped his chin with a grin. "Well, I reckon we can have both." He stepped to her side and pointed toward a pattern of stars rising above a distinctive peak in the distance. "Ain't that the Great Bear?"

She followed his lead, and a smile broke out on her face. "Ah, Ursa Major. The only bear I wish to meet in the woods."

"I never knew the stars had names until the war." He shoved his hands in his pockets and breathed out a sigh. "One of the other boys, Johnson was his name, he knew about 'em, so he'd point 'em out while we laid out under the sky." He shrugged and tossed her a grin. "Well, on the few nights it wasn't rainin'."

"I lived for those clear nights," she whispered. "Especially the quiet ones."

Without the bombs. Or gunfire.

They stood there a few more moments, embracing the view and the silence, nothing but the sound of the wind and the crickets as company. A peace smoothed over him and, for a second, he allowed the stillness to invade all the broken edges and wearying memories that haunted him.

"I reckon we ought to get on along." Jeb gestured toward the path. "It's nigh close to midnight."

She hesitated, casting another look over her shoulder, and Jeb almost smiled. There were many painful and hard things about these mountains, but there was also beauty and community and creativity. Sometimes it took a while to see them, but they waited among the hollows and hills.

The path became easier as they neared more well-traveled areas. Jeb took Miss Taylor on a slightly longer journey, just to bypass

Imogene Carter's place. The last thing he needed was her gossiping tongue causing more trouble than help. Soon the roofline of Reverend Anderson's house came into view.

"Did you build your house?"

Jeb turned toward her and followed her gaze. Moonlight reflected off the second-story windows visible over the tree line. "I built it on my grandparents' land."

"It's larger than any other house I've seen here so far." She looked away with a shrug. "Not that I've seen a great deal of them yet."

He squinted toward the sky, sifting through what to say. His house was one of the largest on the mountain. A fool's errand, his daddy had said, but something in Jeb had needed to build, to create. Every piece, every nail. Something about creating that house and using his hands to carve the little pieces he made in his workshop reminded him that not everything was lost. That something good could come from hard work and diligence.

That not everything was destroyed by fire and bullets and disease.

Good still lived, as surely as God breathed life through these woods.

Jeb drew a great deal of needed hope from the thought.

"It's been good to keep my hands busy." He paused, trying to sort out how to express his thoughts. "I've seen plenty of broken things."

"Yes." Her simple response deepened an unspoken comradery.

"And, well, I. . .I felt as if God wanted me to build it." He cleared his throat, his face suddenly growing warm at the admission. "Like I was proving to myself that something good, something strong, could still come from these hands."

He realized she'd stopped walking, and he turned. She stared up at him, those large eyes searching his. "Thank you for reminding me of that."

"Of what?" The question surfaced on a whisper. He wasn't sure why, but something in the way she looked up at him, all haloed in moonlight after he'd laid out his heart in words, stirred a deep longing inside him.

"That there are others in this world who are trying to create good after living through so much hurt and devastation." She lowered her gaze. "I forget. . .I'm not the only one."

Is that why she had some sort of inner drive in her steps? Some unvoiced passion in her words? Was she trying to find the same healing, the same hope, he was searching for?

She slid a glance up to him and continued the walk. The forest opened to reveal Reverend Anderson's small cabin. Jeb walked Miss Taylor to the door and waited for her to step inside, but she paused.

With a slight hesitation, she took his free hand and pushed the handkerchief into his palm. "Thank you for this."

"You're welcome."

She started to walk across the threshold of the house but then turned back around to him. "I want you to know that I. . .I'm not the sort of woman who cries often."

He looked down at the handkerchief and then back to her, not quite sure how to respond.

"Everything was so unexpected, you understand." She stood a little taller, her chin raised. "I'm not a crier, you see, and I'd not wish for you to think I'm the sort of woman who falls into tears over the slightest provocation."

"I didn't think—"

"I may be a stranger here and unaccustomed to the culture and terrain, but I am not weak." Her gaze held his. "And I didn't mean to lose my head back there in the forest and weep on your shoulder." She released a quivering breath through her nose. "I'm not a weeper."

Those watery eyes of hers didn't seem to pay no mind to her grand protests.

"I didn't see you as the sort." He nodded, and her brow wrinkled with a frown, so he tried for a little more talk. "But I reckon God wouldn't have given tears to us if He didn't mean for us to use them now and again." He scrubbed at the back of his neck and retreated a step. "And it seems you have a fit reason for 'em tonight, Miss Taylor."

Her lips softened into a smile and the movement nearly had him staring at her lips for much too long. Lord, have mercy. No wonder folks around here talked about the moon addling the brain. Jeb was right close to cryin' himself.

"I think, since your sister is married to my brother, which makes us practically family, perhaps we can forgo the formal addresses." She drew in a deep breath and offered her hand. "Please, call me Cora."

Cora. The word in his head sounded delicate and pretty.

He looked down at her hand and swallowed through his thick throat before wrapping his fingers around hers. "Jeb."

"I know that not all men are hard and heartless. I saw all sorts in the war." She glanced up at him. "And even tonight."

Tonight? She meant him? A strange sort of warmth softened in his chest. He nodded.

"Thank you." She released his fingers and immediately pinched her hands together in front of her. "For finding me."

"Like you said. We're practically family and round here, we take care of family."

She nodded, stepping into the golden glow of the house, moving to close the door.

He turned toward the porch steps, pumping his fingers into a fist to shake off the feel of her soft hand in his. Nothing about the sensation felt like any "family" feeling he'd ever known.

"And Jeb?"

He spun back around, bracing his tingling hand against the porch post and raising the lantern so the light shone on her face. "Yes, Cora."

He liked the way it sounded.

And then he grimaced at the thought. Speaking of stars and tears and pretty names. If any man in all eternity had ever been moon-addled, it was him. He needed to get on home and that was a fact.

"Thank you for my scarf."

The expression on her face paused his retreat and his breath. She looked at him in a way that made him feel like he hadn't lost half of himself in the trenches of Europe. That doing something as simple as finding her scarf made all the difference to her world.

He dipped his chin and held her gaze until his breathing grew thick, then he shook off the notion. "Good night."

"Good night."

The cool air hit his face as he marched down the hillside toward home. His thoughts refused to obey his very determined orders. The scent of Cora's hair, the touch of those curls, the feel of her hand on his. . . The thoughts all swirled in his mind as if they were being chased by a cat. He shook his head. Cora Taylor wasn't staying in Maple Springs, and besides, she was a high-society woman.

Women like her didn't choose men like him. Even if he'd been whole.

She didn't belong here. And he didn't belong anywhere else.

Weren't no use for thoughts like those when he couldn't apply them to his heart.

As he crawled into bed, he turned toward the window, the moon glowing over his bed, the stars twinkling in the black sky. He whispered a prayer for Mary Greer. For the safe arrival back home of Jonathan and Laurel. And. . .as his eyes closed, he prayed for Cora.

It was a pretty name.

Chapter Six

A bang from somewhere in the house sent Cora sitting straight up in bed. Her gaze shot to her bag she'd placed on the floor nearby, her pistol tucked within its leather folds. She'd slept so well. Even harbored a few sweet dreams related to starlight and licorice.

Why, oh why, did she have to deal with another catastrophe?

Perhaps, if she pulled the lovely quilt back over her head and refused to answer, whoever rattled the door would go away. She lay back down and proceeded to cover her face with the quilt.

"Cora!"

Her eyes popped wide and she pushed back the quilt. She knew that voice.

"Are you there?" The words came muffled by the door, but her pulse sped up in response. "We only learned last night that you'd arrived."

She stumbled into her robe and down the ladder, missing the last rung and crashing with an indecorous thump onto the floor.

"Where could she have gone?"

Another voice, female, came from the other side. Cora's smile spread wide as she pulled herself from the floor, rubbed her aching backside, and rushed to the door. After removing the wooden bar that, gratefully, bolted the door closed, she jerked the latch up. Her brother's eyes grew wide and then he laughed.

"I wouldn't believe it until I'd seen for myself." His laugh resurrected. "But here you are."

Cora rushed into her brother's arms, burrowing deep. It had been over nine months since she'd last seen him when he traveled back to London for their eldest brother's funeral. Over nine months since she'd learned of his bride. She refused more tears to leave her eyes. It was embarrassing enough that she'd lost her control last night with Mr—with Jeb.

A woman, golden hair in a long braid over her shoulder, stood behind Jonathan, a welcome smile brimming on her face. Cora pulled back, and the woman stepped forward.

"Cora, this is Laurel." He stood a little taller. "My wife."

After two days in Maple Springs paired with a year of her brother's letters about the mountain ways, Cora had conjured up all sorts of ideas about her sister-in-law, but reality proved a pleasant surprise. Of course, she shouldn't have doubted her brother, but Jonathan and Laurel had been forced to marry, and Cora wasn't quite sure what that meant as far as sisters-in-law went. But the smile the other woman donned with such authenticity inspired Cora's confidence.

"It's such a pleasure to finally meet you, Laurel."

Without hesitation, Laurel gathered Cora up in her arms, bringing with her a subtle sweet scent. "It's real good to meet more of Jonathan's family." Laurel stepped back and reached up to touch Cora's hair. "Your hair's as curly as my little sister Suzie's. I ain't seen it such on a grown woman before, but yours looks like something from a fairy tale."

"If you'd written to let me know you were coming, Laurel and I would have met you at the station." Jonathan searched her face. "Is everything alright?"

Cora offered a one-shoulder shrug and then stepped back. "I'd hoped to surprise you." She smiled. "You know how much I adore doing the unexpected."

Jonathan's gaze sharpened. She'd hoped that being apart for a year would have lessened his acute awareness of her talking around the truth, but from the frown puckering his forehead, they'd not been separated nearly long enough for that. "What have you done?"

Cora's entire body stiffened in defense. "What have I done? Why does it have to be something *I've* done? Perhaps you should ask what has Father done. Maybe that would be much nearer the mark!"

"Whoa now." Laurel's smooth voice broke in between them. "Since you've come all this way, I have a feelin' we've got plenty of time to sort out the whys and whats." Her new sister-in-law turned toward Jonathan. "And beins that you ain't seen each other in right near a year, I'd say starting your time with honeyed words rather than salty ones"—she raised her brow to Jonathan—"is liable to get you more of what you want than not."

Jonathan relaxed his shoulders with a sigh. "I am happy to see my sister." He turned his attention back to Cora. "And I'm certain whatever the reason, it is a very good one."

All fight fled from Cora's body and she waved toward the porch chairs. "You may want to sit down for the explanation."

Ten minutes and a dozen questions from Laurel later, Jonathan stood and began pacing the porch. "Dexter Arnold. What was Father thinking? The man and his brothers are scoundrels."

"And more so since coming back from the war, I might add." Cora ran a palm up her arm to stave off an internal shiver. "He lost his older brother, and when he returned, well." She swallowed against the memory of his unpredictable behavior, the haunted look in his eyes. "He'd gone from bad to worse. I've seen the look before in other returning soldiers."

Jonathan placed his hands on his hips and stared at her. "And Father knew this? He knew of your concerns?"

Cora only stared back. Her brother knew their father.

With a groan, Jonathan pushed his fingers through his hair and continued his pacing. "Have his business ventures become so dire?"

"The end of the war was a blessing in many ways, but not for industry. Father needs solid connections in the business world to regain his foothold."

"Which Dexter Arnold provides."

"Exactly."

"And you?" Jonathan paused, studying her. "What could you possibly offer him?"

She lowered her head, a sudden burning in her eyes. No, she'd not cry. She'd already done too much crying.

"Cora?"

She drew in a breath and raised her gaze to his. "My inheritance."

"What?" Jonathan's chest deflated and he took hold of the porch railing. "What could Dexter Arnold want with Grandfather's farm?"

"It's not the farm. It's the property." She smoothed her palms over her skirt. "The water supplies. The lumber."

He groaned. "The coal."

"Why don't your daddy just have you sell your grandpa's farm and get the money that way?" This from Laurel.

"He can't sell it if I'm not there, because I have the rights to it." She shook her head.

"So your daddy can't sell it, but a husband can?"

"According to the law and the specifics of the will, yes," Jonathan clarified. "It's the one loophole. If Cora marries, the property is turned over to her husband."

"So it has become an excellent bargaining chip for my hand in marriage, especially for an entrepreneur like Mr. Arnold."

"But how can your daddy make you marry? Will he pull out a shotgun like my daddy did with us?" Laurel nodded toward Jonathan. "I didn't figure things were done that way in England."

"No, but I'm afraid he'll find other means. Threaten to remove funds he's giving to assist my cousin who came back wounded from the Front." Cora winced. "Perhaps isolate Mother in some way. I don't know. He finds his ways, especially the more desperate he becomes. And Dexter Arnold was just as desperate." She looked up at Jonathan. "Which is why I had to leave. I couldn't let either one of them find a way to trap me in a marriage to that wretched man."

Jonathan gripped the railing and looked out over the front garden. They waited there, quietly, as if taking in the dilemma with nothing but the sound of the wind rushing through the trees and an occasional birdcall.

"Well, it seems you're bound to be with us for a while yet, Cora." Laurel stood. "So, it seems to me we ought to get you properly introduced to Maple Springs with a little home cookin' and pleasant company."

Jonathan's head came up, a look passing between the pair, before Laurel continued. "Preacher ain't gonna get back from his circuit till Saturday, so I think you need to come stay with us. I can help introduce you to life round here and Jonathan can spend time recollecting with his sister."

"That's a perfect notion, Laurel." Jonathan moved to her side, slipping his palm around her waist to press a kiss against her cheek. "She's such a quick thinker when my mind is muddled."

The sweetness between the pair squelched any unvoiced concerns she'd conjured up regarding her brother and his mountain bride. She'd never seen him so. . .what was it? Content? At peace? Though the pairing seemed impossible, perhaps the finite vision of an earthly view paled in comparison to a heavenly one. She paused on the thought and then tucked it away to revisit later.

"Stay with you?"

"Certainly." Jonathan took Cora by the hand and drew her inside the cabin, gesturing toward the loft. "So, go get dressed, pack a bag, and come join us at our house. You can leave a note for Uncle Edward."

Cora shifted her attention between the two of them. No, she didn't want to spend another night alone in this cabin, but join them at their house? "I wouldn't wish to intrude."

"Intrude?" Laurel grinned. "I don't reckon you've been here long enough to realize yet, Cora, that family intrusion is a part of daily life." Her laugh lilted. "You might as well snuggle right up next to the thought and keep it company, 'cause there ain't no gettin' rid of family when you're in the mountains."

Cora hesitated in her turn toward the loft, a little unsure of how to interpret Laurel's words, but then she sighed. It appeared the only way to understand this very strange world was to experience it, and, if it hadn't killed her in the last two days—despite its best attempts—she supposed she'd just have to keep on experiencing.

As she packed her travel bag, her fingers slid over the cobalt beading of her newest frock, a dress her mother bought for her before leaving London. The shape boasted the newest trend of a more sack-like shape cinched at the waist with a belt and, to the shock of the old guard, a calf-length hem. She'd barely reentered the world of ballrooms and dinner parties when her father entangled her in an unwanted marriage match. Her palm glided over the silk fabric and she sighed. After a year of nursing, something about returning to a life of flitting from one social event to another curled a nauseating ball in her stomach. But—her gaze slid to the window—she didn't belong here either. Her eyes wilted closed and she buttoned her bag. Where did she belong if she lived in the in-between?

In only a few more short minutes, Cora had packed a few necessities in her travel bag, written Uncle Edward a note, and started on the trail with Laurel and Jonathan toward their house, she presumed. The day bloomed with color. Whether from the effects of the storm or the loveliness of the season, a vibrancy shone from the earthen hues of green to the autumn splash of golds, reds, and oranges. Beautiful.

A grand vista?

Her lips softened into a smile and her attention pulled to the hillside in the distance, Jeb's roof visible above the tree line. Was Jeb at home? Did he work somewhere during the day? Jonathan's letters told of some men who rarely left the area around their home, and only to hunt food or attend social gatherings. Jeb didn't seem the sort, especially after being in the war. Most likely, he'd been awake for hours, even after rescuing her last night.

Rescuing her? She shook her head. No, not a rescue exactly. More like coming to her aid. She nodded. Yes. Assistance. Not rescue. She didn't *need* a rescue.

"It's somethin', ain't it?" Laurel whistled low as she followed Cora's gaze.

"Oh!" Cora's face flamed hot at being caught staring. "I've not seen anything quite like it since my arrival."

"And not bound to on this side of the mountain." Laurel sighed, walking alongside Jonathan with her arm linked through his. "Seemed he couldn't abide bein' still for too long after he got back from the war, so he worked as hard as a squirrel in late summer, taking all the things in his head and tryin' to make them into reality."

"All the things in his head?"

She nodded. "He's always been the sort that can see and imagine in his mind then make it with his hands, if hard work and tools can do it. He's got a real gift for woodworking, and after spending a spell in Europe, it seemed he came back with even more ideas."

Cora's gaze fastened on the top portion of the house, white plank wood rising to a tin roof that glistened in the sunlight. She wished she'd taken more care to note the inside of the house, the handiwork. The hand-carved squirrel on the mantel in the bedroom where she'd awakened. The intricate carvings on the dresser nearby. Had those all been done by Jeb's hands? "I can't imagine."

Laurel's smile brimmed. "Most menfolk thought he'd gone bloomin' crazy to work up such a fine house for a single man in the mountains, but all the work seemed to help calm his mind." Her attention flew to Cora. "I reckon you'd know 'bout that need too."

Cora's gaze caught in Laurel's for a second and then she looked back at Jeb's house as it slowly disappeared behind the forest. "Keeping busy does help."

"And likely making beautiful things to offset the horrible is good therapy too," Laurel added.

"Or helping others?" came Jonathan's question, his lips tipped into a knowing smile.

"I help others because it's something I've found that I'm good at." Cora raised her chin in mock defiance against her brother's teasing. "Besides, after all that's happened the past few years, all the lives lost, I want to make my time count for more than parties and ballrooms."

"God's prone for using folks right where they are, and since you've seen fit to find your way to Maple Springs, I ain't got a single doubt He's planning on using you and your helpfulness right here." Laurel winked. "Whether you're ready or not."

Cora wasn't certain whether to smile at the ominous comment.

"But I ought to warn you, darling sister, since we weren't expecting you. . ." Jonathan took the bag from her hand and slung it over his shoulder. "I'm afraid we have a bit of bad news."

"Bad news?"

"Don't speak it like that, Jonathan." Laurel nudged his arm. "It's only bad because we want to spend time with you during your visit."

Cora's pulse took a swift upswing. "Aren't you going to spend time with me?"

"Of course we are, especially during the next week," Jonathan said. "But then, Laurel and I will be gone for a few weeks after that."

Laurel placed her palm on Cora's arm. "Ain't too long, but we can't reschedule. We've had it planned for months."

And then her brother's most recent letter came to mind. "Laurel's teaching exam."

Laurel's smile bloomed. "It's a good four-hour train ride from here, and the final training and exam will take a few days."

"Then, while we're there, we're going to spend a week with one of the doctors who has been training me via correspondence. He plans to allow me to join him on rounds at his hospital so I can complete some of my training hours."

Cora held to her smile, though her insides began to tremble. She'd come to be with Jonathan and now he was leaving? But how could she hold it against him? She was the one who'd shown up unexpectedly. And at least Uncle Edward would still be in Maple Springs, at least part of the week.

"But we'll get you as ready as we can over the next week." Laurel's smile softened. "I'll take you to meet Mama. She's a help like none other."

"And we'll introduce you to Mrs. Cappy and her store," Jonathan interjected with an added wink. "She'll have plenty of food you can purchase in the chance that your cooking skills are still the same as they were before I left home."

"Very funny, brother dear." But the truth hurt.

"And, of course, Jeb is here." Laurel tossed a glance behind them. "Besides having the war in common, I can tell you true." Her expression sobered. "Even after all he's seen and the hurts he's known, he's one of the best men I know. If you need anything, he'll do whatever he can to set things right for you."

Cora rubbed her throat as a sudden warmth fluttered to life in her chest. What little she'd come to know of Jeb McAdams inspired not just confidence in Laurel's words, but, well, something deeper. A shared understanding, perhaps?

"And though you're runnin' from a wedding, you showed up just in time for one."

Cora's attention swung to Laurel. "What do you mean?"

"Two of my students from last year are getting married."

The reminder confirmed why Jonathan had come to the mountains last year in the first place. To teach at a mission school in Maple Springs. But when the people had needed medical attention, he had stepped in, earning him the comical title Teacher Doctor. According to Jonathan's letters, the plan was, as soon as Laurel passed her teacher's examination, she'd take over as the teacher of the school, allowing Jonathan to focus on his medical studies. What a strange turn of events from a shotgun wedding to this unexpected and perfect arrangement.

"The festivities take place after church on Sunday."

"As long as it's someone else's wedding besides mine, I will happily celebrate."

"Well, I wouldn't kick your feet up just yet, Cora Taylor." Laurel's laugh burst out. "No siree."

"What do you mean by that?" Cora looked to her brother for clarification, but he seemed just as confused as Cora.

"You might have aimed to run away from marriage, but once the menfolk in these parts get a look at you, you may have a whole mountainside of men waiting to spark you."

"Spark me?" Her voice pitched too high. She didn't need an interpretation for that implication.

"Laurel is teasing you, Cora." Jonathan held his wife's gaze. "Any possible suitors would have to make it by me and Uncle Edward first."

"And I have no plans to run from one proposal into another one."

"Well, there's a wedding Sunday." Laurel shot her a wink. "And a wedding inspires all sorts of matrimonial thinking."

Cora settled in quite well to the day and the visit, basking in the reconnection with her brother and learning more about her sister-in-law as they spoke of the mountains and Cora's experience at the Front. Their home, a cozy stone structure locally known as the Mission House, stood close to Mrs. Cappy's store and made Jonathan and Laurel's house feel a little less remote than Uncle Edward's. As Cora drifted off to sleep, she smiled and thanked God for the remembrance that, even though her introduction to Maple Springs hadn't been ideal, there was sweetness and good people here. Even within Cora's short stay, the comradery and love between the couple put Cora's heart at ease about her brother's new home in the Blue Ridge. She'd never seen him so happy.

She breathed out the tension of the past few days and hovered her thoughts on a prayer. Maybe she'd find her rhythm in this foreign place too, if she didn't run into any more mountain lions or overbearing mountain men.

Cora caused quite a stir in church on Sunday. One reason might have been the fancy hat she wore with a couple of birds perched on top. Jeb's younger brother, Isom, even leaned over to ask if wearing fake birds meant you was high class or just too bad a shot to get the real ones.

She was a stranger for another, and folks in the mountains were always curious about visiting flatlanders.

But the third reason was because, well, she was mighty easy to look at. The green dress she wore brought out her eyes and fit her figure like a glove. And Jeb wasn't the only one who noticed. Every single man in the room kept eyeing her and a few of the married ones too.

Jeb shook off the discomfort with a firm turn of his mind back to the sermon. If what he'd heard from Preacher was true as Jeb walked with him on the way to church, Cora Taylor wasn't only disinterested in sparking any man there, but of all of them, then Jeb wasn't anywhere near the running. Cora was rich. An heiress or some such. And as mismatched to the mountains as her fancy boots. His attention pulled back to her, sitting near the front betwixt his sister Laurel and his mama. He smiled. Mama would be good for her but, of course, Mama was good for everybody.

Warmth swelled in his chest and up his neck, so he squeezed his eyes closed. He wasn't fit for a wife, and especially not one like her. Too many ghosts haunted his dreams. Too many fears he barely controlled.

No, 'twas best for him to keep to himself and his family.

To keep to his right thinking, he slipped from the church at the last song and took the mountain path toward the Jacobs' place, determined to make his appearance at the wedding, but equally as determined to leave early. Nothing wrong with the joys of two folks getting hitched, but at the last get-together Jeb had attended Sue Thompson and Rose Hawes nearly stuck to him like pine resin. Womenfolk outnumbered the menfolk three to one, and Jeb had been running from matrimony since he stepped back into Maple Springs.

He took to helping Claude Jacobs set up some benches from cut logs and tables from wood planks over sawhorses. Matriarch Pearl Jacobs, along with her girls, had decorated the simple front porch with a few autumn roses, mostly red and pink. Dried Queen Anne's lace softened the edges of the aged wood of the house and, framed by autumn trees, the place looked about as pretty as a picture.

Folks started arriving, most with dishes of food to add to what Mrs. Jacobs, Mrs. Hawes, and all the girls related to those families had already prepared. Darrell and Mopey rounded up some musicians, and the celebrating began long before the wedding. Laughter erupted in all corners, children played in the field nearby, and sunlight basked down on the tiny community that felt so far away from Europe.

He grinned. Even with all its hardships, something about the folks and family of these mountains quieted parts of Jeb's heart that had been aching since he'd been in his first battle. Sure, there were folks like the Greers and Carters, but there were also many more folks who loved big and longed to see their young'uns happy. Even if happy took on a simple touch of faded calico dresses, homespun rose archways, and log-made benches.

He caught sight of Rose Hawes crossing the yard, but didn't have time to hide behind the nearby tree. It didn't seem to matter. All she did was glare in his direction, raise her chin, and march in the opposite direction.

That was new. He shrugged. Well, if whatever got her riled kept her away from him, then he'd hope for a similar offense for the next get-together.

Cora came into view among the crowd, strands of her wild hair already coming loose from its pins. He bit back a grin. The fact her hair was about as unruly as the rest of her made him like her even more. He forced his attention away from her and noticed a tall, well-dressed man walking through the crowd in her direction.

Jeb stifled a groan. Well, there'd be no point in wasting day-dreams on Cora Taylor now.

Dressed in his store-bought suit, hair slicked back, and eyes trained on his prize, walked Rowen Hawes.

"You ain't gonna let him dance with her first, are you?"

Jeb turned to find his daddy standing nearby, one eyebrow hitched high. Only a few inches shorter than Jeb, he had his hands tucked into his beige pants, his stomach protruding a bit.

"Ask who?"

"That flatlander." He gestured with his chin. "I seed how you been eyeing her all morning."

Jeb looked away, biting back his denial.

"You don't git over there, Rowen's gonna get to her first."

"Rowe can have a reel with her if he wants." Though his sentence took on more of a growl than he'd meant for it to take.

"You afraid she'll turn you down?" But then his father let out a giant laugh. "Well, lookie there. She's done turned Rowe down on the spot. Even with his fancy suit and greased hair."

Sure enough, Cora's head shook with a "no," her smile kind. Rowe continued with his entreaty, hand extended, but Cora gracefully declined again.

"I like her better for it." His father laughed loud enough to garner attention from a few folks nearby, one being Imogene Carter, the nosiest woman in Maple Springs. "The boy thinks he's somethin' now that he's got hisself a business and all, though he's still just a mountain boy. Ain't no cause to put on airs. With the best folks you can't tell if they's rich or poor, 'cause it don't make no difference to who they are."

Jeb leaned back against the nearby tree and folded his arms across his chest, allowing his daddy's words to settle into silence.

"But I reckon she's too high and mighty for the likes of us, boy." His father placed his palm on Jeb's shoulder and gave it a little pat. "You're probably right not to try for the ones that don't belong here."

Cora looked up then, her gaze meeting his, and the image of her burrowed into his chest, weeping, came to mind. She didn't seem too high and mighty then. Nor when she stood beneath a pale moon framed by starlight. No. She fit right there in the middle of other beautiful things.

Jeb grimaced at the turn of his thoughts and pulled his attention away from those searching eyes of hers.

"I see Darrell's needin' some help with the fiddle." Daddy nodded. "You bound to play today?"

"Naw, I reckon I'll just take it in from here."

"Then I'll give it a go." His father walked toward the porch where the musicians kept the beat for the crowd.

Jeb sneaked a glance back in Cora's direction. Rowen stood nearby, talking to her, and she didn't seem to mind one bit. Jeb released a sigh, training his attention on the music and dancers.

"I don't see how you can show your face round here."

Jeb turned toward the seething voice. Imogene Carter stood nearby, her dark eyes in slits as she examined him. He stood taller, searching the area for an answer to her accusation.

"Don't you play innocent with me, boy. I seed it all with my own eyes."

"I don't mean no offense, Mrs. Carter, but I ain't got one idea what you're talking about."

"You pretend to be this good boy, but we all know what's happened to some of them that's come back from the war. They got used to sin over there and they bring it back here." Her bony finger pointed at him. "Just like you, Jebediah McAdams."

Well, if she'd used his long name, he was bound to be in trouble. He just wasn't sure what for. Imogene wasn't known for a quiet and gentle spirit, so there was no telling what she'd conjured up in that mind of hers.

"I don't know—"

"I seed you with your kept woman. I seed you carrying her to your house five days back." She raised her dark brows, as if waiting for him to deny it. "I was on my way home from Mrs. Cappy's store and spied you through the woods. Followed you to your house and saw you carry her all the way inside."

Jeb opened his mouth to argue but then her implication clicked into place.

Five days ago.

"Her and her fine dress and fancy boots. Ain't never seen the like before. The only womenfolk who wear such finery is the girls down at the hotel in town." She edged closer, the smell of snuff on her breath. "God don't look kindly on the likes of you, Jebediah McAdams, and I've made sure to tell the other womenfolk about your evil doings."

So that was why Rose had glared at him.

Jeb's face went cold.

"You gonna deny what I seen?"

Jeb stared at her. Then, despite his best efforts, his gaze moved back to Cora. If he told the truth and folks found out that Cora had spent hours in his house alone with him, he could only imagine the consequences. As a stranger and flatlander, she was already on the edge of acceptance. If folks found out the truth, she'd never find a peaceable moment in Maple Springs until the day she left.

He squeezed his eyes closed and bowed his head. Without a word, he doffed his hat and walked away from the place. There was no answer to offer without causing harm.

No. If taking the blame protected Cora Taylor, then that was exactly what Jeb would do.

Chapter Seven

The church service was quaint and a bit noisier than what she was accustomed to—well, the men were. Encouraging Uncle Edward with their "amens" and "preach it," and singing with such verve, Cora couldn't help staring at a few of them. Hearing Uncle Edward preach nearly brought her to tears on several occasions. And though Jonathan's letters had described the unique differences of the mountain church, Cora still found herself attempting to take it all in. Women to one side, men to the other. Singing with gusto in full harmony without any instrumental accompaniment, though Jonathan wrote of the mountain people's love of their handmade stringed instruments.

And church gave Cora a wider perspective on the people of Maple Springs. Some arrived at church in dirty clothes but scrubbed hands. Many of the children entered barefoot. The various smells of people in close proximity nearly distracted Cora from thinking of much else, but she'd prayed so fervently for help to try and find good things in this temporary home of hers. Because it would be home for the present. She couldn't return to England. And Jonathan was here, as well as Uncle Edward.

Staying made sense.

So, as she'd had to do so many times during the war, she would train her thoughts. Block out what she *had* to accept and focus on something pleasant. For example, after spending a few days with Laurel, Cora knew without a doubt she'd found a lifelong friend. All the descriptions and examples of his wife's quaint talk Jonathan had shared in his letters came to life in her very person. She exuded a gentle confidence and a ready joy. And seeing her and Jonathan together reminded Cora that there were some relationships, even the least expected or most unique, which were healthy and whole and good. Her parents were not an example of any of those.

She'd found kindness here. From Laurel and her family.

Her gaze slid to the back of the church where Jeb sat next to his father, Sam, and little brother, Isom. She smiled to herself. And, perhaps there were grand vistas, if she could just see beyond all the near-death experiences first.

The walk from the church to the wedding venue inspired even more happy thoughts about the area, especially since Cora spent it walking beside Caroline McAdams, Jeb and Laurel's mother. The woman exuded kindness and wisdom, and in her own unique way, she presented as very much a grand lady. Or perhaps it was the air of quiet confidence that seemed to flow from her smile.

"Laurel and Jonathan mentioned last night that you've been having headaches?"

Caroline McAdams's soft blue gaze settled on Cora. "Oh, they shouldn't trouble themselves with talk like that. It's the same ache my mama used to have 'bout this time of year."

"I've heard that some people experience headaches with the changing weather." Cora glanced ahead, watching as folks seemed to emerge from the trees all around, like forest sprites, all headed to a clearing up ahead. "If there are no other symptoms, then I have headache powder you could take which may relieve the pain a little."

"I heared tell of some headache powders for sale. I reckon Mrs. Cappy's talked of it, but I ain't never took any. I'd be much obliged to you for bringing me what you think works best." Her smile softened. "I reckon you learned a lot about nursing whilst in the war."

"I learned a great deal as a volunteer at the hospital, but when they sent me to the Front"—Cora drew in a deep breath, the taste of death almost revisiting her lips—"well, that sort of nursing teaches you things you'd never learn in a nice, sterile, organized hospital, I don't think."

"I'd say not." Her quiet voice encouraged Cora to continue, like a strange call to her heart.

"It changes one as well." Cora nodded, keeping her focus ahead on the outline of a log house in the distance. "The things I used to think were important or I needed, well, they're not the same anymore." She sighed. "*I'm* not the same."

"Life sure has a way of rolling us around like a clump of dough, don't it?" Caroline kept a steady pace, a graceful procession in her simple calico dress. Her gold hair, mixed with fine locks of silver, wound back into a bun, and Cora could almost envision the woman as a Highland lady or a fairy princess. Something about her seemed… ethereal. "Or, as the Good Book says, a lump of clay." She chuckled. "I ain't never seen a lump of clay turn into a fine cup or plate, but I sure have watched Sam or Jeb carve things from wood. They cut on that wood and beat it somethin' fierce, but when they finish, they've made up a pretty chair, or table, or dresser. All the beatin' and cuttin' and carvin' led to something beautiful in the end."

Cora's smile spread. "So, Mrs. McAdams, you're saying, to be truly fit for whatever God is designing us to be, we must manage the cutting and carving of life in the process?"

"I don't reckon any of us are gettin' out of this ol' world without a bit of carving. Do you?"

"No, I would say not. But I'd prefer a little less of it at the moment."

Caroline's laugh filtered on the breeze. "Wouldn't we all."

Up ahead, the log house they'd been walking toward stood with the mountains rising up almost from the back door, but in front of the covered porch stretched a vast swath of grass, with a large barn to one side and a few outbuildings scattered beyond.

A few makeshift tables held what looked to be dishes of various shapes and sizes. In front of the house logs and benches stood in rows for seating. A melody began to lift toward her. A violin? She searched for the origin of the sound and found a few people standing on the front porch of the house, two men with violins, one woman with a stringed instrument Cora did not recognize, and a man with a guitar. The sound hit her, different than anything she'd ever heard before. The tone in the violins held an edge very different from the sound they made in concerts back home. What was it? Earthier? She couldn't quite describe it, but it fit this world somehow.

Several couples began making a circle in front of the porch, joining together in a series of dances very much like some of the older country dances she'd witnessed when visiting her grandfather's farm. Except, perhaps, with a little less reserve than England.

A young man, probably no more than eighteen, stood near the front of the porch in a simple white button-up shirt and brown slacks. He wore a grin as broad as his shoulders.

"That there's the groom." Laurel sidled up beside Cora, Jonathan at her side. "You remember, we told you about him."

"A good student," Jonathan added, resting his violin case on one of the makeshift benches. "With an equally good heart."

"Come on now, Teacher," came a call from the front porch where the musicians gathered. "That fiddle ain't gonna play itself."

Jonathan raised his violin from the case into the air in answer and then walked in the direction of the house while Cora followed Laurel and Caroline to one of the bench seats. She scanned the crowd, noting Fig and his grandfather not far off.

Then, just beyond the quaint pair, not too far from the forest's edge, she caught sight of a familiar figure. Jeb leaned against a tree, his strong frame relaxed. He had an intriguing profile. Serious. Thoughtful. Steady. He portrayed the best type of returned soldier, she thought. Yes, he still struggled, she could see it in his eyes, but his mind was in the right place. Forward thinking, for the most part. Hopeful. And he was in the business of keeping busy instead of languishing, as she'd seen some do. Yet, he was unique too. Something about his quiet strength drew her.

"Your brother can fiddle like a house afire." Caroline nodded toward the front of the house as Jonathan joined the musicians.

Fiddle? She studied her brother as he placed his violin to his chin, and comprehension dawned. Had Jonathan learned this mountain style? Something about the sound of it, the life in it, had Cora smiling before she even realized it. "He's always been very musical."

"Once he learnt how to keep the rhythm, he took off." Caroline tapped her knee, her profile fragile, but those eyes. They were deep, and strong.

Cora returned her attention to the musicians, particularly her brother. He grinned over at his fellow players and swayed, fiddle and all, along with the music. He was at home here, thriving. Happy. And he did play that fiddle like "a house afire," as Caroline said.

Cora examined the young groom as the music grew in tempo and volume and the crowd began to filter in from all directions, filling the area in front of the house. "He looks so very young."

"Young?" Caroline chuckled. "Why, he's nineteen, I reckon." Her expression softened with understanding. "Though, there ain't much else for young'uns to do round here than to get married and start their own families."

"And when it's slim pickin's, you better git while the gittin's good." Laurel's grin turned impish, joining in with her mother's teasing. "And Jackson's one of the good ones."

"How long have they been intended for one another?" Her smile unraveled at the warmth in the women's comradery.

"Who's to say if sparks were flyin' before, but. . ." Caroline looked up to the blue sky as if trying to draw the information forward. "They've been courtin' a couple of months, I'd say."

"Only two months?"

"Come on now, Cora." Laurel's eyes glittered. "Two months is near dog years around here from makin' eyes at each other to walkin' down the aisle."

Caroline sighed. "It's the way things are done here in the mountains, I reckon."

So many differences between her world and this one. Cora's attention turned away from Jackson Hawes and the couples who'd gathered to dance and back to Laurel. "As I understand it, you didn't follow that path."

"No, I had different plans and that's a fact, but—" Laurel smiled up at Jonathan, who winked at her from the porch. Cora's attention flipped between the pair, her breath bursting out in a voiceless laugh. She'd never seen her brother wink at anyone.

"But God's plans turned out to be even better than mine." Laurel sighed and met Cora's gaze. "It's a wonder why it always takes a body so long to want God's way over our own, ain't it?"

Cora's smile stilled on her face and she turned back toward the musicians. Surely, she couldn't just entrust everything to God. She'd had to fight so hard to make her place in a world where people thought she was too young to manage the devastation of nursing in war and too "female" to do anything but end up as the wife of a rich man. If she'd not taken a few opportunities in hand herself, she may very well be married to a despicable man and holed up in some manor-house-turned-prison. She wouldn't live as the sort who waited for decisions to be made for her. She'd felt the brunt of that life for too long. Oh no, she'd be the mistress of her own life. Her conscience twinged a bit. Though, she certainly wanted God's will and all that.

"Mrs. McAdams, Laurel, who is your new friend?"

Cora looked up to find a man standing before her. His brown tweed suit, complete with vest, paired with his broad smile and dazzling green eyes certainly made him stand out from the crowd. Perhaps she appreciated his presence all the more because she'd been surrounded by men who looked and smelled more like they'd come directly from a barn than a church meeting. Not all of the men, of course. Jeb McAdams cleaned up well in his white button-up and brown trousers, but a large portion of the men fit the former description.

The man before her tipped his head, eyes aglow with welcome.

"Rowen Hawes." Laurel placed her hands on her hips and studied the man from toes to golden head. "Figured you'd be too busy in town to make it up the mountain."

He held on to Cora's gaze for a second longer before deliberately turning toward Laurel. "And suffer the wrath of Granny Hawes?" His Appalachian accent came across a bit more muted, giving it an almost charming sound. "Besides, I wouldn't miss my cousin's wedding for the world."

His attention turned back to Cora, golden brow raised. He offered his hand. "Rowen Hawes, hotel owner in Rock Creek, and one of the Hawes family."

Cora took his outstretched hand. "Cora Taylor. I'm Jonathan's sister, recently arrived from London."

"London?" His brows rose. "And you came here?" His grin etched back up to flare his dimple. "Hard times in London?"

"Familial ties." She pulled her hand out of his and gestured with her chin toward the cabin. "As you are aware, it seems."

"Yes." He studied her, his gaze so intense she fought the urge to step away. She wasn't quite sure what to think of this seeming anomaly of Maple Springs, except that he knew how to wear a suit. "It is a pleasure to meet you. I hope you are enjoying your visit, Miss Taylor."

She refused to give away anything related to the disaster of her first few days in Maple Springs. "There's so much to learn and become accustomed to." She gestured toward the musicians. "Like the food and the music."

"With that in mind." He offered his hand and gave a slight bow. "I'd be delighted if you'd honor me with a dance."

Heat fled her face and she wiped her hands against the sides of her skirt. It was one thing to admire dancing from the safe distance of a log seat, but quite another to engage in whatever the native mountaineers were doing. Besides, Cora knew her limits, and dancing, of any sort, was one of them.

"It's very kind of you, Mr. Hawes, but I don't intend to dance today." Or likely ever.

He took a step back, but his smile never wavered. "I certainly hope it's not the company."

"Oh, don't get your back up, Rowen." Laurel weaved her arm through Cora's, pulling her away from the man. "She ain't even been here a week. You can't expect her to wanna cut a rug when she don't know folks nor ways. Besides, some folks ain't ready to show off any time there's a crowd."

Her obvious slight merely bounced off his growing grin. "Nothing wrong with being proud of hard work and success." He leaned closer to Laurel. "Unless you're holding on to just a bit of regret at turnin' me down all those years ago."

Cora's stare swung to Laurel. Turning him down? Had Rowen Hawes been a possible suitor of Laurel's? But Laurel didn't miss one second.

"The ones with regret talk about it the most, is what I've heard."

His expression sobered, but Laurel didn't leave him there. "But, you ought to be proud of what you've done. You always had top-notch brains, and look how handy they've been."

He relaxed at her teasing. "I suppose we've both found where we belong."

"Woowee, y'all!" came a call from the front of the house. A man with a strange sort of instrument in hand. Like a guitar but with a round bottom. "Preacher's just come in sight. What'ya say we get ready for a weddin'?"

A round of applause and wild calls erupted from the crowd.

"I look forward to becoming better acquainted with you, Cora Taylor." Mr. Hawes tipped his hat and moved to take a seat near the front of the group. Cora raised her gaze back to the forest line where Jeb still stood. The shade of the tree kept her from telling whether he looked in her direction or not.

Although, it shouldn't matter. The last thing she was looking for was a husband. Whether he wore a tweed suit or a simple pair of suspenders over an open-collared white shirt. What she truly wanted was to find a place where she could be herself and make a difference.

About halfway through the little ceremony, Cora noticed Jeb had disappeared. Even when she tried to locate him among the throng, he didn't turn up. However, she did see Granny Burcham hovering around a table laden with what appeared to be various sweets, including a ten-tier cake...of sorts.

After a sweet declaration of man and wife, the groom drove a wagon forward that held various things like chairs, tables, and something that looked like a bedstead. The bride, all smiles, added some linens to the assortment along with one of the most beautiful quilts Cora had ever seen. Hues of red, gold, and green curled into interwoven rings on a background of white.

"What is that?"

Caroline McAdams smiled. "That there's a wedding ring quilt. The bride and other womenfolk get together to sew it stitch by stitch so it'll be ready on the wedding day."

"Wedding ring quilt?"

"Jackson's bringin' the furniture and things to show he's prepared to provide for his bride, and Luanne brings the linens and quilts to show how she plans to make their house a home. Usually the pair would stay for a while in one of their parents' homes, but Jackson's already gone and finished him a little cabin."

"And that's unusual?"

She nodded. "Most times, it is, but Jeb's being back has moved things along. He has a caring heart for helpin' out folks as best he can. And he likes the work."

Cora fingered the scarf at her neck. He had certainly shown her kindness.

"He seems to be the sort to help others."

Caroline held Cora's gaze for a second before she smiled. "Always been such. He brung back all sorts of ideas from things he'd seen over yonder. He even piped in water to our house from the spring." She chuckled. "Wanted to create one of them showers he'd built up at his place, but Sam just couldn't take to it."

As soon as the wedding was finished, the festivities resumed, and Cora made her way through the crowd to find Granny Burcham. The woman stood near a table with several platters of fried chicken. When she caught sight of Cora, her smile caused her face to crinkle into a dozen wrinkles.

"You're still here, I see."

"Much to my own surprise, I assure you." Cora studied the weathered face in daylight. How old could the woman be? Seventy? Eighty? "I suppose I should thank you for sending me out into the night."

A chuckle erupted from the woman and she sat her plate down on the long table. "I was there to tend to a birthin', not tend to a killin'. He ain't the sort of man to cross."

Cora released a frustrated puff of air through her nose. "It seems wrong at every level that Mary should be forced to reside with such a man."

Granny Burcham's face sobered. "He ain't the kind to trifle with and that's a fact, so you best keep as clear of Crow Ridge as you can."

Cora curbed her desire to argue that someone needed to remove Mary and her baby from such a place. "And how are Mary and her child?"

"They're both comin' along as expected." Granny Burcham's thin lips curled into a crooked grin. "A round baby girl, 'twas, though she gave off a weak cry, and that ain't what we want to see."

"A weak cry?"

"Had to give the little'un a pat on the bottom so she'd catterwall. Make them lungs work." Granny Burcham shook her head. "I been catchin' babies for nearly twenty years, and if'n the babes ain't borned fightin' to make it into the world, then you best keep an eye out."

The way the woman spoke paired with what she said kept Cora close. "And why is that?"

Her thin brows rose. "Makes a body wonder, if'n death ain't too far from the door."

Cora braced her palm on the table. "Just because a baby isn't crying when she's born?"

The woman's stare bored into Cora's. "In these mountains, we live strong or we die young. Ain't no in-between. Either the babe was quiet 'cause she tended to some of the spirits in the room, or she ain't got fight in her." Granny Burcham frowned as she picked at her chicken. "Time'll tell."

The spirits in the room? A shiver ran up Cora's arms.

"Clark Greer wun't too pleased by the babe not bein' a boy, but the good Lord gives what the good Lord gives." The elderly woman nodded in acceptance of her words, completely indifferent to her previously ominous statement. "And a girl is a mighty big help to her mama."

Cora tried to take it all in. The memories of her night in the Greer cabin burned in her thoughts, with Granny Burcham's interest a pinnacle point. Granny's familiar basket lay on the ground near the woman's feet. "May I ask you a question?"

The woman offered the subtlest of nods, her eyes narrowing as she studied Cora.

"What did you give Mary to chew?"

Granny placed her plate on the table, reached down into her basket and slowly drew out something that looked like. . .tree bark? She took hold of Cora's hand and placed the bark into her palm. "Willa bark."

Willa? Bark? Did she mean willow? Like the tree? "Willow bark?" Cora had heard one of the nurses speak of willow bark's natural pain-relieving qualities. Here, in the middle of this back water place, a mountain woman used the same?

"Good for pain of any sort." Her lips took a wider tilt. "Flat-landers ain't too keen on our ways up here in the mountains, but plenty of 'em have worked for centuries."

Cora could only imagine some of the things these mountain people believed from what she'd read in her brother's letters, but she knew a little about herbal remedies, and fools refused to listen to solid advice.

Most of the time, she tried not to act like a fool.

"My grandfather often used gentian to aid with his digestion."

"Your grandfather?" Granny's dark brows rose. "A London man?"

"No." She smiled at the thought of her maternal grandfather digging up the fragile root to eat. "My mother's father. Reverend Anderson's father."

Her face relaxed and she nodded. "Aye, Preacher arrived with a mind to the earth around him. 'Twas a good fit, him and these mountains."

Cora fisted her hands at her side, her mind soaring with myriad questions for this woman. She'd learned of only a few other plants or herbs to aid in medical treatment, but what else could this aged mountain woman teach her? Surely, Cora could shift through the superstition and seize on the truth and, in the process, maybe even help the folks here, as her brother had begun to do.

At least until Dexter Arnold forgot all about marrying her.

Cora opened her mouth to ask Granny Burcham if she could come for a visit, but a sudden blast echoed from the direction of the cabin. A woman screamed, and a group of people parted as a man carrying a pistol ran between them and disappeared into the forest.

Jackson Hawes, the young groom, appeared from around the side of the house, his face pale. "Teacher-Doctor! Come quick! Rowen's been shot."

Chapter Eight

Cora took off at a run, catching sight of Jonathan in her periphery as he set down his violin and dashed off the porch. He rounded the corner of the house just before her. Rowen Hawes's tweed suit came into view first. He lay sprawled on the ground surrounded by a group of all ages.

Jonathan knelt by the man, who had a death hold on his stomach. Cora lowered to Rowen's other side, surveying the situation. Blood stained the left side of his lower stomach where he'd pressed his palm. It was a small circle at the moment, a definite bonus of the weapon being a pistol rather than the rifles she'd seen so many of the men toting around.

"Did it go through?"

Jonathan looked over at Cora and then focused on Rowen. "I need to raise you from the ground on this side to see if the bullet exited."

Rowen nodded with a whimper, and Jonathan, with Cora's help from the other side, checked the man's back before giving Cora a shake of his head. The bullet didn't exit.

"It was Clark Greer who done it." A woman stepped forward. "They was arguin' and Rowen started to back away, then Clark shot him."

"I did nothing to the man," Rowen growled. "And now he's killed me."

"Unlikely that he's killed you." Jonathan raised Rowen's shirt to see the wound, blood oozing from the spot.

People pressed in closer, on all sides. Cora stifled a groan. This would never do for medical treatment. They needed space and not a dozen folks breathing down on them.

"We need a table for a solid surface. And we'd benefit from more privacy, if possible." Cora held her brother's gaze, his expression registering surprise for a second.

"Yes."

Her chin raised a little at the realization that she'd impressed him. No, he hadn't seen her change from the naive and idealistic young girl she was when she first volunteered as a war nurse. He didn't know about the long nights of surgeries to save lives or comfort the dying.

"Pearl." Claude Jacobs stepped from the crowd and waved toward his wife. "Git the table ready. We're bringin' the boy inside."

The middle-aged woman ran forward and pushed a hand over her pale hair. With an expression which seemed all too familiar with the scene before her, she surveyed the situation before she rushed toward the house.

"What...what are you gonna do?" Rowen's accent took a thicker turn along with a higher pitch in his voice. "I...I can pay you, if you can save my life. I have money."

"Rowen." Jonathan's voice remained calm. "The bullet is still in you, and our first priority is to manage your bleeding and see if we can remove the bullet."

"Remove it." He started to sit up, but immediately lost all color in his face and fell back to the ground in a faint.

Which was probably for the best. Some men were more prepared for pain than others.

"I'll go inside and see how I can prepare for you." Cora stood, stepping right back into the role she'd served among the war wounded. "Did you bring your bag?"

He shook his head, ushering some of the other men to help him lift Rowen.

"Then we'll make do with what we have." Cora turned and followed Mrs. Jacobs's path to the cabin.

Laurel met her on the way. "Is there somethin' I can do? A way I can help?"

"I'd prefer we had either Jonathan's or my medical bag, but it may take too long to fetch them."

Her face fell. "Our house would take a good half hour or more to git there and back from here, since the trail's so rocky."

Cora seized her arm. "My bag is at Uncle Edward's cabin." She attempted to orient herself based on her limited knowledge of the mountains. "Is it nearer?"

"It sure is!" She gestured toward the right. "There's Jeb, just comin' from the woods. I reckon he heard the shot." Laurel patted Cora's shoulder. "His house ain't a ten-minute walk from here and then he can ride to Preacher's house, git your bag, and be back in ten or fifteen minutes at most, I reckon. The way's smoother from here to there."

Cora stared at the man running toward them. His gaze scanned his sister first and then moved to Cora, his penetrating eyes locking with hers. She could almost feel his concern from across the distance. The gunfire. The blood smear on her gown. It all likely tossed his emotions into the same former life as hers.

She nodded to him, somehow knowing he'd understand that she was fine.

A sigh visibly left his body.

A strange sort of awareness poured through her at the simple connection and she pulled her attention from him. "That's an excellent plan." She stepped back from Laurel. "Yes. Thank you."

She ran up the steps into the cabin just as the men rounded the corner, carrying a still unconscious Rowen Hawes.

Mrs. Jacobs was bustling about, taking things from the long wooden table in the middle of the two-room cabin. "Thank you,

Mrs. Jacobs." Cora studied the space. Though small, it was tidy. And cleaner than what she'd expected. The lighting was lower than her preference, but there was already a lantern lit. That would help. "Is the pot on the fire filled with water?"

"Aye," the older woman responded. "And close to boiling, as is."

"Excellent." Cora pushed her palms down the sides of her skirt and took inventory of the room. "And the table? Has it been scrubbed?"

"Doin' so right now, Nurse Woman."

Cora blinked as the name surfaced again. "Um, thank you." Cora's attention landed on a few bottles tucked together on the lone shelf in the room. By the time Jeb returned with her bag, Jonathan may have finished all he needed to do. "And whiskey? Do you have some?"

The woman's brows came together. "Plenty. The boy could use some for the pain, I reckon."

Cora stopped in her walk toward the fireplace. "Yes, but I also hoped to use it to sterilize our hands and the instruments." Though she'd have preferred her bottle of carbolic acid. "Do you have a very sharp knife? And tweezers, perhaps?"

"Sure do. And I set some cloths there by the fire." She didn't ask any questions, though her eyes searched Cora's before she disappeared into the next room.

Cora tossed a few of the cloths into the hot water just as the men pushed through the door carrying Rowen. She grabbed a bottle from the shelf and approached them, gesturing toward the table. "Mrs. Jacobs has gone for a knife and set of tweezers. I have cloths boiling and"—she raised the bottle—"whiskey here to sterilize as best we can."

"What you need tweezers and a knife for?" Jackson Hawes, a few traces of blood on the sleeve of his Sunday best, stepped forward, studying Cora as if she was the last person on the planet he could trust.

"The bullet is still inside Rowen, Jackson. If we can see where it is, we should try to remove it." Jonathan nodded toward Cora, a soft smile peaking at one corner of his lips. "My sister was a nurse during the war. She knows what she's doing." His grin broadened as he held her gaze. "In fact, she may be more prepared for gunshot wounds than I."

Cora stood a little straighter, returning her brother's smile before focusing on the young groom. "We'll only remove the bullet if it is easy to find. If we cannot see it, we could do more damage from fishing around in his abdomen." She cringed. "Though I'd prefer not to leave a bullet in his body, if we can help it."

Jonathan peeled Rowen's shirt off his right arm and raised him up to loosen it in the back. "You've left bullets inside before?"

She nodded, assisting him with removing the shirt from the other side. "Our lead nurse suggested that the patient often had a better chance at survival the less invasive we were, especially given the less sanitary conditions."

She didn't have to state how their current situation may have matched some of those in Europe.

Cora moved to her brother's side, pouring the whiskey onto his hands and then her own. The entrance wound was small, as she'd expected. Blood seeped slowly from the spot, hopefully another good sign that no artery had been impacted.

"If someone's bound to get shot in the abdomen. . ." Cora lowered her voice to a whisper. "I believe Rowen benefited from one of the safest spots, unless, of course, the bullet wreaked havoc on the inside."

Jonathan's attention shot back to her, his brows raising. "And this from the girl who became sick when Grandfather asked her to help mend a sheep's hoof."

She rolled her eyes. "Do allow me a few years to mature, if you will?" She'd seen worse than cut paws or pistol wounds. Much worse. She lowered to take a closer look at the wound, clearing away some of the blood. "It appears to have been a clean shot to the right of the spleen and just above the left kidney. What do you think?"

He nodded, his smile subdued but shining in his eyes. He looked over at Claude. "Would you bring the lantern close, Claude? So we can get a better look."

The light confirmed Cora's assessment, but the bullet was nowhere to be easily seen.

"Thoughts?" Jonathan whispered after another close inspection before he returned to placing pressure on the wound.

"We bandage the wound and monitor that healing is progressing appropriately." Cora lowered her palms to the table.

"No sutures?" He raised a brow as if challenging her.

"Not if the bleeding is controlled by pressure and bandages," she shot back.

His grin slowly spread from one corner of his mouth to the other, so she continued. "Without proper antiseptic and with no idea where the bullet is, I think he has a better chance of survival and safety without causing him to lose more blood. What about you?"

"I think I have a much-needed assistant." He winked.

Before Cora could fully process what her brother said, Rowen began to move and moan on the table. Jonathan placed his hand on the man's arm, bringing Rowen's focus to Jonathan's face. "Easy there, Mr. Hawes. You'd do well to move slowly."

"What? What's happening?" Rowen mumbled, his bleary gaze moving from Jonathan to Cora as awareness began to dawn in his dark blue eyes. "Am I dying?"

"Not that we think." Jonathan patted his shoulder. "It will take you a few days to get your strength back."

"And the bullet?" His voice pitched high on the final word.

"For your safety we decided not to remove it." Cora stepped back from the table and wiped her hands with the cloths. "You'll get to keep it as a souvenir, Mr. Hawes."

His brows crinkled underneath his sweaty blond curls.

"However, we will need to keep a close eye on your wound for the next few days, so I'm afraid you won't be returning to Rock

Creek just yet." Jonathan straightened, putting his full attention on the man.

"I can't—" Mr. Hawes nearly vaulted from the table, but the sudden movement must have given him enough pain to inspire common sense. He wilted back down onto the table with a moan. "I have a hotel to run. People to oversee."

"Which will both be very difficult to do if you die from an infection." Jonathan's sober tone took root because Mr. Hawes scowled but failed to resurrect his argument. Jonathan raised his head and caught sight of something just over Cora's shoulder. "Jeb, good."

Cora turned to see Jeb a few feet behind her, her satchel in his hands. His gaze locked with Cora's as he offered her the bag.

"Thank you," she whispered.

"Jeb, when you travel to the mill tomorrow would you take a message to Mr. Hawes's hotel and mercantile?"

"My hotel?" Mr. Hawes struggled for only a moment before the pressure Jonathan placed on his shoulder pushed him back down to the table again.

"He's going to be staying at the Mission House with Laurel and me for the next few days, until we can ensure he's healing as he should."

"I can't stay with—"

"I would appreciate it if you could deliver the message," Jonathan continued, completely ignoring Mr. Hawes's protests, his focus on Jeb. "And if you'll assist me in getting Mr. Hawes to the wagon, we'll make our way to the Mission House now."

Rowen raised a palm. "Wait just a minute—"

"Mr. Hawes." Jonathan turned to the man, allowing him to slowly rise to a sitting position. "Do you enjoy your hotel?"

Rowen blinked up at Jonathan. "Of course I do."

"And being young as you are, I imagine you'd like to get married at some point? Have a family?"

Mr. Hawes's attention shifted to Cora for a moment and then

back to Jonathan, his brows furrowing into deep grooves. "Sure I would."

"Then you're going to do exactly what I say." Jonathan patted his shoulder, inciting a whimper from the man at the gentle jostle. "You'll spend a few days enjoyin' my wife's cooking and my sister's company."

Cora's gaze shot to her brother, and the implications of his words met full comprehension. She was staying with Jonathan and Laurel for the next week until they left, which meant...she'd spend the next three days with Mr. Hawes too.

⁂

Jeb steered clear of Jonathan and Laurel's house for the next few days. Firstly, because he didn't care to see Rowen Hawes making eyes at Cora Taylor. He frowned. Nor her makin' eyes at him. And secondly, the less time he spent in Cora's company, the less likely folks would connect her with the "kept woman" rumor that Imogene Carter had already spread over half the mountain.

He nailed another board in place for the clinic building and then swiped the back of his hand across his brow. A few more weeks and the clinic would be dried in and, well, he reckoned Jonathan and Laurel would split their time betwixt the two places. He placed a few more boards, finished off the last wall on the second level, and drew in a deep breath as he stared out the spot where a window would eventually go.

Amos's house caught his attention as it sat just beyond the outskirts of town. Well situated. Only about three miles from Mrs. Cappy's store and the Mission House. An easy ride.

Would Jonathan and Laurel need it?

Amos's sister had tended to it over the years. Kept an eye out. Cleaned it up every once in a while. But she'd moved near to Wilkesboro a few months back, leaving the house to Jeb's care, and he'd not been able to go inside again after his initial visit. Even though it had been years since Amos slept beneath that roof, Jeb knew his friend had carefully crafted each log and each room. Preparing it for the woman he planned to marry when he got back from the war.

Jeb braced his palm against the wall and leaned forward, staring at the house and wrangling his heart into submission. He'd have to go back inside soon. Needed to, for Amos. He sighed. And maybe next time, he'd be able.

After finishing a few last things, Jeb closed up the lower level of the clinic and turned toward Hickory, tied to a hitching post outside.

"Jeb, I was hopin' to see you here today."

Jeb turned from the front step of the clinic to find Key Murphy walking forward, welcome expression and dirty apron intact.

"Key."

"Dale from the diner told me you was workin' today and I'm glad I caught you afore you took back off to the mountain again." The bald man removed a handkerchief from his pocket and dabbed at his shiny forehead. It was difficult not to like Key Murphy. Not only did he run one of the most successful furniture shops in this part of North Carolina, but he was one of the rare folks in the world who never had a bad thing to say about anybody.

"I done sold both of those chairs you sent me and the rocker. A man's comin' in for the bedroom set tomorrow. The whole set." He chuckled and wiped his head again.

Jeb's attention shifted from Key's face down dusty Main Street to his large three-story shop that hovered at the far corner of town. "That's nearly all I sent you, Key."

"I know. And in just three weeks too." He patted Jeb on the shoulder. "Folks is looking for quality furniture with handcrafted details, especially rich folks. With the train stopping in Rock Creek now, well, we're getting more visitors who wanna take a stroll through the mountains or stay in one of them new cabins by Cay Lake, which means more sales."

"Is that a fact?"

"As true as the sun risin'." Key stepped back. "You always made good work, Jeb, but since you got back from the war, it seems you're all fired up with ideas. If this keeps up, I'm bound to hire you for full-time work, unless you go off and start up on your own."

Jeb drew in a deep breath. He loved building. Always had. Learned it from his daddy. But he'd never dreamed of actually doing it for a living. Well, dreamed of it, but didn't reckon that sort of dream would come true, and certainly not nearly this soon.

Surely Key was talkin' out of his head.

But, cash money in the hand proved Key's words true. Enough cash money to buy more materials to create even more of the ideas in his head.

"And Jeb, if'n you make any more of them wood critters and folks, bring them too," Key added as he backed away. "I sold ever last one of 'em, except the coyote. Flatlanders just can't get enough, especially of the foxes and bears. And the ones you made of the mountain folks."

Jeb had spent hours carving forest critters and people from the mountains. Especially when he first returned home. He'd missed them all somethin' fierce, and having the familiar wood beneath his fingers made his return home feel real. Certain.

Jeb stood staring in the direction Key disappeared, shaking his head and sending a look up to the dimming sky. How in the world had going off to that horrible war helped his craftsmanship? That didn't make sense, did it? He should have come back without much skill left after all he'd seen, leastways come back with the same skill as before, but had something changed in his style? His. . .imagination?

Could God really work all things to good? Even something as wretched as his heart, his memories, after a war?

Hickory snorted, nodding his head with such ferocity his black mane swished around his face.

"What'd you know?" Jeb scratched beneath the horse's chin.

"You try to catch flies with your teeth."

He mounted Hickory and started out of town. Evening oranges, pinks, and fading gold cast soft colors across the rising mountains around the town. Rock Creek sat on the evening side of the mountains, so instead of the mountains blocking the light for a good hour before sunset, the horizon glowed into nightfall. It was why Jeb built his house on this side of the mountain instead of the Maple Springs side. Long daylight, when daylight was to be had.

Dried leaves of browns, oranges, and golds crunched beneath Hickory's steps as they made their way along the path just beyond town. Amos had designed the cabin with a family in mind. Two stories, big front porch. And he'd planned to live close enough to town to offer his wife newer conveniences, perhaps even electricity at some point, once it made it this far into the countryside.

Being so close to town, Amos had installed a lock on the outside of the front door and had the backdoor fixed so that it could only be unlocked from inside. Jeb pulled the key from his pocket and fitted it into the lock. With a few twists and turns, the door gave way. Dust floated into the soft rays of sunset filtering through the tall windows Amos had set to bring in as much daylight as possible.

The sparse furniture spoke of the unfinished plans. A large room opened to the left and another to the right with a stairway up the middle, like some house Amos had seen when he visited Wilkesboro and wanted to replicate. Jeb grinned. He'd helped Amos work on the cabin, taking a few ideas he'd learned from his friend to apply to his own house on the mountain.

A kitchen attached to the back, making the lower level three rooms and three upper ones, only a bit smaller than Jeb's. Each fitted with nice-size closets.

His boots clipped against the hardwoods. Jeb drew in a deep breath and stepped to the right, where Amos's bedroom had been. The room held a bookshelf, chest, a bed, and desk—the latter two designed and built by Jeb. He patted the footboard of the oak bed as he moved to the desk, but paused. On top of the chest lay a large Bible. The family Bible? Had Amos's sister left this here on purpose?

He stepped to the desk, which stood as if frozen in time. A pen placed next to paper waiting to be written on. A few books propped vertically by other books on either side. The sudden weight of Amos's loss pressed Jeb down into the desk chair.

Jeb had promised Amos he'd take care of Mercy should the worst happen. That he'd take care of Amos and Mercy's boy too. He'd checked in on her from time to time. Left money for her family. Delivered Amos's last letter and effects to her.

What else could he do? He couldn't bring Amos back, no matter how hard he prayed or tried.

A wooden box nestled so near the books, it almost blended in with the brown bindings. Jeb carefully took the box from its spot and ran a thumb over the top, smoothing away the dust. With a little twist of the golden hook, he raised the lid to reveal a fragile ring. Simple. But elegant too. Amos had chosen it from a shop when they were in France. Picked it 'specially for Mercy.

This belonged to Mercy, along with the Bible.

Amos would want it that way, and Jeb had promised to make things right.

His focus zoomed in on the ring. Like when he asked Mercy six months ago if they ought to get married so she'd be taken care of. She'd told him she needed time to consider if it was best.

But that had been six months ago.

His fingers fisted around the ring and a vision of Cora popped into his head. Heat left Jeb from the head down.

He shook the thoughts away. There was no use pining away for a woman who'd never choose a broken mountain man like him, but if he could do the right thing by Amos by taking care of Mercy? Well, maybe he ought to study on that thought a bit longer. Maybe he could appease his guilt for surviving by making Mercy his wife.

Chapter Nine

It had been three whole days in the same house with a recovering Rowen Hawes, and Cora was in need of distance, quiet, and a really long walk. The man could talk hours on end without stopping, and he rarely required a responsive audience, unless it was to offer smiles of encouragement. Cora's smiles had stopped being encouraging about two days ago.

After some careful questions and a few minutes creating a little map, Cora left a note for Jonathan and Laurel and started up the mountain with two visits in mind. One, Granny Burcham and two, Caroline McAdams, with the plan to stay at Uncle Edward's for the night since the trek back to Jonathan and Laurel's Mission House would likely leave her walking in the dark.

And the last thing she wanted was another evening excursion over these mountains.

Leaves littered the trail, creating a multicolored carpet of oranges and golds and a few reds, almost as if the forest offered an apology for its previous unwelcomeness. She breathed in the cool air, a sweet hint of some unknown scent on the breeze. For some reason, it made her think of Christmas. Pine, perhaps?

Bathed in afternoon sunlight, under a brilliant blue sky, the forest didn't feel as foreboding or terrifying. In fact, the way the light filtered through the trees gave the woods an almost magical glow, especially when leaves floated down in front of her like flying fairies. After a week, perhaps she was beginning to orient herself to her surroundings. At least enough to recognize the trail on the Rock Creek side of the mountain versus the trail on the Maple Springs side.

The incline leveled out for a little while, offering a view to Cora's left. With part of the leaves fallen, she could make out the river of mountains spreading all the way to the horizon. Their smoky hue took a more golden turn, she supposed, from the varied colors of the remaining leaves still clinging to the trees.

Birdsong flittered toward her from various directions. Happy sounds. And then, from among the melodies, she heard a very different tune. A whistle? Recalling one of Laurel's many warnings, Cora raised her palm to the side of her mouth and called out a loud "hello." Evidently, coming upon a mountaineer unexpectedly could lead to disastrous results for the stranger involved. A shiver prickled over Cora's shoulders.

"Halo!" Came a response. Male.

She turned a bend and, up ahead, in the middle of the trail, stood an older man bent over a stack of wood, loading it slowly into a small mule-drawn wagon. Upon closer inspection, she recognized the familiar frame of Mr. Fergus Tate.

"Well, afternoon, Nurse Woman."

His endearment paired with the hint of Scottish in his accent brought a smile. "Good afternoon to you, Mr. Tate." She drew closer and examined his wagon full of logs. "I see you've been hard at work."

"Got just a few more weeks afore the first frost, I reckon." He gestured toward the logs. "Need to make sure the family is set for winter."

"How many do you have in your family?"

"Just me and the young'uns now." He tossed another log into the wagon bed. "Since the wife passed on two years back."

"Oh, I'm sorry." She reached to raise one of the smaller logs into the wagon. "I lost my eldest brother last year. In the war."

He paused and placed his hand on the back of the wagon, those piercing eyes studying her. "Lots of men lost in that war 'crost the way. Young men."

"Yes."

"And you was there?"

"I was." She took up another log. "A hospital first, and then closer to the Front for the last part."

"I reckon war changed you some." He returned to his work. "My father fought in the War betwixt the States when he first came to this country. He'd always been a quiet man, but grew quieter after."

Cora nodded. "Was your father from Scotland, perhaps?"

The man's eyes lit with a smile. "Aye, Argyll, near Inveraray. My mother lived on the edge of Loch Awe, and he used to tell that the first time he saw her, he stood in awe." He chuckled. "After meeting my wife, Lorilee, I felt the same, but without a loch to make the story better."

"I should think that any wife would be flattered at the idea of awing her future husband."

"Aye, she did that." He wiped his head with the back of his hand. "And terrified me some too." He sighed. "But I miss her." He blinked out of a temporary stare and gestured toward the trail. "Where are you off to this afternoon? For a flatlander, you've done come a piece away from your uncle's house by your lonesome."

"I'm hoping to visit Granny Burcham and the McAdamses."

He patted the wagon and moved toward the mule. "I can walk with you a piece, if you like. I heard tell that you have no sense of direction."

Heat crept into her cheeks but she smiled anyway. "I'd be grateful for your company, Mr. Tate, but I feel certain the longer I'm here, the better my sense of direction will become."

He pushed back his broad-brimmed hat enough to scratch his head of snow-white hair, raising an equally white brow as if in doubt of Cora's grand declaration. Stifling a defense, she decided a change of subject may prove more productive and less frustrating. "How many children do you have?"

She walked along beside him, the trail barely large enough for his wagon and her.

"Only had one young'un. She passed on when Fig was borned." He cleared his throat and kept his eyes forward. "Her sorry husband ran off after that, and me and my Lorilee took the young'uns to raise."

So much loss. "I'm sorry."

He nodded. "Lorilee was a sight to behold. Ain't never seen the likes of her round these parts. She came from Tennessee way, but folks didn't take to her too well here."

"And why is that?"

He cast Cora a glance as if measuring her again. "Melungeon."

Melungeon? Was that a disease? "Melungeon?"

He seemed satisfied by Cora's reaction. "Well, there's lots of tales about 'em coming from giants or gypsies. Bein' hateful or lackin' sense, but there are as many folks that lack sense in these parts as there is in any part of the world, I reckon."

Cora had met those sorts of people in her part of the world too, but she kept silent, waiting for him to elaborate.

"But first time I seen her, I was done for." His expression softened, his gaze distant. "I ain't never seen hair as black as pitch, nor eyes the color of the stem of a new daisy. Pale like. And sweet." He drew out the word in a sing-songy way. "Sweetest woman alive, though some folks never took the time to find out onct they saw her."

"Why ever not?"

"Melungeon." He said it again, as if that explained it all. "Mixed blood."

"Mixed blood?" Did he mean mixed races?

"Some say Cherokee and white folks, some say white and black from years ago. Some say they came from explorers across the sea."

He shook his head, his pace slowing. "Didn't matter none to me as long as she stayed with me." He sighed. "And she did. Come all the way from her people to be with me and mine. And there were ones who loved her, and ones who didn't, but you'd have never knowed it from the way she made life good."

The man's tender declaration squeezed Cora's heart. His love and longing pouring out in a simple and beautiful way, which somehow inspired a longing in Cora. For a man to see her in such a way. Mr. Tate's sincere adoration must have been so profound, it tempted his wife beyond her world into his. A love like that would be a worthy temptation for any woman, Cora supposed.

"I should have liked to meet her, I think."

He spared her another glance. "She'd have wanted to hear your fancy talk and see them fancy clothes of yourn. The woman could make any piece of clothin' she set eyes on, if she had the material for it. Mercy got that from her granny, and that's a fact."

"Mercy?"

"My oldest grandgirl. Fig's growed-up sister."

Ah, no wonder Fig looked different than some of the other mountain people she'd seen here. If his grandmother had been Melungeon, her features must have passed down to him in that beautiful olive skin tone. And those arresting green eyes?

"So she lives with you and Fig?"

"Aye." He slowed his pace, his body bending a little more with each step. He must have been tired after all his work, and he wasn't a young man.

"Mercy, Fig, and the wee one."

"The wee one?"

"Daniel. Mercy's boy." Mr. Tate clicked his tongue and nodded ahead of them. "This here be the Twain Trail."

Cora looked ahead where the path split three ways. Right up a hillside, left through a rocky way, and straight ahead along the level path they'd been traveling for a little while.

"Granny Burcham's is not a far piece on the right. The McAdams's is through the left path. My way is straight ahead for a spell, so this be where we part, Nurse Woman."

"Thank you for allowing me to join you."

He sniffed and, if she didn't know better, tried to stifle a smile. "Git on, now. You'll run out of daylight afore too long as it is."

He tapped his hat and continued on, and Cora hoped "not a far piece" truly meant so.

She'd barely traveled five minutes before a dark figure emerged in front of her at the turn of the path. At first, she thought the forest light played a trick, but then the figure turned, in all its tattered cloth, head shrouded. Cora's breath seized. The figure wasn't necessarily tall, and certainly not wide. Barely a waif of a soul, but the way it poised in the center of the trail, covered from head to foot in black, brought all sorts of gothic visions into Cora's head.

A stick crunched beneath Cora's boot and she froze, waiting.

The shrouded head turned, eyes in shadow, and all Cora saw was a pale face before the figure took off at a run down the hillside, disappearing into the forest depths.

Cora didn't move. In fact, she couldn't. She had to wait for heat to surge back into her limbs before her body obeyed her brain's command to take another step forward. When she finally could move, she kept her attention riveted on the place the figure had disappeared until she'd moved far past the spot and, only then, realized her fingers had wrapped around her pistol in her jacket pocket.

Not far ahead, the smallest house she'd ever seen nestled into the side of the hill as if built into the mountain. A porch, matched to the house's size, lined the log front, covering a single door and window. The breeze blew cool up from the valley below, rustling the trees like a thousand whispers. Cora pulled her coat closer and looked back over her shoulder down the trail. Nothing but loose leaves tumbled across the lonesome path.

She held up her skirts and climbed the steps to the porch. It took a few minutes for the woman to respond to Cora's knock on the door, but when she did, her whole face registered surprise. She didn't say anything, but looked past Cora and then focused the full attention of those dark eyes back on Cora's face, nearly sending Cora back a step. "You've come a ways to my door."

"Yes." Cora managed the word. "And I'm sorry I arrived unexpectedly."

"Careful roaming these mountains on your own, girl. There's no tellin' what you might find."

Another shiver danced up Cora's spine, but she refused the impulse of shrinking back. "Do you mean like. . .like people shrouded in black or mountain lions?"

The woman's eyes flickered wide for a second and then narrowed. "Haints. Painters. No tellin' with the stories that cover these hills and hollers."

Cora refused to be baited, even if she was beginning to wonder if the figure in black was real or imagined. . .or worse.

Granny held Cora's gaze for a moment longer and then stepped aside, ushering for Cora to enter the dark room. Cora's first assessment of the house proved true. The front may have been made of logs, but the back of the house opened into the mountainside, with a stone floor leading back into an indention into the rock. Granny Burcham had just put a house-front on a cave! What an idea.

Drying plants strung from various places in the room, hanging down like laundry. The scent of earth and something sweet filled the air.

"I must be mighty important for you to traverse s'far." She turned and took a seat in a ladder-back chair by the fire.

Cora stepped closer, lowering herself and her shaking legs into a similar chair across from the woman. "I wanted to talk about. . . well, your herbs. Your healing remedies."

Granny Burcham picked up a piece of darning from near the hearth and began working on it, as if Cora hadn't said a thing.

"While I was nursing near the Front in the war, I befriended a nurse who spoke of natural remedies for various ailments. Some she used while there, but others, she tried to explain. Vines. Flowers, even weeds, that served healing purposes." Cora smoothed her palms down her skirt. "I think there's value in knowing the synthetic creations of doctors and chemists, but also what nature has to teach us."

Granny paused her darning and stared at Cora. "I heard tell you nursed in the war."

"Yes, not for long. I worked for the longest time in a hospital for wounded soldiers, who. . .who could have benefited from some natural remedies, in my opinion."

"What sorts?"

"I would wager you know many sorts." Cora raised her brow. "However, many of the men I saw suffered from difficulty breathing due to consequences of breathing in the mustard gas. My fellow nurse mentioned certain natural teas that were used particularly for breathing difficulties."

"Aye." She nodded, slowly. "Some."

"And some for wound healing and stomach pains?"

"Aye. Same."

"Similar to things like you gave Mary? To assist in childbirth?"

"There is many a remedy, but most city folk don't want to learn the mountain ways." Granny Burcham resumed her slow movements with the yarn. "They got their own notions 'bout what needs doin'."

"Well, I believe in learning as many ways to help sick people as possible, and while I'm here, I mean to help folks."

The woman chuckled.

"You don't think I'm able."

"I reckon you're as able as the next." Her eyes narrowed. "Maybe more so than some, but they won't take you here."

"Won't take my help?"

"Not most folks." She lowered her gaze back to her work.

"Whyever not? If I have the skill and desire, why wouldn't someone want my help?"

"'Cause you're a flatlander, and a single woman besides."

"Single woman?" Cora sat up straighter in her chair. "My brother is a flatlander, and when he first arrived, was a single man, and he was allowed to go about these mountains without any trouble." At least, none that Cora remembered him stating in his letters. But had it been difficult for him?

If Cora didn't know better, she'd say the old woman's lips twitched. "Folks didn't take to him at first, but onct he married a mountain girl, things got easier for him. That makes a difference round here. Folks who knows his woman and her family are more likely to trust him."

That made a little more sense, from what Cora had been learning about the suspicious mountain folks.

"And he's a man."

Cora ground her teeth. "And how does that change things?"

"It just does," came the quick reply.

It always did, didn't it? Well, she'd proven herself in her flatlander world, over and over again. She'd just have to prove herself in these mountains too. She raised her chin and almost smiled. A worthy challenge, if she'd ever seen one. "If you're willing to teach me, I'd like to learn your ways."

Granny looked up, stare-to-stare. The silence built, but Cora held the woman's gaze. Something in her told her she had to find a way to earn this woman's trust, and if the only way meant stubbornness, then Cora knew she had plenty of that.

"We'll see, Miss Taylor." She put her darning down and stood, Cora following suit. "We'll see."

She ushered Cora to the front porch without another word, a dismissal. It took everything within Cora not to turn back around and reiterate to the woman how much she wanted to learn. Surely, if she proved her interest, the woman would see the value in teaching her, wouldn't she?

Granny Burcham stepped out on the porch and stared down the trail, her graying hair spinning around her face in the cool breeze. "Rain's comin' this eve." She whispered it as if to herself, and then her dark gaze shot to Cora. "Trillium helps move the baby along when it's a woman's time."

Cora blinked at the sudden change in topic. Trillium? The delicate three-prong flower? Without a pause, Granny Burcham reached to the left of the door and plucked a drying, white plant from its place. "Ever seen this afore?"

Cora examined the flower, which looked like a long collection of tiny white balls all strung together to make a blossom of some sort. "No, but I have a few of my brother's books to review, and they have writings about some of the medicinal benefits of mountain plant life in them."

"Black cohosh." Granny sniffed and placed the plant in Cora's hand. "See if'n you can find out what it does in your book, then come find me when you don't."

She left Cora standing on the small stoop, staring at a closed door. Cora looked down at the plant, examining it for a moment longer until another rush of wind blew against her face and alerted her of the fading day. Maybe making such a promise to herself wasn't the smartest idea in a land where specters walked the forest, lions roamed the cliffs, and men shot each other at the slightest altercation, but she'd lived through worse. Perhaps. And surely, Maple Springs couldn't throw anything at her worse than ghosts.

"I'm namin' this'un after Sadie Long." Isom held up the hook from his fishing pole. "She's the girl for me."

Jeb chuckled at his little brother's sincere trust in an old wives' tale and carefully pulled a worm from the jar he'd brought with him to the fishing pond. "Sadie Long?" Jeb pulled up the girl's face in his mind. Big smile. Pretty eyes. Friendly. Made sense Isom would take a shine to her. "You think you've found your lifelong sweetheart at ten years old?"

Isom shrugged a shoulder and tossed his line into the small pond on the back end of the McAdams's property. "Don't seem you're in a hurry to catch a wife, so I reckon I'll have to be the one to do it."

Jeb wrangled his smile into a straight line and nodded. "And why do you think Sadie Long is such a fine catch?"

Isom raised his brows in a superior way and looked out over the pond. "She runs real fast, smells like apples, knows about critters, and's gotta voice like a bird."

"Those are wife-building qualities for sure." Jeb turned his face back to the jar to keep Isom from seeing his struggle with his grin. "Unless she can run faster than you. Then you won't be able to catch her."

Isom stared out at the pond, evidently studying on Jeb's words, and then his face brightened. "Lookie here." He pulled at the pole in his hand. "I done caught a fish on the hook with her name, which means she'll be mine no matter if I can catch her or not."

Jeb allowed his grin's release and tossed his own line out into the water. "It probably don't hurt that she's a might bit pretty too, does it?"

Isom took the small bass off the hook and tossed it in the bucket of water they'd brought with them to hold their contributions to dinner. "I ain't got no cause against it. Makes lookin' at her a whole lot nicer, don't it?" He sighed and took another worm from the jar. "What do you reckon makes a good wife?"

Jeb stared ahead, refusing the turn of his thoughts to a woman who smelled like flowers and a pair of eyes that made his chest ache when he thought about 'em too long. "I'd prefer if she had all her teeth."

Isom took the teasing comment with a sober expression. "That's a good one."

"And I'm partial to a woman who can cook now and again."

"I reckon Sadie Long knows 'bout cookin', since her mama's so good at it."

Jeb sobered. "And I'd like a wife who has a good mind and a sweet heart. A woman to talk with. Share stories and dreams and life with."

His pole tightened in his hands, and he tugged it forward.

"Where you gonna find a growed-up woman like that?"

Jeb took the trout in hand and worked the hook loose. "Since you're so good at wife-catching at such a fine young age, how 'bout you keep your eyes out for the right girl for me too?"

Isom's pale eyes lit and his grin followed close behind. "I'm not sure who would have you, Jebediah McAdams, but I can tell you true, if'n there's a gal out there for you, I'm gonna find her."

Chapter Ten

A pair of dogs rushed off the porch of the little cabin, howling and running directly toward Cora. One looked familiar. She squinted. Was that Puck? She raised her bag up to her chest, ready to use it to beat back the dogs if necessary, but a call from the porch brought both dogs to a stop.

The large frame of a man stood above her in the shadow of the porch. She couldn't make out his face, but something about him seemed familiar. Puck shifted closer, so she removed her glove and the dog gave her hand a sniff and then buried his nose into her palm.

"Mr. McAdams?"

The man shifted closer to the porch railing, enough to move into the late afternoon light. "Ain't used to seeing fancy flatlander women traveling alone on these mountains."

"I'm Cora Taylor. We met on Sunday at the wedding." She slowly removed her hat in hopes of giving him a better view of her face. "I'm Jonathan's sister."

Sam leaned against the porch railing and peered down at her from his lofty height, stumbling a little. Another silhouette joined Sam, a bit taller and with the same strong frame.

"Cora?" Jeb's deep voice cradled her name, and the sound carried some kind of strange warmth with it. He turned to his father.

"She's family, Daddy. Remember? Her brother's married to Laurel."

The older man released some sort of grumbling sound but Jeb ushered her forward, casting a look around the forest. He met her at the bottom of the steps. "It's awful late for you to come this far, ain't it?"

"I made a stop at Granny Burcham's first and didn't realize how long it would take."

He stepped aside for her to pass him on the steps. "Mama'll be happy as a bird in a water puddle to see you."

Her lips tugged upward at his phrasing. Something about the way he spoke, the quaintness of it, settled over her with a sweet touch.

"But you'll have to overlook Daddy tonight." Jeb's tone sobered. "He ain't at his best right now."

Before she could ask for clarification, she was met at the door by Caroline McAdams, who held a little boy on her hip. A little girl stood at her mama's skirts, smile shy. From the look of those curls, Cora guessed this must be the Suzie that Laurel had talked about. The older girl, Maggie, from what Cora remembered, peeked around the door holding another little boy in her arms. Ah, yes. The twins. James and John. And these were only the youngest of the McAdams children. From what Cora had gathered from conversations with Jonathan and Laurel, Sam and Caroline had an eldest daughter, Elizabeth, who was married and lived somewhere else. Then, there was the mysterious Kizzie, a sister who fit between Laurel and Maggie, but. . .well, Cora wasn't quite sure what happened to her. All she had gathered from the bits of information was that Kizzie hadn't died, but wasn't married either.

And, any mention of her came with sadness or whispers.

"You come just in time for supper," Caroline announced, taking hold of Cora's arm and drawing her inside the house. "Jeb and Isom brung us some fresh trout."

"And a bass, Mama," came a boy's call from the back door, his wild golden hair in all directions. If anyone ever embodied the look of a Barrie's Peter Pan, it was definitely this freckle-faced youth. What had Jonathan said his name was? Isom?

"And a bass," Caroline corrected with a grin. "So there's plenty."

"Oh, I didn't mean to intrude on your meal."

"Don't talk nonsense," Caroline reprimanded gently. "You're family. You always gotta place here."

Cora looked from the curious faces back to Jeb, whose brow creased into a dozen wrinkles. The previous warmth dissipated. Did he not want her here?

"I brought the headache powder I mentioned to you on Sunday."

"Well, that's awful nice of you." Caroline led the way through the large front room which doubled as a sitting room and a bedroom. A narrow set of stairs twisted up beside the fireplace and disappeared out of sight. Likely leading to a loft for the older children's room. The only other room in the house held a cookstove, cupboard, and large rectangular table with ladder-back chairs all around it. "I'll take some with our sassafras tea."

Sassafras tea?

"Caroline makes the best sassafras tea this side of the mountain."

Sam McAdams entered, his words too loud and a bit slurred. That was when Cora smelled the alcohol. A sudden change fell across the room. Maggie stepped back from him, drawing the two youngest boys with her. Caroline tugged Suzie near her side and Jeb moved nearer, almost as a barrier between her and Sam. The movements had been small. Barely noticeable, if Cora hadn't been paying attention, but almost in synchrony. As if it wasn't the first time.

A hollow feeling spread through her middle. Familiar. She knew that horrible dance. The careful adjustment to cover a father's sins. Of course, her father's drunkenness hadn't been as bad until after her older brother died, but then, it was as if he gave in completely to the need. Mother and Cora had learned to adjust, cover for his behavior, shift their expectations and redirect questions.

But here? In this culture, she wasn't quite sure how things might look different. Be different.

"Why don't you sit on down, Sam." Caroline broke the sudden silence. "I'll get the food on the table."

Sam nodded and gestured toward Jeb. "You too, boy. And act like you got manners. Sit that girl down too."

Jeb turned to Cora, his eyes searching hers, apologizing, attempting to explain.

Cora forced a smile. "I'll be happy to try some of that sassafras tea."

Jeb's smile crooked, and something in Cora's heart pulsed with an awareness, a connection. There was something about Jeb McAdams that paused her, or pulled her, or. . .something, she couldn't quite define. Maybe it was a sense of safety? Kinship?

Jeb led her to the table, making sure to place her as far away from his father as the table allowed, then the rest of the family took seats as Caroline and Maggie placed various bowls filled with food on the table.

"Jeb." Sam's voice boomed into the bustle. "Since you're here tonight, you say grace."

Grace?

Cora glanced around the table as the children bowed their heads. Even in his mental state, he'd remember grace? Drunkenness was such a dizzying spiral of contrasts, but habits remained, even if the mind proved foggy from alcohol.

Jeb cleared his throat. "For this food, we are thankful. For Your goodness, we are grateful. May You use this food to strengthen us so we can do Your will, just as Your Word gives strength to do the same. And. . ." He paused. "Bless the guest within this house. Protect her wherever she goes. Amen."

Cora stilled the desire to look over at him. His gentle and simple entreaty to God along with his mention of her touched her heart in ways few things ever had. Perhaps it was the combination of feeling so unprotected in this new world and the quiet strength this man beside her exuded that brought tears to her eyes, or maybe, it was the fact that such a man, so different from the men her father wanted her to marry, cared enough for her to pray for her. She didn't know.

But no one seemed to notice her internal struggle.

Instead, movement happened on all sides, dispersing food to each person. Fish, potato cakes, beans, and corn bread. She wondered what a sacrifice her presence created in portion sizes for the rest of the family, but neither Caroline nor Sam gave any hint of concern. Despite her initial misgivings at the novel meal, it was probably the best one she'd had since arriving in Maple Springs.

And though Sam spoke too loudly for the setting and talked over others as if he didn't hear them, the meal moved forward with some fun antics from the twins, James and John, while little Suzie, who appeared to be around five, sent Cora adorable smiles. Her double-dimpled cheeks framed in by golden curls won Cora at first sight. Isom's face was so expressive, it was easy to note his thoughts, even though he didn't speak unless to ask for another helping of food. Maggie, the eldest daughter in the house, kept a quiet, gentle demeanor as she took turns with her mother going back to the cookstove for additional food.

"You come from England way?"

Cora turned her attention to Sam and smiled. "Yes, London, but I spent many summers on my grandparents' farm in Derbyshire."

Sam's brows rose and he gestured toward his wife with his chin. "Caroline's people are from yonder." Cora met her hostess's gaze. "Are they?"

"My grandparents was from there," she answered, helping John with his food. "I have the tea set passed down from my granny who come from there."

Cora followed Caroline's nod to a cupboard in the room, its three shelves boasting items that must have been family treasures. A pieced-together array of various china along with other painted containers lined the shelves with a beautiful tea set, complete with simple blue flowers against a white background, at the center.

"It's beautiful." Cora smiled back at her. "I would think that keeping such a family treasure would make you feel connected to your grandmother?"

"Aye," came Caroline's reply. "I know there's some folks that ain't got no interest in the old ways, but there's good to be found in them."

Cora nodded, considering her words. The quiet and simplicity had certainly turned Cora's thoughts toward a more heavenly direction than she'd experienced in a while. Though the great trials of caring for wounded soldiers increased her prayers for help, this mountain world brought with it a quiet introspection. A look into who she was in God's grand world and how she fit. What was her purpose? What had He created her to do?

Being the wife of a self-absorbed money-hunter was definitely not it.

But nursing? Yes. Helping others? Most certainly.

She looked around the table at the simple love shown in this family, even with Sam in his semidrunk state. Family? A smile warmed her face. Someday.

She'd planned to excuse herself after helping clean up the dishes, but she was ushered into a chair in the front room of the house. Without ceremony, Sam McAdams took up his violin—fiddle— and began playing a tune. Isom joined him, holding some strange instrument similar to a guitar but with a round belly.

"It's called a banjo," Maggie answered when Cora asked about it. "He learned hisself how to play one when he saw Fig Tate with one."

The first tune was a haunting one about a dying man who wanted to see some woman named Barby Allen. Words like "yonder" and phrases like "out of his bosom grew a red rose" swelled as story rose in song, and Cora stared, fascinated by the longing in Sam's voice, as if he, himself, was grieving the death of the young man in the song. With each tune, Sam became more like the man Cora had met at the wedding—jovial, witty, ready to laugh, and affectionate with his family.

How sad what drink took from a person. Were these sweet memories clear to him or a blurry "something" in his thoughts?

Her attention shifted to Jeb, who sat nearby, his profile pensive as he tapped his knee to the rhythm of the music. His profile was worth viewing, dark hair waving around his forehead to curl behind his ear, a matching close-shaved beard over a strong jaw, and lips set in a straight line, but ready for a crooked smile.

Heat rose up her neck and she turned back to the music. Sam and Isom began a "picking war" as Caroline called it, and took turns passing increasingly complex melodies back and forth to each other. Cora half-wished a piano stood in the room so she could join in the fun too. At least then, she might contribute something, otherwise there was nothing to do except enjoy.

She was much better at *doing* something, but as the songs continued on from one to the other, the nervousness of "just sitting" began to disappear into the awe of the music. Each tune or ballad told stories of various sorts, as if they'd come from books Cora might have read as a child. Tales of fair maidens and dashing heroes, horse thieves and daring escapes, hangings and chases, and, of course, lost love.

Sorrow and beauty mingled together through the strums and the voices, much like life seemed to do on a regular basis. Sorrow *and* beauty. And attitude and perspective changed, depending on which Cora set her mind on. The difficult and sad, or the beautiful and lovely. Maybe that was exactly what she needed to do in this hard place. Find the beautiful and lovely among the everyday, because it was around her, from the rainbow of trees shrouded in earthen tones, to the endless view of mountains, to the tenderness of family.

Jeb sat nearby, tapping his knee and humming to the tunes. Suzie and John danced in the center of the room, giggling if someone fell to the ground, only to join in again.

What an intimate setting. A family gathered around a fire listening to music together, as if the songs were bedtime stories.

Not long into the music, Maggie joined Sam and Isom by bringing out a long, thin instrument with strings. Cora must have looked curious, because Caroline grinned over at her as she rocked James in her lap and nodded toward the instrument. "That there's a dulcimer. Sam's brother made it for Maggie since she's taken a shine to music, like the rest of the family."

A dulcimer. The sound was almost harp-like, adding a magical quality to the other instruments. Without preamble, Caroline began singing, a beautiful, soprano tone. Her lone voice filled the room, accompanied by the gentle strumming of the other instruments. She sang about two lovers who parted and longed for each other but were confident in their commitment to each other, only able to rest once they were back together again.

"One, I love.

Two, he loves,

Three, he's true to me."

And then, the verse turned to how the couple rested in each other's arms when together again. So simple, yet lovely. Cora had never heard anything like it, yet the style sounded vaguely familiar. What strange beauty to find in the middle of this small house on the back side of a mountain in the middle of nowhere. But, as she'd learned from the past year of the war, God had a way of placing beauty in the most surprising places. Perhaps it was His way of reminding His children that He was never far away. That good still lived, even when the darkness of war and the agonies of death surrounded all sides.

He still walked among those places with as much care and love and beauty as in the sunlit ones. Like these ballads, both the beauty and the hardship played a part in the grander story of God's work in hearts and lives. Even now. Even here.

"Take over the playin', young'uns," Sam said, placing his fiddle to the side. "And give me a dancin' tune."

Isom started off on some quick tune as Sam left his spot by the fire and approached Caroline. With a shuffle forward and a bow, as if he were a nobleman at court, he offered his hand to Caroline. She smiled the broadest Cora had seen in the woman and, after a shake of her head, set James down on the floor and took Sam's hand. Off they went, dancing about the tiny room with Suzie, James, and John attempting to keep up. Cora couldn't help but clap along with the beat out of sheer pleasure in the sight, all tenseness gone. Even quiet Maggie giggled in pleasure.

Then Sam, with his bride in hand, danced over to Jeb and spoke to him so low, Cora couldn't hear.

Jeb shook his head, but Sam spoke again, and Jeb's entire body stiffened before he stood.

It wasn't until he'd turned toward her that she began to understand the hushed conversation. All heat slipped from her body and her clapping froze in midair. Jeb McAdams was going to ask her to dance. And what was worse, she'd have to tell him no.

❧❦❧❦❧

Jeb stared up at his father for a full five seconds, his father's words slowly bleeding into comprehension. "Go ask Cora to take to the floor with you."

The last thing Cora likely wanted was a dance with him. And the last thing he needed was another reason to spend more time with her. She already took up too much time in his head, especially when he was trying to work up the courage to ask Mercy Tate to marry him. The whole idea just seemed wrong as wrong could be.

Jeb shook his head.

His father didn't so much as flinch. He looked to his mama, but she merely smiled in that sweet way which really said, "Listen to your daddy," though Daddy made the statement again, with a little wink tossed in to inflame Jeb's face all the more.

He was a grown man, for goodness' sake. He didn't need his parents helping him spark a woman who didn't have no intention of sparkin' back. And yet, when he looked over at her, sitting in her purple dress, curls slipping loose from her bun and framing her face and those eyes all wide and wondering—well, his feet made up his mind.

He stood. Her eyes grew wider. He took a few steps toward her. Her bottom lip dropped. And then, like his daddy—without the flourish—he offered his hand.

She stared at him, blinking. He swallowed through the gathering lump in his throat, waiting.

"I. . .I can't, Jeb," she whispered.

His shoulders deflated a little. Of course. Why on earth would she want to dance with him, even if it was in the privacy of his parents' house? He lowered his hand.

"I'm a horrible dancer." Her words tumbled forward. "My eldest brother attempted to teach me to dance several times and it was absolutely devastating. My feet and my mind don't seem to speak the same language."

He released his breath in a chuckle of relief. It didn't have a thing to do with him. "This dancin' is likely something different than he was trying to teach you."

"Certainly." She looked over at Isom and blinked again. "Much faster. I barely made it through the waltz without squishing his toes to jelly."

Energy zipped through his whole body. She needed a bit of rescuing from her own worries, didn't she? Well, he could certainly try to do that. "Miss Taylor, you deserve another chance at learnin'." He reached down, took her hand, and pulled her up to him. "And I give you permission to squish my toes to jelly all you like."

She opened her mouth to protest, if he guessed right, but before she uttered a word, he brought her into a turn.

"Now, link hands with Mama," he nudged.

"What?" Cora turned to his mama who had her hand out and ready. "I take her hand and keep yours?"

He nodded, attempting to keep his grin under control. Her uncertainty, her vulnerability, had him tightening his grip on her hand. "That's right, and we'll go round and round for a bit. Nice and easy-like."

Her brows rose, a few more curls dropping loose from her bun, and she took Mama's hand. He took Daddy's, and they circled round, his daddy's chuckle in time with the music while Suzie danced in the middle of the circle, her happy laughter joining in with the banjo and dulcimer.

"There you go, girl," Daddy called.

Cora stumbled but Jeb tightened his grip, steadying her.

"Now we step in toward each other," Jeb said, moving her forward toward his mama and daddy. "And then we go back." They followed suit, her body slowly beginning to relax into the music.

"Let's circle about a few more times, Daddy," Jeb said. "So Cora can find her feet."

Cora shot him a look of gratitude, stumbling a little less as they circled about, just the four of them. It wasn't going to be like an actual reel, with just the four, but, maybe he could help her along when she danced again.

They changed directions with the circle and Cora didn't stumble as much. Jeb felt plumb proud of her.

"Now we're gonna pair off," Daddy called, as if announcing to a crowd.

"Pair off?" Cora repeated, breathless.

Mama let go of Cora's hand and Jeb let go of Daddy's, drawing Cora closer to him. She searched his face, her flowery scent invading the small space between them so well he nearly lost his train of thought. "I'm gonna spin you round real slow like, so you can know what to do next time."

He raised their braided hands above her head and guided her

into a spin.

She grinned. "I didn't fall!"

"Not even a little," he said, tightening his hold on her hand as she wavered a second. "Now, let's do that turn once more."

Slowly, he guided her through it and led her, with a little hesitation, toward his daddy, as the partners were supposed to trade. Daddy was in the beginning of his drunk, having a little bit more every night, but the full-on madness of his problem waited only a few days away. Daddy would lose his mind, taken over by the liquor.

Jeb shook his head and returned to the song. Daddy wasn't there yet. Jeb had grown up with the signs. He knew the difference between the father and the drunk. And his father still held court over the madman.

Daddy carefully turned Cora around twice and then they all gathered hands again for a circle, repeating the dance until Cora returned as Jeb's partner. Her cheeks bloomed pink and her eyes glistened in the lantern light. Heaven on earth, he was done gone and over the moon.

The circuit happened a few more times before the song came to a close and the four dancers, along with the three little'uns, clapped their gratitude for the musicians who each took a bow, Isom's the most dramatic.

"See there." Jeb led her back to her chair. "You danced just fine."

She relaxed down into the chair with a sigh. "I'd always thought I *couldn't* dance, but, well, it seems I just needed the right teacher."

The way she looked up at him with those big eyes and her sweet smile left him more befuddled than he cared for anyone to know. He shoved his hands into his pockets and cleared his throat, looking back over at his siblings getting ready for another tune. "Maybe just the right kind of dance, I'd reckon."

"Or a good combination of both," she added, so softly, he looked back down at her.

The expression on her face paused him for a second too long.

If he didn't know better, he'd say she looked at him almost as if. . . Well, he wasn't quite sure, but the look she gave him hit him square in the chest and left a strange kind of tightness.

No, no, no! He didn't need to spark on a woman who wasn't plannin' on stayin' in the mountains, no matter what her eyes said. She was an heiress, and though he wasn't a hundred percent sure what that all entailed, he knew his fairy tales and history well enough to know heiresses didn't go around sparkin' mountain men. And spending any more time with her would likely do one of two things, neither good: one, cause these sparkin' feelings to catch fire; or two, ruin Cora Taylor's reputation to the point of hurting her. Neither of which he wanted. Well, for sure he didn't want one of 'em.

Besides, he was plannin' on asking Mercy to marry him. He needed to do right by Amos in death, since he couldn't do right by him in life.

"Jeb, I'd say if you're gonna make it home, you might wanna get on down the trail." Mama's voice pulled him around. "It'll be dark afore long."

Jeb nodded and backed away from Cora, headed toward the jacket he'd left by the door. "Sure 'nough."

"You can walk Cora on down the mountain too," Mama added, the little twinkle in her eyes promising trouble of the courtin' kind. "Ain't no cause for her walkin' alone when y'all are goin' the same way anyhow."

Jeb tightened his jaw and gave his mama a long stare. He knew good and well she'd heard the rumors as well as anybody else. Why on this side of eternity was she encouraging closeness with Cora Taylor? The woman wasn't bound to stay in the mountains nohow. It was a fool's errand. But as soon as the thought came to mind, he frowned. No, ain't nothin' foolish 'bout his mama. Wistful and wanderin', maybe, but not foolish.

The only one feeling foolish was the man trying to button a jacket he'd buttoned just fine the past five years of his life.

He pushed a hand through his hair and raised his gaze to Cora, who'd stood from her chair. "Do you mind, Jeb? Since we are going the same way?"

"'Course not." He shot his mama another look, trying to communicate the danger in her suggestion, but she only grinned wider.

"Isom, why don't you go on down with Jeb tonight so you can help check his rabbit gums in the mornin'." Mama's lips twitched ever so slightly. If he didn't know she was such a good woman, he'd conjure up words like *meddlin'* and *busybody* in his head. "Then you can head on home after school tomorra."

"Woohoo!" Isom jumped up from his spot and placed his banjo down. "I get to sleep in the big house tonight!"

A strange mixture of relief and disappointment snaked through Jeb and he stifled a growl. If sparkin' meant his brain and his heart spoke two different languages, then he was in a heap of trouble.

"Come on, then." He shot a glance to Isom and jerked his chin toward the door. "We wanna get Miss Taylor on home before it's too dark." And in enough light for any mountain spy to see clear enough that Isom was walking in betwixt the two of them.

Cora bid everyone goodbye, receiving a hug from the twins, Suzie, and Mama, a shy smile and wave from Maggie, and a hearty nod from Daddy, before joining Jeb and Isom down the front steps and onto the trail. Jeb kept his distance and Isom easily filled in the space between. Red hues of sunset slipped through the trees, causing what leaves remained to glow like some of the electric lights he'd seen in Europe and on the ship coming home. Except, this glow came naturally, soft and welcome, like a cool breeze on a hot day or a warm house on a cold night.

Isom spent the first bit talking about some fox he'd captured a week back that got away this morning and then he went off on something about Dandy Bruce's dog having a new litter of puppies.

"You oughta git you a good dog, Miss Taylor." Isom lowered his chin as if he knew best. "Ain't no cause for bein' in the mountain without a good dog."

Cora sent a grin to Jeb before tempering it when she looked down at Isom. "Well, with all the dogs you know, I would assume you're an excellent person to know about dogs."

"I am." Isom stood a bit taller. "In fact, I can tell you 'bout any critter in these mountains. I've caught nearly all of 'em."

"Or nearly been caught by them," Jeb added, catching another glimpse of Cora's smile when he spoke.

"Well, I'm glad I know someone to ask about the critters."

The way she said the word "critters" with her fancy accent nearly unfurled Jeb's grin all over again, and he had the odd notion to just hug her. Maybe he was going bloomin' crazy.

"That's right. Just ask me." Isom nodded again but then caught sight of something up ahead. "Did you see that up yonder? Looked like a white owl." And off he ran, conveniently taking away the barrier Jeb hoped to keep between his feelings and the Englishwoman.

They walked in silence for a little while as Isom dashed back and forth ahead of them in the fading sunlight. Trees crouched closer in the shadows. Night noises grew louder and the sound of their footsteps among the freshly fallen leaves kept time with the crickets.

"Your family was very kind to me."

He looked over at her, but her face remained forward. "They're a good sort, for the most part."

Her lips twitched into a crooked grin. "I especially like your mother. She's someone I'd wish to, I don't know, learn from."

"Ain't many like her, that's for sure."

"There's a gentleness in her that calms those around her." She released a sigh. "I think you must have gotten that from her."

He laughed. "You think I'm gentle?" With the fury going on inside his mind most days, *gentle* wasn't the word he'd choose to describe himself.

"You don't think so?" She looked up at him, searching his face. "Perhaps, then, it's a sense of safety? Or kindness?" Her lips pursed in a frown that wrinkled her brow. "I haven't sorted it out yet, but it's a good thing, Mr. McAdams."

He shook his head and stared heavenward, breathing in the scent of earth and leaves and evening air. "It ain't easy to keep folks safe."

An owl's call permeated the quiet between them.

"Jeb, it's impossible to keep everyone safe, especially in a war."

He shot her a look. He hadn't mentioned Amos to her, but the understanding in her eyes told him she knew. Understood without him having to explain.

"The world isn't safe, no matter where you are or what's happening." Her voice softened. "I lost a good friend, another nurse. She took my shift since I'd worked a double the night before. For a while I blamed myself. It should have been me."

"That ain't so," came his quick response.

Her fingers played with the scarf at her neck. "True. Life and death are in the hands of the Almighty." Her gaze met his. "But sometimes our hearts are much too broken to recognize the truth in our heads."

He held her gaze, allowing her words to sink into his aching spirit. "Then what do we do?"

He knew the answer but wanted to hear her say it. Confirm it. Remind him. And herself.

"I was thinking about it while I listened to your family play that wonderful music. Trust. That's what we do." Her heart strengthened at the voiced declaration. "We trust that God's love for us and the people we've lost is even bigger than ours for them. And so, whatever He's chosen for their lives is a much better plan than one we can imagine."

Her words voiced the truth with much more eloquence than his mind. "Preacher says the world is a broken place, and broken folks leave more broken people behind."

"Which should cause us to long for heaven, but I'm afraid my first reaction is anger." She released a sad chuckle. "I want to mend the world, but it's impossible to navigate all the many things only God can." She shrugged a shoulder. "I'm bound to try."

His smile grew from one corner to the next. "I bet you are."

Her gaze lingered in his, all golden and beautiful, until her smile fell and his breath stalled. Then she stumbled over a limb on the trail. He caught her, drawing her against him, and every ounce of her scent and softness crashed against his good intentions. Her body melted into him. His arms naturally caged her in, and that tiny spark took up such a flicker he felt it shooting up through his whole body, and then. . . He realized what was happening and jerked back, nearly sending her sprawling to the forest floor.

Luckily, he caught her before she fell and steadied her back to her feet before slipping back—with extra distance between them.

"I'm—I'm sorry." He shook his head, distancing himself even more.

"No harm done." She sounded breathless, and he liked that sound too much.

He pinched his eyes closed. *Lord, help me.* "Hopefully not, but there's no tellin' who's watchin'."

"Watching?" She turned toward him, her eyes widening. "What do you mean? Watching?"

He growled and rammed his fists into his pockets. Stupid talk. He needed to keep his mouth shut. "Nothin'."

"Jeb." Her tone firmed. "What do you mean?"

He released a sigh and turned to face her. "Some folks in these mountains, especially the busybodies, keep a lookout for anything worth gabbing about."

"And they have a reason to *gab* about us?"

"I just don't want to start any trouble for you, especially since you're an outsider and folks round here aren't keen to take too kindly to strangers."

She studied him with such intensity, he just kept on talking like he knew what he was saying. "We don't want no rumors to start for you that might lead to wrong thinkin' about you and—" He cleared his throat. "Me. If folks thinks there's anything sinful goin' on betwixt the two of us."

"Sinful?" She laughed out the word.

He cringed. "It ain't like there's anything sinful going to happen." His face heated. "But if someone thought we was in a romantic way without goin' about it properly then things might not turn out so good for either of us."

"Good heavens! How would anyone imply such a thing? And why would it matter to them?"

"It shouldn't, but it does, and since you ain't of a matrimonial mind, I'm tryin' to keep you clear of any possible misunderstandings." He'd butchered this conversation worse than any hunting mistake he'd ever made. He raised a brow. "Safe, if I can."

"What are you not saying, Jeb McAdams?"

He looked away and prayed for help.

"You ain't got no notion to get married?" Isom emerged as if from nowhere, but clearly he'd heard enough.

Cora blinked, effectively releasing Jeb from her stare, and turned to Isom. "I would love to get married someday, Isom, but I'd like to choose who that person would be."

"You don't get to choose where you're from?"

"Not as easily as I ought, I'm afraid." She smiled at Isom but narrowed her eyes up at Jeb.

He conveniently looked away.

"Well, it's a good thang you come all the way here then." Isom's confident stride returned as he kept in time with them. "Fellers and gals ain't got no qualms choosin' and marryin' a'tall."

"That's a relief to know." And though Cora focused back on the walk, her tight smile sent Jeb a clear message she wasn't finished with their conversation.

"You took care of folks in the war, didn't you?" Isom continued, oblivious to the tension in the night air.

"I did." Cora retied her scarf. Double knot, and Jeb had the strange notion she wished his neck fit behind it. "For my part."

"Which means you're the caring sort?"

Isom's words trickled through Jeb's frustration to reach recognition. The caring sort?

"I like to think I am." Her words returned to their gentle tone. "I hope so anyway."

"Caring, easy on the eyes, and good at talkin'?" Isom drew in a deep breath and sent Jeb a rascally grin. "That's an awful nice list for a gal worth marryin', ain't it?"

Chapter Eleven

Cora wasn't certain whether her brother truly wanted her to drive the wagon so she could get accustomed to the mountain road to Flat Creek or if he'd noticed her avoidance of Rowen, but no matter the reason, magnanimity or practice, she wouldn't complain. Besides, she'd driven all sorts of conveyances while at the Front, so this experience proved one of the less shocking of her time in the Blue Ridge.

Laurel sat in the bed of the wagon, keeping Rowen Hawes entertained as he sat propped by blankets to soften the dips and bumps of the ride. The timing wasn't ideal—her brother leaving only a little over a week after she'd arrived—but she couldn't fault him for it. After all, he didn't know she'd taken a ship then a train to Appalachia to escape a very unwanted future. But still, she'd barely gotten enough time to bask in his nearness after almost a year apart.

But since he and Laurel had asked her to tend house for them while they were gone, Cora would, at least, have some time to delve into Jonathan's medical books.

"I hate we're leaving you just as you've arrived." Jonathan sat by her side in a dapper suit. His felt hat was poised too far back on his head, but he still managed to look above reproach. Well, except for the mischief tipping his smile. "Who will be here to keep you out of trouble?"

"And you automatically assume that I'm the one who causes all this trouble, are you?"

His grin broadened and then he sobered. "It is quite the adjustment, Cora. This place." He glanced to the back of the wagon. "But at least you'll have the McAdamses and Uncle Edward. There's some relief in that."

"I'll be alright, you know?" She nudged him with her shoulder. "I've grown up a lot in the past year."

"Be that as it may. . ." He nudged her back. "You're still my little sister, and there are things about these mountains and these mountain people that you may have never encountered in the war."

She nodded, allowing him that. "As strange as it sounds, helping you with Rowen's bullet wound has been the most natural thing that has happened to me since I arrived here."

He released a laugh. Oh, how she loved his laugh. It had been so long since she'd heard it. "If that doesn't tell you how topsy-turvy the world is right now, I don't know what would." His expression sobered. "But do be careful. I'm glad you can tend to the house, but go to Uncle's at any point you feel unsafe. Won't you?"

"I'll certainly keep that in mind."

His cheek twitched at her lack of commitment. "And don't forget that Mrs. Cappy and her store are available to you. You can see her store from the front of the house."

"Jonathan." She settled her gaze in his. "I know I've never lived here with all of its many differences, but I have been on my own, somewhat, and in a dangerous place, I might add. You must trust me a little."

His shoulders slowly lowered with the release of a long breath. "I know you're right, but. . .but I'm so glad to have you here that I want you to remain safe and. . ." He shrugged. "Well, just remain for a while, I suppose."

"That's my plan." She grinned. "After a mountain lion, a shooting, and a childbirth in the middle of a storm, I feel as if I've passed some sort of test already." She refused to mention the "haint," mostly because she didn't believe in them, but also for the simple fact she didn't want Jonathan to know the idea of the shrouded woman unnerved her.

"Let's hope those are the worst of it." He looked ahead. "Yes, let's hope."

She flinched at the foreboding in his response, determined to end on a lighter note. "Of course, there are things about this place that have been"—she almost said "frightening," but refused to admit such aloud—"surprising and that I've felt ill-equipped to manage at first, but the longer I'm here, I think I'm beginning to see a little of what kept you in this place."

"Besides Laurel, you mean."

"Yes, besides Laurel." Cora grinned. "There's a need, but also a beauty. And the way some families find joy in the smallest things, well, it's refreshing, isn't it?"

"And if you know where to look, you'll find goodness, creativity, intelligence. So many things." Jonathan shook his head slowly. "The handiwork these mountain folks create with the meagerest of resources is astounding. I can't seem to sell their crafts fast enough. Have you seen Jeb's woodcrafts?"

Cora turned toward her brother, her mind flipping back to her first day when she'd awakened in Jeb's cabin and saw the woodland creature carvings on the mantel in the bedroom. Had those been his? She pressed her lips together to keep her smile under control. How could she be both surprised and not so surprised by this knowledge? "I don't think I've seen much of them."

"The shopkeepers and craftsman in Wilkesboro snatch up his work as fast as I can bring it to them. And he's not the only one who creates quality products. There are dressmakers, quilters, basket weavers, potters, so many things."

"Now if we could just get them to improve their hygiene and diet, we can say we've discovered a lost colony of renaissance men and women."

He raised his brow.

"I read all of your letters over and over again." She pointed at him. "I remember almost everything you've written about these people, and now I have my own information to add. They need more vegetables than potatoes and corn whiskey."

He rolled his eyes skyward as his grin grew. "When I get back next month, I will show you all the gifts they have *and* the changes that are slowly happening, and then you'll bite your tongue."

Flat Creek proved nothing like any town Cora had seen back home. No cobblestone streets, limestone, thatched-roof character, or picturesque alleys. In fact, she didn't see any thatch, cobblestone, or limestone at all. Few trees, though there were pockets of them, but the entire conglomeration of box-shaped buildings were framed in by the mountains in which she'd spent the last week.

The buildings lined both sides of the street, many brick, some white-painted wood slabs. A church steeple rose at the far end of the street with a large, gray building with stairs leading up to tall columns pitted across from the church. A government building, perhaps?

The entire scene reminded her of a photo she'd seen once related to the "Wild West" towns nearer the West Coast of the United States.

"There's the town clinic Jeb has been working on." She followed Jonathan's gaze to a three-story wood-slab structure at the edge of town. "The plan is to use the lower floor for the clinic, the middle floor for living quarters, and the top floor as additional space for storage or housing, as needed."

"Your hope is to be in town, instead of up in the mountains?" An unexpected decision, given his passion for the mountain people.

"Only part-time and until we can add another doctor." He looked ahead. "Rock Creek is as in need of a doctor as Maple Springs. Their long-time physician passed away about six months ago and I've been staying in town for a few days when I take crafts to Wilkesboro."

What doctors would come to this place? Jonathan needed help now. It was evident from the vastness of the place. From the stories she'd heard. From Jonathan's own tales.

A large white house stood out from the other shops as they passed, its grand wraparound porch and varied rooflines jutted in typical Victorian style. Jonathan must have seen her staring.

"That is the mayor's house," he said. "He's quite proud of it, from what I hear."

"And rightly so." Cora nodded to people as they passed, their attire less stylish than London, but much more up-to-date than Maple Springs. Her attention dropped to the feet of the pass-ersby—they all wore shoes. Something about that mental acknowl-edgement pierced her in a way she didn't expect. A need. A longing. A. . .purpose sparked to life inside her. Was this the same type of desire her brother had felt a year ago when he'd come into this wild place to teach school?

His comment from the day Rowen was shot came back to mind. *I think I have a much-needed assistant.*

Could the people of Maple Springs be her calling too?

"Back there is Rowen's house."

Cora followed her brother's gesture to a massive three-story, whitewashed house on a hill a street behind Main. It felt as if it towered over them, even though it wasn't as large as the mayor's house. Close, but not quite. And *tower* seemed the appropriate word, because there were three of them, jutting up from the house's roofline as if to garner attention in castle-like fashion.

"You like what you see, Miss Taylor?"

Cora swiveled on the wagon bench to the sound of Rowen Hawes's question, the potency of his confident smile unscathed by the weakness in his body. The fact the town road allowed for her to hear his voice from the back of the wagon attested to the smooth-ness of the packed dirt.

"It's a beautiful house, Mr. Hawes."

"Stop puttin' on airs, Rowen Hawes." Laurel shook her head and added an exaggerated eye roll. "Everybody in this wagon knows where you're from, so no need to get high on your horse." She may look the part of a town lady in a navy suit and matching hat Cora gave her, but the mountain shone through in her speech.

Cora grinned. That accent was growing on her.

"Our train leaves shortly." Jonathan glanced at Laurel and then looked at Cora. "Would you mind taking us to the train station before returning Rowen to his home?"

"My hotel," Rowen corrected. "I need to check on things there first."

Jonathan sent a look to Cora, searching her face.

"It's fine, Jonathan." Her smile softened. "I'm certain I've seen worse than a small-town hotel."

His brow darkened but he didn't respond.

Once Jonathan and Laurel retrieved their tickets, Jonathan took Cora by the arm and pulled her aside. "Be careful in certain parts of this town. It's good mostly, filled with good people, but there are places. . ."

"As there are everywhere." She patted his hand on her arm. "I'll be careful, brother dear."

His smile crooked at her childhood nickname for him. "Mind you do, or I'll be forced to have Uncle Edward give you a thorough tongue lashing." He raised one brow. "And those are uncomfortable no matter how old one is."

She laughed and gave Jonathan a hug before seeing him and Laurel off on their train. Even though she'd navigated field hospitals without him, a sudden loneliness swelled through her as she watched the train disappear around the bend. Of course she had Uncle Edward, but his schedule proved as malleable as Jonathan's.

She pinched her eyes closed and straightened her shoulders. She would just have to make do, wouldn't she? Her life had changed so much in the past two years, she barely recognized the lighthearted, whimsical girl she'd been before the war changed so many things. But she'd learned to fight for herself and others. To push beyond the fear and discomfort. And she'd do the same now.

As she approached the wagon, Rowen greeted her with his typical grin. "Just the two of us, Miss Taylor."

"I suppose so." She paused before him as he sat up from his pillowed place among the quilts. "But I will make our time together as short as possible since you need to rest and I mean to get back to Maple Springs before dark."

"You can always stay in my hotel." His grin teased wider. "Much finer accommodations for a fine lady like yourself."

Before the war, if she'd been thrust into the world of Maple Springs and someone had offered her a warm room, carpeted floors, and a bed with a real mattress, she'd have pounced at the opportunity. But now? Well, she'd learned how to manage simpler expectations and recognize rascally intentions.

"That is very kind of you, Mr. Hawes, but I really—"

"I think we've gotten to know each other well enough that you can call me Rowen, don't you?"

Her smile hitched but she held it intact. "Thank you, Rowen, but I need to start on back."

He caught her arm as she moved to pass the wagon bed. "That mountain ain't for the likes of you, Cora. You're meant for grander things. And I'm sure you're used to 'em. Soft beds, warm rooms, excellent meals." His fingers tightened ever so slightly. "I can promise to take real good care of you."

Her body tensed. Unfortunately, she'd also experienced the sting of being manhandled. She pulled her arm away as easily as possible and forced a smile she didn't feel. "Again, thank you, Mr. Hawes." She enunciated his name. "But I find that war has taught me that the grander things, as you call them, are rarely related to how soft the bed is or how excellent the meal, though I have a keen appreciation for both."

His smile faded, so she attempted to lessen the blow.

"But, perhaps, when I return to see to your healing, you will indulge me in a tour of your hotel and, perhaps, one of those excellent meals?"

He recovered his grin as well as the glint in his eyes. "It would be my pleasure, Cora."

Her stomach knotted in unexpected revolt, but she held to her expression long enough to take the wagon ride down the street and help Rowen into the lobby of his grand hotel. For a small-town hotel, it held an element of grandeur she hadn't expected. The four-story brick edifice stood tall, its roofline visibly taller than the steeple from the church across the street. A glossy black-and-white checked floor led to a massive grand staircase, splitting at the landing and disappearing up on both sides.

"Care to change your mind now?"

She looked at him as he leaned against her for support. Though with the way he'd been healing, he likely didn't require her help. Her cheeks flared hot and she carefully led him toward one of the posh, red high-backs that stood facing a marble fireplace. What an anomaly! All of it! And how was he able to maintain such a place in the middle of nowhere?

As if reading her mind, he said, "Sawmills are all around, and with the development of Route 421 for access from east to west, we get a surprising amount of stopovers."

"You must," she whispered, taking in the grand room and accommodations.

"I can have a room readied for you, if you'd like to reconsider your plans." His low voice edged close to her ear and she nearly dumped him in the chair.

"Mr. Hawes." A young man dressed in a white button-up and starched brown trousers ran forward. "We heard you planned on returnin' today. We got your office all set up for you, sir."

Rowen made to wave the man away but Cora raised a hand

to stop him. "Sir, Mr. Hawes requires further rest, so I insist he is driven home within the hour." Her gaze landed on Rowen, and he frowned. "If you hope to recover well enough to stay in your office for a full day, you'll do as I say."

"What on earth happened?" the young man asked. "You know every time you go into those mountains, it causes trouble."

"Nonsense," Rowen grumbled, returning his attention to Cora. "Trouble finds me. Folks green with envy that one of their own could turn out so well."

"Is that why you were shot? Envy?"

He looked away and tapped the arm of the chair. "That and a simple matter of someone not wanting to pay their debts." His gaze came back to her. "Don't trust those mountain people. They'll turn on you as soon as look at you if you're an outsider."

"Aren't you one of those mountain people, Mr. Hawes?"

His jaw tightened. "Not anymore, I'm not."

Cora excused herself from the hotel after Rowen made another offer for her to stay. As lovely as a hot bath and a grand room sounded to her in her current dirt-dusted state, the idea that Rowen Hawes held the keys to the place sent her in retreat. The longer she knew him, the less comfortable she became in his presence.

After a stop in the mercantile to purchase a few needed—and unneeded—items, including some candy, a few small toys for the McAdams children, some hearty boots, and some cloth in hopes of convincing one of the ladies to make Cora a few more "fittin'" dresses for mountain life, she started on her way back up the mountain. Even leaving when she did, the short autumn days offered little hope she'd make it all the way to Jonathan and Laurel's house by nightfall. Well, she'd just have to stop off at Uncle Edward's for the night and then on to the Mission House in the morning.

The afternoon clouds blew across the sky, slowly gathering into darker hues as she kept a steady pace up the trail. Her pistol waited in her pocket, ready for any repeat of her first day in Maple Springs, but apart from birdsong and a rustling squirrel here and there, the only thing the cool breeze brought to her was the scent of rain.

The long quiet ushered all sorts of thoughts which turned into prayers as Milkie, the mare, kept a steady pace up the trail. After almost two weeks, the initial shock of the mountains had given way to a curiosity, maybe even a desire. She hadn't reached an understanding of these people yet, but her initial distaste had worn away, replaced by the same drive that had sent her headlong into a war for which she'd been ill-equipped.

God knew, she was more equipped now, but she hadn't realized how much until Rowen thrust introspection on her in the form of a comparison. The lavishness and relative ease of his world—similar to the one she'd known in London—and the harder and simpler life. In that moment, without thought, she'd chosen the latter. No hesitation.

She chuckled at the unexpected realization. Even though she'd narrowly escaped death, been terrified, and come face-to-face with some sort of "haint," something about these people, this world, had taken root in her heart. Between her work with her brother and the long medical conversations she enjoyed with him, the endless acres of plant life from which to glean herbal remedies, and her visit to the McAdamses. . . She paused as warmth crept into her face. She'd danced. Her thoughts spiraled back to the way Jeb's hand warmed her waist and to his gentle directions as the firelight bathed his face in a soft glow. She cleared her throat and glanced around the wood as if someone read her mind.

Despite her life experiences and the fact she wasn't as green to relationships as she'd been before she volunteered, she'd never experienced the strange mix of comfort and exhilaration she'd felt while in his arms. In fact, if she thought about it, the dance hadn't been the first time she'd felt those things. Jeb's presence since her arrival had slowly grown into an expectation. She trusted him.

Even more than that. . . She *cared* about him.

She shook her head. What a ridiculous thing to happen! Caring for a man she'd barely known two weeks! And not only the short time, but she didn't have any plans for romance or matrimony. She'd promised herself so faithfully since leaving Dexter Arnold in London. Yet, while running away from a very wrong decision, had she run directly into a right one?

She pinched her eyes closed. No, of course not. Jeb had no interest in a stuff-shirted English woman such as herself. What good would she do for him in this place? She couldn't even cook, barely danced, and proved stubborn to a fault.

"I know You have perfect reasons for Your timing." She looked heavenward. "But now? Here?" A quiet roll of thunder echoed in the distance and she grimaced as a drop of rain hit her hat. "Ah, I see Your humor is well intact."

She urged Milkie into a faster pace as the dark clouds deepened the shadows of approaching evening. Less than a half hour before she reached Jeb's house and another fifteen minutes or so to Uncle Edward's. No doubt, by that point, she'd end up thoroughly drenched.

Cora suddenly sat straight, her fists tightening on the reins. Up ahead, on the side of the trail, a dark mass waited. Not a rock. No, this looked like—she squinted—cloth? A chill descended down her body. Fur?

She reached for her pistol as the wagon neared. The huddled mass didn't move.

Cora tugged on the reins, slowing Milkie down a pace, but not enough to keep her from escaping quickly should she need to. As the wagon approached, the mass became more recognizable. Definitely cloth. And the shape took form. Human.

She closed in and the pale, beaten, still face of what appeared to be a black-shrouded young woman came into view in the fading light. A gasp escaped Cora before she could catch it. She pulled Milkie to a stop and jumped from the wagon bench. Was she dead? A touch to her throat revealed a weak pulse.

Alright. Clearly, she'd been beaten, but how badly? Cora began a careful examination, pulling back the first layer of black cloth. The woman's threadbare shirt showed a large stain at her side, likely blood. As Cora moved the woman's arm so she could get a clearer view of her torso, the stranger released a moan. Very well, then. Her arm may be broken.

The rain came with more intensity, pelting down on the top of Cora's hat, but she continued her exam. The girl's foot was twisted in an awkward direction. She cringed. Who would do something like this to a woman?

Well, they couldn't stay here in the middle of the trail in the rain.

Cora stood and evaluated the next steps. She'd helped move men twice her weight into beds before, but not without some support from another nurse. Still, perhaps she could get the woman into the back of the wagon.

Her first attempt ended in the unconscious woman crying out in pain as Cora tried to drag her toward the wagon. Her second attempt, by using two long tree limbs for support, ended in some slow progress but the stranger rolling off.

Cora sat down in the mud beside the woman, praying for a third option, when the sound of a rider broke into the rainfall. Her hand instinctively went to her pocket. Who would be riding up the path this late in the afternoon? And on a horse? There were only a few folks in the mountains who had horses at all, and even fewer who lived on this side of the—

She shot to her feet. Jeb.

She ran to the middle of the trail and waved her arms, but there was no need. As soon as she'd stood, he'd pushed the horse from a trot into a canter. She started talking before he even reached her.

"There's a woman who's been beaten on the side of the path."

His attention moved down her, as if checking her well-being before focusing in the direction she pointed.

"I think there may be some internal bleeding, but I'm not certain, and a possible broken wrist and probably a few cracked ribs as well."

He slid from the horse and followed her over to the woman, whom Cora had been able to pull beneath the back of the wagon so that her head and shoulders were protected from the rain. The woman's face looked so pummeled and swollen, Cora couldn't imagine her being identified, even if Jeb might have known her, and her dark hair lay matted against her head from a mixture of mud, blood, and rain.

"What do you need me to do?"

"We've got to get her inside as soon as possible. I need to give her a thorough exam." Cora knelt down and pushed some of the woman's hair from her forehead. "If she's unconscious, she likely has a head wound as well."

Without another word, he bent low and carefully took the woman into his arms. A moan bubbled up from her, but she didn't open her eyes. Of course, her eyes were so swollen, she couldn't have anyway. Cora adjusted the damp blankets to try and make a more comfortable spot for the stranger, and Jeb placed her as Cora directed.

With a look to Cora, he took his horse and tied the reins to the side of the wagon.

"I'll drive the wagon to Preacher's so you can keep an eye on her."

"No, Jeb." Cora caught his hand as he turned toward the front of the wagon. "I don't know if she'll survive to Uncle's. The way the mountain slants and the rough path?" Cora looked back down at the woman. "It could worsen her wounds, even kill her."

She met his gaze, pleading. "We have to get her to your house."

"My house?" Jeb's voice took an uncharacteristically harsh turn as he pulled his hat from his head. He stepped back. "Ain't no doin', Cora."

What was wrong with him? This was a person in need, and she'd seen Jeb's compassion on display enough to know what sort of person he was. "Jeb, I don't know the extent of her wounds, but there are many. There's no knowing how long she's been beside the trail or how much blood she's lost already. Even moving her from the ground to the wagon could have worsened her injuries. How can you not help?"

"It's only another fifteen minutes to Preacher's." He cleared his throat. "And I can drive it faster if I have to."

"Faster would be worse!" Cora firmed her voice, matching his tone. "This is a very real Samaritan moment, Jeb McAdams. And I know you are the type of man who will rise to the occasion."

His brow creased into a dozen wrinkles. He slammed his hat back in place and studied her for a full five seconds, as if weighing every other possible option. With a slight growl and something mumbled under his breath, he marched to the front of the wagon and started them toward his home.

Chapter Twelve

L ord, help him!
  Jeb shot a glance heavenward as he carried the unconscious woman up the steps of his house and into his bedroom, placing her carefully down onto the quilt his mama had given him as a house-warming gift.

There was a good chance that taking Willow Greer into his house would be the end of him. Or at least a confirmation of what part of the ridge thought about him already. What awful thing had Jeb done in his life to suffer such a fate!

After having very untrue rumors of him entertaining kept women in his house, he carried a kept woman right into his house without one notion of...entertaining her or taking advantage of her... profession. Sometimes, he really did wonder what in all creation God was working for good, because there wasn't nothing good going to come from Imogene Carter catching sight of him carrying an actual kept woman into his house with Cora on his heels.

He groaned and left the room as Cora replaced him beside Willow.

No, he hadn't recognized Willow at first. The bruising and cuts distorted her features, but then, as he placed her in the wagon, recognition dawned. Last he'd heard, she'd taken up as a "lady" for Rowen's hotel, and he thought he'd seen her a few times while in town—not that they'd talked. She knew better than to proposition him and he knew better than to be seen in her company. Unless she'd been forced upon him by a stubborn Nurse Woman, of course.

Thistle slipped by his feet, her tail at alert.

He scooped the cat up and gave her a scrub beneath the chin in hopes of calming her, or even himself, down a little. She was as unused to visitors as he was. He placed Thistle down on the porch and took care of his horse, then brought all the quilts from the back of the wagon and hung them over the porch railings to dry. Cora's purchases were safely housed in the wagon box, so at least they'd keep mostly dry until the two of them could get Willow down to Preacher's.

And what if they couldn't move her?

His stomach revolted at the idea, but he forced his emotions under control. War had taught him the need for extra caution with specific wounds, and moving Willow at the wrong time could lead to more damage, or worse. He released a long sigh and scanned the forest around the house, his gaze pausing on his workshop. He couldn't see anyone peeping through the trees, but that didn't mean no one was looking. Well, in the chance that a peepin' Tom or Imogene happened to wait in the woods, he'd ensure he tried to protect Cora's reputation as much as he could. His shoulders drooped and he looked down at Puck, whose head tilted to the left as if in question. "Be glad you're a dog today, boy."

With a sigh, he turned into the house and took the stairs two at a time. He marched into the large room to the right which held a simple chest in the far corner beside a bedstead he'd recently finished. All it needed was a quilt or two. Mama promised him one so the young'uns would have a place to sleep when they visited. He opened the chest and took out an old quilt, its age failing to dim the brightness of the patchwork's colors. He breathed in the cedar scent and then tucked the quilt under his arm, pulling out a pillow next. Returning downstairs, he poured some water from the kitchen sink into a pot and placed it on the cookstove. If he knew anything at all, Cora would want clean, warm water to wash Willow up.

He'd just stepped out on the porch, hands laden with his items, when the front door opened and Cora joined him. More of her wild hair had come loose, strands falling around her face in unruly curls. She rubbed at her eyes and walked toward him, reminding him a little of one of the twins when they were fighting a nap. He moved away, toward the steps, doing an awful job of keeping a hold on his heart. Something about her grabbed at him and wouldn't let go.

"She's not awake yet." Cora's gaze found his and she pushed back a strand of hair. "From what I can tell, besides the bruises and cuts, she has a few cigarette burns, a broken right wrist, and her left ankle is swollen, but I don't think it's broken." She squeezed her eyes closed and shook her head. "Why would someone do something so horrible to her?"

"It ain't a common occurrence, and that's a fact." Jeb leaned back against the porch post and sighed. The idea that some boys had gotten so drunk to beat a girl senseless didn't seem right either. This was a lynching, but what would cause folks to get so all fired mad to beat Willow? "If a woman is beaten a'tall, it happens behind closed doors. This ain't normal."

Cora grimaced and folded her arms across her chest, her eyes searching his face. "Who is she?"

He looked out over the yard as rain pelted down around them. "Name's Willa Greer."

"Greer?" The word escaped like a whisper.

"Clark Greer is her older brother. Daddy's Ozaiah Greer." Jeb cleared his throat before moving on to the next part. "She ain't been in the mountain for over a year or more, I reckon. Disappeared around the same time as—" He swallowed as emotions rose in his throat. "Just before I left for the war. Folks learned she'd took up with Rowen's bunch down at the hotel as a kept woman."

"Rowen keeps prostitutes in his hotel?"

Jeb turned his attention to Cora. "I reckon it brings in good money, don't you?"

She squeezed her fingers in front of her and looked away from him. "I saw her a few days ago, when I went to visit Granny Burcham. She ran from me, but it was her. Why would she be here now? And in rags?"

"I don't know." He waited until she looked back at him. "But I've got a mind to send you down to your uncle's and let me take care of this. Messin' with the Greers ain't somethin' you need to put your hands in, Cora. And with her history, I got a bad feelin' about keeping her here."

"She needs medical attention." She moved closer, fire lighting her eyes. "Just because she has the history that she does, doesn't mean we cannot take care of her. I should think our Christian duty calls for it even more so." Her chin tipped, her stance stiff. "I can't believe you'd cast her out."

"I want her to have help, but there's a chance what she's gotten herself into has caused this trouble, and I don't want to see you in the thick of something neither one of us is fit to fix."

"Why do you assume she brought this on herself? Are you saying she somehow wanted to be hurt?"

Lord, help him. He knew he was in trouble when a woman started asking rhetorical questions. "Now, Cora—"

"Why is it that women are always thought of as ridiculous or irrational?" Her voice rose. "Or worse, it is automatically assumed that the trouble was brought on by something she did or didn't do?" Those eyes narrowed at him and he almost jumped off the porch and ran for the workshop. "Are we so foolish? Is it such a hardship to imagine that we have thinking brains and can manage our own emotions to the point of rational thought?"

"Cora, I don't know what's caused such a stir." He raised his hand. "But I ain't never said nothin' nor thought nothin' like that—"

"How can you know what it's like to be moved about like a pawn just because you're a woman? That people make decisions for your life, your future, and you're just supposed to follow along blindly into a miserable marriage when you have the capabilities of finding your own future?" Her words trembled, half angry, but there was a whole lot of hurt in them. "You. . .you can't know."

He moved toward her, face-to-face. "I ain't trying to make a decision for you. Willa Greer brings a whole lot more trouble than you can underst—"

"I understand that there's a woman who has been beaten to the point of her possibly dying and your concern is about what people are going to think if they find her in your house." She shook her head so hard her curls bounced.

"That ain't the only reason—"

"I should hope if. . .if one of your sisters, heaven forbid, was beaten on the side of the road, you'd want someone to help her, instead of respond like you're doing in this begrudging manner, regardless of her history and choic—"

"Don't put me in one of your boxes, Cora." His words seethed out between his teeth.

Her eyes shot wide.

He stepped back, drawing in a calming breath. "I may not understand the plight of a woman, but I sure know what it's like to feel helpless." His jaw tightened. "And you can be sure, Willa's background ain't got nothin' to do with me wanting to take her down to your uncle's house. Not a thing. Because I can tell you true, I pray every day that if somebody found my lost sister on the side of the road they'd take care of her as good as I'm sure you will Willa." Air shook from his nose and he took another step back. "I can't know how you've been hurt, but using your hurt to believe the wrong things ain't good neither."

Her large eyes blinked up at him, and maybe there was a tear or two on those long lashes. He backed down a porch step. "I put water on the cookstove to boil. I reckoned you'd need it." He took another step and the rain hit him, cool against his hot head. "There's canned beef, some biscuits, and a few baked apples for you in the kitchen."

He gestured for Puck to stay. "And keep Puck in the house with you. His bark'll let us know if someone's coming and he'll keep an eye out for you."

"Where are you going?" The fire in her voice had quieted.

"I'll stay there." He waved a hand in the direction of his workshop. "Close enough to help but far enough to, hopefully, quit waggin' tongues." He bowed his head. "Good night, Cora."

He turned and walked across the yard to his workshop, praying God kept all of them safe, especially with Willow Greer under his roof.

⁂

Cora stared at Jeb's retreating back, fighting back a sudden rush of tears. He was right. Instead of being a rational woman, she'd allowed all the hurts and insecurities of her past to bubble right out of her mouth and speak in such a way that she not only hurt him, but practically accused him of being as heartless as the men who had left Willa Greer on the side of the trail. Her shoulders wilted forward. Why, oh why? Her head knew Jeb McAdams was nothing like her father or some of the lewd soldiers who treated her as either an object at which to gawk or a person without a thinking mind.

Of course, after her reaction to poor Jeb, she was beginning to question how little her mind was involved sometimes. And his lost sister? Was that the one called Kizzie that she'd only heard about in passing conversations, in whispers?

Oh, Cora! You are such an idiot! She squeezed her eyes closed and contemplated going after him, but a sound from inside the house pulled her attention away from the little building into which he'd disappeared. She rushed inside, Puck at her heels, and rounded the doorway to the small bedroom.

Willa, as broken as she was, had managed to push herself to a sitting position, and in spite of the fact her eyes were still nearly swollen shut, she'd moved as if to get off the bed.

"I wouldn't attempt to stand if I were you, Miss Greer."

The woman's head jerked up, her dirty brown hair matted against her forehead. The smallest peek of gray-blue peered between the slits of swollen and red flesh around her eyes.

Cora approached, carefully, keeping her distance. "My name is Cora Taylor. I'm Preacher Anderson's niece and Jonathan Taylor's sister. I'm also the one who found you along the trail."

The woman tried to sit up straighter but winced. She *had* to be in pain.

"I'd advise you to stay where you are, Miss Greer. Your wounds are significant, and it would be very difficult for you to walk. Your ankle is swollen, likely a sprain."

Another movement, almost in rebellion against Cora's warning, sent the woman nearly fainting. Paleness hovered beneath her bruising, and beads of sweat pearled on her forehead. She rested her head back on the pillow, leaving mud smears. Cora frowned. Jeb's pillow.

She nodded. She'd clean them. Everything. It was the least she could do after taking over his house and accusing him so ruthlessly.

"Why are you helpin' me?"

Cora took a step farther into the room. "Because you need help and God placed me within your path at just the right time to help you."

Her head came up again and the slightest tremor quaked her bottom lip before it hardened into a thin line. The girl couldn't be very old. Not even nineteen, if Cora guessed rightly.

"Where. . .where am I?"

"You're in Jeb McAdams's house. He came along as I was attempting to get you into my wagon bed." She waved toward the room. "You were too injured to travel far, so we brought you to the closest place in order to spare you more injury and to get you out of the rain."

A visible quaver shook the girl's body.

"Miss Greer, we need to clean you up and get some clean clothes for you to wear. The last thing you need is a cold to weaken your body even more than it already is."

But what clothes would the woman wear? All of Cora's clothes were either at her uncle's house or her brother's. Her gaze went to the window. Would Jeb ride to Uncle Edward's for her?

"You shouldn't keep me here," Willa's raspy voice breathed. "I'll bring trouble if folks knows I'm here."

Her declaration shot a chill over Cora's already damp body. "And why is that?"

Willa didn't answer.

"Well, I am a nurse and it is my job to help people. So that is exactly what I plan to do." She brought her hands together and set her mind on her task. "Besides, you won't be able to leave on your own for quite a while, so if Jeb and I are careful, no one needs to know you're here."

The woman's swollen lips tipped in something resembling a smile. "You ain't been here long, have ya?"

Willa didn't elaborate. "Who did this to you?"

The woman looked away, her lips pinched closed.

Cora shook her head and took a step toward the door. "I'm going to speak to Jeb and then come help you get cleaned. For now, continue to rest so you'll have enough energy for your sponge bath."

Willa kept quiet and merely watched Cora leave the room. After a few weeks in the mountains, Cora had a slight fear that Willa could escape, even with a twisted ankle, a few cracked ribs, a body full of bruises, and a broken wrist. She likely was suffering from a concussion too.

Cora snatched a couple of biscuits and a piece of beef, wrapped them in a clean handkerchief, then poured a cup of milk. The rain had slowed as she made her way across the yard to the little building. Puck followed close behind, as if he knew to keep watch over her. She almost smiled at the thought.

With a timid knock, she waited as the remnants of rain

dampened her already wet hair and, likely, unloosed it even more than it already was. She would have attempted to control the curls a little if her hands hadn't been full of biscuits and milk.

Jeb opened the door, his white work shirt open at the collar and his own hair in disarray.

"I'm—I'm sorry," Cora said as she thrust bundle and cup toward him.

Without one look at her offering, he peered skyward and then took her by the arm and pulled her into the little building. It consisted of a large room with three windows, one on each lateral wall, and a large one on the back. Two long tables created an *L* shape along two of the walls and were covered with various wood creations in different stages of completion. A chair, a table, a bookshelf, a bedstead, and then small things. A couple hand in hand. A woman in a simple dress holding her hat with one hand and smiling heavenward. A little boy studying a frog on his palm. Cora's thorough apology died on her tongue as she scanned the room.

"You. . .you made these?" She shifted forward, her hands still full. "They're fantastic. Works of art, truly." Her gaze swung to his as if seeing him anew. "You have such a gift."

He studied her without moving, his expression unreadable.

"I've put you in a box again, haven't I? Surprised at your handiwork." She sighed and lowered the cup and food to one of the tables before turning to face him. "And I've taken over your house and wrongly accused you." She hoped her plea mattered to him. "Please, accept my apology."

His gaze measured her. What did he see when he looked so intently at her? A stubborn, headstrong, ridiculous woman? She stifled her cringe at the thought.

"Mama thought I should try my hand at sellin' these in town, along with the furniture I make." He gestured toward the figurines of the couple and the boy with his frog. "I figured folks would want the furniture but hadn't reckoned they'd take to these carvings so well."

She blinked at his change of topic but determined to follow along. "I can't imagine why they wouldn't sell. You've done such intricate work." She ran a hand over the head of a carved dog that looked like Puck. "And you sell your furniture too? It truly is remarkable, Jeb!"

He shoved his hands in his pockets, his hair curled at the edges because of the rain. "Started sellin' both about three months ago in Flat Creek."

Silence swelled between them, and Cora reviewed a few other woodcrafts. One was of a man, who looked a great deal like Sam McAdams, kneeling in prayer. Cora's heart squeezed. The expressions on the faces of the figurines drew her in, so real and emotive. And the furniture! Detailed and even elegant in simple ways. Why was she surprised to see such beauty come from a man she was beginning to realize held a great deal of heart behind his quiet demeanor?

"Willa's. . .profession is one of the reasons I didn't want her in my house, but it's not like you think." He looked out the nearby window before turning those azure eyes back on her. "I don't want to see her hurt a'tall, but I'm trying to protect you."

"What do you mean?"

He released a long sigh and gestured toward a stool near one of the tables. She lowered to the seat. He followed suit by sitting on a ladder-back chair by the door. He rubbed his palms down over his knees and cleared his throat, clearly uncomfortable. Maybe she should leave.

"I reckon you heared some of the women at church or at Mrs. Cappy's store tell 'bout me having kept women?"

She'd heard something like it in passing but didn't pay much heed to it. "I don't believe it though." She answered so quickly he grinned.

"It ain't true." His brow rose. "Lest you count me carryin' an Englishwoman into my house when she fainted on her first day in Maple Springs."

"What?" She thought through his statement and her mouth

dropped wide. "Do you mean to tell me the rumor started when you brought me here that day?"

He folded his arms across his chest and nodded. "Imogene Carter saw me carryin' you with your fancy boots into my house and talked like she had sense to whoever would listen."

"She doesn't know it was me?"

"And I'm hoping to keep it that way for your sake."

She blinked. "My sake?"

"So long as she thinks what she does, then most folks'll treat you kindly and let you doctor 'em." He held her gaze. "But onct they think we've been. . .together, they'll call you as fallen a woman as Willa Greer. Then folks'll shun you, at best."

And then what would she do in Maple Springs? It was difficult enough to get people to trust her as it was.

"My frustration's got a lot less to do with hurtin' Willa and more to do with—"

"Protecting me," she finished, closing her eyes as the truth weighed through her. And she'd accused him of narrow-mindedness and cruelty. How idiotic could she be? Her attention fastened back on him. He was such a good man. "What happened to your lost sister?"

"Kizzie." Jeb whispered the name and then leaned back in the chair. "Headstrong. Always dreamin' of life outside the mountains." He shook his head, his gaze softened with memory. "Willa and Kizzie was good friends and talked big plans together. When Kizzie went off to work in the flatlands for a tenant farmer, she got in the family way." Jeb's chest pulsed, his jaw tight. The story was clearly difficult for him. "Daddy cast her out. Wouldn't even hear of her stayin', because she brought shame on the house. He was on a drunk at the time. Didn't have any reason." His lip curled as he spoke. "So he sent her away. All by herself." His gaze came up to Cora's. "We ain't seen nor heard from her since."

"I'm so sorry, Jeb."

"So you can be sure, Cora, that I pray ever day someone would show the same kindness to my sister as you showed to Willa today."

Her guilt pained her even more. No, there was no box for Jeb McAdams. "I don't understand much about this place, but. . .but life is so hard here."

"Life is hard everwhere." He shrugged a shoulder. "Maybe we can't choose our hard, but I reckon we can choose how to live with it the right way."

"Very true." She ran a finger over the little figure of the boy and the frog. "I suppose with that in mind, we can choose joy instead of anger, can't we?"

"Aye." His soft answer brewed across the distance between them.

"One of my patients in the war, he'd survived an explosion." Her finger slid over the couple holding hands. "But the damage left behind altered his brain. He wasn't safe." Heat stung her eyes, but she continued. "I'd told the doctor of my concerns for others' safety, but he wouldn't listen. After all, I was merely a young female volunteer. What did I know of war and broken men?" She swallowed as her throat closed. "One night, I heard screams coming from a nearby tent. When I entered, I found the patient stabbing the other soldiers, thinking they were the enemy." She pinched her hands together in her lap, squeezing her fingers together. "Then he turned on my friend, a fellow nurse."

Jeb leaned forward in the chair, his focus on her face, his expression showing an understanding she felt all the way through her.

"I—I had to shoot him." Her voice broke. "There was no other way. To save the others, I had to shoot him." She looked down at her hands, the feel of the gun, even now, burning her palm as it had when she'd fired it.

Warmth surrounded one of her hands. Jeb's fingers, rough and strong, covered hers. "You did the right thing."

She knew that. There had been no other choice. But to hear the words spoken aloud broke something inside her and loosened all the tears. Before she even realized it, she'd been pulled into his arms. She nestled in close, resting her head on his shoulder and allowing the pain to release in a way she'd never done before.

He smelled of rain and sawdust and the slightest hint of that licorice scent she couldn't quite decipher, and the way his arms encircled her made the world outside seem so far away. What was it about this man? Surely, her brother would have comforted her. Her uncle also. But Jeb? His expressions, his embrace, opened a place in her heart no one had ever touched, and all she wanted to do, at the moment, was burrow closer into his warmth.

The tapping of rain on the tin roof permeated the silence with a gentle rhythm. Her sniffles punctuated the beat. His breathing smoothed out a gentle tone underneath it all, and a wonderful swell of comfort wrapped around her with as much potency as the feel of his arms. A new revelation bloomed out of an older thought. Could she love Jeb McAdams?

She pulled back and looked up at him, their faces so close she could make out a dark rim of blue around his irises. He searched her eyes before brushing his thumb over her cheek to remove a tear, his caress so tender and gentle, a new swell of tears blurred her vision. His palm spread at the base of her spine and took her breath away with the simple movement. Her fingers tightened around one of his suspender straps, holding him close, and she instinctively rose on tiptoe as if she needed to get closer to him. His attention dropped to her lips and her entire body trembled in anticipation of something she felt like she'd been waiting for her whole life.

"You're. . .you're cold." He drew in a shaky breath. "You need to get back into the house." He shook his head as he stepped back and reached for a jacket he'd tossed on a tiny bunk near a potbelly stove in the far corner of the room.

The jacket did little to replace his warmth. "Please forgive me, Jeb. For all of it."

He didn't meet her gaze. "Of course." He shifted back again. "Has she woke up yet?"

"Yes, but she won't talk about who attacked her."

"Ain't no surprise."

She pinched the jacket close around her shoulders. "It's frustrating though."

"Some of the stubbornness may be 'cause of family, but I reckon most of her quiet is to try and protect us." He looked out the window. "It's the way things are around here."

Cora took a deep breath to attempt to clear her head and abate the heat in her cheeks. "She needs dry clothes, and mine are either at Uncle Edward's or Jonathan's house."

Jeb soared to attention, maybe a little too quickly, if she thought about it. "I can go get what you need."

"I must admit, I was hoping you would." She dashed a remnant tear from her cheek, immediately sorry that it wasn't Jeb's fingers against her skin again. Why did his touch make all the difference? It wasn't as if she hadn't been courted by a man before. But nothing came close to how it felt to be with this quiet mountain man. "There are some dresses in my trunk in Uncle's loft. Please bring the green one, the blue one, and the purple one. My clothes may be too big for her, but they'll work for what we need them to do."

"And Mama or Mercy could stitch 'em up, if you needed."

"Mercy? Do you mean Mr. Tate's granddaughter?"

His eyes grew wide and he almost stumbled to the door. "Sure do. She. . .she's good with dressmakin', from what folks say."

Why on earth was he behaving so strangely? Did it have to do with this Mercy woman? She narrowed her eyes. And if so, *why* did it have to do with this Mercy woman?

"You git on back up to the house." He waved toward the door as he tugged a hat onto his head. "There's wood by the fire, so you can keep the place warm without gettin' back out in the rain."

She followed him out the door and watched as he nearly ran to the barn. Maybe she didn't want to meet Mercy Tate as much as she thought. She raised her chin and started marching toward the house. Well, if it meant a little healthy competition, she could turn up the charm and turn down the stubbornness.

Her chin drooped. Maybe?

Her shoulders slumped. How charming was Mercy Tate after all?

Chapter Thirteen

Thankfully, Willow hadn't moved from where Cora had last seen her. In fact, she appeared to have dozed back off, so Cora got to work ladling the hot water into a basin she'd found on Jeb's washstand. A bar of soap, which smelled nothing like licorice, waited by the washstand, so she took it as well, but the water was still too hot to use, so she took advantage of Jeb's absence to explore his home.

All she'd noticed on her first day in Maple Springs had been the simplicity, but now that she wasn't terrified for her life and she'd become more acquainted with both the mountain people and this particular mountain man, the house spoke of him at every turn. Especially after witnessing the craftsmanship in his workshop.

The mantel in the front room showcased ornate designs, complete with something like a sunburst at each corner. The stair rail leading to the second level boasted a beautiful oak color and curved at the ends with as much style and grace as in any of the grand houses Cora had known. And yes, the house was much bigger than the others she'd visited in these mountains, but somehow, it held more charm than the others. Upstairs a hallway stretched down the center with two doors on either side opening to large rooms, each with closets, large windows, and built-in shelves. Two of the rooms had beds. The others stood vacant except for a chair or a side table. One of the more furnished rooms held a beautiful cedar chest designed with all sorts of woodland creatures.

And then there were the small hand carvings. A squirrel, a fox, a rabbit, a bear. There was even a set of blocks and a rocking horse. All made by the same hand, if she guessed. She leaned her head against the post of a four-poster bed and stared out the window. The faintest tips of the mountains came into view just above the tree line. A hint of sun attempted to break through the clouds in the distance and dusted the blue mountains with the faintest hint of gold.

A grand vista.

She shook off the daydream and made her way down the stairs. The water had cooled enough to bathe so, with soap, cloth, and two bowls in hand, Cora slipped back into the bedroom. Willow had removed her outer dress and was wincing through a failed attempt at removing her stockings.

"Let me help you."

Her gaze shot to Cora and she pulled the bedding up over the simple underdress covering her chest, suspicion riddling her young face. The swelling around her face had subsided a little, revealing even more of those piercing blue eyes.

"I'm sure you're strong, but I'm here to help, so you might as well let me." Cora took a step closer.

"You ain't afraid the likes of me will sully the likes of you?" Her frown deepened into a sneer. "Keep you from gettin' into heaven."

"No one has that sort of power, Miss Greer." Cora placed her hands on her hips. "Because, as I understand it, my heavenly future is based on Christ's history, not mine." She tipped a brow. "Nor yours."

The girl's eyes filled with tears. "Preacher said words the likes of that when he talked to me."

"Uncle Edward spoke to you?"

She nodded, her speech still slurred from her swollen mouth. "He. . .he came upon me at Granny Burcham's a few months back. Wasn't preachin' down to me and my hell-bound ways. He said God still loved me, even now."

Cora slipped down on the bed, her eyes watery. For heaven's sake, she couldn't seem to maintain her composure more than three days at a time. "From what the Bible says, we are all broken, Willa, and that is why we need a rescuer."

A crooked smile appeared on her puffy lips as she lowered the blanket to accept Cora's assistance. "That's what Preacher said too, and that's why I was glad all the more I ran away."

Cora gave the girl a cloth and gently poured water over her hair, catching the dirty water in a large bowl she'd placed on Willa's lap. The poor girl sighed as the water slipped over her head. How long had it been since someone had taken care of her like this?

"Ran away?"

The muddy brown slowly cleared into a beautiful strawberry blond.

"I knowed I was sinnin' by being one of Mr. Hawes's girls."

Cora finished up with Willa's hair and then gave a clean cloth to her, carefully pulling back the blankets so she could attend to herself with her one good arm. That was when Cora noticed the small roundness of the girl's abdomen. The bulge had been easily hidden beneath the layers of loose cloth she'd used to cover her tiny body, but now, as Cora helped her raise her chemise to wash, her pregnancy became clear. How advanced was this pregnancy? Women with first babies sometimes carried smaller, from what Cora had heard.

"I couldn't come back to my brother. He wouldn't have nothin' to do with me." Willa ran a hand over her head. "I reckon they hit me in the head with a stick, 'cause it's achin' like my back."

Cora cringed at the idea. Willa had lost consciousness somehow, but from the clarity of her words, Cora wondered if she hadn't passed out from pain rather than a head wound. She hoped for the former, at any rate. It likely meant less long-term healing from a concussion.

Cora helped Willa adjust in the bed. The girl continued to move slowly, wincing every now and again at the way her body shifted.

As the dirt came off, some of the wounds, old and new, shone more clearly on her skin. Scars in hidden places.

Cora pinched her eyes closed as her fingers fisted the cloth. What had this poor child endured? "And the baby?" she managed to ask.

Those blue eyes rounded, and Willa placed her palm over her extended stomach. "They would have kilt the baby if'n I'd stayed, like they did to the last 'un."

Cora wrung out Willa's hair and wrapped a towel around it. "What do you mean? Last one?"

"Last time I got in the family way, they gave me somethin' to drank that made me awful sick. Said it would git rid of the baby too." She shook her head. "I was plannin' to leave anyhow, once Paul saved up 'nough money for us to git away."

"Paul?"

The girl leaned close as if someone else was in the room listening. "You cain't tell a livin' soul about him or we mightn't get away."

"So Paul is the baby's father?"

A smile brightened the girl's face. "I hope so. He does too, 'cause he wants to marry me onct he earns 'nough money at the sawmill to get us away. Granny Burcham took him a note two months back, so he'd know where I was, but we cain't risk seein' each other till he's ready to leave town."

Could this Paul be trusted? Was he truly interested in marrying Willa or was he another heartless man stringing a young girl along? Cora helped Willa to the edge of the bed so that they could finish cleaning her up and prepare her for some new clothes, but a trail of blood lined the bottom sheet as Cora moved her. All heat fled Cora's face. Had the beating caused something unexpected to begin? Or worse, hurt the baby?

"You've been to Granny Burcham's?" Cora worked the words through a drying throat, trying to sort out her next steps.

Willa nodded.

"And she told you when to expect the baby?"

The girl whimpered and rubbed at her lower back. "Late November's what she said."

Late November? Well, at least the baby wouldn't be too premature, perhaps?

"Willa, I know you are hurting in many places, but are you having discomfort in your stomach?"

The girl's gaze came up to Cora's. "I've had pains in my stomach for a day or so, but I reckon the boys really beat up my back, cause it's a throbbin' awful bad."

As Willa moved again, she gasped and, evidently forgetting her injuries, attempted to stand, but wilted back onto the bed. "Law, I'm losin' my waters right here in front of an English woman."

And sure enough, a trickle of blood-tinged fluid followed her movements on the bed. Cora shot a look heavenward. She would have appreciated a few lessons from Granny Burcham before she was thrust into helping birth another baby, but it looked like she'd have to rely on her book reading over the past few days, because Willa Greer was in labor.

"Willa, I think you're getting ready to have your baby."

The girl's eyes went as wide as the swelling allowed.

"And your body is already wounded, so we must be extra careful for your sake and the baby's."

Willa nodded, eyes growing wider by the second.

Cora could do this. She'd tended dying soldiers. Reattached limbs. Removed bullets. Surely, she could help do something as natural as having a baby.

Except this wasn't natural at all. Willa should have a few more weeks of pregnancy and a much healthier body than her current state. Broken ribs? Was she already having internal bleeding?

Oh Lord, be with this girl! Her eyes pinched closed. *And whatever happens next.*

A sudden rumble of horse's hooves came from beyond the

window and Cora shot to a stand. Jeb! A smile nearly broke free on her lips. Yes, surely Jeb would know what to do.

What on earth had he done? Hugging her like that! He'd never in his life hugged a woman that wasn't family, and those hugs were a sight bit different than holding Cora Taylor in his arms. Have mercy! At first, all he could think about was helping comfort her through an ache he understood so well, and then, well, she felt so nice in his arms the urge to kiss her nearly shocked him all the way to his boots.

Besides, he was supposed to be making plans to marry Mercy Tate. But how could he make plans to marry Mercy Tate when he wanted to take Cora Taylor back in his arms and kiss her till he learned how?

He frowned. What if *she* already knew how? He turned Hickory back up the trail and attempted to navigate with one hand on the reins and the other holding enough frilly garments to decorate a dress shop. Or so it seemed. "I ain't got no problems with her teachin' me none. Not nary a problem."

Hickory snorted.

What did a horse know 'bout kissin' talk nohow?

An old sayin' from his granddaddy came to mind. If your lips itch, it means you want to be kissed.

Heat shot into his face and his mouth twitched. His lips were itchin' something fierce.

Thankfully, the rain had stopped for a bit, though the clouds still weighed dark with another storm or two, if he guessed right. Well, at least the dresses would arrive dry. He squinted at the turn of his thoughts. He'd never in all his days imagined thinkin' such a thought, let alone being the one carryin' the dresses.

Ain't no tellin' what Imogene Carter would think if she witnessed him carrying an armful of frilly dresses into his own house.

He frowned. And it was probably a good thing none of the menfolk from the mill could see him now too.

Puck leaped off the porch just as Jeb dismounted. Thistle followed close behind. What in the world was wrong with them critters? Why were they actin' all skittish?

"It's alright, y'all." He ran a hand over Puck's head as he passed. "It's just two womenfolk." As he said it, the statement took root, and a shiver tempted a climb up his spine. He shook it off and opened the door just as Cora, with all her wild hair flyin' in every direction, bounded toward him.

Alright, maybe the critters were on to something.

"Jeb, I'm so glad you're back." She stopped only a few feet in front of him, her eyes so big and round, his lips started itching all over again.

He pinched them tight.

"I need you to fetch Granny Burcham."

"Granny Burcham? But ain't you a nurse?"

She took the dresses from his arms and nodded, her gaze meeting his. "Yes, but not for delivering babies."

The itching came to a dead stop. "Delivering babies?"

Surely she hadn't said what he thought she'd said. He repeated it just to be sure. "You need me to fetch Granny Burcham for delivering babies in my house?"

She placed the dresses on the wingback chair nearby. The one he'd purchased special from Flat Creek. His reading chair. He blinked. None of this fit into his head. A woman giving birth in his house? Frilly dresses on his reading chair?

Maybe he was the one who got hit on the head.

"Willa is pregnant," Cora whispered, leaning so close he got a whiff of her flowery scent. His lips started itchin' all over again.

What had she said? "Willa is pregnant?"

"Quite pregnant," she repeated. "I believe the beating may have sent her into labor."

All kissing thoughts flew right out of his head. "That cain't be good, Cora. Not with the way we found her."

"I know," she whispered. "I'm not sure if she has any internal wounds besides the cracked ribs. I hope not, but I can't be sure, and to go directly into birthing?" Her gaze searched his, as if he had an answer. "That's why we need Granny Burcham."

He took a step back from her and pushed his hand through his hair, or meant to, but his hat was still on his head and he proceeded to shove it right off. The sound of it hitting the floor sent him into motion.

Cora swept his hat off the floor and handed it to him. "It's already sunset, Jeb. Be careful."

A sweet warmth spilled from his head to his damp toes at the sound of her gentle entreaty, but he didn't have any time to bask in the glow, because a cry from the next room reminded him of his purpose. "Light the lanterns," he said, backing toward the door. "And if'n you think about it, light the ones on the porch."

"You have lanterns on the porch?"

He nodded with a grin as he crammed his hat back onto his head, opening the front door. "Saw 'em in England and thought 'twas a good idea if a body was comin' home late."

"I hadn't noticed until now." She looked around him to examine the nearest porch lantern. "They're lovely." Her lips tipped up on one side. "Well, at least there are some good things that come out of England."

"Yes, ma'am." The pull to draw closer to her shocked him back a step and he nearly fell over Thistle as she slipped in between his feet. "I reckon there are a few good things from England."

The soft smile that lit her face flamed up all kinds of itchin'. He nearly jumped off the porch in retreat toward Hickory. How could something that sounded as good as kissing her nearly terrify him to his bones? With an easy mount of his horse, he breathed in the cold air to clear his head, but his thoughts remained a muddled mess until he took the fork toward Granny Burcham's. He gave his head another shake. 'Twasn't right at all to harbor kissing thoughts about one woman and contemplate marrying another. So one or the other had to be wrong.

He growled and turned his mind back to his task. Jeb didn't know much about women in the family way nor the entire process of a baby's birth, but he knew it took a good deal of strength from the woman. And Willow Greer had quite a bit of her strength beaten out of her already. He shot his gaze skyward. *Be with her, Lord*—he drew in a breath—*and help Cora know what to do in the meantime.*

Granny Burcham's house came into view in the fading daylight, the faintest glow in the window letting him know she hadn't turned in for the night. She met him at the door before he even made it up the steps to her porch, her doctorin' basket already in hand. "It has to be something awful grand for you to come boundin' to my door, Jeb McAdams. Is it your mama?"

"No, ma'am." He took off his hat. "It's somethin' a bit trickier than any of my folks."

Her expression sobered, those eyes peering into him with an almost otherworldly look. Sometimes, Granny Burcham scared Jeb all the way down to his kneecaps.

"Willa?"

He nodded.

"She alive?"

"Cora got to her in time with me not far behind, but she wasn't in good shape. I reckon they left her for dead."

"Did they?" Granny frowned.

"But her baby's comin'."

Granny's brows shot high and she pushed past him down the steps. "Well, let's git goin'."

Jeb rushed away and took the horse's reins, guiding Hickory closer to Granny.

"Don't you look at me like I'm gettin' on that critter." She waved a hand at him. "These legs have served me just fine gettin' over these mountains all these years. I ain't bound to tempt the good Lord now with your foolery."

"It's a horse, Granny. Not some wild critter."

"I'm old. I ain't blind." Her look turned fierce but for the twinkle in her eyes. "I know it's a horse, but I ain't got a mind to die today since I'm needed for doctorin' and all. Besides, I can get there lickety-split cutting through places your horse cain't go."

"It'll be dark afore you get to the—"

"Hush your jawin' and move on." She started down the trail. "You think I ain't walked in the dark afore?"

Jeb sighed and stepped up toward Hickory, but Granny caught his arm. "Here. In case you get there a might bit before me." She shoved a dried piece of something into his hand. "Tell Nurse Woman to have Willa chew on this till I get there."

He took the proffered item. "She'll want to know what it is."

"Smart girl." Granny's grin tipped. "Willa bark. She'll know what to do."

Jeb nodded and mounted Hickory, turning him to face the trail.

"Jeb?" Granny walked toward the forest's edge, away from the trail, likely choosing her own secret ways to get wherever she was going. "How bad was she beat?"

"Pretty bad."

Though the woman's expression didn't change, her dark eyes softened with the concern of the loving granny she was. "Ain't a good start to a birthin'."

"Cora's been tendin' her."

Granny paused, studying him a second, and then she straightened her shoulders and gave him a nod. "Well, what are you doin' stayin' around here gabbin'? Git on down the trail." She winked. "Lest you want an old woman to beat ya there."

She slipped into the darkening trees and Jeb took off down the trail, hoping Willa Greer had enough of her granny in her to survive the trials ahead.

Chapter Fourteen

Cora had drawn from every bit of experience she possessed, attempting to make Willa prepared. She'd read that a woman should walk as long as possible during delivery, but with a sprained ankle, or at least a bruised one, walking wasn't the best option. Cora had managed to help Willa into a sitting position and even helped finish her bath with the hope that being clean might make everything else a little easier.

It was likely a ridiculous notion, but it certainly made Cora feel better when she had to face something difficult.

The girl bore the brunt of the contractions with remarkable fortitude. Though Cora hadn't borne any children, the idea of the actual process paired with stories she'd heard from experienced nurses had her offering up all sorts of extra prayers for Willa's relief. The warm water against her stomach appeared to soothe a little. Willa had even asked for a stick to put between her teeth to bite on during the painful moments, which were growing increasingly more frequent.

Sweat beaded across the girl's pale forehead, but she didn't offer one complaint. In fact, she kept quietly thanking Cora with each small task Cora completed to attempt to help her. Cora wasn't sure what she'd expected from a "kept" woman, but Willa Greer didn't match.

Every once in a while the resident gray cat stopped at the door, peering in with its purplish-blue eyes, before dashing off when Willa's pain brought out a cry. Jeb didn't seem like a cat person, but she hadn't expected him to be a master craftsman either, so perhaps she needed to hold her assumptions loosely. Some things about the mountains fit—her face heated at the memory of their moment in his workshop—and others didn't.

A sound outside had her exiting the bedroom and turning the corner of the living area as Jeb entered the front door.

"Oh thank God, you're back." She rushed to him and peered out the open doorway. Hickory waited at the steps, but no sign of the help Cora had been waiting to see. Had she not been home?

"She's on the way." He gestured toward Hickory. "Didn't take too keen to the idea of ridin' here."

Cora's shoulders sagged. "I don't think Willa has much longer."

"Don't worry none." His lips crooked. "Granny Burcham'll be here in time." He offered a small piece of stick. "Granny said to have her chew on this."

Cora took the offering, examining it.

"It's willa bark," Jeb said.

Cora's gaze shot up. Willa? "Do you mean willow bark?"

One brow rose. "Aye. Willa bark."

"Willow." Air burst out of her. "How do you spell the girl's name in the other room?"

Jeb's forehead wrinkled, his eyes narrowed as he studied her, and then his expression cleared. "W-I-L-L-O-W."

"Of course. Her name is Willow." Cora released a long sigh. "And I've been calling her the wrong name all along." She shook her head.

"Sounded right to me." He shrugged a shoulder, his grin crooked.

She chuckled and held up the bark. "Thank you for this and for fetching Granny Burcham."

He dipped his head and took a step toward the door as a pained cry came from the other room.

"Wait, Jeb. I think an axe may help Willow."

The smile slid right off his face. "You need an axe to help with a birthin'?"

She stared at him, processing his question, and then almost laughed again. "No, no, not anything brutal. I think it's some sort of folk remedy to provide comfort."

His whole body sighed. "To cut the pain." He nodded, and that gentle gaze came back to touch hers. "I'll leave it by the front door for you, then I'll tend to the fires. But I'll be in hollerin' distance if you need me."

"Thank you, Jeb." She slipped back a few steps and held up the bark. "For everything."

Within five minutes, Granny Burcham burst through the bedroom door, basket on her arm and a stern look deepening the creases on her face. She marched forward, and very much like their first meeting, raised a little hatchet into the air then drove it into the floor by the bed.

Even though Cora knew what was coming, the whole scene still left her a bit unsettled, but her gratitude at having Granny Burcham present quickly overcame any discomfort at these "old wives' tales," as Caroline McAdams called them. She had winked and added, "The young wives use 'em too."

"Get open that window, girl." Granny Burcham waved toward the lone window in the room.

"The window?" Cora looked from Granny Burcham to the window and back. "But it's cold out, especially now that it's dark."

Granny Burcham released a sound like a growl, placed her basket on the side table, marched to the window, and opened it wide. Then she approached the bed and placed a hand to Willow's head. "Now, that'll open up things for you, won't it, girl?"

Did opening the windows have some sort of magical connection to opening the birth canal? Cora refrained from arguing the ridiculousness of the point for fear of being forced from the room.

As much as her insides wanted to flee seeing Willow in pain, the nurse inside her needed to learn from a woman who'd been doing this for decades.

"Baby's close," Granny said, casting a look to Cora. "I see you got water and cloths ready. That's good."

Cora quelled the desire to preen a bit in the woman's favor.

But then Granny did the most unusual thing. She pulled a quill out of her bag, shook a red powder into it and then put one end of the quill near Willow's nose. The girl's eyes grew wide. Cora's probably matched.

Then Granny Burcham blew into the quill, sending the red powder into Willow's nose. Willow coughed and then sneezed five times in a row.

"There we go." Granny Burcham nodded. "Now we're making good progress. Faster."

She must have noticed Cora's horrified expression, because she leaned close. "Quillin'." She examined Cora's face. "You ain't never heared tell of quillin', I reckon? Well, just some red pepper and a quill." She leaned close to Cora, lowering her voice to a whisper. "The sooner we git that baby out, the easier it will be on the girl. If her ribs is busted, she's bound to be in a heap of pain."

So blowing pepper into Willow's face caused sneezing to induce faster labor? Cora had never read that in the medical books. And Cora was likely not to try the technique herself, if she could help it. What an experience!

"Now, instead of standin' there with your mouth open, why don't you make up some nettle tea?" Granny handed Cora a small bag with dried leaves inside.

"Nettles?" Cora slowly took the bag. "But aren't they a weed?"

"Aye, but God knows how to use all sorts, weeds and flowers alike." She moved her palms over Willow's stomach as she talked. "Helps slow the bleedin'."

Cora stared at the woman, taking in the information. She'd

gone from a volunteer to assisting nurses with wounded, without any "proper" training, but the fieldwork taught her so much that she'd been promoted to the Front more quickly than some of the other volunteers. And though she valued the knowledge housed in books, she knew the benefits of practical experience too. Granny Burcham offered the latter.

"Git on, now. Afore we have a baby and the nettle ain't as much use."

Cora rushed to the kitchen, fumbling around to find the teapot… or rather, coffeepot in Jeb's case.

She rushed back, cup in hand, and only managed to help Willow get in a few sips before another contraction hit, followed by another. Within a few minutes, and several contractions later, the loud cry of a healthy set of lungs filled the air.

"Yes, sirree. A fine baby boy, right here." Granny Burcham's grin widened, showing off a smile with a few missing teeth. She raised the small newborn in her wrinkled hands, giving him a good pat on the bottom to increase the cries. "Strong cry."

Her chuckle turned into a laugh before she turned to Cora. "Wash 'im up, Nurse Woman, and wrap him tight afore we let his mama hold him."

Cora froze as Granny Burcham offered her the red, squirming bundle. She had as much practice with holding babies as she did with birthing them. However, she refused to allow Granny Burcham to take her for more of a birthing fool than she already felt. Rubbing her palms together to warm them, she reached with a towel and engulfed the little body.

His crying quieted as he nestled within the folds of the cloth and Cora drew him close. Murky blue eyes peered back at her from the tiny face. Would they stay blue, like so many of the other Appalachian folks she'd met?

"He's. . .he's alright?" Willow's voice quaked with exhaustion.

"Looks as fine as can be," Granny answered. "We'll finish up here and then you can hold him for a spell, but you got more work to do afore you rest, girl." She rounded the bed and placed her hands on Willow's stomach. "I'm gonna press down. It won't hurt nothin' like what you already done."

Cora washed up the tiny body, those eyes watching her as she moved the cloth over each little crease and dimple. A miracle, truly. In so many ways. After finding Willow beaten and unconscious, there was no knowing if the mother or the baby would survive, but right now, to have them both alive, well, Cora couldn't help but offer a grateful smile to heaven. Something in her heart settled into the moment like a view of home.

The little fingers reached up and snagged one of Cora's loose curls, giving it a healthy tug before puckering his lips into a frown. The smallest whimper escaped him and Cora raised her gaze to Willow, who, though sweating and pale, smiled the sweetest smile in Cora's direction.

Granny Burcham tugged the blankets up around Willow, closed the window, picked up the pan of dirty water, then nodded toward Cora. "You better hand that young'un over to his mama, girl, or he's gonna take ta catterwallin'."

Cora had no idea what catterwallin' was, but she didn't mean to find out. In a few steps, she gently placed the baby into Willow's arms.

"Oh, look at 'im, Granny." Willow ran a finger down the baby's cheek, and Cora almost lost her emotions again. "He looks good and healthy."

"He sure does." Granny patted the bed. "And you did a fine job. One of the best first births I've a witness to."

"Zat so?" Willow's smile widened and she peered back down at the baby.

He began to nudge close to her, so Granny took time to teach Willow how to feed the little one, all the while giving Cora little tips and instructions, like a teacher to a pupil. She added a few things about how an herb would work for helping milk come in or a certain tea would reduce after-pains, all of which Cora wrote down in a notepad she kept in her nursing bag.

"Havin' a baby will be good for her." A smile softened the woman's features as she stared at Willow. "Plumps up a woman in all the right places. Menfolk like that in a wife. Meat on the bones worth cuddlin' up to."

Cora tried to cover her chuckle with her hand, but Granny raised a brow, taking her time giving Cora a look from head to toe. "Ain't no man wants to warm up at night next to a gal as skinny as a new tree." A twinkle lit her eyes. "But we'll fatten you up if you're here long enough. You got a good start."

A good start? On becoming a "Granny Woman" or of being cuddle-worthy? Her attention shot to the window and the little building on the other side of the "yard," as Jeb called it.

"I reckon that boy's about fit to be tied."

Cora snapped out of her thoughts and met Granny Burcham's much-too-aware gaze. "Why would he be? It isn't his child."

"Naw, but if'n I know that boy a'tall, him and his tender heart's flustered enough to need some reassurin'." She tipped her chin toward the window. "I reckon you ought to go set him at ease, so he'll git some sleep tonight." Her grin grew. "Lord knows, we won't git none, and somebody ought to."

<hr/>

Jeb took another load of firewood to the front porch, just to have something to do. After hearing Willow's moans of pain through the window of the house, he'd worked. Sometimes, loud enough to cover her hollerin' for a little bit. Then all got quiet. That was when he felt the compulsion to double up on firewood. Or maybe triple up.

The porch lantern lit the front of the house, but he kept clear of the bedroom window, no matter how much his curiosity burned. Were they alright? Did Willow make it through the hardest part? The baby?

He turned in time to see the front door open and Cora step out. Her gaze searched the front and then found his, a tired smile pulling at her lips.

"A boy." Her grin spread wide. "A beautiful baby boy."

Jeb rested back against the porch railing and crossed his arms. "And Willa?" His lips tipped. "I mean Will*ow*?"

Cora moved near him, shooting him a weak glare. "Willow is doing well as far as I can tell." Her expression sobered. "It's amazing what a mother's body can endure in order to bring a child into the world."

"I reckon neither of 'em would be here, if you hadn't come by."

"I couldn't have gotten her here without your help." She looked over at him and then back out into the dark, her palms pressed against the railing, face forward.

The tapping of Puck's paws against the porch sounded into the silence until he came to rest at Jeb's side. Jeb placed a hand on the dog's head and listened as the night critters continued their evening sounds.

"Granny Burcham didn't shoo you out of the house, so she must like ya a little."

Cora laughed and pushed back her hair, the lantern light glowing gold in her eyes. "She's tolerated me at least, but I'm grateful. She's already shared so many things about the medicinal uses of plants in this area, and I've tried to take as many notes as I can." Her eyes grew wide as she leaned closer to him. "Did you know that wild hydrangea can help with kidney troubles? And sumac assists in reducing fevers? She recalled from memory the recipes for sweet gum salve and wild cherry cough syrup. Her knowledge is remarkable."

"Well, she's bound to know most everything. She's nigh two hundred years old if rumors can be trusted." He shot her a wink, and a sweet blush crept up into her face. *Lord have mercy.*

He looked away to keep his head clear and his lips from itching.

194

"Two hundred or not, I'd hate to be on the wrong side of her anger."

Jeb laughed at her raised brows, her smile lighting her eyes. "She'll use some of her potions on ya and turn you into a frog or some such."

"Believe it or not, I imagined such things before I arrived here." Her chuckle turned into a sigh as she leaned back against the porch post facing him, her hair tumbling over her shoulders, her white blouse a mess of stains.

He nearly grinned at how perfect she looked. How at home.

"Jonathan's letters held such warmth and beauty, but he also spoke of the wildness and brokenness." Her smile dipped. "I thought so many wrong things."

"I reckon some of them were right." He knew the rumors, the stereotypes laid up for his people. Appalachians. The South. After the War betwixt the States, some of those rumors got bigger and uglier too.

"Perhaps, but most not." She met his gaze. "Joining the war hospital and then nursing near the Front, well, it seemed to temper those imaginings with a bit of realism, and, after my first few weeks in these mountains, I'm glad it did."

His stomach clenched at her words. No, she didn't have no place here, did she? How could she love this mountain and these people from all the wrong she'd seen?

"I grew up during the war, but more than that." A gentle smile curled her lips. "I think I started learning what was important and what mattered most. I didn't understand it really. Not before, when my life had been all about pampered rooms and careful conversations."

"This ain't an easy life. That's for sure."

"No, it isn't." Her gaze bore into his, brows low. "But I've felt more alive and more myself in the middle of the hardest days, than I ever felt in the easiest. There was purpose and this. . .this joy in making a difference, in offering even the smallest hope to those who were hurting or heartbroken." She glanced out into the night, her profile pale and pensive. "I don't think I would have seen it before in my gilded world, but I do now. And I don't wish to go back to what I was before."

"You got a good heart for helpin' others."

"And a hard head." She winced. "You've seen the worst of me, I'm afraid. I can't imagine the impression I've left."

He cleared his throat and rubbed at the heat climbing the back of his neck. Oh, she'd left an impression alright. "Takes a strong person to manage life round here, especially strong women."

"That reminds me, Jeb. Willow spoke of what happened for her to be at Rowen's." The smile on her face faded slowly. "She said her brother, Clark. . ." Cora paused, and Jeb tensed. "She said he sold her to Rowen Hawes to pay off his debts."

Cold spread through Jeb from his forehead to his toes. A brother selling his own sister for debts? Jeb's fingers fisted the porch railing. Ain't no cause for any soul to think so lowly of another to sell 'em.

"From the horrified expression on your face, I'll assume enslaving siblings to pay off debt is not a common occurrence in these mountains?"

"No."

"I can't tell you how happy I am to hear it."

He responded to the lighter tone in her voice. She likely needed a turn from the dark topic as much as he did. "Tradin' wives has been heard of. Huntin' dogs has been done a few times."

"Trading wives?"

"Most times the wives didn't complain none." Jeb shrugged a shoulder. "But this ain't like nothin' I've ever heard, and I'd wager Willa's daddy don't know 'bout it either."

"What do you mean?"

"Willa's the oldest gal young'un in the family." He cleared his throat. "I mean, the oldest daughter, and despite Ozaiah's meanness, he would have seen it as a high offense to sell off his young'un to be one of Rowen's girls instead of havin' her marry and carry on the family line."

"Do you think Clark did this without his knowledge?"

"I can't see no other way." Jeb looked out into the night, sifting through possibilities. "But how? What lie would have convinced his daddy that Willa up and ran off?"

"How long ago was it?"

"She went missin' 'bout the same time as Kizz—" His gaze came up to meet Cora's. "Kizzie was sent off the week afore Willa left."

Cora's eyes grew wide. "Do you think he somehow used Kizzie's disappearance to explain Willow's? Maybe he claimed Willow had gotten the idea from her friend, perhaps?"

"Mayhap." He ran a hand through his hair. "It'd make sense with a dark mind like his."

"She said there's a man who works at the mill who wants to marry her. Someone named Paul."

"Paul Russell?" Jeb stood from his leaned position. "He was workin' there when I came back from Europe. Good worker. Quiet. Is he the daddy?"

"Who can know?" Cora raised a brow. "But she believes he truly wants to marry her and take her away from here."

Jeb paced across the porch. Getting Willow away from this place was probably the best option for her, but was Paul serious about his intentions toward her? He turned back to Cora. "I can try to find out some more tomorrow at the mill."

"Good." She straightened. "And we can hide her here until we can sort out what to do next?"

He stared down at her, a grin tugging his lips despite himself. "I reckon we'll have to."

"I'm sorry, Jeb." She nibbled her bottom lip and stared up at him. "I've caused so much trouble for you."

His hands fisted at his sides to keep from reaching for her. "You're worth the trouble, I reckon."

"You reckon?"

The sound of a baby crying made its way to the front porch and sent him back a step. "You need to get some rest." He gestured toward the door. "If you can." He looked down at Puck. "Stay, boy." He walked to the edge of the porch.

"Jeb." He turned at the steps. Cora stood with her hand on the door latch. "Has there been any news about Kizzie?"

"No." The weight of the declaration pressed in on him. "But I sure hope wherever she is, her and her baby are as looked after as Willa and hers is."

Chapter Fifteen

Jeb left at dawn, without making a visit to the house for fear of disturbing a new mama and the ladies who'd helped her. Instead, he loaded up a few pieces of furniture and a carving or two, then made his way down the mountain as morning woke around him. Frost glistened off the leaves in the sunlight, making the whole world sparkle like light on glass.

He'd slept hard for a few hours, more soundly than he'd slept in a while. And over the course of the last two and a half weeks, he hadn't needed one dram of whiskey. He stared up at the lightening sky with its pink and orange hues growing paler with the rising sun. Maybe he wasn't cursed with the drinking sickness of his daddy.

Perhaps, all he needed was enough time to heal from the hardships of war and—his thoughts paused on Cora and the way she'd looked on the porch yester eve—a new perspective? It didn't sound a'tall like she planned on leaving Maple Springs. In fact, from her conversation yesterday, the whole idea of mountain life seemed to be growing on her, and Jeb was tempted to find a whole herd of needy folks she could rescue just so she wouldn't get any ideas of leaving. But, of course, he had to consider his promise to Amos. He had to keep true to it, no matter what direction his heart pulled.

"Ain't right, Hickory," he growled out. "I gotta make things right betwixt Mercy and me and that's all there is to it. She wasn't ready to talk about it when I first got home, but time's passed." He straightened. "And I'm bound to give up on it altogether if I let much more time pass with a certain feisty female around."

Hickory snorted.

"Females is right." Jeb shook his head. And now, with all these females in his life, he was tasked to find out if Paul Russell wanted to marry Willow Greer. Lord, help him! He'd never been one to get involved in other folks' affairs. It just wasn't something that was done, but here he was, planning a way to find out if Paul Russell had serious intentions toward the young woman who'd just had a baby in his house. Bringin' a heap of women into a man's life certainly sent everything into a tailspin. For months, he'd barely had a visitor on his side of the mountain, and over the course of a day, he'd gone from quiet, solitary bachelor to hosting a gaggle of women and not even being able to sleep in his own house.

But, despite it all, he couldn't help but grin. Truth be told, he hadn't grinned so much before Cora Taylor came into Maple Springs, and the very idea that the craziness felt perfectly right proved he'd lost every bit of sense he'd ever had.

He dropped the furniture off at Key Murphy's shop first and then traveled on to the mill, arriving early enough to find only Elias starting up everything.

"Early today," Elias commented as Jeb stepped right in to help him check all the equipment before beginning the saw.

"Had some things to do in town, so thought I'd get an early start."

Elias grinned. "You know you can't hide nothin' from me, don't ya, Jeb? You're flustered up to your eyeballs 'bout somethin', and from a few things you've said here and there while at work, I've a mind to think it's about some English woman."

Jeb shot his attention to Elias. "You got nothin' better to do than to make stuff up?"

Elias broke out into a full body laugh, deep and loud. Jeb glanced around the mill, glad to see none of the other boys had shown yet. "We've known each other too long, and spent too much time working with each other, for you to hide it from me, friend. What'll you do about Amos's woman now that you're sparkin' some foreigner?"

"Elias Harris." Jeb leaned close, his whisper harsh. "You'd be hurtin' something awful if I walked right out of this mill and didn't come back, wouldn't you?"

Elias's expression sobered a little, but his dark eyes were still lit with more teasing to come. "I'm afraid I'm bound to lose you soon 'nough with all your furniture making."

Jeb pushed one of the trunks into the waterway that led to the saw, Elias helping at his side. "Don't count ya chickens on that one yet." Though the more he spoke with Key Murphy the more hopeful he became for a future in woodwork as full-time work. Folks, more and more, seemed to be looking for handcrafted pieces, and if Jeb could spend his time doing something he loved, stay in the place he loved, *and* keep food on the table doing both, well, it just seemed too good to be true. He drew in a breath. "And it's 'bout time I pay Mercy a visit, and that's a fact." His shoulders dropped. "She told me to give her six months to think on things, and that come and gone two weeks ago."

"A lot can happen in six months' time, Jeb." Elias placed his large hand on Jeb's shoulder. "I ain't never met Mercy, but if she's one of Fergus Tate's bunch, she's got a good head. She'd understand if you've had a change of heart, I'd wager."

Jeb studied on the thought a second. Mercy would be kind and understanding, as she always was, and that was the very reason Jeb needed to keep to his promise. Hold to his word. Mercy was a good woman. And she deserved to have somebody take care of her instead of becoming an old maid in the backwoods without the chance to keep her own house and family.

No, he couldn't cultivate these feelings for Cora until he'd found out what Mercy needed. He'd make his visit in two days. Sunday.

He nodded to himself, as if it fixed everything, when all it did was tense up his muscles even more than they already were.

"You still got some chickens you're wanting to sell?" Elias changed the subject out of compassion, if Jeb judged rightly.

"Sure do."

"Good, cause Dolly's taken a fancy to two of ours and cries a storm when I talk about cookin' them up for dinner." Elias offered a helpless shrug. "I don't got no idea how to raise that girl on my own. I reckon we both got trouble with the females." He winked. "But I'll take mine over yourn any day."

Other workers started filtering into the mill, each taking to their usual stations and working in tandem from weeks, months, or years of practice.

Jeb found Paul during lunch break, the young man sitting outside on a makeshift bench overlooking a view of the town, his lunch sack at his side and coffee cup in hand. He couldn't have been much younger than Jeb. Twenty, at most. Came from Sparta way, with family still in that part of North Carolina. Not too far, if the boy had plans to take Willow back with him. He proved a hard worker and smart, and if Jeb recalled correctly, wanted to build houses in the future.

How was he supposed to start this conversation? A man didn't pry into another man's business.

"Good place to sit and think." That seemed easy enough.

Paul looked up, his dark eyes registering surprise, and he offered a small smile. "Sure is."

Jeb shifted closer. "Mind if I join you for a spell?"

Paul moved over, giving Jeb space.

"You do good work." Which was true, so might as well say it.

"I like the work."

"You hope to stay for a while?"

Paul breathed out a sigh and took a sip of his coffee. "I plan to move back toward Sparta and start up my own business, if I can."

"Well, you got the skills for it." Jeb glanced out over the view and prayed for the right words to say. "The times you've helped with the clinic shows you know what you're doing."

"I learned a lot from working with you there."

Silence. Jeb cleared his throat. Paul took another drink of coffee.

"There's a gal I met a few days back." Alright, got out a little of it. Now to use some of what he'd learned from Willow's story about Paul. "Said the two of y'all are plannin' a big future in Sparta."

Paul's attention shot to Jeb. Yep, that hit the nail on the head. "Zat so?"

"Yep." Jeb kept his voice low. "Said she's missed seein' you for a few months' time and hopes it'll change soon."

"Willa's alive. I ain't heard nothin' in a month." Paul's eyes widened. Even became a little glossy. Well, now. That wasn't just your average man after an easy night with a woman. "You seen her?"

Jeb raised his hand and glanced around them, lowering his voice. Ain't no tellin' who might be listening, and Jeb didn't need more trouble in his direction, what with housing Willow and trying to keep Cora safe. "Found her beat up in the woods. She's doin' better now. Had the baby."

Paul's grin spread. "She had the baby."

"Sure did. And they're both doin' as well as can be expected." Jeb looked around them again. "But I come to find out what your plans are."

Paul stared at Jeb and suddenly straightened. "I mean to marry her. Always have."

"That's good to hear." Jeb nodded. "She seems to be mighty fixed on that too."

"Can I see her?"

Jeb drew in a breath, trying to sort out the next plan. He'd only worked out this part in his head. "You can, but not just yet. We need to work out a safe time and all." He raised a brow. "And you need to start making some quick plans to git away from here, if I know anything about what all this is about."

Paul's jaw tightened. "Some of Rowen's men found me. Tried to bully me into tellin' if I knew anything, but I could honestly say I hadn't a clue. All she had time to send me was a note that she'd find me when she could."

Were those the men that attacked Willow? It didn't seem to fit Rowen a'tall. No, whatever happened to Willow likely came more from some angry mountain men. Rowen wouldn't have wanted one of his girls to show up beaten when she had a job to do to win men's favor.

"Then hold this news close to your chest and keep workin' as if we ain't talked about it at all." Jeb stood. "And don't try to find her lest I take you. We need both of y'all to stay safe, you hear?"

Paul nodded, his grin spreading wide again. "I'm just glad to know she's alive."

Jeb started back toward the mill.

"Jeb?"

Jeb turned back toward the man.

"Gal baby or boy?"

Jeb's expression softened. "Boy."

Paul beamed bright enough to light a room. Now all Jeb had to sort out was how to get Paul, a crippled Willow, and a newborn out of the mountain without Clark finding them or Rowen's men catching them. Well, nobody knew where Willow was except Cora, Granny Burcham, and Jeb. At least, in that way, they'd keep her safe for a bit longer.

⁂

Jeb settled Hickory in the barn, washed up, and then made his way to the house. The last rays of daylight glowed rose and orange through the trees, but a breeze deepened the chill in the air. Jeb gave a quiet knock on the front door, and when no one responded, he cautiously opened it. A sound from the kitchen drew him forward to find Granny Burcham washing up and the scent of chicken in the air. Jeb's stomach growled loud enough to turn the older woman from her work.

"Sakes alive, boy. Get you some food afore somebody mistakes you for a mountain lion." She gestured toward the small table nearby where a plate covered with a cloth waited. "Last thing we need is another person for Nurse Woman to tend, and that's a fact."

Jeb sat down at the table and breathed in the scent. He'd learned to cook basic things for himself, but fried chicken and mashed taters? Not yet. With a grin of gratitude heavenward, he took a glorious first bite, then looked up at Granny Burcham, her comment finally registering over his pangs of hunger. "What do you mean by another person for Cora to tend?"

Granny Burcham turned from the cookstove, wiping her hands on a towel. A towel with flowers on it? When had he ever bought towels with flowers on them?

"She went down yonder to the Preacher's house to fetch a few things this mornin'. Wasn't there no time and Coon Roberts showed up carryin' his least 'un in his arms. Said she'd got burned real bad on the arm and needed some tendin to." Granny Burcham shook her head. "And the girl wasn't halfway done tendin' Coon's little girl when Avis Jones showed up with a bad cut from a wrong swing of an axe."

Jeb winced at the thought.

"She had one other visit, from Posey Smith 'bout some female troubles, then she finally got back up here to tell me all 'bout it. Said folks knew Teacher Doctor was out of town and heard she'd tended to Rowen Hawes's wound so fine, they figured she had a smart or two 'bout doctorin'."

Jeb crammed another bite of chicken into his mouth to hide his frown. The more folks she met in these mountains, the less likely she'd be to stay. Avis Jones? That man could cuss the beard off a sailor, if he had a mind to. And Posey Smith was always ailin' from one thing or other, whether she really was or not.

"It beat all, Jeb." Granny Burcham chuckled. "That girl came back up here grinnin' like she'd just won a mule race."

Jeb looked up from his plate and stared for a full five seconds at Granny Burcham. "She was happy 'bout it?"

"Sure was." Granny's chuckle turned into a laugh. "She looked a mess for the likes of a city girl. That wild hair of hern shootin' in all directions and her clothes smeared from one end to another with what all, but you'd have never knowed it bothered her a bit."

Taking care of his mountain people all day made her happy? Jeb stood from the table. "Where is she now?"

"Well, she washed up and then seemed to see some laundry that needed tendin' to so she's out on the back porch still, I reckon. Out of sight of pryin' eyes, as much as one can be round here."

Jeb stood, plate in hand, digesting the information that city girl Cora Taylor from across the waters found joy in doctoring his simple mountain people. He needed to see this for himself.

"Go on." Granny took the plate from his hand. "You ain't no use just standin' there with your mouth hangin' open."

Jeb shot the woman a grimace and then sighed. "Thank you, Granny Burcham."

She just grinned like a cat on a mouse's trail and turned back to her work.

Jeb shrugged off the woman's reaction and made his way to the back door of the house, careful to open the door quietly. Cora stood over a basin of water, hands pressing—albeit slowly—some type of cloth. A sheet, perhaps? She'd wrangled her hair back into a bun, but sprigs of curls spun around her ears, and her shoulders dropped lower with each scrub.

She raised the back of her hand to catch a yawn and then went back to her work.

Night crouched in. She had to be freezing.

"Don't you reckon it's about time to get inside for the night?"

She turned and offered him a sleepy smile. "I hadn't cleaned up the blankets after the baby's birth, and I didn't want to leave them soiled for you."

He stepped closer, the lantern light haloing them with night on all sides. He'd seen pretty women before. Stared a little too long at one or two, but never had he thought to linger. Till now. Till her. Mercy deserved to have Amos's ring, but Jeb's heart was already filled with somebody else. "I can finish up here, Cora."

Her brow wrinkled and she switched her attention from the washtub to his face. "But—but it's not your job to clean up this mess."

Her words came slowly, weak. It was a wonder she could still stand upright. "I've lived on my own a while, so I can tend to this. Seems you've been tendin' to many more important things today."

When he drew her hands out of the tub, she didn't argue, only stared up at him in a sleepy way that made him want to pull her into his arms and kiss her smiling lips. "It's been good, Jeb. Truly. That feeling of being useful and doing exactly what I'm meant to do. Do you understand what I mean?"

"Aye." He took the towel from her shoulder and wrapped it around her hands, warming them as he dried. For a split second, he nearly brought her delicate fingers to his lips.

Great day alive! She would have taken him for a loon, for sure, if he'd done something like that. But then, when he looked down into her face, he wondered. . .maybe she wouldn't? "I feel that way when I'm handcraftin'."

Her smile bloomed. "Yes, I can see that. You have a gift."

"So do you."

Her expression softened. Her eyelids dropped a bit. Cuddling up close to her sounded better and better all the time. She yawned again and he took his cue. "From what I understand, folks with big hearts need to make sure they get good sleep." He placed his hands on her shoulders and turned her toward the door. "Which means, you get on inside and I'll finish up here."

She took a few steps and stumbled. He steadied her, and one of her palms caught his hand in the process. "I think you might be right, Mr. McAdams. I'm so tired, I can't even seem to walk straight."

He stepped with her to the door, but she didn't release his hand. Their palms touched, skin to skin. His lips took to itchin' like he'd landed face-first in a natural bouquet of poison ivy, then she turned at the threshold and looked up at him. "You need sleep too, because I am quite certain you have a wonderful big heart."

"I'll get some when I finish." His voice barely worked.

"You promise?" she whispered.

"Aye," he said, and then impulse took over. As he kept his gaze focused on hers, he brought her hand toward his face. Her expression transitioned from sleepy to curious, watching his slow movement. His fingers smoothed over hers and he gently turned her hand over in his. Without being certain if what he was doing was sweet or not, he pressed his lips to her palm.

Her breath hitched and heat spilled from his mouth all the way down his body. He looked back at her from his bowed position over her hand, not too sure whether to smile, apologize, or give in to the itching, because instead of that one touch dousing the desire, it had sent the need into full flame.

She stared up at him, neither smiling nor frowning. Dark shadows hovered beneath her eyes, sending sense back into his head. He sighed and lowered her hand, finally releasing it. "Good night, Cora."

She blinked and looked down at her hand, then slowly brought her fingers into a fist before drawing in a deep breath. "Good night, Jeb."

Cora woke to daylight filtering through her window. For the second night, she'd slept in one of the upstairs rooms, the one with windows looking out over the view instead of facing the forest. Bringing an extra duvet from her travel chest had proven a wise choice, since the heat from belowstairs took much longer to reach the second floor, but at least it stole some of the chill out of the air. It had taken much too long for her to fall asleep, even though her body ached with weariness.

Jeb had kissed her.

Yes, it had only been the palm of her hand, but the gentle expression paired with the look in his eyes nearly buckled her knees. She'd had poor experiences with men who'd been attracted to her. Either they'd presented as domineering cretins, played sport with her heart while entertaining interest in other women, or they'd bumbled about with an immaturity of both emotions and mind. But Jeb? She had no script for him. His strength calmed her. His tenderness drew her nearer. His kindness had her wishing to vanquish all propriety so she could take his face in her hands and kiss him senseless—. She pressed her palm to her chest and breathed out a slow breath as heat flooded her cheeks. Which was highly inappropriate. But nonetheless appealing.

She smiled up at the ceiling, watching the pale light dancing about the room to tease her from the bed. Caring for him meant a shift in her plans, didn't it? A full embrace of this life. One day of "doctorin'" couldn't be enough to decide on a possible lifetime, could it? But... Could such a man be enough?

Jonathan had seemed to acclimate to this foreign world with surprising joy and readiness, even bringing his own ideas into Appalachia to help improve people's lives. Could she do the same? Had God called her here? To teach women hygiene? To tend the wounded? To birth babies and assist her brother?

She pushed past her aching muscles and got dressed, following the scent of bacon all the way to the kitchen and feeling slightly guilty in her lack of culinary abilities. However, she had learned how to make fried chicken from Granny Burcham the day before, so at least that was something. Well, once Granny had de-feathered and cut up the bird then brought it inside for frying. Cora would have to learn the preliminary steps on another day.

"Well, you almost missed greetin' the mornin', girl." Granny gestured with her chin toward the table. "But at least you'll have company this mornin'. She was mighty determined, so I helped her git up and at 'em, then brung the babe to her. Good for her to move round. Good for healin'."

Cora turned to find Willow sitting at the table, dressed in the gown Cora had left out for her. The one with buttons down the front to make feeding the baby easier. Though cuts and bruises still deepened parts of her face, the natural beauty of the girl shone through. There were even a few freckles speckling her cheeks.

"What a pleasant surprise to see you up and about, Willow. And you look lovely this morning." Cora took a seat across from the girl, who boasted a beautiful blush.

What a strange dichotomy. A girl who'd lived as a prostitute for over a year blushing at a simple compliment. Perhaps the tenderest parts of her innocence were still intact? Cora pondered over the idea for a moment. She may have never spoken ill of women in such a profession, but she'd never considered their various reasons for being there. Or if they wished to leave or not. She'd always supposed the profession was a choice, a regretful one, perhaps, but not something in which the women longed for freedom, or normalcy, or even love.

Why had she never considered them before? Was it because of society's cry of the evils of such a life? For surely, even though payment for carefree intimacy was not within God's best plans for His people, these women were still women created in His image. Their souls needed love and grace and forgiveness no less than Cora's.

Just shifting her thoughts from labeling Willow a prostitute to a woman created in the image of God changed everything. It took the learned piousness away and replaced it with something sweeter and more meaningful, more like compassion.

"I thank you kindly for the dress, Miss Cora." Willow gestured with her wrapped wrist toward the skirt. "I ain't never worn nothin' so fine and that's the truth."

Cora smiled and placed one of the serviettes she'd cut from an old sheet she'd brought with her from home over her lap. No one else seemed to use them here, but Cora had made up her mind to model etiquette in hopes of it catching on. "It's yours for the keeping. I have no need for it."

"I can't keep your dress."

Cora nodded a thanks to Granny Burcham as she placed a heaping plate of eggs, sausage, and American biscuits before her. Her stomach growled in thanksgiving. "You very well can, because I have no need for it and it fits you much better than me." She smiled and slathered a greedy amount of strawberry jam onto the biscuit. "Besides, that shade of blue is perfect with your eyes."

Her blush deepened. "Paul wouldn't mind introducing me to his parents if I wore something so fine as this."

"He shouldn't mind introducing you to his parents at any rate." Cora raised the biscuit to her lips. "Not if he loves you enough to marry you."

"Oh, he does, Miss Cora." Willow nodded. "He's worried somethin' fierce about me. That's what Jeb told me when he got home last night."

Jeb had spoken to Paul? "And what other things did you discover from Jeb?"

"That he's plannin' to have Paul come up to see me and the babe tomorra, if'n you don't mind none." She looked over at Granny Burcham. "Granny said should be safe tomorra, since the menfolk'll be off huntin' on the far mountain 'stead of church goin'."

How did Granny know what the menfolk were doing, unless... Cora's gaze shot to Granny Burcham. Where had she gone when she'd disappeared yesterday? And moreover, with whom had she spoken? Surely, Granny Burcham could be entrusted with Willow's welfare and Jeb's secrecy, couldn't she?

Granny raised a brow in Cora's direction, as if she knew just exactly what Cora thought. "They heard tell of a herd of deer over yonder. Can't let a good hunt go by with winter on the way."

Cora held Granny Burcham's gaze a moment longer and then turned back to Willow with a smile. "I should very much like to meet him, if I may?"

"Sure as shootin'." Willow's grin brightened even more. "And he'll be right happy to see his son. I've been waitin' to name the baby till Paul can see him, but I got a hankerin' for the name Peter."

"That's an excellent name." Cora took a sip of milk. "Is that name special to you?"

The girl's pale eyes glistened with a sudden sheen of tears. "It's 'cause Peter in the Bible broke Jesus's heart with his sinnin', but Jesus loved him still." Her bottom lip wobbled. "And I reckon, if Jesus can love me still after I've gone about breakin' His heart, then I want a reminder of that love ever day of my life."

Cora's smile quivered alive. How tender. Surely Willow's phraseology wasn't as refined as it could have been, but her theology was sound. God did love His children. Anyway and always. No matter how broken or lost.

"What an excellent reminder." Cora cleared her throat and took another sip of milk. "Paul will think so too, I'd guess."

After breakfast, Cora helped Willow to the sitting room and returned to assist Granny Burcham in cleaning up after their late breakfast. Then they straightened up the bedroom Willow used, careful to do so quietly as little "Peter" slept, wrapped in blankets, in one of the dresser drawers near the bed.

Cora hadn't been back long after gathering supplies at her uncle's house, when a knock came to the back door of the house. She looked across the room to meet Granny Burcham's knowing gaze. What had Granny done?

The older woman raised a palm in warning and walked quietly to the kitchen. Cora followed. Who would be coming to visit Jeb's house with those dark clouds threatening in the sky? Without a word, Granny peered out the kitchen window which gave a view of the back door, if one stretched enough to see. Cora followed Granny's movements and caught a glimpse of a thin older woman in a threadbare coat. The wind bent the trees, and the slightest sprinkles of rain, mixed with a hint of snow, spun in the air.

Granny walked to the back door and opened it to allow the woman into the house. Wind followed the woman, bringing a foul odor of human waste with it. Cora stifled the urge to raise her hand to cover her nose. Who was this woman and why was she here? She sent Cora a wary look, wringing her thin hands in front of her. Deep lines etched her face and her pale hair twisted back with hints of gray interspersed within the blond.

"Mama?" Willow called from her chair in the sitting room, baby in arms. "Mama? Is that you?"

The woman's nervous expression fell into a shaking smile.

"Go on, Merla." Granny Burcham nudged her forward. "She's been achin' to see ya."

Merla Greer rushed forward and took Willow's free hand into both of hers. "Oh, girl. I didn't know." Her voice quaked. "I didn't know what your brother done."

Cora turned to Granny Burcham. "You told her to come." Did this place them all in danger somehow? This one act of reuniting a daughter and mother?

"She won't tell nothin'." Granny nodded toward the endearing scene. "But a Mama needs to see her young'un. 'Specially when she thought the girl lost for nigh two years."

"Lost?"

"Their daddy cast her out when he heard tell she was one of Rowen's girls. They hadn't heared from her since then. They weren't sure whether she was still there, had moved on, or was dead." Granny's

213

frown deepened all the wrinkles of her face. "Merla said Clark even told the family he'd tried to keep Willa from goin' to Rowen's."

"Making himself out to be noble in some way?" Cora's lips curled. "How vile."

Granny stepped close. "Now, I don't expect Merla to tell nobody, but that don't mean she wasn't followed, so I want you to do somethin' for me."

Followed? Cora turned to the nearest window, squinting to view the forest beyond the yard. Rain and snow still spun with the wind.

"Cora." The sharp edge in Granny's voice brought Cora's attention back around. "I'm low on aloe and elderberry, both I need for makin' salves." Her stare bore into Cora's. "Caroline McAdams keeps extra and is generous in sharin' it. I need you to go get some for me."

"What are you hiding, Granny?"

The woman dared a little smile. "I ain't hidin' nothin, but I think if trouble was to start, there'd be a lot less hurt if you wasn't here."

"You think I'd want to hurt anyone here?"

"No, but you bein' a flatlander female livin' in Jeb's house might cause more trouble to the situation than either one of us wants to add."

Cora narrowed her eyes at the woman. "That's a good half hour walk." She pointed toward the window. "In freezing rain."

"Won't hurt you none." Granny's grin grew. "You've shown you're tough, and I reckon you've been through worse than a walk in the cold rain, ain'tcha?"

Cora only glared.

"Plus, you'll need the aloe salve to give to the Roberts' young'un."

Cora sighed. She *had* told the couple she'd bring by additional salve on her next trip to Mrs. Cappy's store. Granny had hit on Cora's nursing nerve. She was out of aloe salve, a concoction meant to help ease the pain of the burn as well as disinfect. "Fine, but I mean for you to explain yourself, Granny, when I get back. Do you hear me?"

"You'll do just fine." The woman chuckled. "Just fine."

Despite Cora's slight annoyance, Granny's words sounded very much like a compliment of sorts.

Granny Burcham walked toward the sitting room without another word, leaving Cora to go upstairs and locate the weatherproof coat she'd gotten from one of the nurses at the Front. Of course, it was meant for the soldiers, so it hung loose and large, but it kept damp away much better than a wool coat. Besides, an umbrella would prove useless in such wind.

With a last look into the warm sitting room and the consolation of seeing Willow so happy at the sight of her mother, Cora dashed out into the rain. The chill of the air hit her in the face and she pulled her scarf up over her nose and cheeks, offering a little added protection. The forest provided some slight protection from the heavier rain, and most of the precipitation came in light doses.

She marched at a clipped pace, her pistol in her pocket and her face forward. Oh, what she wouldn't give for a horse at the moment, but Jeb had taken both Hickory and Milkie with the wagon.

About three quarters of the way into her walk a strange scent reached her. It only passed as a hint, but a minute later, it came again. Stronger this time. Smoke? Ah, good, the McAdams house was close. She drew closer and the smoke smell grew. But it wasn't the smell of smoke from a fireplace.

Cora started into a run up the incline toward the house and that was when she saw it. Large, black billows of smoke rising from the far right of the McAdamses'. She pushed up through the last bit of forest and reached the clearing to see a building on the edge of the forest surrounding the house completely engulfed in flames.

Cora ran up the front porch and pushed open the door.

Caroline McAdams stood in the middle of the room, Suzie in her arms crying, and James and John huddled to the side with Isom poised in front of them. They all looked in her direction, eyes wide.

"Are you alright?"

Cora's frantic question sent Caroline into motion. "You need to git out of here, girl."

"What?" Cora followed her toward one of the windows where the silhouette of a man walked from the burning building toward the house. Was that Sam?

"Sam ain't gonna take too kindly to you bein' here, and he's done burned down the place the children hide."

"Burned down..." Cora repeated. Hide?

"Why are they hiding? What can I do to help?"

Caroline looked around the room, her gaze taking a frantic search.

"Sam ain't in his right mind." Caroline marched across the room and gathered a blanket up in her arms. "He ain't safe. I gotta git the young'uns outta here."

"You can come to Jeb's. You should be safe there."

Caroline fixed her full attention on Cora and then slowly started nodding. "That's good." She bolted the front door. "That'll give us a little time. He'll come front first then go to the weaker door in the back."

Cora looked from Caroline to the front door, trying to digest her words. What was the woman doing? In answer, Caroline began pulling coats on the two boys before giving Isom directions to put his on as well.

"Maggie's at Mrs. Cappy's store tonight or I'd have her take the young'uns." She handed Suzie her coat and then continued to help James with his. Cora rushed forward to assist John. She wasn't quite certain what was happening, but imminent danger hung in the air like a fog.

A loud crash came from the front door, sending Cora stumbling back with John in her arms.

"Don't you dare lock me out, woman." Sam's words slurred and thundered. "Give me my liquor now." Another slam shook the door, causing dust to fall from the ceiling. If John hadn't been in her arms,

Cora would have reached for her pistol. "I don't abide no sass from my young'uns. I'm gonna have to teach 'em all a lesson."

Caroline nudged Suzie and Cora toward the front door. "Onct you hear him comin' in the back, run out the front. Get 'em down the trail as fast as you can." She nodded toward Isom. "Isom'll help ya with the least'uns."

Cora followed Caroline's gaze, but Cora's understanding emerged slowly and halfway. "Aren't you coming?"

"No." The woman looked at Cora as if she'd lost her mind. "Somebody's gotta stay here to tend to him."

Tend to Sam? The man who burned down their building and now had them shivering in fear? "You must come to be safe."

"He won't hurt me none." She pushed Cora toward the front door. "But I don't know what he'll do with them."

A crash came from the back of the house along with a loud string of threats and expletives. Caroline nudged Isom and the twins forward. "Git on. Now."

Glass crashed.

"Mama?" James cried as Caroline opened the front door.

"Isom, get 'em now."

The older boy took James by the hand and Cora grabbed Suzie's while still holding a wide-eyed John. What was happening?

Another crash shook from the kitchen.

"Go, Cora. Save my young'uns."

Without full comprehension, Cora tugged John close to her chest, tightened her hold on Suzie's little hand, and ran from the house, Isom and James at her heels, and the sound of Sam McAdams's voice following on the freezing air.

Chapter Sixteen

I t was a good thing Paul Russell didn't have to wait long to lay his eyes on Willow. One more day, and then he could put the boy's mind at ease. Shucks, Jeb had often chuckled to himself about men who'd gone loony over a woman. The idea of barely being able to wait to see her seemed like a fool's head and a weak man's heart, but the past few days, he found himself making the horses ride a little harder than usual just to get a chance to talk to Cora.

They hadn't seen each other since the kiss passed betwixt them the night before, and he not only wanted to make sure she'd gotten the rest she needed, but also study on whether that simple touch started a hunger in her heart like it did in his. Could she care for someone like him? He wasn't a rich man, nor very romantic. He didn't even know what a grand house looked like apart from the ones he'd seen in France, and most of those were partially destroyed; but if Cora Taylor could care about him even a fraction of the bit he cared about her, he'd play the fool.

The iced rain took on a whole new severity as Jeb neared home, pelting to the point it nearly stung. The horses sped up without Jeb's nudging, likely as interested in getting under shelter as much as he. The back porch lanterns lit the way to the barn and Jeb made quick work settling the horses in before setting off at a run to the house. He'd studied on a few new woodcraft ideas he'd likely tend to by lantern light tonight, but first, supper and a chance to see Cora.

He rushed into the house, careful to keep the door from slamming as the wind took hold. The savory scent of ham and biscuits flooded toward him with such force, his mouth started watering. What a welcome from the cold!

"Good you're gettin' out of the cold."

Jeb followed the voice to a chair by the fire where Willow sat cradling a little bundle in her arms. "I see you escaped the room." He edged closer, attention moving from Willow's face to the sleeping babe in her arms. "I reckon both of you needed to see a bit more of the world than those four walls."

Willow's grin spread from cheek to cheek. "I won't complain none, Jeb, if I had to stay in that room for another month or two. I'd rather be 'bout anywhere than where I was."

He shrugged out of his coat, familiar heat coursing through his veins at the idea of what the girl had endured for the past year. He couldn't help but think of Kizzie and wondered if she'd suffered some same fate just to stay alive. "Well, I hope we can do better once you and your man can take to figurin' out what to do."

"He's really comin', ain't he?" Her pale eyes nearly glowed.

"'Ats what he said. Tomorra, in fact, if you're still keen on it."

"Oh, I am." She looked down at the baby. "He'll be proud as can be for a son."

Jeb placed his jacket and hat on the rack he'd fashioned by the door. "The sooner he can git both you and that babe away from Rowen, the better for all y'all."

"Rowen ain't so bad, Jeb."

His gaze came back to her, fingers fisting at his side. "Ain't so bad? To use a girl the way he used—"

"He takes care of the women real good." She shook her head. "Don't want you thinkin' otherwise. Most of them girls came 'cause they had nowhere else to go. They was starvin' or beaten by their men, and he gave 'em a job and place to stay."

"And killed off one of your babies." He didn't mean for the statement to come out so sharp, but the idea turned his stomach.

"He didn't know 'bout it, I don't think." Willow lowered her head. "The lead woman, Sally Ann, she's the one who keeps the girls in line. She gave it to me. But I ain't sayin' I want to go back to that life. Not now as I've found religion and a good man. I wished I could get all them girls out, but some don't want to leave, 'cause Rowen treats 'em so good. There ain't no beatings."

Jeb stiffened at her words. How awful that a whorehouse proved safer for her than her own home. "Rowen should have never taken you for your brother's debts, Willa. It ain't just awful, it's agin' the law."

"He didn't know I was Clark's sister."

"What?"

"Rowen ain't seen me in so long and I'd growed into my womanhood, he didn't know." She rubbed a hand under her nose, her voice dissolving to a whisper. "Clark told me that if I didn't go and tell Rowen I come of my own free will, then he'd take Daisy instead, and she was barely fourteen at the time."

Jeb stared at her, his fists and shoulders tightening. If he ever got his hands on Clark Greer, it might take all God's angels to keep him from committing murder. "Are you tellin' me he threatened to take Daisy if you didn't tell Rowen you was joinin' his girls of your own free will to pay his debts?"

She nodded. "My daddy's mean, but Clark is worse."

Sure 'nough, Ozaiah Greer was known throughout the mountain as a mean man, but it was one thing to be mean, foolish, and hotheaded. It was another to be mean, cunning, and hotheaded. And the latter was much more dangerous.

Jeb knelt down in front of the girl, placing his hands on the arms of the chair and holding her gaze. "Who attacked you, Willa?"

She sat quietly for a few seconds, rubbing her palm over the baby's back. "Some of Clark's friends. They knowed I'd run off from town, and Clark had told 'em to teach me a lesson if they come acrossed me so I'd git back to town for help." Her bottom lip wobbled. "I—I can't go back, Jeb. I'd rather die."

"You ain't goin' back and that's a fact." He shot to his feet and ran a hand through his hair before turning back to her. "And if Clark or his boys try to make you, I got a rifle that'll end any argument 'bout it." He released a long breath, trying to calm down. "You ate already?"

"'Bout an hour ago. Granny made the ham, but she done taught Cora how to cook some biscuits."

Jeb smiled a little. He'd have paid good money to be a fly on the wall to watch Cora learn biscuit cookin' from Granny Burcham. "We'll make her a mountain woman yet."

Willow smiled. "You like her just as she is. I can tell it. No need to be puttin' mountain in her."

Jeb sent the girl a mock glare that bounced right off her smile. It was good to see her happy after all the trouble she'd been through, even if the grin came at Jeb's expense. Without another word, he walked into the kitchen to find Granny Burcham where she'd been the evening before, doing the exact same thing as before, but Cora wasn't in sight. Where was she? She couldn't tend to no laundry on a night like this.

"She ain't here."

Granny's words stopped Jeb in mid-sit. She did not say what he thought she said, surely.

"I sent her off to your mama's for some herbs a couple hours back."

Jeb stood, slowly, staring at Granny Burcham. She had the good sense to look guilty. "I didn't know 'twas gonna git as bad as it is or I wouldn't have sent her."

Everything clicked into place and Jeb ran from the room toward his coat and hat. Good night! Anything could happen to her. Sure 'nough, it was barely nightfall, but the dark clouds made everything seem much later and pushed temperatures colder.

"She had on some fancy coat," Granny added, following Jeb to the door. "And them boots she bought down at town, which were a heap better than the city boots she brought—"

He closed the door on her words, snatched a lantern from the porch, and burst off the porch toward the trail, Puck on his heels. What on earth was Granny thinking, sending Cora out into the cold? Mayhap the iced rain wasn't coming hard when she'd left, and the darkness hadn't closed in, but Granny knew how fast weather changed on the mountain in winter.

Jeb picked up his pace to a run, the wind lashing rain against his face in stinging hits. The last time he'd visited his parents, he'd danced with Cora and his daddy hadn't succumbed to the darker power of drink yet. Maybe they'd keep Cora up at the house until the storm passed.

A bark erupted from Puck who then took off at a dash up the trail. Jeb followed, the lantern light casting a mixture of glow and shadow against the dark forest.

"It's Puck," came a familiar voice.

Isom? The lantern's light caught the silhouette of several figures ahead and, as Jeb grew closer, recognition grew. Cora held John close, while little Suzie shivered against Cora's side and Isom had wrapped James inside his own jacket.

Their clothes hung with dampness and the twins' lips quivered in the pale light. Cora's hair clung in wet ringlets to her face. Jeb held the lantern out to her and pulled Suzie into his arms, the little girl shivering against him. "Isom, run on to the house."

Isom pulled James tighter against him and took off. Cora stumbled at his side, but Jeb steadied her with his free hand.

She offered him a small smile, her face as pale as the rest, and his jaw tightened. He could only imagine what brought all of them here in such weather. With Cora holding the lantern and Jeb keeping a steadying arm at her back, they rushed toward the house.

Neither spoke as they made it inside and Jeb led the way to the fireplace.

"We need to get the wet clothes off of them," Cora said, already unbuttoning John's soaking wet coat. "Do you have extra blankets?"

"Aye." He started unbuttoning Suzie's coat, her little body shivering uncontrollably. The twins had been carried against Isom and Cora's body warmth, but not Suzie. He rubbed his palms over her arms and encouraged Isom to help James remove his coat. "There's chests in both rooms upstairs with more blankets and an extra nightshirt that'll work for Isom."

"Good." Cora shrugged off her coat, a man's coat, like the ones he'd seen at the Front. "I'll get Suzie settled in one bed, if you and Isom can get the boys into the other."

He nodded, moving from John, who stood in his damp nightshirt, over to James, as Isom took care of himself. "Get on up to the Maple Room, Isom. Got two quilts in the chest."

Isom nodded and ran toward the stairs.

"I fixed up a batch of ginger tea for y'all." Granny Burcham emerged from the kitchen. "I'll fetch a tray and take some upstairs."

"With honey?" Cora pulled Suzie into her arms, her underdress stuck with dampness to her little round body.

"Sure thing."

"Perfect." Cora moved around Jeb and up the steps. He followed close behind, James in one arm, John in the other.

She turned to Jeb as they parted ways, one to the left and one to the right. "Let's pray the chill doesn't take hold. That's what we must do now."

The boys' skin was so cold, Jeb crawled into the bed with them after they'd had a few sips of tea and let them cuddle up next to him, drawing from his warmth. Even Isom burrowed as close as he could to Jeb beneath the blankets. Something in the moment stilled him. It had been years since he'd rested like this, all cocooned together, and the sweetness of it rushed through him. The dark days called his daddy to the drink, but, by God's grace, Jeb didn't feel the need. At first, after he'd come home, he'd used liquor to get to sleep, but as the nightmares moved into blurry memory and his prayers grew louder than his fears, he'd found more peace without it.

Which was something his daddy had never known. Not really. Not to his soul. He offered up a silent prayer, encompassing his mama and the children and Cora. Who knew what was going through her mind at what she'd seen? With her thirst for justice, she was bound to invent some awful ideas as to why things were as they were, and the whole situation likely turned her off to any such love for these mountains or their people.

He pressed his eyes closed and prayed. Well, it felt akin to a prayer, but he didn't really know what words to say. But, if he'd learned anything from the last few years, God knew the words whether Jeb did or not.

In no time at all, the deep breaths of sleep alerted Jeb to the resting boys, so with careful movements, he slipped from the bed and took the last quilt from the trunk, in case Cora needed another. If she was even still awake.

With careful steps, he left the room and gently closed the door behind him. A lone lantern in the hallway answered his curiosity about the lovely flatlander. She stood by the window near the landing at the top of the stairs. It was his favorite window, large and pointing toward sunset, when sunset could be seen.

Her attention was focused somewhere in the distance, her hair partially wrangled into a braid at the side, her arms folded across her chest. She'd changed into a simple white blouse and brown skirt, and thick socks peeked from beneath the hem.

"How long has he been this way?" She didn't turn around, just kept staring out the window, and something about her stillness put him on guard.

"It started gettin' bad like this 'bout ten years ago, I reckon." He stepped closer.

"Ten years," she whispered, hugging her hands around her arms.

"It's why we moved further back up on the mountain. We used to live closer to the church and Mrs. Cappy's." Jeb stepped closer, taking the blanket and draping it over her shoulders. "The drunks started gettin' so bad, we moved farther away to keep folks from seein' 'em."

"He seemed so. . .so pleasant just a few days ago."

He stared out the window too, his own reflection looking back at him from the dark night. Cora's reflected face showed no emotion from what he could tell. "It's 'cause he don't stay drunk but during the dark days of winter. The rest of the time, he hardly takes a dram."

At this, she looked up. "He only stays drunk for three months out of the year? How is it even. . . I've never heard of something like that before."

"It's how some of the men in the mountain take to drink." Jeb pushed a hand through his hair before returning his gaze to hers. "It's a sickness, I can't rightly explain. Some darkness comes over him when winter hits. When the days get short, a wild desperation takes control."

"So he uses drink as medicine? To self-treat this—this sickness?"

"I've studied on it 'cause I feared I'd be like him." Jeb shook his head. "I thought the war would bring it out in me, but the more I get back into handcrafting and being with my people, the more I realize that sickness ain't in me. And I'm grateful. Maybe it's 'cause of his past or some other shadow that haunts him. I don't know."

"Why?" Her voice trembled. "Why does your mother stay?"

He should have expected this question from her. "Love, mostly."

"So she loves her violent husband over her own children?"

The accusation stung, and Jeb took a deep breath before answering. "She loves 'em both. Mama loves 'em all somethin' fierce, but I understand your thinkin'. After all, you're from a different world than—"

"Yes, from one where women living with atrocious men should take their children and flee."

He drew in another breath and stepped back. "And that's what happens where you live?"

Her gaze immediately faltered and she looked back out the window.

"Where would you expect her to go, Cora? A mountain woman with five young'uns?" He shrugged a shoulder. "It takes money to feed mouths, and none of us'll be beholden' to charity. Should she take 'em down to Rowen's for his special brand of care?"

She flinched, and his eyes withered closed with a sigh as he wrangled in his emotions.

"Before I come home from the war, Mama didn't have a whole lot of choices." He softened his voice, praying for words, for understanding. "This is the first winter I've been home since leaving for the war so *now* there's a safe place for the young'uns to be, but before that. . ." He shook his head. "Around here most folks barely have enough to feed their own families, let alone six or so more. Besides, Daddy saves up for his drunk. Cans meat. Chops firewood. Makes sure he takes care of as many things as he can before the darkness comes."

"He plans for it?"

"Every year since things got so bad," Jeb answered, a sting coming to his eyes at the thought. He remembered the quieter times, and watched his daddy's struggle. Almost felt empathetic pain as he thought about him. "And Mama stays for the man he is all the other months of the year. Because nine months out of the year, he's the man who makes folks laugh at get-togethers, and the husband and father who makes sure his family's stomachs are full. He's the husband who dances with Mama by the fireplace or tucks Suzie and the twins into bed with a tall tale." He cleared his throat and looked back outside, the darkness deeper. "I'm not excusin' him. He's broke bad. But he's also a man I'm proud to call my daddy because I've seen how hard he works and how much he loves his family and how hard he fights to stay away from the darkness."

Cora looked up at him with a watery glint in her eyes. "And she stays?"

"Because he needs her. She knows he does." The stinging in his eyes intensified. "He'd never survive without her, and, as crazy as it sounds, her life would be an awful lot harder without him."

"What sort of history could cause this type of brokenness?"

"First off, he don't have Jesus to help him, 'cause he thinks he ain't fit for God's heaven." Jeb swallowed through the tightening in his throat. "But his mama died when he was seven and then...then Granddaddy left him on the side of the road when my daddy was eight."

Cora drew in an audible breath.

"The only family that would take him in was run by a farmer who beat Daddy regularly, over the smallest offense. He beat him so bad that when Daddy was eleven, he ran off to town and started working in a furniture factory."

"Which thrust him into an adult world with adult influences."

"And no woman to tend his heart till he met Mama." Jeb shoved his hands into his pockets, remembering how Daddy told the story. How his whole face softened when he mentioned that during their first talk, he handed his heart right over to her.

She brushed back a tear escaping down her cheek and Jeb wondered if he'd ever seen anything more beautiful than Cora Taylor standing in lantern light crying over his daddy. "It's a horrible situation, but I can't find fault with your mother, because I've met her." Cora sniffled. "Though I wish I could because it would make the ache easier to bear and the horribleness of it more manageable."

"I'm glad to have my own place now." He pulled his attention from her face. "'Twill be easier for Mama and the young'uns, until..."

"Until he dies from his sickness?"

"Or God saves him." Jeb locked eyes with hers. "'Cause there ain't no way he's strong enough to fight his own darkness and win. I've watched him try. The only way beyond his sickness is God's rescue."

It seemed that Cora had barely closed her eyes to sleep when a resounding thud shook her awake. Suzie still slept at her side, rosy cheeks and deep breaths revealing the contented slumber of the young. Cora gently pushed to a sitting position and the thud resounded with frantic rhythm. What was happening? She blinked the window into view, the faint light of dawn barely showing the outline of trees. Was someone at the door?

Her eyes popped wide.

Someone was at the front door of Jeb's house in which she was currently sleeping. As was an unwed mother of a newborn. She jumped from the bed and wrapped one of the quilts around her shoulders as she rushed out the bedroom door in time to meet Jeb coming from the room across the hall. His nightshirt hung open at the neck and draped down to midcalf where it met a pair of tan breeches. Cora froze and pinched the quilt more tightly at her neck. His hair stood in all states of erratic, dark chest hair curled from his open collar, and his eyes blinked back at her, as if still waking up. The embarrassment of the intimacy in the moment was only curbed by the pale light shadowing a clear view of either one of them and another loud banging from the front door.

"Someone's at your door?"

Brilliant, Cora. State the most obvious thing to show your massive intelligence.

He stared at her, his expression taking on a strange look that somehow brought heat to her cheeks and then the door knocking came again, followed by the sound of a muffled young voice on the other side.

The noise shook him from his stupor and sent him down the stairs, with Cora close behind. She stopped at the bottom of the stairs and peeked around the corner of the wall for a view of the front door. As soon as Jeb opened the door, in rushed a boy, so bundled with cap and jacket, she couldn't sort out who he was until he pulled the wool cap from his head. Fig.

"You gotta come. Grandpa's real bad off." Fig pulled Jeb by the arm toward the door. "The iced rain felled a tree right into the cabin this mornin'. Landed on—" The boy's words broke off on a sob. "Grandpa."

Cora rounded the corner. "I'll be ready in five minutes."

Fig's attention landed on her, his pale eyes glittering with unshed tears and gripping Cora's heart. "Nurse Woman? You're here too." He sniffled. "Praise be."

She caught Jeb's stern look and glared back. "What does it matter if he knows I'm here when someone needs help, Jeb?"

He rolled his eyes heavenward, then approached her, towering so close she caught the faintest hint of that licorice smell again. "Can you ride?"

His question didn't fit with what she'd expected. "Y–yes."

"Astride?" His gaze searched hers. "Safer on the mountain trails."

She raised her chin, attempting to prove more confident than she felt. "Yes."

"Then take Hickory. He's familiar with the trails more than Milkie is." He stepped back and looked to Fig. "I'm gonna git my boots and coat so I can get Hickory saddled and ready. Fig, you're gonna ride with Nurse Woman so y'all can get back lickety-split."

"Th–thank you, Jeb."

He nodded to the boy and sent another look to Cora. "You're gonna need to get dressed for ridin'."

She looked down at her nightgown, and heat shot back into her face. "Yes, of course."

Granny Burcham rounded the doorway from the kitchen. "I've got some salves here for you, Cora-girl. I'll have Fig put 'em in your bag." She marched forward with a pitcher in hand. "Here's some water for washin' up so's you can git on yer way."

"Excellent. Thank you." She took the pitcher in the hand that wasn't clutching the quilt and rushed past Jeb up the stairs and found Suzie stirring awake. With quick work, she washed up, dressed, and brought Suzie downstairs. Isom and the twins met her in the kitchen.

"What about the children?"

"Caroline'll come git 'em when it's safe." Granny helped the twins onto the bench by the table. "She knows where they be."

Cora packed up her bag with the salves, her own medicines, and some gauze, her pulse hammering with the familiarity of this life, this purpose. Though she'd never expected to experience such dramatic needs in such a short amount of time in the mountains. And she'd never taken care of anyone hit by a tree. She wasn't even certain what to expect. She added extra bandages, freshly cleaned.

Fig already waited on Hickory by the time Cora made it to the barn. The horse snorted a welcome. Jeb moved to her side and took her bag. "The children are with Granny Burcham."

He nodded, set the bag on the ground, then braided his hands together to give her a boost onto the horse.

"Settle that bag betwixt the two of y'all." Jeb handed her the bag and she did as instructed. "I'm gonna follow behind you with the wagon so we'll have it in case we need to carry—" His gaze went to Fig then back to her. "In case we need it."

She nodded, taking the reins in hand.

Jeb stepped close, his palm resting against Hickory, his gaze searching hers in that breathtaking way of his. "Fig knows the way and you can trust Hickory to keep you on the path." He took a step back, still holding her attention, and then patted Hickory on the hindquarters. "Now, git on."

Chapter Seventeen

The world glistened as the dawn touched frozen leaves and frosted trees. Within five minutes, Cora missed the warmth of cuddling up next to Suzie in bed. The chill of the morning bled through her coat, absorbing any heat that may have come from the growing sunlight. Though Hickory's pace brought an added breeze to her cheeks, she appreciated the speed. The path that had taken her so long last night sped by on the back of the horse.

Last night? Had the McAdamses' house been just last night?

Jeb's explanation, his evident love for his family, even his father, flowed through each word. Cora knew all too well the trapped state of women, whether by cultural expectations or financial dependence, but Caroline McAdams proved a strange mixture of something she couldn't quite define. The woman wasn't weak by any stretch of the imagination. She ran her house with confidence and even joy. Nor was she so beaten down that she couldn't make her own decision. No, she didn't present either fault.

Cora had known men whose sickness drove them to respond badly or out of character. She cringed. She'd killed one. The "darkness" lived deep in some people, so deep, that as Jeb had said, only the light of Christ's love could reach them. And brokenness took all types of shapes and forms. No, perhaps she couldn't understand Caroline McAdams's choices, but neither could she fault her for them.

"Do you know where your grandpa is injured, Fig?"

He sniffled, as he'd been doing during the entire ride. "Mercy said it got him right in the middle."

"The tree?" Cora attempted to keep the horror from her voice.

"What the tree done to the house. The roof parts." He tried to turn to see her face, his hands going up as if to show her. "One of them big roof logs."

Cora nodded, envisioning the scene. "And did he talk to you at all?"

"Onct me and Mercy got him out from under the hole in the roof so the iced rain wouldn't keep fallin' on his head, he whispered some words none of us could hear, then he ain't talked since." Fig's bottom lip wobbled and he turned back to face the path. "Mercy says she'd want him to go on to God if'n it meant he wouldn't hurt long. We watched Granny hurt long and none of us wants that sort of dyin'."

Cora squeezed her eyes closed at the pain in his voice. So young, and what had this boy experienced? What was he yet to experience?

"I reckon ain't no cause for it now." Fig released a sigh too big for a boy his age. "Mercy'll have to marry Jeb if Grandpa dies, won't she?"

His words came so softly Cora couldn't have heard correctly. Jeb marry Mercy? Why?

She didn't have time to spend on those thoughts, because a cabin came into view.

The damage from the tree became obvious immediately. The center of the small cabin bent beneath the weight of the mass, splitting the house in half. The fact no one else had been injured proved a miracle, but if the roof was basically destroyed, where had the family taken Fergus and where were the rest of the Tates?

Cora slid from the horse and then helped Fig down. The boy ran toward the crippled house, so Cora tied Hickory to a nearby fence and followed. Part of the front porch pinched beneath the tree, lowering the porch roof so low, Cora couldn't enter what she presumed was the front door. Fig ran around the back of the house, where a corner of the house stood erect and relatively unscathed.

"I brung Nurse Woman," he shouted before shoving open the back door and entering. "Jeb's on the way too."

Cora held to the doorframe and took the large step into the house, or what was left of it. Daylight crept in from the gape in the ceiling, allowing cold air to run so freely, there was no temperature difference between outside and inside. The crushed remains of a bed, table, and some other pieces of furniture lay beneath rubble and tree, but golden light flickered from the dark, existing corner of the house.

A fire flickered in the hearth of an intact fireplace and a small group huddled around its warmth. Cora stepped closer, noting a body laid out upon the ground, a quilt covering Fergus Tate to the chin.

One of the figures rose and stepped forward so that daylight illuminated her face with more clarity. Dark hair tumbled, wavy and long over the shoulders of her simple green dress, framing an olive face and piercing green eyes. There was a mesmerizing, almost exotic, beauty about her and a grace in her movements Cora had only noticed in Caroline McAdams and Laurel.

Mercy Tate.

"Real glad you could come." She stepped closer. Her accent held a softness to it. "I've heard good things 'bout you."

"There are some kind people here." Which was true.

"Some bad ones too." She raised a brow and turned to lead the way back to the fireside. Mercy Tate held a calmness, a steadiness, about her, even in the way she spoke. Was that part of being Melungeon too? Or merely her character?

"We been trying to save the lantern light, since most of our other ones were destroyed by the tree." She lifted a lantern from the mantel. "You'll need more light, I reckon, but. . ." She paused and swallowed. "But I don't know there's much to be done."

If Fig's account proved true, Cora wondered the same. Internal bleeding. Broken bones. Who knew what else? "Well, I'll be happy to see if there is something I can do."

Mercy smiled, a gentle smile, and nodded. "Grandpa said you was the good sort, and I can tell 'tis true."

She lit the lantern and brought it close as Cora knelt by Fergus's still body. It wasn't until then that Cora noticed a smaller person standing close to Fig's side. A little boy. Mercy's son? Had Fergus called him David? No, Daniel. Cora smiled at the little one, likely only three years old or so, but he nudged closer to Fig.

As Cora reached to draw back the quilt, she stopped. A faint trail of blood slipped from Fergus's left nostril. Not a good sign. And then she listened. Over the quiet crackling of the fire, she caught sounds of his breathing. Shallow. Barely wisps. She knew that sound too well.

"You feel it too, don't ya?" Mercy lowered to her knees, frowning. "Felt it the same with Mama and Granny. It's close, ain't it?"

Cora touched Fergus's forehead. She wasn't sure why, but she needed that physical connection to him as the end drew close. Mercy seemed to recognize the same, because she reached beneath the blanket and took his hand in hers, then turned back to Fig.

"Come hold Grandpa's hand as he goes on."

Fig's bottom lip wobbled afresh and he looked to Cora. "Can't Nurse Woman do nothin' to keep him on this side?"

Cora offered her hand to the boy. How she wished she had such power. "I'm sorry, Fig. So sorry."

"You know, Fig, what we talked about with Granny." Mercy's soft voice rasped the slightest bit. People dealt with grief in so many different ways. Some wore their wounds better than others. Some sank beneath the pain, others soared. Mercy Tate was one of the latter.

So well, she had to pay close attention to the tiniest shift.

"God calls folks home on His time, and Grandpa was sure fit to get on to heaven, wun't he?"

The boy nodded, taking Cora's proffered hand and kneeling at her side. The younger of the boys shuffled over to Mercy and she took his little hand and pressed it between Fergus's and her own. Cora followed suit with Fig's.

"Grandpa sure liked talkin' of heaven," Fig whispered, staring down at the old, wrinkled hand wrapped around his own.

"Liked the idea of bein' able to sing," Mercy added, with a slight grin, even as tears invaded her eyes. "He ain't never been able to sing nary a note, and, he sure was lookin' forward to impressin' Granny."

The breathing shallowed even more. A slight trail of blood dripped from Fergus's ear. Cora's eyes dropped closed in prayer, for Fergus's passing, for this little family, for her own heart, because no matter how many times she watched death visit, it never left without pinching at her soul. Why this man? Why now? Why, when he had suffered so much, to die in such a brutal way?

But yet, she knew the "whys" bowed to an understanding that if God took one of His own from such a broken world, it was a greater mercy. A sweeter transition from a dark, cold, and only fleetingly joyful place, to a world of ever-sweet.

"What wondrous love is this, O my soul. O my soul." Mercy's voice broke into the silence, a haunting, simple sound, soft and clear. "What wondrous love is this, O my soul."

She closed her eyes and bent her head back, face heavenward, and Cora sat mesmerized, her hand and Fig's clasped within Fergus's on the floor of this dilapidated cabin.

"What wondrous love is this that caused the Lord of bliss, to bear the dreadful curse for my soul, for my soul. To bear the dreadful curse for my soul."

Tears invaded Cora's vision. What a song, much like these people. It sliced through the fluff and got directly to the heart. Christ bore the curse of pain, of brokenness—she looked down at Fergus's still face—of death, because of wondrous love.

"And when from death I'm free, I'll sing on. I'll sing on. And when from death I'm free, I'll sing on. And when from death I'm free, I'll sing and joyful be, and through eternity, I'll sing on. I'll sing on." Her voice caught and the final words emerged on a whisper. "And through eternity, I'll sing on."

The melancholy melody paired with such hopeful words shook through Cora with a powerful rightness. Sorrow twined with hope. Weeping mixed with joy. Life in this world with a glimpse of a better world. Heaven was the goal of God's people, the dazzling glory of eternal light, yet with eyes only fit for this world, its beauty seemed so far away. So distant, and a chasm crossed by grace and faith.

Yet, in those simple words, the Gospel rang with beautiful truth, and the chasm shrank. Fergus Tate would sing on. In fact, as the silence confirmed Fergus's passing, perhaps he sang even now, more alive than he'd ever been while trapped in humanity. He was truly whole and home.

Fig seemed to know, because he turned into Cora's chest and buried his face against her, his little body shaking with his tears. Cora wrapped her arms around him and looked at Mercy, who stared down at her Grandpa as tears slipped, silently, down her cheeks.

Cora had witnessed dozens of deaths. Many tragic, like this, but rarely had she felt the presence of God so near, so close, as here and now.

The sound of wagon wheels sounded from beyond the walls of the house.

"That is likely Jeb," Cora whispered.

Mercy stood, bringing Daniel along with her to sit on her hip, and Cora followed, giving another glance around the room. How long had Mercy and the boys huddled by the fire to stay warm through the night? When Fig had mentioned morning, had it still been dark out?

One bed stood in the corner, unscathed, which must have been where Mercy and Daniel slept. A lone chair remained, but there was no evidence of a cookstove, hutch, or dresser, unless those lay in the same heap as Fergus's bed and the kitchen table.

Cora met Jeb at the back door. With one look, understanding dawned on his face and he sighed and lowered his head. Uncle Edward followed close behind, his riding coat and hat in place.

Jeb entered the house and walked toward the Tates while Uncle Edward paused. "I got your note and went directly to Jeb's this morning." His arm came up around Cora's shoulders and he tugged her close. "You've had a busy week."

Her eyes burned anew but she refused another display. "Indeed, I have."

"Jeb said you've done remarkably." He pressed a kiss to her head. "I was wrong to worry. You have your mother's clear-headedness and strength, thank God." He gave another squeeze to her shoulders and stepped back, looking at the remains of the house and finally fixing his attention on Fergus's body.

Removing his hat, he stepped forward, years of these moments a part of his story. Years in these mountains, bringing comfort and hope. Though she'd have never imagined such a simple existence as full enough to last a lifetime, the past week had proved to brim over. Painful, horrible. Her gaze landed on Jeb. Sweet and good. Then she looked to Fergus. Tragic, yet. . .tender.

"I don't need a wake," Mercy said to some question of Uncle Edward's. "We don't have folks who'd likely come this far and no house fittin' to give it proper." She looked around the room. "As long as he's got a Christian burial on his land, Preacher, I reckon that's all he'd want."

Uncle Edward nodded and looked to Jeb, some silent understanding passing between them, before Uncle spoke again. "If that is your wish, Mercy, then Jeb and I shall tend to the grave, if you'll choose a spot."

She bowed her head in assent.

"I want to help with the diggin'," Fig said, standing tall, his expression grave.

"That'd be good." Jeb placed his hand on the boy's shoulder.

"Your grandpa would like it."

The boy seemed to age before Cora's eyes, taking on the death with a solemnity beyond his years.

"We'll need to sort out where you'll go after the burial." Uncle Edward looked up at the hole in the ceiling and then turned back to Mercy. "This is no place for you and the boys to stay in winter, Mercy."

Cora met Jeb's gaze and he must have read her thoughts, because his eyebrows rose in unison. She nodded, as if he'd asked her a question aloud. With a slump to his shoulders, he turned to Mercy.

"We got room at my house." The words emerged slow and stiff. "There's an empty room upstairs that'd be just for the three of you and your things, if you're willin'?"

"Jeb." Mercy looked from Cora to Jeb. "What would folks think if they knew I was stayin' in your house?"

Jeb shrugged a shoulder and shook his head. "To tell you true, Mercy, if folks ain't talkin' by now, then you don't have nothin' to worry about."

She shot a quizzical look to Cora, who hoped she smiled in response, and then Mercy's grin bloomed again. "Just till we find a new place is all." She stepped close to Jeb and touched his arm, her look softening. "Thank you, Jeb. You're always so kind."

Something pinched in Cora's middle.

Oh dear. Mercy Tate was a single mother, who'd recently lost her livelihood and home. One sure way to find stability for her future was to marry, and from the look Mercy fastened on Jeb, she already had her choice.

Cora had stayed much too quiet for the Englishwoman he'd come to know. From the wagon ride home to helping Mercy and the boys get settled in his house, Cora not only had grown quieter, but somehow distant. Had Fergus's death grieved her to such a depth? Were the miseries of mountain life finally taking a toll? He had no time to sort it out, because no sooner had they gotten back from the Tate cabin and unloaded a wagonload of Mercy's things, than Paul Russell showed up with Elias Harris much too early on a Sunday morning for any visitors.

And Jeb had forgotten all about the meeting in the wake of his siblings staying the night and Fergus's death. Granny Burcham told them Jeb's mama had come to collect the young'uns round dinnertime, so Mama must have felt Daddy had calmed down a bit for now, so at least there were four less people under his roof, but he'd replaced those with three more.

It was the right thing to do, but, Lord have mercy, he didn't even recognize his life from a week ago. Elias didn't help. He kept grinning and occasionally bursting out into laughter for no apparent reason, but Jeb felt the reason all the way to his boots. Jeb's house had turned into a home for unwed mothers and orphaned young'uns, with Granny Burcham and Cora Taylor keepin' watch.

Though Cora wasn't near as bossy as she should have been with such a houseful of needy folks.

While Willow and Paul made eyes at each other and Paul took to bein' a father like the good man he was, Granny Burcham offered everyone stack cake and sun tea, effectively turning Jeb's house into a get-together place. He squeezed his eyes closed and just accepted his life. What else could he do? 'Twas a good thing he had a job or two.

Then something unexpected happened. Mercy had kept to upstairs when Paul and Elias first arrived, tending to all her personal belongings with Cora's help. But then Mercy had walked down the stairs and Elias Harris stopped talking in midsentence just to stare at the woman. He didn't even care that his tea was about to spill right out of his cup. Mercy didn't seem to notice Elias's gawking at her. Likely her head was too full of her new grief, but nobody else in the room could git by without seeing the man was 'bout as dumbstruck as a body could be.

Jeb bit down on the inside of his cheeks to keep from laughing.

And over Mercy Tate.

How come it had never occurred to Jeb to introduce the two before? Didn't matter that Elias didn't seem interested in remarrying after becoming a widower five years before. Didn't matter that Mercy stayed as deep in the mountains as a body could, so Elias had only heard tales about her but never seen her.

What mattered was right now, and, well, if Jeb had been much on matchmaking, he'd have taken to matching the two of them like bees to spring flowers. His thoughts turned to where Cora sat holding Willow's baby as Paul and Willow enjoyed a private meal in the kitchen so they could discuss future things. Cora Taylor. She'd been through so much in her short time in Maple Springs. Any sound person would likely run off, but thanks to her stubborn streak and some sort of crazy love for. . .crazy, she fell right into the world here. Didn't make sense to Jeb, but who was he to argue with God's plans and all.

As Mercy spoke with Cora and Granny Burcham about the baby, who still needed a name, Daniel attempted to "sneak" around the room and surprise the grown-ups. He was a real pretty boy, if boys could be pretty, with dark curly hair like Amos but his Mama's wild green eyes. He squeezed behind where his Mama sat, then crawled past Preacher, his double-dimpled grin at full tilt, and then he tried to sneak around Elias, but tripped.

Evidently Elias had been watching the boy's antics too, 'cause he easily slipped an arm beneath Daniel to keep him from hitting the wood floor, then, with the practice of a father, he swung the boy up on his shoulder to the sound of Daniel's giggles.

A welcome sound after such a morning, and it was, still morning. Early. Barely ten. The laughter was a reminder of joy and life and the next generation.

That was when Mercy finally took a good gander at the tall mill owner, and Jeb had a front-row view. He'd heard about love at first sight, and never put much mind to the notion, but if a look could tell a feeling as big as love, then he was witnessing all kinds of sparkin' going on.

From the glint in Elias's eyes as he stared back, Jeb felt pretty sure Elias was dealing with his own lip itchin'.

"Cora and I are going to return home to get ready for church, Jeb." Preacher stood from beside Jeb and gestured toward Cora. "Seems you've got enough women here now to keep the mountain rumor mill fed for weeks, so I don't want to add a tardy preacher and his single niece to the list."

Jeb groaned and stood, taking Preacher's hand. "The only mill I'm interested in being a part of is Elias's."

"I know you couldn't have foreseen all of this and, well. . ." Preacher sighed. "If you were a married man, no one would have much of a problem with you taking mountain folks in, but being a single man puts your reputation in all sorts of danger."

"And Cora's too," Jeb whispered, looking across the room as she handed the baby over to Mercy and stood. "I don't care much for mine, but I ain't keen on hers gettin' sullied. You know that can't be good for her in these parts."

"I know." Preacher shot Cora a look and grinned. "But I'm beginning to realize she is much more resilient and capable than I gave her credit for when she first arrived."

"She is that." He hoped his stare didn't resemble Elias's to Mercy. To make sure he kept his focus away from the distracting English brunette, he walked with Preacher to the hooks by the door where Preacher and Cora had placed their coats.

Jeb helped her with her coat, breathing in her scent.

"I plan to stop by Laurel and Jonathan's house on my way home from church," she said. "To see if everything is still in order during their absence."

"I've checked on it a few times. Fed the chickens. Milked the cow," Jeb offered.

She turned toward him and started buttoning her coat, her

smile spreading to add a glimmer to those fascinating eyes of hers. Sure 'nough, he probably looked just like Elias had a few minutes ago. Maybe even worse.

"Can you bake biscuits too? Make stack cake?' Her grin grew. "You better be careful, or no mountain girl will think you need her as a wife."

"If I was thinkin' in the wifely direction, Miss Taylor, her stack cake makin' wouldn't be at the top of my list." He shrugged a shoulder and continued staring like a loon. "Though, I wouldn't complain none if she was good at makin' 'em."

Cora's attention flickered behind him and Jeb suddenly realized when her odd behavior started. Maybe grief didn't have so much to do with Cora's quietness as did Mercy Tate.

A warmth swelled up through his chest and caused him to stand just a bit taller. Was there a chance Cora Taylor sparked him just enough to be jealous of Mercy?

"Preacher, afore you go," Willow called from the doorway of the kitchen, "Paul's got a question for ya."

Everyone turned to the young couple. Paul supported Willow as she stood at his side, the two of them smiling like they'd won the biggest hog in the Flat Creek fair.

"What is your question, Paul?"

The young man looked down at Willow, shuffled a little, and then raised his attention back to Preacher. "We was wonderin' when you would do the honor of marryin' us, Preacher."

Elias's big laugh resounded through the room.

"I'd be happy to fulfill that wish. Are the two of you free to wed?"

They looked at each other and then back, Paul gesturing toward Willow for an answer. "I don't know if'n I'm beholden to Mr. Hawes down at the hotel or not, but. . .but I can't go back there."

"You won't," Paul interrupted, turning back to the room. "There ain't no reason for her to go back to that place, is there?"

Preacher exchanged a look with Jeb, who'd filled the man in on the real reason Willow had been at Rowen's hotel in the first place.

"Based on the circumstances of the situation, I would say Willow need not adhere to the manipulative agreement of her brother any longer." He placed his hat on his head, his grin crinkling at his eyes. "If the two of you can be ready to marry by next Saturday, I will happily perform the wedding. . .here?" He looked to Jeb.

"That would be fine, Preacher."

"And we'll have train tickets to leave town right after," Paul added. "I'm anxious to get Willow as far from Flat Creek and Maple Springs as I can."

"Very good." Preacher brought his hands together and stepped back toward the door. "I look forward to the festivities on Saturday, then. A good ending to a situation which could have become much worse. Praise be to God."

"For truth," Paul shouted. He took Willow into his arms, giving her a sweet kiss on the cheek before helping her return to one of the nearby chairs.

The room responded with similar jollifications, and before Jeb could even bid Cora a good night, she took her uncle's arm and followed him out the door.

As she stepped from the house, her bag in hand, she looked back over her shoulder. Their gazes held for a few seconds as the door closed, and Jeb knew, sure as shootin', he was ready to take all this lip itchin' and put it into action.

Chapter Eighteen

Cora nestled into the wingback chair in front of her Uncle Edward's fire, a cup of tea warming the palms of her hands as she breathed out the tension of the past few days. Her mind and body thrived off the service these mountain people required, even the hardest parts, but the frantic pacing of the last few days finally hit. How would she usher up enough energy to make it through a church service?

"Are you missing the activity of Jeb's house?" Uncle Edward took a seat in the matching chair across from her, his smile soft and teasing.

"At the moment, I'm basking in complete inactivity." She sighed and took a sip of her tea. "Even if it's going to end when we ride to church in a little while."

He chuckled. "I have a feeling you are not satisfied with inactivity for very long."

"When I discovered how fulfilling service can truly be while at the London hospital, it changed everything for me. It wasn't that I doubted God had a purpose for me, but it was as if my mind and my soul had been craving the usefulness and challenges the hospital introduced." Cora brought her cup down to her lap. "I believe I needed to serve them as much as they needed my service."

"I'll not place a sheen on life here." He stirred his tea and offered her a measured look. "You've seen enough to know this place is hard and the people, at times, even harder."

"It is, more than I imagined." She looked back into the fire, her thoughts pausing on the bittersweetness of Fergus's death as Mercy sang. "But there is strength and beauty too. At first, I was so appalled by so many things, I refused to see those."

"I've always said that these mountains either call your heart or repel you." He grinned. "There is no in between. Your soul is either made for the work of these mountains, or it is not. I knew within a few months that I was meant to be a part of this place and these people." He shook his head and chuckled. "Though they fought against me on so many fronts at first. I was a stranger, spoke funny." He winked. "And brought a different view of Christianity than they'd ever heard with their strange mixture of Calvinism and humanism and superstition."

"I saw true faith today at the Tates', but in such an unconventional way. Through a song Mercy sang." Cora swallowed as her throat tightened at the bittersweet memory. "And that's how this place has seemed on all fronts to me. Unconventional. Surprising. Hard. Broken." She blinked as tears invaded her eyes. "Yet, I—I want to be here."

"It's a hard calling." His gaze softened with his smile. "But the most fulfilling ones usually are."

As Cora got ready for church in her little loft space, her prayers flooded in a wild mixture of comfort for the Tates, gratitude for her uncle, direction for Willow and Paul, and then, as her thoughts went to Jeb, she tried very hard not to pray unkind things against his connection with Mercy. After all, if God had thought Cora strong enough to call her to the Blue Ridge Mountains, surely He knew she was strong enough to handle whatever disaster might happen to her heart too.

Maybe.

What a strange thing to have a man she'd known for such a short time take up so much space in her heart. She couldn't seem to help it. Somehow, since the very first, she'd felt a connection to him, a shared understanding, and then, the little thoughts about his gentleness and subtle humor grew into big thoughts. . .which then settled deeper and sweeter.

She peeked toward the window, the sun brightening the sky with much-needed warmth. "But I'd be perfectly content if You didn't make a disaster for my heart, Lord. In case You were wondering."

The noonday church service came with its own sense of partially fitting in and also standing out. Before Cora even made it inside the church, Coon Roberts brought his daughter forward for Cora to check on her burn, then Eliza Lewis asked for Cora to take a look at her eyes, which were riddled with trachoma, a condition Jonathan had written to Cora about over the past few months. Cora had researched the condition a little, and encouraged the girl to increase her facial cleaning to twice a day and try to keep her hands away from her eyes, if possible. She told Eliza that Jonathan would be home soon and would give further instruction, but in the meantime, Cora truly needed to delve into more research. As she looked around the church, she noted many more with the same condition. Oh, what a little hygiene education could do for the people here!

Mr. Roberts had left three jars of canned venison and a small basket of various dried fruit as payment for Cora's services she'd given to his daughter. Another family she'd helped by stitching up a gash in their son's head brought a winter rosebush to her that they'd dug up because "English folks likes gardens, from what we hear tell from Preacher." Cora also had a delightful conversation with Mrs. Cappy, who sat next to her on the women's side of the church. By the beginning of the service, Mrs. Cappy had promised to order Cora additional soap and rubbing alcohol. All in all, a very good start to the day. Cora still had to adjust to the boisterous singing style of the hymns, but was grateful that with the colder weather, the body odor around her was considerably reduced. Or perhaps she'd begun to see the people more than the annoyances, and it changed her focus.

The McAdamses weren't at church, an absence Cora would ask Jeb about when she saw him next. Were they safe? Had Sam experienced another fit?

Uncle Edward preached a wonderful sermon about how sin separates people from God and leads to eternal downfall. He encouraged them to be a light to those within and without their community who needed guidance toward Christ's salvation. And, as Uncle Edward added, "Sometimes it's gentle ways the Lord uses to usher people into His kingdom. Other times, for those of us who are particularly muleheaded, as you folks would say, or hard-hearted, as the Good Book describes, God may use trials to bring the truth of our need for Him to the forefront of our minds."

Cora offered up a silent prayer for Sam McAdams. If he'd turned from God for so long, after having such a God-fearing wife and family, then he must be one of the most muleheaded men in Maple Springs. Cora's shoulders sagged. She knew what muleheaded was like on a personal level, and God had used war, her own father's drunkenness, and the threat of marrying a horrible man to push Cora into finding His way.

Lord, if the only way to save Sam McAdams is to break his hard heart, then, Lord, break his heart to save his soul. Whatever it takes. For his good, as well as his family's.

As the congregation stood to sing the final hymn, a commotion erupted just behind Cora.

"Preacher, I got some words that need to be told."

Imogene Carter. A woman Cora knew very little about, but by all accounts was the local gossip and an all-around unpleasant person. Wasn't she related to the Greers in some way? Had Granny Burcham said that Imogene was Merla Greer's sister?

Uncle Edward stiffened. "Mrs. Carter, is this something that needs to be discussed in church or can it wait for a private conversation?"

"All folks here need to know it, Preacher. 'Cause it will keep them from fallin' into the sin you was just speakin' 'bout."

Uncle Edward attempted to interrupt her again, but Mrs. Carter's voice boomed through the room, echoing off the rafters with more "wind," as the folks here might call it, than even Cora's uncle.

"Preacher's words were true today, speakin' of how sin leads to the downfall of a soul." She raised a finger in the air, her volume growing. "And it corrupts those who tolerate it livin' amongst us."

Mrs. Carter took a detour, away from the heart of Uncle Edward's sermon.

"There's one amongst us that's carryin' sin and sickenin' those who dare listen to her words."

Her? Who? Cora looked to the ladies around her, who seemed to be wondering the same thing.

"'Tis known throughout most of the mountain that Jeb McAdams has been keepin' kept women at his place and pretendin' to be a man of God, but seems his sinnin' ways was brought in from the outside, as most sinful ways are."

A chill spread through her body in preparation. Oh no! What was Imogene Carter doing?

"Mrs. Carter, that is quite eno—"

She completely ignored Uncle Edward.

"I seen the woman who he kept in his very house for the whole world to know about. Unashamed of his sin. Though I didn't know who she 'twas at the time, I recollected her clothes and shoes today when she walked into the church."

Imogene's gaze bored into Cora.

"That woman who's been treatin' our young'uns. The one you called Nurse Woman." She pointed her bony finger directly at Cora. "She's the kept woman. She's the one livin' in sin."

Cora froze for a full five seconds and then heat soared through her body, shooting her to a stand. How dare this woman falsely accuse her when she knew nothing about the situation?

"I can assure you, Mrs. Carter, I am no such thing."

"And then I seen her comin' and goin' from Jeb McAdams's house like they was married and all." Her wicked smile curled at the edges like some evil doll's. "But ain't no marriage took place as I know of. So what would you call it? Her spendin' the night at his house."

A gasp waved through the crowd.

"The night in question was when I helped take care of—" Did folks know of Sam McAdams's behavior? Cora paused. Surely, she wouldn't be the one to wound the family by announcing his struggle. They needed to be the ones to do so. "A local family whose children needed a place to stay from the ice storm."

"Mrs. Carter, I think it's time we dismiss from the church—"

"Which family, so we can go and ask 'em? 'Cause we'd trust them over the likes of you. Besides, you been there for more than one day. I seen you, carryin' in another'n of your kept women, 'cause I reckon one wasn't enough for Jeb McAdams."

Murmurs rose around her, and Cora fisted her hands at her sides. "I've only done things to help the people here, with no reason for your slander, Mrs. Carter." She stood taller. "As to the other woman, who was wounded, I was helping take care—" Cora caught sight of Merla Greer only a few pews away, her terrified expression halting Cora's confession. If she told the truth of who the woman was, the whole mountain, and any of the men who beat Willow, would know exactly where to find her. Cora forced her lips closed. She had to bear the brunt of this false accusation or put Willow in danger of being discovered before she and Paul could leave town. After years of fighting to be heard, every justice-focused bone in her body fought to clear her name.

But for Willow's sake, she couldn't.

"We are finished here," Uncle Edward announced. "This conversation is not leading in a direction that will glorify God or help this community."

"You'll protect her 'cause you're family. Just like you'll protect that nephew of yourn who taught devil's magic in the schoolhouse last year. All y'all are bringin' sin to us."

"Imogene, Teacher's been real good to folks here. Helped folks, taught good things," came a quick response from one of the men on the other side of the room. "We ain't got no cause with him nor Preacher. Both have proved true."

Cora didn't wait for more. Lengthening the torture would only make things worse. Grabbing her bag and rosebush, she walked from the church with her head high, sending her uncle a reassuring look before she left. Her gaze lifted heavenward as she marched down the church's path to the forest trail. Just as she'd accepted this crazy life, God had allowed that! She gestured back toward the church as if He were staring down at her from His heavenly throne. False accusations and no way to defend herself without hurting others!

She breathed out a sigh. What had her mother always said? The truth comes out, perhaps not as soon as we wish, but eventually. Well, she hoped much sooner than later, because if the people of Maple Springs took Imogene's slander to heart, Cora wouldn't have anyone to nurse, because they'd refuse to come to her.

Though the breeze blew cool, the late autumn sky shone with its remarkable azure blue, allowing sunshine to bathe her with a little warmth as she moved up the path. She'd only gone a short way when she noticed a figure up ahead running toward her. A girl, from the flow of her pale pink dress.

Cora slowed her pace and shielded her eyes from the sun to get a better look. Was that. . .Maggie McAdams? Cora picked up her pace to reach the girl more quickly.

"Miss Cora," Maggie gasped between breaths, her gaze frantic. "Mama said I might find you at church."

Caroline sent Maggie to find Cora? Something was definitely wrong.

"I'm just on my way from there." She placed her hands on Maggie's shoulders, searching her face. "What is it, Maggie? What's wrong?"

"Mama thought 'twas nothin' at first, but last night Suzie got real bad off. Mama says it's the croup." Maggie shook her head, her soft golden braids wiping back and forth. "And—and ain't nothin' helpin'." Her voice cracked and she turned back toward the way she'd come, pulling Cora along. "Granny Burcham's been by, but Mama thought to ask you too."

A rush of dread spilled through Cora and pushed her into a faster walk. If Granny Burcham had already seen Suzie, and Caroline was still concerned enough to send for Cora, it didn't bode well for Suzie's symptoms. How had she gotten it?

And then the memory of their walk from the McAdams cabin in the icy rain solidified the answer.

"What about your brothers?"

"They ain't showed no signs of it." Maggie kept her face forward. "Just Suzie."

Croup, what did she know about croup? She had a cousin who lived with her family for a while and she'd developed croup, but all Cora could remember from that incident was the barking cough and a sterile hospital surrounded by a whitewashed world. Nothing like what she'd find at the McAdamses'.

"And it started the day after the ice storm?"

"But wasn't much of anything at first. Mama thought 'twas a cold till the fever started."

Most of the rest of the walk progressed in silence until the little McAdams cabin came into view. The smell of burnt wood still lingered in the air, but a few winter roses vined up one side of the log cabin, softening the aged look to something more quaint. Cora scanned the surrounding forest, almost expecting a wild-eyed Sam McAdams to emerge from the thicket with rifle in hand, but everything remained eerily still, like the calm after a storm.

The first thing Cora noticed was that one of the front windows stood open with a white curtain blowing in the gentle breeze. True, the temperature proved unseasonably warm only a few days after the ice storm, but the air still held a chill.

Maggie led the way inside the front room with its lower lighting, except for the fire.

"You're here." Caroline came forward from the little bed in the corner, her eyes weary with dark shadows beneath. She took Cora's hands in her own. "Thank you."

"Of course." Cora squeezed her fingers. "I'll try to help in any way I can."

"I know you will." Caroline nodded, her eyes glossy for a second before she turned and led Cora to the bed.

A sound erupted from the body that was covered in quilts, a horrible cough, like a barking sound, followed quickly by a rasped breath. Wheezing. Cora's chest tightened at the noise. She'd heard similar sounds from soldiers after being exposed to gas. Dying breaths.

Oh, Lord. Please don't let this be the same.

Pots of steaming water sat along one side of the bed, evaporating into the air beside little Suzie. Or a frail semblance of the little girl who'd slept in Cora's arms only a few nights before.

Her pale face flushed bright pink, a stark comparison with her gold locks, and her rosebud mouth held a pale hue. Not quite blue yet, but not healthy.

"When did the cough start?"

"Night before yester eve." Caroline sat on the bed to smooth Suzie's hair as she coughed again. "The first night 'twasn't so bad, but then she kept gettin' worse and worse until last night. Then she'd only take a few spells to rest afore she'd start coughing again."

Cora dipped her hand into her bag, thankful she'd had the sense to purchase a stethoscope and a few other items before making her trek across the ocean. She stepped close and looked down into Suzie's bright eyes.

"Hello, darling." Caroline stood so Cora could take her place. "I'm so sorry you're sick."

"My froat hurts." Suzie's voice emerged strained and hoarse.

"I'm sure it does, from all that coughing you're doing." Cora forced a smile to hide her concern. "I'm going to listen to what your breathing sounds like, which means I need to raise your dress just a little and place this over your lungs." She brought Suzie's little hand up to touch the chestpiece of the instrument. "Is that alright with you?"

The little girl attempted a smile, and Cora almost lost control of her emotions right then and there. With a deep breath, she moved some sort of poultice from Suzie's chest and listened to her breathing as she lay still. Some stridor, but not as much as she'd expected from the severity of the cough, so perhaps the infection was higher in the airway than the lungs. Her skin burned hot though. Much too hot.

Upon request, Caroline brought a lantern nearer, and Cora asked Suzie to open her mouth and say "ah." Even in the dim light, Suzie's throat looked red and swollen. So, whatever was causing her breathing obstruction appeared to happen above the lungs but just beyond the back of the throat, directly where the airway started.

"I heard your heart beating loud and strong." Cora tapped Suzie's nose, and the little girl attempted a responsive grin before dissolving into coughs again. Cora made out a slight indentation between the ribs as she breathed. Not good. It meant her struggle to breathe was becoming more effortful.

"What have you and Granny Burcham tried already?"

Caroline pushed back a stray hair and blinked as if trying to wake up. "Well, we gave her some clover blossom tea with honey. Then some ginger tea with a bit of peppermint." She waved toward the cloth on Suzie's chest. "And that onion poultice to ease the cough, but I don't see as it's worked."

Cora gave Suzie's hand a little squeeze and then stood, lowering her voice as she stepped closer to Caroline. "I've never treated croup before, but I have a few ideas that may help."

"I'll do anything to save my young'un," Caroline raised her chin, ready for the fight.

"It doesn't seem the infection is in her lungs, but her throat, so the poultice isn't likely helping, as you've gathered already."

Caroline's lips tipped in the smallest smile. "Well, I'll git rid of it directly, 'cause none of us is too keen on the smell."

Cora's smile flamed wide for a second at the woman's attempt to add levity. "Unless fried with beef."

"Mmm hmm." Caroline's tired gaze softened, tears reemerging in her pale eyes.

"Infections have a tendency to cause swelling, and if the swelling is in her throat, then it's going to make breathing harder."

Caroline nodded, understanding.

"If you could get some cold water from your springhouse, and even some ice, we could let the cold water go down her throat to help ease the infection a little, I hope."

Caroline turned to Maggie who had been listening and, with nothing more than a nod, Maggie ran out the door.

"And we need to close the windows and close off this room, if we can. Or move Suzie to a room we can close off as much as possible." Cora waved toward the room. "The more steam we can have filling the air, the more she will breathe it in."

Caroline went to the window and closed it without a word, then waited for the next instruction.

"And tonight, I wonder if we can try and give her a tea that will relax her, because the more anxious she becomes, the more difficult it will likely be to breathe."

"Got some lavender," came Caroline's quick reply.

"It may do good to add some cool cloths to her head also."

"We'll do whatever you say, Cora."

Cora smiled at the sweet woman and then turned back to Suzie, gaze taking in the small girl as the sound of her wheezing filled the room. "And we'll pray. . .and wait."

"And pray some more," Caroline added.

"Yes, and pray some more."

Chapter Nineteen

Jeb sat out on the porch steps in no hurry to return to a house full of women. He breathed in the cool mountain air and welcomed the peaceful familiarity of the night noises. An owl in the distance. The rush of residual leaves in the wind.

He leaned back against the porch post. Had Cora Taylor cared enough about him to be jealous? He smiled up into the starry night.

"Well, well, that grin's wide enough to mean you're up to somethin', I'd say."

Jeb looked up to see Mercy stepping from the house, a blanket wrapped around her shoulders.

"Just enjoyin' the night."

"Likely the quiet, if I know you." She took a seat beside him on the porch and allowed the stillness to pass between them.

They'd known each other their whole lives. Gone to school together, as long as Mercy had attended. Met at corn shuckin's and apple harvests Mercy felt comfortable attending. They both understood this world.

"Thank you for letting us stay here."

He leaned forward, resting his elbows on his knees. "I told you six months ago that I'd take care of you."

"I recall you asked if we ought to consider gettin' married too."

Long before he'd met a flatlander from England. "And you said you needed to study on it a bit."

"I did." She leaned her head back against the post and stared up into the sky. "And I have."

Stars winked down at them, bright and sprinkled all across the skyline. Jeb held his breath, waiting.

"But I don't reckon it's a good thing to marry a man who's spar-kin' somebody else."

He groaned and hung his head. "That clear, is it?"

"As spring water."

He looked over at her. "I'm sorry, Mercy."

"Jeb McAdams, you know the only reason you even courted the idea of marriage with me was because you thought Amos would want it." She rolled her eyes before staring back at him. "But you're wrong. Amos would have wanted us both to find somebody to love forever, if we could. This life's hard enough without adding on regrets when we can help it."

He studied her a moment and nodded. "Amos would have wanted that for true."

She hugged her knees close, looking as much like a little girl as she had back in their school days. Law, Amos had sparked her for right near a decade before getting brave enough to court her. Just before the war.

Time had a strange way of stealing and giving, and there wasn't a way to predict which way it would go. Only God knew. And there was comfort in that.

Jeb sighed and then reached into his pocket. "I have something for you. From Amos."

Her lips wrinkled into a confused frown as she took the small box from Jeb and opened it. She gasped as moonlight and lantern light glinted off the simple little ring.

"He bought it in France. Wanted to bring it back to you. I'd placed it in his house with most of his other things and forgot about it. I'm sorry."

"I ain't never seen nothin' as beautiful in all my days." She smiled up at him. "It's like he caught starlight and put in on this here ring."

"Amos would want us both to marry someone we love, especially you, when your heart is healed, but at least you can have a part of him with that gift."

She carefully took the ring from the box and slid it onto her finger, staring down at it with such wonder on her face, Jeb couldn't help but smile. With a sigh, she turned to him. "Amos is always going to have a sweet place in my heart. He gave me Daniel. And I'm real glad to have this treasure from him." She looked back up at the sky. "But today's reminded me all the more how valuable life is and. . .and I want to try again. I think I'm ready to try." She looked back at him, one brow raised and a teasing glint in her eyes. "Love's worth being brave, ain't it? Brave again and again and again."

Jeb's attention moved to the trail that led down to Preacher's cabin and nodded.

Love certainly was worth being brave. . .with a little bit of crazy thrown in.

Jeb drove Hickory harder up the trail through the early morning light, prayers and possibilities pouring through his mind. Preacher had found him just waking up in his workshop before dawn, the man almost desperate. Cora hadn't come home last night. At that moment, Jeb felt as if someone had punched him hard in the stomach.

Not come home?

Preacher assumed Cora had stayed at Jeb's house, but she'd never come back there either.

The story got worse when Preacher relayed what had happened at church with Imogene Carter, which kept him at the church much longer than he'd anticipated. Folks had questions and concerns. Some wanted to know more about Cora's coming to the mountains. Others swore they'd never let the "Nurse Woman's" sinful hands touch anyone in their family.

After all of the attempted peacekeeping, Preacher hadn't gotten back to his cabin until nightfall, and just thought Cora had stayed at Jeb's to tend to Willow. Had some of the same men who'd attacked Willow come after Cora?

With quick work, Preacher and Jeb decided to part ways with Preacher riding out to Jonathan and Laurel's house to see if she'd stayed there and Jeb heading to his parents'.

With Cora's talent for getting lost, although she'd gotten better over the past week, he hoped his instincts proved right. He caught sight of the burned corn crib at the back of the house as he brought Hickory to a stop near the porch. It was the first time Daddy had succeeded in burning down an entire building, though he'd attempted it a few times before.

Butter greeted him on the porch, the greyhound dancing around with excitement as if all was well with the world, but when Jeb knocked on the door, the look on his mother's face showed that all was not well. He'd seen his mama tired or worried, but the tightness around her eyes gripped him more than her unkempt dress. Without a word, he pulled her into his arms, and, to his surprise, she let him.

His mama wasn't one for a great show of physical affection, though she poured love into most all she did, but as she rested against him for the briefest embrace, he knew the situation boded much worse than even Granny Burcham described.

She pulled back almost as soon as she'd hugged him and ran a hand through her hair, which fell halfway loose from her bun.

"Come on in." She ushered him into the room, and he immediately heard the strident breathing from the corner. He'd heard similar sounds only on the battlefield. With the dying.

He shifted farther into the house, forcing one foot forward then the other, and then he saw her. Cora, bent low over Suzie, giving her a drink of something. He sighed out a breath he didn't even realize he'd held. At least Cora was safe and found.

He almost smiled. And doing what she loved to do.

"She's good at doctorin', I tell you that," Mama whispered by his side. "She even stayed up with Suzie so I could get in a little sleep, since it seemed I was fallin' asleep nearly standin' up."

"How bad is it?"

"Ain't improvin' like we want." Her expression told him more than her words. "Poor thing's scrapin' for every breath with only a small piece of time without a cough, and that usually comes after Cora has her suck on ice for a might bit."

"I'll take a turn, girl." Mama stepped toward the bed. "You been at it most of the night."

"I'm happy to try and help." Cora stood, stretching out her back. "Suzie and I are becoming good friends, aren't we, darling?"

His little sister attempted a smile, but it ended in another barking cough. His chest squeezed, his body shifting forward to help, but. . .but what could he do?

"Is there anything I can—"

"Pray, boy." His mama's soft voice broke just a moment. "That's all we can do right now asides what we've been doin'."

Cora walked forward, stiff, most likely from being crouched for too long. "Though, at times, it feels a little like I can't trust my prayers to make it past the ceiling."

"He's proved Himself all through my livin' days." Caroline's gaze drifted to Suzie. "And we trust God's holdin' my girl in His hands now, just like He's been holdin' her all her days." She blinked and turned back to Cora with a sad smile. "But I learned a long time ago that prayin' ain't mostly 'bout gettin' what we ask for, is it? Praise may be for the Almighty, but all the rest of prayer is for us."

"What do you mean?" Cora looked from Mama to Jeb. "For us?"

Mama nodded toward him and returned to Suzie's side, so Jeb answered. "Mama's always said that God uses prayin' to change us more than us changin' anything else."

"Change us?"

"What do you s'pose happens when we pray, Cora?" This from Mama, who was sponging a cloth over Suzie's head.

"Our requests and confessions and…" She waved toward Mama. "Praises are heard and God…" She paused, her brow furrowing.

"By all accounts, folks should think we was all a bunch of loons, talkin' to somebody we can't see nor ain't never seen afore. Believin' that this somebody hears us when we do." She smoothed back Suzie's hair and offered her another sip from the cup. "But prayin' is where we admit we ain't the lords of our own lives, nor of any lives, to be true. And, as I study on it, God uses prayin' to change my heart into what He's wantin' it to be in sun or rain, 'cause I'm trustin' His love and His plan."

Cora stared over at his mama, her bottom lip trembling the slightest bit, and he just had to put his hand on her arm. He didn't rightly know why he needed to touch her, but he did, and she turned those beautiful eyes on him, all teary, sad, and maybe even grateful, and he knew all the way down to his boots he wanted to look into those eyes for the rest of his life.

"Your uncle sure will be glad I found you."

Cora's eyes rounded. "Oh no! I—I didn't even think about telling him where I'd gone. He must be worried to pieces. Maggie met me on the path and all I could do was—"

"We'll meet him at the house and he'll know then." Jeb touched her arm again. Why on earth did he keep doin' that? Though he liked it just fine. But he wasn't one to go about touchin' on women's arms nor anywhere else on the spur of the moment.

"I can't leave here, Jeb," Cora whispered.

"Preacher moved up the wedding, Cora, to protect Willa." He drew her closer, his volume lowering to match hers. "Preacher said word got out after church about Willa bein' in the mountain, and all trouble points to you and me. Some folks ain't too friendly in their thoughts on me…" He raised a brow. "And you neither. They left a pair of sliced rabbits on my porch this mornin'."

"Oh no, Jeb." She stepped closer, searching his face. "They did something similar to Jonathan when they didn't like his teaching at the school."

"It's a warning, and that's a fact, but they'd do worse by you, 'cause you're a flatlander and ain't got ties to mountain folks." He pushed a hand through his hair. "And I ain't sure what they'll do if they get their hands on Willa, which is why Preacher plans on marryin' Paul and Willa off this afternoon so they can get out of town."

"Marryin' sure is one way of protectin' folks round here," Mama said so soft, Jeb barely heard it.

Cora turned in her direction and then looked back at Jeb, a flicker of sadness crossing her features before she pulled out of his reach. "I hate to leave you here, Caroline."

"I'll be fine, girl." Mama smiled. "You helped me get some sleep last night and that'll do."

"I promised Willow I would come, but as soon as the wedding is finished, I'll be back." Cora stepped forward. "Then you can rest tonight a little too."

"Do I need to take some of the young'uns with me?" Jeb offered, but his Mama shook her head.

"You already got a houseful. Besides, Maggie and Isom have been good help."

"And Daddy?"

Her shoulders bent a little. "I ain't seen him since the fire. The good man inside him likely knows what he done and cain't abide layin' eyes on us right now."

He stared at the scene, offering a silent prayer, while Cora gathered a few items and then followed him out the door, glancing back a few times as she went. He took Hickory's reins and led him down the inclined yard to the level path and then turned to her, braiding his hands together for her to use as a footrest to mount.

Her eyes widened all over again and she looked from him to

Hickory and back again. "I can walk." She waved toward the trail. "And you can ride along to the house."

He tilted his head, studying her. "Did you hear me tell you that some folks left rabbits on my porch?"

Her brow crinkled. "Yes?"

"That means I ain't leavin' you alone till all this is settled. You ain't safe as an unmarried flatlander who has a history of being a kept woman."

"I am not a kept woman, Jeb McAdams." She folded her arms across her chest and narrowed her eyes. "Of which you know quite well."

"All the important folks know." He gentled his voice and leaned a little closer. "But I ain't worried about the important folks."

She studied him for a moment, sent a longing look down the path, wrung her hands a little, and then released a long sigh. "Alright. Fine." Her voice dropped to a grumble. "If only I'd remembered my pistol."

He bit back his grin as she mounted, the ache of what commenced inside his parents' house dimming a little at the thought of spending time with this lady. And lady she was. He settled into the saddle and took the reins, his arms caging her in, another type of touching he was taking quite a fancy to. Though she sat straight as a ladder-back chair, her body eased against him every once in a while as they started down the path.

"How are Mercy and the children?" Her voice sounded strained. Was she uncomfortable on the horse?

"They're settlin' in pretty well, I reckon."

"Oh." Her back bumped into his chest and she shot straight again. "Well, I suppose it's a good thing, isn't it?"

"I'd rather them have whatever comfort I can provide in their time of grief than worry about a roof over their head too."

"Yes, of course." A sound like a whimpering kitten slipped from her. "You're so very good."

He wasn't sure if she'd meant to comment out loud, but those words hit him square in the chest and all he wanted to do was tug her a might bit closer.

"I'd say spendin' the night takin' care of my baby sister shows a heap of goodness too."

She leaned back again, this time resting for a second longer against him. "She is so small and dear." Her words trembled ever so slightly and he nearly leaned forward and kissed her head. "I want to help the people here so much, Jeb, but I fear. . .I fear my reputation may have ruined my opportunities."

"It'll pass in time."

She shook her head, the curls waving right before his face. "How much time? Can't they understand, I feel as though I belong here in these mountains and with—" She shot straight again. "Well, with these people."

He studied the back of her head in silence, wishing he could see right into her thoughts. Did she want to be with him? A strange bubbling started in his stomach and nearly erupted in laughter, but he turned it into a cough before it took hold. Now was the time to be brave and tell her how he felt. Seize the moment. Be romantic.

'Cept, he wasn't quite sure how to be romantic, so he switched the reins to one hand and brought his arm around her waist, burying his face into the bend of her neck. What a feeling, to settle this close to her. "Cora."

She shot so straight, her shoulder slammed him in the nose.

"I need to get off." She reached for the reins in his hand and pulled, not even waiting for him to stop before slipping off the horse. She took off at a fast walk. "Go ahead, please. I'm certain I'll be fine the rest of the way."

He shook off the sting in his nose and dismounted, leading Hickory along to catch up with her.

"What on earth is wrong with you?"

"It's just. . .well. . ." She stumbled, but found her feet and kept right on moving. "It's not proper."

"What's not proper? Ridin' on a horse together?"

"No." She turned toward him and then seemed to think better of it, and started off at a march again. "And yes, I mean, perhaps."

"Cora, what's the matter?"

"Nothing." She sent a smile faker than Rowen's whiskey over her shoulder. "I just feel more comfortable walking. I like to walk. It's excellent exercise."

He caught up to her and reached down to take her hand. "Cora."

"Stop doing that." She turned on him, eyes ablaze. "You are going to be married."

He blinked as if she'd hit him square in the nose. "I'm gonna be married?" Not that he was against such an arrangement, but she didn't seem too pleased by the notion.

"Of course you are. I heard Isom talk about your plans with Mercy and then I saw the two of you together, and Fig said something about it, and then it all made sense." A wounded expression crossed her face and she started walking again. "Which is the reason you cannot do things like you did."

That bubbling feeling started all over again and he grinned. Now he was beginning to understand. "What things?"

"The closeness and the neck and the hand-holding." Her words squeaked at the end. "You should know better, Jeb."

"I do know better." His words caused her to pivot back around to him.

"It's not that I don't think Mercy is lovely." Her chin trembled a little. "She is probably the most beautiful woman I've ever seen, but. . .but you ought to know for certain without this shilly-shallying about with my hands or my neck or—" She raised her hand. "Kissing my palm."

He stepped closer, dropping the reins. "Why don't you come right out and say what you really want to say, Cora, 'cause it don't sound like you've made it there yet."

"Very well, I shall." Her shoulders stiffened and she drew in a breath, only to hold a long pause before stating, "I want what makes you happy." She ended with a little nod as if she was proud of herself.

"What makes *me* happy?"

"Exactly." Her word breathed out as he stepped closer. "What makes you happy, Jeb?"

He didn't have to think too hard for the answer. With a growl like a hungry bear, he caught her by the waist and pulled her to him, catching her gasp with his lips. Her entire body stilled against him and then, with the tiniest of murmurs, she relaxed, allowing him to keep kissing her for a little while longer. Lord, have mercy! She had the best lips and cheeks and hair.

He pulled back slowly, already ready to try the whole kissing practice again.

"Jeb?" Cora breathed out his name, her breaths shallow. "You... you kissed me."

"I sure did." His grin spread wide, and he tightened his grip on her waist again. "And I'm surefire gonna do it again."

"You can't." She pressed a palm to his chest. "You...you're marrying Mercy."

"Don't you know not to listen to wild rumors, Cora?"

Her frown deepened and she shook her head. "You're not marrying Mercy?"

"Nope, and the ring you see on her finger when we git back to the house is from Daniel's daddy. My best friend, Amos. He bought it for her in France but never got the chance to give it to her."

Cora kept studying him as if she didn't know what to do next. "So you're not marrying Mercy?"

"She ain't quite got what I'm hopin' to find in a wife." He took her hand from his chest and brought it to his lips.

Her eyes rounded. "And what is that, exactly?"

"Wild hair." He pulled a rebel lock through his fingers and

watched it curl against his skin.

Her breath shivered and his lips took to itchin' like crazy.

"Stubborn and a good shot works right well for me too."

A smile started on one side of her lips.

"A big heart is to my likin', and I find I'm mighty fond of the sound of highfalutin talk too."

Her smile grew a little more.

"And I'm partial to a good dance partner."

One of her brows shot high, smile in full bloom. "A good dance partner?"

"Aye, especially if she steps on my toes."

She laughed, grabbed him by the jacket, and pulled in him right into another kiss. Her lips had to have been itching something fierce too, 'cause she didn't let go for a long time.

⁂

Jeb McAdams wanted to marry her. She leaned back against him as they rode the last stretch of the path to his house, some sweet sense of relief and comfort wrapping around her like the feel of his arms. *This* is what right felt like. What being accepted as yourself meant between a man and a woman, the humor and tenderness. The honesty and trust. Her smile pinched into her heated cheeks. The kisses.

And, if kisses meant yeses, she had definitely agreed to the match, several times over. Her face heated at the wonderfully recent memory. Somehow, even in their short acquaintance, everything fit into place like a part of her life she'd been waiting to enter and didn't even know it. Is that how God worked? Once she walked into His plan, she felt a sense of rightness? Or perhaps, it was only in this case, because she'd known going to the Front had been the right thing, but never experienced the calmness like she did being loved by Jeb.

Loved by Jeb. Even as she thought it, he nuzzled the back of her head with his nose, as if she smelled delightful. She stifled a cringe. The likelihood of that seemed fairly impossible after the night she'd had. He didn't seem to mind, though, and she had no intention of stopping this gentle affection. All she wanted to do was close her eyes and sink back into him, but the house came into view.

As he helped her down from Hickory's back, he refused to release her immediately, keeping her near him, with Hickory blocking the view from the house to them.

"You really did kiss back on the trail, didn't ya?" He searched her face with such tenderness, she rose on tiptoe and pressed her lips against his as answer.

A quiet growl erupted from his throat and sent wonderful tingles over her skin. Oh, she liked kissing him! She had the overwhelming urge to wrap her arms around him and bury deep into his strength to drown out all the trouble. What a beautiful combination of strength and tenderness!

"I want to make sure for myself too." She kissed him once more, and his arms tightened around her so they lingered a bit longer than planned, but neither seemed to mind.

"You git on inside to help folks prepare for the wedding." He nudged her forward. "I'll put Hickory up."

She looked behind her as she mounted the porch steps only to find him watching her with a ridiculous grin on his face. Perhaps she wore the same, which only caused her to smile even more until she turned toward the front door.

Lying at the threshold was the mangled remains of. . .a cat?

"Jeb!"

She pinched her eyes closed to gather her emotions and then looked again. Thistle? Upon closer examination, the fur looked too light for Jeb's cat, and she heaved a sigh. But what a horrible thing to do to a poor creature. The sound of Jeb's boots hit the stairs and she turned in time to watch realization dawn on his face.

"It's gettin' worse."

She hugged her arms around her shoulders. "Yes."

"Go on round back." He scanned the grounds. "I'll clean it up and meet you inside."

Cora rounded the house and entered through the back door to the sound of raised voices. The group didn't appear to notice she'd entered. On one side stood Willow holding the baby with Paul by her side. Elias Harris had positioned himself nearby, somewhat blocking Cora's view of Mercy and Daniel. Fig crouched on the stairway, peeking between the railings, and on the other side stood Merla Greer and a short man with beady dark eyes who pointed a gun toward Willow and Paul.

Granny Burcham stood in between, her arms out as if to shield one side from the other, in direct path of the gun, which may have been the reason the older man hadn't fired.

"I can't let you keep bringin' shame on our house, girl," barked the man. "I'm gonna take you back to where you belong."

"I ain't goin', Daddy." Her response grew in volume, in strength. "It wasn't my fault I was at Rowen's. I tell you true."

Daddy? A chill settled over Cora's skin. Ozaiah Greer, a man she'd heard enough about to know he wasn't to be trifled with.

"I ain't got no time for your lies, girl."

"It's not a lie, Mr. Greer." Paul shifted to stand in front of Willow, his palms raised. "I went to Rowen myself yesterday and spoke to him. He'll verify every part of Willow's story. He didn't know it at the time Clark first brought Willa but found out later that Willa was Clark's sister. He learnt the truth when he confronted Clark back at the wedding."

Ozaiah paused. "Rowen said Clark traded in Willow for his debts?"

"He did, sir." Paul rushed on. "Said he'd tell you the same or anyone else who come to talk to him, it bein' against the law and all, and he didn't want to cause no trouble with his business."

"Clark was gonna take Daisy instead, Daddy." Willow's voice

broke. "I couldn't let him."

Ozaiah lowered the rifle a little and looked from Paul to Willow. "You tellin' me my own boy shamed our family by visiting a whorehouse and then sellin' his sister to one?"

Silence answered him and he lowered the rifle more, his jaw tightening. "You hear this now and spread the word. We ain't got no son named Clark Greer no more. And since the boy is borrowin' my horse and land, we'll be takin' that from him too." He turned to Merla. "We're done here, woman. Say yer goodbyes and don't be long 'bout it. I need to go have myself a talk with Clark Greer."

He marched from the house and out the front door without a look back.

Mercy approached Cora as Willow and her mother exchanged goodbyes.

"I saw the cat outside the door just before the Greers arrived."

Cora nodded and breathed out a long sigh, her body tired from her long night. "It seems to be getting worse."

"This news 'bout Clark'll help some, at least until they learn me and the boys is here." She pushed back a strand of her ebony hair and Cora noticed the lovely detailed stitching on her sleeve.

"Do you mean because you are unmarried and with Jeb here?"

"More 'cause he's unmarried." She shook her head. "Folks don't always think sensically do they? Don't mind that Jeb is staying out in the workshop at night and only comes in for meals. Folks only see trouble."

"So. . .so if he was married, it would help quell some of the anger, even if they all thought we were living in sin beforehand?"

"Ain't that a sight? But it's how some folks think round here. As long as the marryin' happens, then it fixes all the wrongs afore." Mercy chuckled and rolled her eyes, then her smile softened into a welcome comradery. "But ain't everybody like that. There's a lot of good. Your uncle and brother, they've seen it and come to bring good change. I think you've come with the same heart 'cause even in the hard, you've found the worthwhile and good. That takes a special person."

The back door burst open and in walked Jeb carrying a furry bundle in his arms. Puck.

"They shot my dog," he growled, and it was nothing like the growl he'd made before kissing her. It was dangerous and dark and ready to fight.

Cora followed him into the kitchen where he placed Puck on the table. On the table? She bit down to keep from protesting and determined to scrub the table very well later.

Puck whimpered as Jeb gently adjusted him to the center. "It was a warnin' shot. They got him in the hindquarters. A coward's shot. Ain't no 'cause for shootin' a perfectly good dog."

Cora set her bag on the table and began pulling out cleaning materials and gauze. She'd bandaged a horse before, but only once, though the same procedure applied as it did for humans. "I'll tend to him." She gestured toward Jeb's blood-soaked shirt and hands. "You go get cleaned up."

He stared at her for a long moment, myriad emotions shifting across his features from anger to concern to gratitude. "Thank you, Cora."

She offered him a smile and he walked past her, leaving her in the kitchen with Mercy. What would the angry, ignorant people do next? Hurt a human? Each warning grew worse. Would Uncle Edward become a victim of the superstitious mountain folks?

Mercy stepped close. "I'll help in any way I can, Cora."

Cora's attention shifted down to Mercy's hand. A beautiful and simple ring shone on her finger. *"Marryin' sure is one way of protectin' folks round here."* Caroline's sentence came back with full meaning. If she loved Jeb and he loved her, and marriage would fix this ridiculous quandary, then why wait?

Chapter Twenty

J eb scrubbed his hands with more force than necessary. Even the chill of the air in the barn on his damp skin failed to douse the fury burning beneath. Yes, he loved this mountain and these people, but he hated how some of them were still so lost in their own superstitions and small-headedness. It made him more and more thankful he was raised by his parents, a couple who knew some of life beyond here, of ways outside.

There was good. Wonderful good housed within these forests and hollows, but meanness and bitterness shared an equal amount. He squeezed his eyes closed, war memories surfacing unbidden. No, it wasn't just here. Dark hearts lived everywhere. He supposed it was why the beautiful hearts shone even brighter and were even more worth the winning. But shooting his dog? The only cause for it was pure meanness, and that was what bothered him most about the whole thing.

Getting Willow out of Maple Springs would help a little, but it wouldn't change the minds of folks set in their old, twisted ways and unwilling to believe the truth. But what else could be done? Mercy and the young'uns had nowhere else to go, nor any means of taking care of themselves for the moment, and it would take him a few months, even with Elias's help, to get a cabin built to suit them. So the rumors would stay strong and likely bring more meanness to his door.

He rubbed a hand across his face, his hair still damp from a cold washing, and made quick work of trimming his beard and mustache. Having not been to church for a few weeks kept his whiskers longer than usual, but he figured a wedding deserved a good trim. Besides, it gave him something to do with his hands besides searching the woods for the folks who shot his dog and give them a good throttling. His front porch couldn't compare to a church, but it was the least he could offer to the young couple who weren't getting the typical wedding treatment of family and celebrations.

He'd just pulled on his white button-up when the barn door creaked open. Expecting Preacher, he turned, hands on the buttons of his shirt, to find Cora entering. She'd changed into a soft green dress—like the look of the evergreens when bathed in sunlight— and she'd pulled her hair up in such a way that a few curls spilled from the top.

His hands froze on his buttons and for a second he forgot all about meanness and gunshot wounds and sickness, and focused his full attention on her. Had kissing made her prettier somehow, or maybe it was the sweet way she looked at him, like. . .well, like he was something special. He stood a little taller and made it through another button.

Her gaze dropped to the movement of his hands and then a sudden flush rushed into her cheeks and she turned a little to avert her gaze. "I. . .I should have knocked. I'm sorry."

"Ain't nothin' I'm sure you've seen afore in the war."

She cleared her throat and drew in a deep breath. "Yes, well, it's a little different when it's you as opposed to a wounded soldier."

Despite himself, he grinned and took a step closer. "Zat so?"

She looked up, keeping her attention focused on his face. "You know very well it's so. If you'd walked in on me getting dressed, I don't think you'd have been unmoved."

Heat shot all through him at the very idea, and kissing took on a whole new idea. "Have mercy! Why'd you have to go giving me thoughts like that, woman?"

"Exactly." She smiled, the rose in her cheeks deepening. "So, careful Mr. McAdams, that you don't take too much pleasure out of my current discomfort."

He slowly fastened the next button. "I'm still gonna enjoy it, Cora."

She raised her brows and blinked, her gaze flickering back to his hands for a moment before returning to his face. "I came to talk to you about Puck and a plan."

His smile disappeared. "Is he alright?"

"He is, or will be. The bullet passed through and I bandaged him."

"Thank you."

"And Uncle Edward is here." She wrung her hands in front of her. "Willow and Paul are keen to get on their way."

"If you hadn't come to distract me, I'd be ready much quicker."

Her lips curved in a saucy smile which made kissing thoughts nearly take over again. "Ah, I see I'm not the only one who's distracted."

"You're much more distractin' than me."

"I would beg to differ." Her breath grew shallow for a second and she swayed closer to him. He moved to meet her halfway and then she blinked and seemed to remember something. "But. . .this attack on Puck proves this wild hatred of Willow's former occupation and our presumed sinfulness is getting much worse, and a human may very well be next."

"I've thought about that too."

"So I have a solution, or at least the start of one."

She squeezed her hands again, so he finished the next few buttons and leaned down to take one of her hands in his. "You're gonna rub the skin off your hands if yer not careful." He smoothed a thumb over the soft fingers and she shivered. "What's got you all worked up?"

"I. . .I have a proposal for you."

He raised a brow.

"I. . .well. . ." She cleared her throat. "As you well know, it's rumored you have kept women and that I'm one of those kept women. Willow leaving will not completely calm the rumors, since Mercy will still be with you for the time being."

"Aye." What had her so nervous?

"And we understand one another and. . ." She cleared her throat again. "Are fond of each other, even after such a short acquaintance."

"I'm glad to hear you're right fond of me, 'cause I'm so fond of you I plan on kissin' you again once you stop talkin'."

Her bottom lip dropped in the most fetching way, he nearly started kissing her before she finished what was ailing her. "Well then, I'd better get to the point."

"I wouldn't mind none."

She raised her chin. "Jeb McAdams, would you marry me today?"

Now it was his turn to have his mouth drop open like a fish. She wanted to marry him! Today! Christmas just came early and he hadn't even put his wish into words yet.

She rushed ahead at his silence. "I know it's not typical, of course, and a church wedding would be preferred."

She pulled away and began pacing, but all he could do was stare and wonder and repeat her question in his head. *Would you marry me today?*

"I know it's a bit unconventional, but we're not exactly living in a conventional place, so. . ." She kept wringing her hands as she walked.

Her hair sure was pretty. And her nose, small and feminine.

"You've already alluded to the prospect of marriage, and I'm certainly amenable to it."

Green was a nice color on her. Made her eyes stand out even more. He'd surely purchase some more cloth so Mercy could make Cora a whole closet full of green dresses if she wanted. And he'd build her a room onto his house so she could treat sick folks to her heart's content.

"So if you're. . .amenable too, then we can enjoy the fruit of matrimony while also curbing the sting of the rumors. It would kill two birds with one stone, so to speak."

He didn't understand some of her prattle, but he got the gist of it and decided he knew exactly how to answer her. He caught her by the waist as she passed by and kissed her until she melted against him. Maybe he was getting better at the whole kissing thing, 'cause it didn't take near as long to get her to join in as it did the first time.

She drew back with such a satisfied smile, he 'bout started kissing her again. "You seem quite amenable to the idea."

"Sure am." He ran a hand down her arm. "Zat why you put on this pretty dress? For our wedding?" Speaking those words out loud nearly had him laughing to the skies. What an idea!

She smoothed a palm over the material. "Mercy gave it to me. One of her newest creations, and I'm determined to get her dresses in one of the shops in Flat Creek. They're remarkable."

"Well, it sure looks remarkable on you."

"Thank you." She smiled shyly up at him and his heart nearly burst from his chest. "I wore it to help my cause."

"Miss Taylor, you could've shown up in my dirty overalls and I'd said the same answer." He brushed his palms against her cheeks, her skin soft and warm. "But are you sure you're gonna be happy with a simple mountain man like me?"

"Jeb." Her fingers dug into his shirt, and he liked the security of the touch a whole bunch. "You're not simple, and I can't imagine anyone not falling in love with someone who has such a wonderfully tender heart as yours. I know I have."

She loved him too. Shoot fuzzy! Well, she deserved a lot more kissing for saying something so sweet.

Having the weddings on the front porch of the house promised two things: a beautiful view of sunshine and mountains, and the hope that any eavesdroppers would spread the news of the nuptials. Cora hadn't expected to feel particularly impressed by such a sparse display, having been to much grander weddings in London, but something in the simple Appalachian tradition of handfasting, followed by Jeb surprising her with a lovely ring he'd purchased in France at the same place Amos had purchased Mercy's, shifted this moment into a tender affair.

She regretted not having Jonathan with her, or their mothers, but down deep, she knew she'd made the right choice for everyone involved. She smiled as Jeb held her cold fingers in his warm ones. Especially for her. Life afforded hardship and unexpected turns, but something in Jeb McAdams's forthrightness and gentleness assured her she'd never find anyone like him again, and she wasn't one to waste time on a decision when the right one fell directly in front of her.

Of course, their wedding day proved as atypical as their courtship. They'd barely finished some coffee and stack cake, provided by Granny Burcham and Mercy, when the inevitable came. Jeb and Elias planned to drive Paul, Willow, and the baby to the train depot, and Uncle Edward agreed to escort Cora back to the McAdamses'.

"Promise me you won't leave Mama's house till I come for you." Jeb tugged her into a private hallway of the house as Paul and Willow settled in the wagon outside.

He slipped a thumb over her cheek and she leaned into the touch. "I promise."

"I don't like this a'tall." His fingers slid down to cup her chin. "I can't take care of my wife if she's all the way across the mountain from me."

His wife. Her eyes drifted closed against the warmth in his touch. Oh, the way his deep voice cradled those words nearly puddled her to the floor. "They'll feel safer with you at the lead, Jeb." She looked back up at him, raising her own palm to touch his face. What an intimate gesture, but she held this freedom now. He was hers and she was his. "They're the ones most in danger of an attack.

Plus, your mother needs me."

He swallowed so hard his Adam's apple moved. "Take your pistol."

"I will."

With deliberate and slow progress, he leaned over and touched his lips to hers, gentle, lingering, warming her from the kiss all the way down through her body. She clung to the sweetness of belonging to him, having his arms around her. No, this wasn't how she'd always dreamed of her wedding or wedding day, but life rarely turned out the way one expected, and if it had, she would never have known Jeb McAdams.

He lowered his forehead to hers, a smile tipping his lips. "Law, woman, I like those lips of yours a whole lot."

She grinned at his endearing directness. "They're at your disposal whenever you like."

He raised a brow as if doubting her answer. "I'm afraid that just ain't so, 'cause I know exactly what I'd like, and I cain't make it happen right now."

The hooded gaze he sent her incited all sorts of wonderful sparks through her body. Was that why the mountain folks referred to the romantic interests of man and woman as sparking? It made perfect sense now.

He kissed her once more and she walked with him to the porch, watching him take his seat beside Elias in the wagon and then head down the trail. Uncle Edward came to stand beside her. "He's a good man, Cora. One of the best I know."

"You would have objected with more determination, I believe, if you'd thought otherwise." She grinned up at her uncle, who'd teased Jeb about the rushed wedding.

"I would have." He rubbed his bearded chin. "And he wouldn't have been fit for you six months ago. Not with all the healing he needed from the war, but, I suppose. . ." He looked down at her. "Neither were you."

He was right. She would have balked at the idea of living in Maple Springs, let alone marrying a mountain man, six months ago. She carried her own scars and pride from the battlefield, her own stubborn way of thinking. But when she looked back on the young woman who'd volunteered as a nurse over a year ago, she barely recognized herself.

The sky bloomed with late afternoon colors and the cool wind blew against her cheeks. She drew in a breath and turned to her uncle. "Let's get on our way. Caroline will need me, and I pray Suzie is on the mend."

But the painful reality hit Cora as soon as she stepped over the threshold of the McAdamses' house. Suzie's cough had grown worse and her striving for air nearly inverted her ribs. Her lips had taken on a more purplish hue and sweat dampened her golden hair into tight ringlets.

"Ain't no relief for her," Caroline said, her voice strained, her eyes red-rimmed. "She's coughin' so much, she ain't hardly breathin'."

Cora scanned the room, and her attention fastened on the kitchen. The smaller space might allow the hot water to remain in the air around Suzie longer. She turned to Uncle Edward. "Would you help us move her to the kitchen table?"

"What?" His brows shot high. Caroline didn't even flinch.

"The kitchen is smaller and closer to Caroline's cookstove. Perhaps the smallness of the space and the fact we can boil water directly on the cookstove to keep the pots of water hot around Suzie may help." She met her uncle's gaze. "What we're doing isn't working. We have to try something different."

He scooped the little girl up in his arms and they moved everything into the kitchen as Isom and Maggie kept James and John entertained in the loft. Uncle Edward stayed, fetching water and bringing firewood, until evening started to settle in. He paused a moment to pray over Suzie before taking his leave.

Caroline spoke little as tears waited at every turn, and Cora worked hard to ease Suzie's position and attempt to get some ice into her. Suzie took a few pieces and even sipped on some water before she began coughing again. Her face flushed bright and her responses remained small. Cora prayed like she'd never prayed in her life. Begging for healing, asking for wisdom, searching for strength. Every symptom pointed to one end, and the very idea tore at her need to heal and help. To fix things. But she had no power to fix this no matter how hard she tried.

As evening fell, she convinced Caroline to try and sleep a little. Cora ached for rest herself, but from the droop in Caroline's step to the weariness in her eyes, the woman needed a respite much more than Cora.

The other children had gone to bed and the house fell silent except for the sound of Suzie's coughing and the crackling fire. Cora patted Suzie's head with a cloth and waved the steam toward her face, hoping the moist air would finally make a much-needed difference. Butter, the dog, lay by the table as if guarding Suzie, and the sight nearly had Cora laying her head against the table and weeping.

"God, where are you?" she whispered. "Can't You see how much Your little one is suffering? How much her family is suffering? Won't You please help?"

She must have dozed off a little, because a loud sound woke her from her crouched position at the table. Butter shot to his feet and the sound came again, from the back of the house.

The back of the house. Cora's blood ran cold. Hadn't Caroline said the easiest door to break open was the back door? She stood and pulled her pistol from her pocket as she rounded the table, placing herself between whoever entered and Suzie. Would one of the folks angry about Jeb's kept women break into the McAdamses' house to exact some sort of judgment? She couldn't see anything out the dark window. Butter stood to attention, not growling.

Could it be someone he knew? She took a step toward the door. Jeb, perhaps?

And then the door burst open. Standing in the doorway, eyes wild and bottle in hand, stepped Sam McAdams. His gaze fixed on Cora then shifted to Suzie and back, the look on his face darkening from surprise to fury.

"What have you done to my young'un, flatlander?" He shifted forward and slammed the bottle against the doorframe, causing Suzie to jump. "You hurt my kin, and now I'm gonna hurt you."

Chapter Twenty-One

Cora shifted a step back, bumping into the table, the gun quivering in her palms. "Mr. McAdams, Suzie is sick. I'm here to try and help her."

"Lies." His bleary eyes held no reasoning. "I heared tell about you, woman. I know what kind you are. You're full of lies, and you're bringin' your sin into my house. What did you do to my young'un?"

His hand swept to grab her, but his uncoordinated and slow movements gave her time to sidestep him, leaving his fist to crash into the wall nearby. He released a roar, and Suzie whimpered, distracting Cora long enough for Sam's fingers to dig into the upper flesh of her arm. She cried out as his grip tightened and the pistol fell from her grip.

"Sam McAdams, you let that girl go."

Cora swung her attention to the doorway where Caroline marched forward. The shock shook Sam's hold from Cora and he stumbled back enough that Caroline positioned herself between Cora and Sam.

"That woman's brought sin in our house. She ain't got no cause to be—"

"What would you know 'bout it, Sam McAdams? You've either been gone or too drunk to know what's been goin' on in your own house the past few days." Caroline's response was as surprising to Sam as it was to Cora. She'd never heard Caroline raise her voice, but from the tension on her face, she looked like she could fight her husband and win. Cora thought of articles she'd read about how mother bears or lions protect their offspring to death, if necessary, even from the father of the cubs.

"You don't talk to me like that, woman." He growled, gaining volume again.

"If you can't behave yourself, you need to leave the house, Sam." Caroline pointed to the back door. "We ain't got time to deal with your foolery when we got a sick baby to tend."

"I ain't leavin' that woman in this house—" He marched forward but Caroline moved to block his path to Cora.

"Get out, Sam. Now."

He turned wide eyes on his wife and raised his hand with another roar, keeping it in the air as if he was uncertain what to do next.

"It's right you think twice afore hittin' me, Sam McAdams." Caroline braced her fists on her hips and stood taller, her eyes glossy with unshed tears. "'Cause if you hit me, you better kill me. If'n you don't, I'm gonna git up and kill you."

He stared, frozen in place.

"I know the drunk is up front, but the man can hear me. You want to know why our young'un is gaspin' for every breath?" Her voice rose, strained, holding back who knew how much fury and grief. "You and your drunk. That's what done it. You keered more about your liquor than for your own kin, and now she may be dyin'." Caroline's voice broke on the last word and something in that show of weakness impacted Sam.

He looked over at Suzie, her labored breath scraping across the tension-singed air, and something flickered within his expression. Realization? Regret? Horror? He turned his gaze back to Caroline and stumbled back as if she'd struck him. With a sound like a wounded animal, he rushed out into the night, leaving the door open and the night air swarming into the room.

Cora rushed to Suzie and wrapped blankets around her.

Caroline followed where Sam disappeared, staring out into the darkness before closing the door and returning to Suzie's side.

"You alright?"

Cora nodded. "Are you?"

Caroline looked back toward the closed door and then ran a hand over Suzie's head. "You think a bit of lavender tea might bring some relief?"

"Is it possible to mix lavender with some more of the goldenrod?" Anything to make a difference. Suzie's little body couldn't maintain this fever much longer, and if the swelling didn't reduce in her throat. . . "Granny Burcham says it may help reduce swelling in muscles, and since the place I think is swollen is the muscles of her voice, then maybe it will help."

"Been giving it to her since you mentioned it yester eve."

"Good." Cora looked back at the little girl. "Hopefully, it's doing some good."

After warming more water to fill the pots surrounding Suzie, Cora adjusted the little girl's position by lengthening her neck in an attempt to open the airway. Caroline had tied another onion poultice to Suzie's feet in order to reduce her fever. Maybe this time?

Cora leaned her weary head back against the wall, listening to Suzie's breaths. Praying the next one would be easier. Or the next. Another noise from the front of the house shook her from her momentary stupor and brought her to her feet.

Oh no! Not again.

Caroline raised a palm for Cora to remain in the kitchen and then disappeared into the front room. Cora stepped to Suzie's side, something different in the girl's pallor. Her heart seized in her chest and she stepped closer. The room had grown quiet. Much too quiet.

Jeb had never seen his mother look so weary. He wrapped an arm around her shoulder and she leaned into him for longer than a brief embrace, almost as if she drew from his strength. He held on and walked with slow steps toward the kitchen. Her head even dropped against his shoulder, and he squeezed her closer.

"It's bad?"

She answered with a sigh.

Jeb steadied his shoulders and pressed his emotions deep, readying for the task of comforter. He barely knew Suzie. The little girl had been only three when he left for war, but the loss struck a deep blow nonetheless. A little life. A mother's grief. He had no concept of such a soul-shaking ache.

"Caroline." A harsh whisper brought his attention up to the kitchen doorway, where Cora stood, her gaze taking him in. Some sound like a sob erupted from her throat, which didn't match the smile on her face. "Her fever's broken. She's breathing easier."

Mama stumbled forward and Jeb caught her, guiding her by the shoulders into the kitchen. With a quiet whimper, she collapsed beside the table and quietly shook. He'd never seen his mama cry like this. He stepped forward and knelt beside her, placing his hand on her back. Within seconds, he felt another touch near his fingers. He looked up and Cora had done the same, her palm on his mama's back next to his. Their eyes met, hers glossy with tears, and he placed his hand over hers then closed his eyes to thank God. Thank God for keeping one little life in this world for now. For answering his mama's pleas. For bringing Cora.

The raspy sounds of Suzie's breaths punctuated the silence, but a sudden sense of peace washed over him. After all he'd been through, and the hours he'd beat himself up over not being fast enough or strong enough or brave enough, God held him as assuredly as he held Suzie and Mama and Cora, even if God's answer was "no" or "wait." He'd answered "no" with Amos and "wait" with Daddy. He answered "no" with Mercy, but given Jeb much more than he'd ever imagined when Cora entered his life. He'd thought, at first, he'd lost all his joy and hope in France. There had been so much loss and hatred and human brokenness, he'd forgotten how to see beyond the grief and the hour ahead. But, little by little, God had taken Jeb's natural gifts and passions, like his woodworking and his drive to protect others, and used them to bring a future business and a rescue-turned-wife. Both beyond what he deserved or even dreamed.

So maybe, with the situation about the rumors, Mercy, his daddy, and even Kizzie, God was shaping situations and circumstances to form a better story with grander vistas than Jeb could ever imagine.

After a little while, he helped the ladies to a stand and Mama served warm milk and molasses cookies as Cora continued to monitor Suzie. With each passing minute, her breathing became gentler and the cough less. Cora's eyes were heavy and the night well spent when Jeb and Cora finally bid Mama good night, mounted Hickory, and started the trek toward home. *Their* home, plus a few extra folks.

This time, she cozied right up next to him as they rode together, her body wrapped in a wedding ring quilt mama gave to them when she'd learned they'd married. She rode sidesaddle, "due to the type of skirt she wore," she'd said, but he didn't mind. He could see her face this way.

"Mama said you gave the twins a bath while she was tendin' to some chores."

Cora's head tottered forward, eyes dropping, before she snapped her head back up. "I thought it might be a help to her after all she's been managing."

She shivered and he tightened his hold around her, shifting her so that she could rest against him a bit better. Her head dropped against his shoulder, and she sighed. He rested his chin down against her head for a second.

"Did some house cleanin' too, as I understand."

"Mmm hmm. . ." Her forehead brushed against his neck and she nestled her cold nose closer. "Oh, your neck is warm."

He chuckled, enjoying this unhindered display of affection and trust from her.

"The twins' hair was such a pretty red color underneath the dirt they'd been in." She yawned and shivered again. "I like...your arms... around me like..."

With a little purr of a sound, she grew silent and nestled her forehead against his neck. Lord help him. He wasn't quite sure he ever wanted to reach home if he could keep her nestled all close and soft against him.

Mercy had lighted the lanterns, so Jeb slipped Cora from the horse. She woke for only a moment before smiling up at him and dozing off again. This time, he carried her into his house knowing full well who she was and where she belonged. Puck's paws tapped against the porch and hardwoods as he followed them inside, Jeb attempting to be as quiet as possible. Mercy, Granny Burcham, and the young'uns must have gone to bed hours ago. Question was, where would he put Cora?

As if in answer, Mercy stood from the wingback by the fire, her dark hair in a long braid and a shawl around her shoulders. "I fixed up the downstairs room for y'all."

She moved past him and opened the door to the room so he could slip in and place Cora on the bed. She murmured something, but he didn't have any idea what it was.

"Thank you, Mercy."

She smiled the sweet smile of one friend happy for another. "It's a good pairing, Jeb. The likes of you two. I wouldn't have picked it, if I'd been choosing, but in hindsight, it's real good."

He nodded and she stepped from the room, closing the door behind her. With gentle hands, he took off Cora's boots, coat, and shirtwaist, then placed the new blanket on top of the ones he already had on the bed, tucking it around her.

She yawned and blinked up at him. "Are you staying with me here?"

What a question! His throat tightened and he smiled. "You go on back to sleep. I'm gonna go take care of Hickory."

"Then you'll be back?" she murmured, eyes drifting closed. "I'm a lot warmer when you're next to me."

Lord, have mercy. "Yes, ma'am. I'll come right back."

Hickory likely thought Jeb had lost all sense from the frantic speed at which he got him to the barn and took care of him. The horse didn't complain none, just snorted a few times, but someday he'd understand. Well, maybe. Jeb wasn't quite sure of all the feelings shooting through him, nor exactly what was going to happen next, but just the idea of holding Cora close all night long had him running around like a fox in the chicken coop.

He slipped back inside the house, bolted all the doors, put some extra logs on the fire, then washed up in the kitchen before making his way back to the bedroom. Cora's deep breaths made the only sound in the room, and the moonlight haloed the space with bright white. He undressed to his nightshirt and, with a deep breath, crawled right in beside her. She hummed a sweet sound and curled up against him, her eyes still closed, but somehow she managed to use his shoulder as a pillow. He didn't mind none. In fact, he liked it so well, he lay there enjoying it for a good while before falling asleep.

At some point in the night, or early morning, he woke to the feel of something warm and soft against his neck. Surely he'd closed the bedroom door so Thistle wouldn't come into the room and make trouble. But when he pulled back just a bit, something tightened around his chest, and the soft warmth moved from his neck to his jaw.

Then he remembered all that had happened and he opened his eyes to find Cora's arm wrapped around his chest and her lips against his jaw. Her lips against his jaw! He instinctively pulled her closer, and she moved to raise up on her elbow, staring down at him with her long hair splayed all around her in a heap of curls. At some point, she'd undressed down to her nightgown, the thinness of the material more evident as the moon's glow bathed her body.

She didn't say anything.

They stared at each other in the silence, his palms moving to rest at the curves of her waist, her palm moving over his chest. He allowed his thumbs the gentlest caress across the cloth of her nightgown, and her breath caught, sending a sense of need through him. She seemed to feel the same, because without a word, she bent low and brought her lips down to cover his. Despite the worries and excitements of the day, neither went to sleep for a while, and when they did, it was the most contented sleep Jeb had known in a very long time.

Chapter Twenty-Two

"Law goodness, what are you doin' to that poor bacon?"

Cora jumped at the sound of Granny Burcham's voice and blinked out of her happy daze to look down at the browning bacon in the frying pan. She snatched a spatula and rescued the bacon from a crispier demise.

"You got your head in the clouds, girl?"

Not exactly the clouds, though "heavenly" might have been a near-accurate description of her memories from last night or early this morning, whichever it was.

"I know I taught you better since you been here."

But this time, Cora caught the glint in Granny Burcham's eyes and heat flew into her cheeks. "I'm just having an off morning, Granny. I'm sure to adjust."

She chuckled and shooed Cora out of the way toward the half-made biscuits on a small table by the window. Cora floured her hands and began pushing the dough, attention focused outside. The object of her thoughts emerged from the barn, white shirt sleeves rolled up even as his breath puffed in the morning air. Puck limped along behind him, not as energetic as usual, but on the mend.

He shoved the barn door closed and started toward the house, giving Puck a pat on the head as he walked. Cora grinned. She'd always found suspenders particularly attractive, but somehow Jeb wore them better than anyone she'd ever met. Perhaps it wasn't solely about the suspenders anymore.

She lost sight of him as he approached the house and devoted her attention back to the dough despite the fact she felt Granny Burcham's eyes on her.

"I don't reckon you'll be wantin' Mercy to stay round now that you're the woman of the house, will ya?"

Cora shot Granny a look. "I don't know why that should change anything. She needs a place to stay, and there's plenty of room in this house."

"Now that Willow's gone on, I reckon I'll be goin' too." She whistled low. "Ain't no lovin' gonna make up for your cookin' though, so you'd better start payin' attention to your bacon instead of moonin' over your man."

Cora's lips tipped. "Maybe I can do both."

Granny shook her head as if Cora was a lost cause, but Cora had a feeling the woman held secret pleasure in the pairing.

Cora took the metal biscuit cutter and divvied out the dough, placing the circles on a baking pan just as the back door opened. She slipped the pan in the oven and turned as Jeb walked by the kitchen door on the way to their bedroom. He found her gaze as he passed, and his expression softened into a knowing smile she felt all the way through her.

She turned back to her work with a happy sigh and Granny mumbled something unintelligible, but Cora thought she heard "addlebrained."

Jeb showed up to the kitchen just as Cora was pulling the biscuits from the oven.

"Those smell good."

How the man's voice suddenly took on extra power, Cora had no idea, but she sent a smile heavenward just so God knew she didn't mind.

"Hopefully, the smell will overpower the lingering scent of burnt bacon."

His presence warmed her from behind and she leaned back against him, sending the kitchen a quick glance. Granny had conveniently disappeared.

Jeb buried his face into her neck, and she closed her eyes to the newly familiar sensations. "It's awful nice to wake up with you in my bed, Mrs. McAdams," he murmured low, near her ear. Her knees weakened.

"I believe you're going to be very helpful in keeping me warm on these cold nights."

She turned in time to see his eyes darken. "I'm happy to be helpful."

Noise from the other room sent them apart and Jeb started setting plates out for anyone who wanted to join them for breakfast.

"I thought you might have been gone for the mill already."

He looked up from pouring a glass of milk. "I think I'll change up my hours a might bit so we can see one another in the mornings."

"I like that idea."

"But I am going to the mill for a while today. Want to talk over an idea with Elias."

"I want to visit your mother and Suzie today." She raised her brows, waiting for him to protest. "I need to see how her recovery is coming along."

He breathed out a long breath and looked toward the window. "I'm not keen on you goin' up there alone. Not just yet."

"Granny said something about returning home," Cora said. "What if she walks with me part of the way?"

"And you come back alone?"

"I'll take my pistol and I'll make certain to come back in broad daylight."

He stared at her a few seconds and then nodded. "But take Puck with you, alright? He's a good warning dog, even if he's a bit slow right now."

"Alright." She covered his hand with hers as she reached for another plate. "We can't live in fear, Jeb. It's easy to with life being so very unpredictable, but. . .but if we trust God's love at all—"

"I know." He squeezed her hand and stepped back, offering her a crooked smile. "I'm just getting used to having you around."

The look in his eyes didn't match the levity in his voice. He cared for her deeply. She hadn't imagined such care from a man. And the way he'd shown it last night with such tenderness and passion—

Her throat squeezed as wonderful flutters erupted in her stomach. He seemed to follow the direction of her thoughts, because his expression sobered and he stepped toward her, attention focused on her lips.

"Who burnt the bacon?"

Jeb and Cora turned to see Fig standing in the doorway, hands on his hips and dark hair sticking out in all directions. Breakfast followed in a flurry of busy conversation, nothing like the stilted quiet of her home growing up. She liked this constant flow of conversation and even laughter, though Granny Burcham muttered later that she'd grown up to believe children should be quiet at the table.

But Cora loved the energy and joy Fig and little Daniel brought to the meal, and from Jeb's happy response, she imagined their future could involve similar encouragement, should God bless them with a family.

Jeb left, after a prolonged goodbye in the barn, where only Hickory witnessed the thoroughness of both parties to ensure each remained at the forefront of the other's thoughts while apart. Cora felt certain their kisses held all sorts of promises for later. So, with a lighter step, she returned to the house.

Only an hour later, Isom and Maggie stopped in on their way to school to let Cora know Suzie was sitting up in bed, talking and laughing, and the cough had almost completely disappeared. When

Cora asked if they'd seen their father, Maggie shook her head. "Not one sight. Mama's gonna send Pike, one of Daddy's friends, out lookin' for him to see if he's alright."

"If Mama's sending Pike, then we know she's worried," added Isom. "She ain't never sent Pike afore."

Maggie lowered her voice. "She thinks she heard some wailin' early this mornin' not far off in the woods. Ain't sure whether it was Daddy or not. Ain't never heard him cry, let alone wail, but there's somethin' botherin' her about him and that's a fact."

Cora sent the two off with some molasses cookies Mercy had made for the wedding and then Cora took a survey of her new home. The sparseness hit her afresh, but once she retrieved her trunks from Uncle Edward's *and* made a trip to Flat Creek, she imagined she could soften up the space a little.

Granny Burcham disappeared some time midmorning, after learning that Cora didn't plan to walk to the McAdamses' after all. So Cora checked on Puck's wound and cleaned up the house a little more while Mercy washed some laundry. It was a welcome quiet and routine after the past few days. Then, only an hour later, Lizzie Spencer, a woman Cora had met at church and someone of whom her uncle and Caroline spoke highly, showed up with a little boy in her arms.

"I heared tell you got some doctorin' skills. Jeremiah's all covered up with poison ivy." The woman spoke gently, not overly anxious, but the fact she'd walked however far to get to Jeb's house spoke of her concern. "I done tried a sodie water bath, but it ain't done no good. He's awful eat up with the sores."

So the Spencers must have heard of the wedding, since Lizzie had come to Jeb's house for Cora. Cora guided Lizzie and Jeremiah through the house and into the kitchen, the only spot she really had to work with her herbs and medicines at the moment. "Have you tried an oatmeal bath yet?"

Lizzie blinked at Cora. "An oatmeal bath?"

Cora explained the concept while she created a small concoction from some of her own knowledge and incorporating elements she'd learned from Granny Burcham. "It helps with the itching." She washed Jeremiah's arms and chest, which held the worst of the rash. "It's important to keep the rash clean to remain free of infection, so I'd suggest washing it a few times a day with a cool, damp cloth."

Lizzie nodded.

"And here's a little cream to apply in the meantime." She placed a small jar in Lizzie's hands. "It's a mixture of aloe and witch hazel."

"It smells good 'nough to eat." Lizzie smiled, her eyes so golden-brown they reminded Cora of freshly brewed tea.

"Oh, well, that would be a bit of peppermint oil. Besides adding a lovely scent, it also helps cool the skin and provide some relief, I hope."

"Thank you kindly, Nurse Woman." Lizzie took the salve and placed it in the basket she carried on her arm. "And I brung some things for you as you set up house."

From the basket, she brought three jars of a dark substance and a tall bottle of some purplish liquid, followed by three of the most beautiful lace doilies Cora had ever seen. "That there is some strawberry and blackberry jam." She pointed to the jars, then the bottle. "And some elderberry wine."

"And these?" Cora touched one of the doilies.

"Thems made by my mama." Lizzie's smile widened with pride. "Irish lace. She sends 'em with her congratulations."

"Thank you so much, Mrs. Spencer."

"You can call me by my front name, if you like." She rubbed Jeremiah's back and then tipped her head toward Cora. "And we don't believe none of the rumors 'bout you and Jeb. We've knowed him since he was borned, and they ain't no better family." She sighed. "'Twill all pass soon 'nough."

She headed toward the door before stopping to turn back. "My man, Cade, he's bringing a new mattress for y'all as a wedding gift. Him and his brothers learned how to make them newfangled cotton mattresses, and they're worth havin'." Lizzie smiled, took Jeremiah's hand, and went out the door.

"Figured out how much someone like you's needed in these parts yet?" Mercy asked, drying her hands on a towel as she stepped into the room.

"I can't imagine Jonathan managing all this on his own."

"He can't." She shook her head. "'Specially after Doc Ashe passed last year. He's been runnin' around like a chicken to git it all done, plus teach school. It'll be a mercy when Laurel gits her teaching license and can take over his spot." She raised a brow. "Not that she hadn't been doin' more and more teachin' over the past six months nohow. And Fig says anytime there's a doctorin' call, Laurel will step right in."

"They make a good team, don't they?"

"Aye. And I feel you and Jeb'll make a fine team too." Mercy tossed the towel over her shoulder. "You ain't afraid to learn our ways." She gestured toward the herbs on the table. "And Jeb ain't afraid to learn the ways outside here and invent all new thangs I've never seen afore. Did you know he has a shower out back?"

"A shower?"

"That's right. He has a small buildin' with buckets sittin' atop and strings attached to the buckets. Four buckets." She laughed. "I ain't never seen the like. The rainwater fills the buckets and then you go into the building, lock the door, use two of the buckets for wettin' yourself and the other two for washin' off the soap. Craziest thing."

And brilliant. Not exactly something she'd want to investigate in winter, but a lovely option for warmer temperatures, and an excellent reminder that her new husband did think outside of his world. Maybe that was another reason they fit together so well, even from the start. Their shared war experiences. Her desire to reach into his world from hers and his desire to reach into her world from his.

In late afternoon, the sound of men's voices brought Cora out to the front porch. Jeb and Elias stood to the side of the house, gesturing and talking, with Jeb making marks on a piece of paper as they did.

"What are you two up to?"

Jeb looked up from his paper, and Elias's grin split wide. "A wedding gift." Elias laughed. "Your husband has thought of the perfect wedding gift for you, though I ain't sure any other woman would call it a gift."

Cora walked down the steps toward the pair. "What on earth could that mean?"

Jeb returned to his scribbling, and Elias walked forward. "He's buildin' you on a clinic space, so you can set up what you need to see folks in the mountain." Elias added on a wink. "Not quite what most women might see as a romantic gesture, but Jeb seems sure it'll do the trick."

Comprehension dawned slowly, and when Jeb raised his gaze to her, a laugh burst out and she ran to him, throwing her arms around his neck.

"Looks like you guessed right, friend." Elias's laugh echoed back to them. "I'm gonna let y'all celebrate while I look for some of those molasses cookies I was promised."

Cora barely heard the door close as Elias disappeared into the house. "Are you certain about this? It means people will be coming here all day long."

"At least I'll always know where you are." He grinned, a sweet light sparkling in his eyes. "Besides, it makes a lot of sense if you're going to be doctorin' that you have a place for all your things."

"And, I'm less likely to stink up the whole house with the smell of them."

He wrinkled his nose in mock disgust. "That too."

"Thank you so much. It's wonderful." She hugged him close again. "Now I need to sort out what gift I can offer you that would carry such a sweet sentiment."

"I'm a pretty simple man, Cora." His fingers came up to play with one of her loose curls, gaze holding hers. "I'd be real content with similar pleasures of last night whenever you're so inclined."

"I think that we are both equally rewarded with such activity, my dear." She fisted his jacket, tugging him closer.

He kissed her, long and deep and so thoroughly, she stood breathless by the end. Oh yes, there was definitely mutual reward in loving Jeb McAdams.

They walked hand in hand into the house to find Elias and Mercy in deep conversation as Daniel played on the floor nearby. Cora looked to Jeb, but he only stared at the pair with a small smile on his face.

As if aware of the interruption in their conversation, Elias stood and turned toward Cora and Jeb. "She likes the idea."

Jeb's smile grew but he didn't clarify.

"Are you certain, Jeb?" Mercy stepped around the chairs to face him. "I. . .I can't imagine you not wanting to sell."

"It ain't mine to sell, Mercy." He shook his head and stepped closer to her. "Amos left it in my care, but he built it for you. It was always meant to be yours. It's all a matter of whether you want to live near town or not."

"I want to start new." She covered her smile with her hands, her green eyes brightened with tears. She laughed and looked over at Elias. "Elias said he'd keep watch on me and the young'uns. He knows the couple who owns the dress shop in town. Says he thinks I won't have no trouble a'tall selling my dresses." She wiped at her eyes, her smile continuing to grow. "And thank you, Jeb, for offering to let Fig stay here if'n he wants during the school week. Then he won't feel so far away from his friends."

Cora began to put the pieces together. Jeb was giving Mercy the house he'd told Cora about that belonged to his friend Amos. A fitting and tender gift, since Amos had designed it with Mercy in mind all along.

"And, if y'all are fine with makin' another trip into town. . ."
Elias scanned the room. "We could load things up in your wagon
and get her there tonight."

"Tonight?" Cora echoed.

"I think it's time for ya'll to have your house back." Mercy sent
a shy look to Elias before turning her attention back to Cora. "And
now that I got one of my own, I'm excited to make a new start."

The sun had only begun to set as Cora and Jeb made their way back
up the mountain from town. Gold and orange light gave the forest a
magical glow, or that was what Jeb had always thought of this time
of evening. If fairy folks was to live a'tall, like the old folks said, then
they likely lived best "in the gloaming," as his great-granddaddy
used to say.

Cora cozied up next to him on the wagon bench, her arm through
his and the breeze blowing curls around her face. Witnessing her
joy at the idea of the clinic addition brought a heap of pleasure. In
fact, he was already trying to figure out other ways to surprise her.
Would she like a porch swing? He'd meant to make one for months,
but never got around to it. He studied her profile and smiled. She'd
likely be the sort to find pleasure in a porch swing. In fact, the idea
of sitting beside her on one and watching the evening fall sounded
almost as pleasant as what could come later. Almost.

"Can you believe how many new orders Mr. Murphy had for
your furniture?" Cora pushed back her hair and looked over at him.
"You're going to have to cut back on your mill hours if you're going
to have time to meet all the orders."

"I've had a talk with Elias 'bout that. We've agreed on three days
at the mill and three days making furniture, for now." Jeb snapped
the reins to increase Hickory and Milkie's pace as the trail steep-
ened. "Which means I'll be home working in the shop on those
days, so if you need help, I'm there."

She squeezed close and pressed her cheek against his shoulder. "You're such a good man. I can't believe you'd want to marry me with all my stubbornness."

"That's a fine trait to have in a place like this." He pressed a kiss to her head. "Most of the best survivors I know are the stubborn ones."

She chuckled and sat up. "But I think you should increase the size of your workshop, Jeb. If you're going to have more time to make furniture, you should have more space for it. And you know how much Fig wants to help you. When he's with us during the school week, you'll have more space to show him. In fact, imagine how many young boys you could apprentice in your shop." She squeezed close again. "Oh, what a wonderful idea. You'd make such an excellent mentor for any boy, both in craftsmanship and in heart."

He wasn't rightly sure how long he'd be able to handle all this sweet talk. It wasn't that he didn't like it, especially from the woman he loved, it was just he didn't have a lot of experience knowing what to say in response, so he nodded and let her continue happily planning.

She seemed to like planning and fixing things anyway.

"Oh, since it isn't too late, do you think we could stop in at Uncle Edward's so I could gather the last of my things?"

"How much more do you have?"

"Oh, I don't know. A whole trunkful, probably."

His grin stretched wide and he kept his face forward. "I'm gonna have to make one of them wardrobes next, so you'll have a place for all them dresses of yourn."

She turned to him, brow furrowed into deep lines. "Are you making fun of my clothes, Mr. McAdams?"

"Not one bit, Mrs. McAdams. You look mighty pretty in 'em."

She snuggled right back to his side, letting the beauty of the evening pause their conversation along the path.

Preacher's cabin sat quietly in place among the growing dusk, giving off an empty feel. He must have left for his circuit. Jeb helped

Cora down from the wagon and scanned the area, something pricking beneath his skin. What was it? The windows of the house were dark. The chicken coop door closed and bolted. His attention moved to the barn and the prickly unease intensified. The barn door stood ajar though. Did Preacher usually leave the door open?

"I'll walk you to the house, then I'm gonna go check on the barn, alright?"

That quick mind of hers must have caught onto his caution. "What's the matter?"

"Probably nothin', but sometimes folks'll take up residence in empty barns on cold nights, if they don't got a place to stay." He gestured toward the building. "I just want to make sure all is safe and in place. Your uncle's real careful about making sure the buildings are closed up when he's gone."

He opened the cabin door and stepped in first, glancing around the darkening room. Nothing seemed amiss. Cora came in behind him and as he turned back toward the door, she grabbed his hand. "Be careful." She squeezed his fingers. "I have my pistol, if you need it."

He shook his head and offered her a reassuring smile, he hoped. "You keep the pistol. It's probably nothing a'tall. I'll be right back."

The light from sunset turned from golden to purplish gray, bringing the shadowed forest in closer. He wished he'd brought Puck with him. The dog's warning growl had proved useful more than once, and not just for snakes neither. Jeb pushed the barn door wide, allowing as much light into the space as possible before he stepped inside. Nothing seemed out of place, as far as he could tell.

Then he heard it. The smallest sound, like a whimpering babe.

What was a babe doin' out in this barn? He followed the sound to a stack of hay, and froze. A baby, a newer one, lay bundled in rags within the hay, and beside the babe lay a young woman, pale. He reached down to touch her and felt the cold skin of death. It was too dim to make out who she was. She couldn't have been there long, since Preacher must've only left after the wedding for his circuit. He leaned closer.

She looked familiar, but he couldn't place her.

Jeb turned toward the door to light the lantern and a shadowy figure rose from one of the stalls. Before Jeb could react, something hit him across the head. Jeb paused his approach. The world stilled. The shadow moved. And the last thing Jeb saw before darkness seized him, was the silhouette of a man turned toward the house. Cora!

Chapter Twenty-Three

Cora really had too many clothes.

She stared at the overflowing trunk by the door and tossed a few more items inside. Perhaps she could offer Maggie a dress or two. She was almost Cora's height. And Laurel would look lovely in the one with the blue shirtwaist. Yes, she'd give a few away and then—her smile took an uptilt—she could order something special from Mercy.

With a firm push, she closed the trunk and looked toward the door. Dusk crowded in from the forest, even darker than usual with the growing clouds. She took the lantern from the table nearby and walked out onto the porch. The hint of rain dampened the air. She'd better fetch Jeb and get them on their way, if they meant to make it back to the house before the storm.

The barn door still stood ajar, but there was no sign of Jeb, nor of any lantern glow in that direction. A sudden chill swept over her shoulders. She held the lantern up with one hand and reached into her skirt pocket with the other, slowly making her way toward the barn. Her fingers slipped around the handle of her pistol and then, she heard it. The sound of a baby's cry.

She picked up her skirt, took a tighter grip on the lantern, and dashed toward the barn door.

"Jeb?"

Her lantern light brightened the view and stole her breath. Jeb lay on the barn floor, blood on the side of his head. She ran toward him, but someone caught her by the arm, twisting it to the painful point behind her back. She bit back a cry and swung the lantern toward her assailant, twisting out of his reach as the lantern hit some part of his face.

He grunted and she stumbled back, lantern light shining full on her attacker's face. She'd only seen him once, at the Hawes wedding, but she remembered his face. Clark Greer. Cora fumbled for her pocket, but Clark lunged at her, pushing her back against the stall wall and knocking the lantern from her hand. It crashed on the floor near her and immediately some scattered straw caught fire.

"I'm 'bout done with the likes of you, flatlander," Clark roared, stepping slowly toward her as she continued to grapple for her pocket.

Her fingers slipped into the slit and fitted around the handle of her gun. Another whimper from a baby pulled her attention to the left where a woman lay in the straw next to a wriggling bundle. Was that Mary Greer? Cora's eyes widened and she looked back at Clark.

Something wasn't right about the way she lay, or her pallor. Cora's stomach seized. Was the girl dead? The lantern light fell on Mary's pale face and Cora's breath paused. She'd seen enough dead bodies to recognize the lifeless hue.

"She's been sickly since giving birth to that gal baby." Clark Greer spat out the words. "I ain't got no use for sickly womenfolk nor gal babies. Better off she died than slow me down."

The flames flickered brighter, catching onto the barn wall. Cora tried to process what to do. There was no way she could pull Jeb out of the barn quickly, even as near to the door as he was. The baby lay nearer the fire.

"You brought trouble with you from the first day you came to this mountain, just like the rest of your family." He moved a step closer. "If you'd just left Willa to die, then I'd have my home back.

My life back. But there you went, rescuin' her, and onct my daddy found out the truth, he took everything from me. Cast me out. And it's your fault, woman." His words slurred from drink, his eyes red-rimmed. "So I reckon you'll be my warnin' to the rest of your kin. What would your uncle do if he found you dead in his house when he got home and your brother found his house burned to the ground?" His lips took a wicked tilt. "I can finish what my kin started with the schoolhouse last year, 'cept there won't be nothin' left of that house when I'm done."

Cora freed her pistol from her pocket and pointed it at Clark. "Leave me and my family alone or I will shoot you."

The end of the pistol quivered. She swallowed through her dry throat and attempted to steady her hand as visions from the last time she'd fired the gun shook through her.

"You ain't got it in you." He stepped closer, his smile distorted and eerie in the growing firelight.

But when he lunged this time, she pulled the trigger. He bent from the impact and Cora ran for the baby, pulled her into her arms and then dashed out the barn door. Sprinkles of rain hit her face as she ran for the cabin. What could she do? She took the steps to the porch and looked back. Firelight flickered through the one window of the barn.

She had to try and save Jeb.

Carefully, she placed the whimpering baby inside the cabin on her uncle's carpet and then dashed back out into the rain, pistol in hand. But just as she reached the barn door, it slammed open, hitting her so hard in the shoulder, it knocked her to the ground. Before she had time to regain her footing, Clark Greer had her by the arm. Blood stained the lower left of his shirt and, with quick movements, he twisted the pistol from her fingers then backhanded her with it.

The impact blurred her vision and shot blinding pain up the side of her face as she landed on her right hip. He staggered toward her, but she crawled a few feet until her head cleared and then she stood, taking off at a run toward the cabin. She'd barely gotten inside and closed the door when she heard boots on the porch. The baby's cries rose behind her.

Cora slid the bar into place just as Clark made impact with the door. It shook beneath his weight a few times before all grew quiet, except for the baby's cries. She took a step back, breaths slowing, and then a chair from the front porch crashed through the side window. Cora picked up the baby and placed her on Uncle Edward's bed, away from the arms grappling through the broken window glass. Then she ran to the kitchen for a knife.

"Too late, woman." Clark's voice emerged as he made it through the window, his body scraped and bleeding. Was he surviving off fury alone? Like some Old Norse Berserker? He grabbed her by her wrist and twisted her arm behind her. "All trapped in by these walls now. Ain't nowhere to go."

<hr/>

Jeb coughed, thoughts coming slow and painfully. His head ached and he felt sick, or maybe he was floating. His eyelids weighed too much to open, but he needed to open them. Something was wrong, or had been wrong. What was it?

His memories slipped away from him like water through his fingers. A dead woman. A baby. He coughed again, the smell of smoke overwhelming. Something cool and wet hit his face. Was Cora crying over him?

Cora? Her face cleared in his head. Cora. Where was she?

He forced his eyes open and found himself seated with his back against a tree. The world blurred again so he pressed his eyes closed and tried to make sense of things. Last he remembered, he was with Cora at Preacher's house. He'd gone to the barn. And then. . .

His eyes opened wide. Cora!

"Git up, boy." Before him hovered the silhouette of a man with a familiar sturdy frame, but his face remained hidden in the darkness. "He's done gone after her."

Was that his father's voice? Jeb tried to stand, but swayed. The man caught him under the arm. "You ain't in no shape to rescue your woman, but you're gonna have to try. I reckon it's gonna take both of us, 'cause he just broke the front winder to get to her while I was pulling you from the fire."

Fire? Jeb focused on the man's face and his father's familiar features cleared. Then his daddy's words clicked into place. Cora was in trouble. Jeb pushed forward, half stumbling, half running toward the cabin, but just as he reached the steps his father caught him by the arm again.

"Ain't no help you rushin' in like a crazed fool." There was clarity in Daddy's eyes, sense in his words. Was Jeb dreaming? Where had the drunk gone?

"I'm gonna go in the front to distract him." He nodded toward the porch. "You round the house and surprise him from the back."

A baby's cry grew louder, clearer through the broken front window. Another crash followed by the sound of a woman's cry. Jeb jumped to the alert, his mind clearing, and he ran around the back of the house. He froze when he caught sight of Cora through the back window. Clark Greer had her pinned against the wall, hand to her neck, as she struggled to free herself. Her fingers dug into Clark's thick hand, her eyes rounded, almost bulging.

Jeb rushed to the door. Did she bar this one? *Lord, please no.* He had to make it in time to save her. He couldn't be too late for another person he loved.

He pushed forward and the door swung wide, slamming against the wall as Jeb rushed to Clark. The commotion pulled Clark's attention toward the door and his eyes widened as Jeb barreled into the man, hitting him with such force he dropped his hold on Cora. Jeb drilled him into the nearby wall. Clark's fist slammed into Jeb's stomach, loosening Jeb's hold on the man, but he rallied quickly. Noting the bloody side of his shirt, Jeb thrust his fist into the wound, sending Clark to his knees, just as Daddy made his entrance through the front window.

He kicked Clark as the man tried to rise back on his knees, and the man fell face-first and didn't move.

Jeb crawled to Cora's side where she lay in a heap. The baby continued to cry and thrash on the bed, the sound muffling Jeb's attempt to hear Cora breathing. He drew her into his arms and nestled her head against his chest, his palm moving down her face to her neck.

"Wake up, Cora," he whispered. "Come on, darlin'. Wake up."

She groaned and then coughed, shuddering against him, and he pulled her into him, holding her close and burying his face into her neck. When he pulled back, her eyes fluttered open slowly.

"Jeb?" the word rasped from her. Music to his ears.

"Good to see those eyes." He brushed a thumb over her cheek.

She blinked and then her vision seemed to clear and she dug her fingers into his shirt. "You're alright!" She pressed her face into his shoulder, wrapping her arms around him. "I. . .I couldn't pull you from the fire in time. I thought. . .I thought. . ." Her voice trailed off as she clung to him, her warm tears dampening his shirt.

He looked up and found his father watching, a softening expression on his tired face. "Daddy pulled me out."

Cora sat back and stared at Daddy, who lowered his gaze, almost as if he was ashamed. Without another word, Daddy pushed Clark over onto his back, the man barely conscious, likely dying.

"He don't deserve to live," said Daddy. "But if anyone knows how important a second chance is, it's me." He looked over at Cora and shrugged. "You reckon you can do some doctorin' enough on him that we can send him back to his family? That'll be enough punishment all its own, if I know Ozaiah Greer a'tall."

⊰❦☙◖◯◗❧❦⊱

Clark Greer didn't live an hour, despite Cora's attempts at helping him. The gunshot wound followed by his multiple other injuries inevitably led to his death, and despite fighting against the sliver of guilt at shooting the man, Cora knew she'd done the right thing. Sam and Jeb wrapped Clark in an old blanket Cora found then loaded his body into the back of the wagon as rain continued to fall. Uncle Edward's barn continued to burn with a dying flame, Mary Greer's body a part of the ashy debris.

Cora closed her eyes and thanked God for the miracle of life. That this little baby was taking cow's milk from some makeshift tubing Cora had configured in order to feed her. That Sam McAdams had shown up in time to pull Jeb from the barn when Cora couldn't. That this little baby somehow survived all the horrendous circumstances of her first few weeks of life.

Jeb and Sam tended to the barn fire and then boarded up Uncle Edward's broken window to keep animals out until Jeb could return to repair the damage, so it wasn't until deep into the night when they finally arrived back at Jeb and Cora's house.

The baby had fallen asleep along the way, finally full enough to rest, her body still shaking with residual sniffles from her long crying. Sam McAdams hadn't behaved like the wild man she'd seen a few days ago. He'd sat in the back of the wagon sober and serious, head bent, quiet.

There was something different about his countenance, softer, maybe? Cora couldn't quite put her finger on exactly what.

As Jeb helped her from the wagon, baby in tow, she looked back at Sam. "You should stay with us until morning, Sam. It's a wet walk back to your cabin, and we have space here."

Sam's eyes grew wide and he sent Jeb a searching look. "It's a good notion, Daddy. Git some rest afore you head home. Besides, whatever you need to say will be better said without waking the house to do it."

Sam looked between the two and then gave a nod. "I appreciate it."

Then he helped Jeb move the wagon and Clark's body into the barn while Cora took the sleeping baby into the house.

Cora breathed a sigh of relief when she stepped over the threshold, and nearly broke into tears. A dying fire attempted to provide a little heat in the room and the lantern light glinted over the place she already called home. But she'd cried enough for one night, so she sniffled, raised her chin in defiance of the tears, and walked to the bedroom. She pulled out a dresser drawer in the bedroom, like Willow had done, and used one of her woolen scarves to cushion the base. Then she placed the little one into the drawer to sleep while she herself changed into dry clothes. Tomorrow, she'd ride to Flat Creek and invest in some bottles, just until she and Jeb sorted out what to do with the infant.

Cora started up a pot of coffee and had set out some ham and biscuits by the time the men entered the house. It wasn't until the three of them sat around the table that Jeb asked the question niggling at Cora's mind.

"How'd you find yourself at Preacher's tonight?"

Sam placed his coffee cup on the table and braided his large hands together in front of him. "Don't make a lot of sense, I reckon, but after what happened with your mama and Suzie, I ran off. Thought I'd drink myself into forgetting how I hurt my family, but I'd lost my thirst for drink. Even when I tried, it turned sour in my mouth. All I could hear was your mama's voice tellin' me I'd caused Suzie's sickness and. . ." He paused, swallowing. "And Suzie's breathin', it just kept echoin' in my mind."

He stared down at the coffee cup between his hands and shook his head. "Then all the things your mama and you young'uns and Preacher said over the years started rolling round in my head. I couldn't get 'em out. 'Bout God savin' sinners, even the worst ones. 'Bout hope and. . .peace." He cleared his throat, his hands tightening and loosening their grip on the cup. "The words weighed on me like I ain't never felt afore. I could barely move my feet, didn't even know where I was goin'. I just knew. . . I just knew I needed savin' from myself."

Cora didn't realize she'd covered Jeb's hand with her own until she felt his fingers wrap around hers. Something deep and rich warmed the air around them, this story different than one of Sam's tall tales or family stories. This. . .this had the scent of a miracle.

"So I wandered around like a lost man, finally finding may way to Preacher's place." A sound like a quiet chuckle came from him. "And that's what I was. Lost. Found my way to Preacher's cabin, thinking he might be home to tell me them words again that he'd told me afore. But he wun't there and I. . . Well, I couldn't keep walkin'. The weight was too much and I. . .I felt it."

Cora's vision blurred, her eyes stung. Words failed to grasp the depth of what she was hearing, but her *soul* seemed to understand.

"Felt what, Daddy?" Jeb's voice rasped. Did his soul understand too?

The older man looked up then, tears swirling in his eyes. "I can't rightly explain it 'cept to say I felt God call me." An expression of awe filled his features. "Heard Him in my head so loud that. . .that somehow I felt it all through me." His hand shook as he rubbed his beard and then returned to his cup. "Then, I knew. Them weights was from my sin, the sin I'd carried my whole life. They'd wrapped round me like chains, and I didn't see no way out. Then. . .then my heart just. . .knew." He released a shaky breath and pinched his lips closed for a moment as he gathered his emotions. "The Spirit of God fell on me so hard that I dropped to my face on the ground just outside Preacher's yard and gave my heart to Jesus right there." A single tear rolled down one of his leathery cheeks. "The chains. . .they're gone."

Cora looked over at Jeb, measuring whether he'd heard the same thing she just did. It sounded like some sort of Saul-to-Paul moment directly from scripture.

Jeb's jaw tightened and he nodded. "Mama will be real glad to hear it."

He dropped his gaze back to his hands. "If she can forgive me. I. . .I've been hard on her."

Jeb reached out and covered his father's hand with one of his own. "She ain't never lost hope God would find you, Daddy. Maybe some of the rest of us might have, but not her. Never."

"Even after I caused my baby girl's death?" His voice broke.

Cora and Jeb exchanged another look, and Cora nearly sobbed out a laugh.

"Sam, Suzie didn't die. She's recovered."

His gaze shot to Cora's and held it with such intensity, she couldn't look away. "My baby girl's alive?"

Cora nodded, her own eyes stinging with tears at the awareness dawning on the man's face. "Yes, she should make a full recovery. And Caroline has sent people out looking for you since you ran off, so she wants to find you too."

Sam looked from Cora to Jeb and then, without warning, leaned his head over on his hands and began to sob. Loud, aching, grateful, hopeful sobs. And somewhere in that moment, Cora realized she'd witnessed another miracle. The greatest of all miracles.

A broken lost soul found. Forgiven. Rescued.

Epilogue

"Y'all don't believe in doin' nothin' by halves, do ya?" Sam McAdams laughed.

The older man sat at the new table Jeb had built for Cora, so it would fit more people around it, and with Sam, Caroline, Maggie, Isom, Suzie, James, and John, it already looked crowded.

A happy sight. Cora smiled at the assembly. Suzie sat on Sam's lap, nestled close. Both Jeb and Cora had waited for Sam to return to his drinking, but it had been two weeks since that night, and there was no going back. Caroline didn't seem to question Sam's change at all.

"What do you mean?" Cora placed some potatoes on the table with Caroline bringing the ham.

"Well, you showed up from across the waters just over a month ago, and within that time, you and Jeb met, married, almost got yourselves killed, and now ya got a baby to boot."

Cora met Jeb's gaze, his smile so wide she thought he might break into a laugh. He didn't laugh often, but it was one of the best sounds. As if on cue, the baby girl in Jeb's arms started to wriggle awake. The Greers hadn't wanted the baby. Said she was sin-borned, so, after a very short discussion, Jeb and Cora took her as their own. And Cora, with a desire to combat the awful superstition of "bad blood" in the mountains, asked Jeb if they could name her Faith.

He agreed. And so, Faith Caroline McAdams joined their very new family.

"You do have a point, Sam." Cora took her place next to Jeb. "But I've always been the strong-willed sort, so I imagine this was God's way of making a joke."

Sam's laughter burst out again and some of the rest joined in. What a lovely sound after so much hardship, but things had finally started settling down a little.

Jeb and Elias had started the clinic addition to the house, and Maggie was stopping in a few times a week to help tend Faith while Cora did her "doctorin'." She was kept quite busy now that the news had gotten around about all that had happened with Willow and Paul, and then Mary and Clark. Imogene Carter had still refused to look her direction in church, which might have been because everyone had stared, shocked and amazed when Sam McAdams entered the building that morning for worship. His salvation story, which he told to anyone who would listen, sent Jeb and Cora's rumored and distorted tale to the back of everyone's minds, and what a worthy replacement.

They were halfway through the Sunday meal when a knock at the door pulled their attention toward the front of the house. Cora took Faith from Jeb to finish giving her a bottle and he went to the door.

Uncle Edward entered first, all smiles. "Look who I found at the train depot, just in time for Sunday supper."

Jonathan and Laurel walked in behind him, still in their traveling clothes but looking no worse for the wear.

Cora shot up from her seat and moved toward the door, baby in arms.

"Uncle has been filling us in on the ride up here." Jonathan shook his head and stared at Cora, then the baby, then Jeb, and back to Cora. "I feel as though I've missed an entire year of your life, and we've only been gone three weeks."

"It's truly a novel-worthy story as only the best mountain tales should be." Cora sent Laurel a wink. "Perhaps your wife can spin it into one of her magazine series."

"Ain't a soul who'd believe it." Laurel laughed and teased baby Faith from Cora's arms. "So I'll have to make it fictional for sure."

"Though she may have to cut back on her writing schedule since she passed her teaching test with flying colors," Jonathan announced. The whole room erupted in a mixture of shouts, applause, and laughter.

"Which means, Teacher Doctor here," Laurel said, nudging her husband with her elbow, "will start the year off just doctorin' folks, and I'll take over the schoolin'. With the progress Elias and Jeb are makin' on the Rock Creek Clinic, seems he'll have a spot there readied for work real soon."

"I reckon it should be fit for folks by the New Year," Jeb said. "With an apartment on the top floor for y'all when you need to stay in town."

"Come, we can finish this conversation at the table." Cora waved them forward. "I didn't have Jeb make such a giant table for nothing, and the bench seats allow us to cozy up to one another so we'll all fit."

And they did. All close and welcome, just missing Cora's mother who would have loved this small feast and feisty company. She caught Jeb's eye and wondered if he thought the same about his sister, Kizzie. They talked of Jonathan's medical training, which would continue in Greensboro in intervals over another year before he could take his licensure test. Jeb shared about the last things he needed to do for the Rock Creek Clinic. Cora bragged about Jeb's wedding gift to her and let Jonathan know he could use the space along with her so they could share the load. And then, the room grew quiet as Sam shared his tale once again, and the same misty-eyed response that had moved Cora and Jeb and all other listeners touched Jonathan and Laurel too.

"Look!" Isom stood from the table, his attention focused at the front of the house. "It's snowin'."

All the children, except Faith, of course, dashed to the front windows where the world outside was already growing white from the thick flakes drifting down. Soft, full, and blanketing the world in a lovely sheen of icy wonder.

Folks started taking their leave. Uncle Edward, first, who had another visit to make before ending his day at home. Then the McAdamses, with Sam bringing up the rear. Cora watched him pause on the porch and stare out on the frosty world, a sweet smile on his face, and she wondered if he pondered on the verse, "though your sins be as scarlet, they shall be as white as snow." He caught Cora watching and tossed a grin over his shoulder, as if in answer to her own musings, before he joined his family on their trek back up the path. Suzie danced alongside him a few steps before taking his hand, and Cora nearly started crying all over again.

Perhaps there was something about these mountains that encouraged nonweepy women to become weepy. Or maybe some things were too painful or beautiful or powerful to keep inside and tears became an automatic outlet. They didn't prove she was weak, but that her heart felt for the needs and brokenness of others, a truth any "Nurse Woman" should keep well aware of.

Jonathan and Laurel stayed a little longer, asking questions about Jeb and Cora's adventures, then sharing a few of their own. It was a sweet reunion and, in many ways, a fresh start for them all. As they bid the couple good night, Jonathan drew her to the side.

"I was worried when Uncle Edward told me what happened." He searched her face and draped an arm about her shoulders. "I thought you'd been forced into a decision, somehow trapped or desperate, and feared you'd be miserable."

"With your history, I can understand why." She leaned into his hug. "But I do believe God worked out your forced marriage quite well for the two of you, if my skills of observation are worth anything."

Jonathan looked over at his wife who was cooing over baby Faith asleep in Jeb's arms. "I am certain I am exactly where and with whom I'm supposed to be."

Cora sighed as her gaze drifted to her quiet, gentle husband, who had somehow become even more special to her with each day. Watching him tend to a baby with such tenderness may have helped matters along, but Jeb already had all the makings of a wonderful father. "Yes, as remarkable as it sounds, so am I."

Jeb placed Faith in the crib he'd made for her and walked with Cora, Jonathan, and Laurel onto the porch. The snow covered everything with its wintry white, giving the forest a magical look.

They stood on the porch watching Jonathan and Laurel ride away and then Jeb turned toward her. "Care to swing for a spell and watch the snow?"

Her husband didn't realize how romantic he truly was. She smiled up at him and led the way to the porch swing he'd put into place only a few days before, as an "early Christmas gift," he'd said. She was learning that gift-giving, even in the smallest ways, brought him the greatest pleasure.

He wrapped his arm around her and she leaned her head on his shoulder, the swing barely moving as they watched the whitening world in silence. These moments were her favorites. She'd never appreciated them before, the quiet. She'd always thought her world needed to be busy and active, proving herself in every second, but definitions and needs changed. Everything changed when one rested in the confidence of being loved well and in walking in the calling God had placed upon one's life.

Troubles came, and were sure to still come, but the truth of being held by God's loving hands somehow steadied her heart in ways she'd never realized before God brought her to this place and these people. No, quiet wasn't bad at all. And sitting on a porch swing with her husband watching the snow proved one of the delicacies of life.

"Your brother was worried 'bout you, I reckon," came Jeb's quiet comment.

"He was." She turned toward Jeb, his face so close. "But I set him straight about it all."

Jeb kept his face forward. "Told him I didn't kidnap ya, nor hold the baby for ransom so you'd marry me?"

Cora's laugh burst out. "Is that the newest rumor?"

He sent her a wink. "You know how tall tales get taller here in these mountains."

"What if *I* kidnapped *you* and held the baby for ransom so you'd marry *me*?"

"Yep." He nodded. "That's more believable."

She chuckled and he turned to her, breaching the short distance between them for a lingering kiss. She kissed him right back, burrowing close to his warmth.

"You think we ought to take this inside?" Cora touched his cheek, enjoying the way his eyes lit with understanding.

"I won't complain one bit if we did."

She kissed him again and then something in the distance caught her attention.

The glow of lantern light shone from the forest just beyond the fence line, growing brighter as it came nearer. Cora stood with Jeb at her side, and the silhouette of one man holding up another came into view among the snowflakes.

"Nurse Woman?" came the call.

Jeb sighed and Cora nuzzled her lips into his cheek before leaning near his ear. "I promise, I'll make it up to you later. Will that help?"

His grin slipped crooked and he snuck a quick kiss before walking backward to the porch steps. "I'm gonna hold you to that promise, Mrs. McAdams."

She smiled and watched him run toward the pair struggling forward in the snow before she went inside to prepare to do what God had created her to do. Here. In this wild place she called home.

PEPPER BASHAM is an award-winning author who writes romance peppered with grace and humor. She is a native of the Blue Ridge Mountains where her family has lived for generations. She's the mom of five kids, speech-pathologist to about fifty more, lover of chocolate, jazz, and Jesus, and proud AlleyCat over at the award-winning Writer's Alley blog. Her debut historical romance novel, *The Thorn Bearer*, released in April 2015, and the second in February 2016. Her first contemporary romance debuted in April 2016.

You can connect with Pepper on her website at www.pepperdbasham. com, Facebook at https://www.facebook.com/pages/Pepper-D -Basham, or Twitter at https://twitter.com/pepperbasham

Other books by Pepper Basham

HOPE BETWEEN THE PAGES
Visit a great American landmark while spending time in both the present and the past. Will a reclusive book-store owner and a dashing Englishman find romance during their travels from the Vanderbilts' grand estate in North Carolina, to Derbyshire, England, in pursuit of a century-old love story?

Paperback / 978-1-64352-826-7 / $12.99

THE RED RIBBON
Ava Burcham tends to court trouble, but when her curiosity leads her into a feud between an Appalachian clan and the local authorities, her amateur sleuthing propels her into a world of criminal cover-ups, political rivalries, and a battle of wills. The end result? The Hillsville Courthouse Massacre of 1912.

Paperback / 978-1-64352-649-2 / $12.99

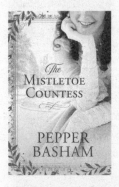

THE MISTLETOE COUNTESS
He was never supposed to become an earl. She was never supposed to marry him. But when the nevers become reality in the Christmas of 1913, Frederick and Gracelynn team up in love, life, and a little bit of amateur sleuthing to solve a Christmas murder mystery.

Paperback / 978-1-64352-986-8 / $15.99